Sweets and Sycamores

ARIANNE NICKS

ISBN 979-8-9988892-8-8

Cover design by Alina Bobilova

Editing by Alexandra Leonhardt

Proofreading by Ramona Mihai

To the readers who love falling in love

Chapter 1

FIRE!

Allie thought hell would freeze over before the coven Magistra allowed her inside the potions room. Since joining the Silverbarks, Allie had been living from one mishap to another: getting the words of a spell wrong, running late for rituals, falling off her broom. She only fell *once*, but Lydia, the Magistra, made sure to remind Allie about it often. All her mishaps were rooted in her inability to control her power—fire. Her mother's fire.

"Whatever you do, my love, don't choose a lonely life."

Allie kept her mother's words close to her heart and had taken them as guidance to join her mother's coven as a legacy. If only Petra had lived long enough to teach her about this fire, which had manifested later than it did for the average Witch. By about twenty years.

A couple of months ago, Allie joined the coven shortly after she came back to Pearls Fields from her years in Green Creek that she would rather forget. Confident and excited, she'd knocked on the manor's door thinking she would get all the help and support from her new sisters.

She was wrong.

Allie was the only elemental Witch in the coven, while the other Witches were gifted with mental talents like telepathy, mind reading, transcending the worlds between the living and the dead, and various otherworldly skills that sent cold chills down her spine when she thought of them. She had begged Lydia and all her sisters for some guidance, but they refused every time, saying they had no experience with elemental magic and would hate to steer her wrong.

Allie did her best, and sometimes Freya, one of her sisters and the closest thing she had to a friend, watched over her practice. It was always short-lived; as soon as Allie's power grew remotely out of control, Freya would bail on her, too. At least she was nice to her, as the newest arrival to the Silverbarks before Allie.

And that was why this very early morning, long before dawn, as they climbed down the stairs together from their rooms on the second floor of the manor to the potions room in the basement, Freya was the only one cheering her on.

"You'll do great with the potions, Allie," Freya said, linking their arms, but no comfort came from her words. "I got my first potions assignment at the same time as you, a few months in. Lydia knows what she's doing if she's assigned you to potion-making."

Allie nodded absentmindedly, trying to ground herself in her friend's touch. She rotated her rings mindlessly, taking turns between the four hoops on her index and pinky fingers. But her hands trembled, and her breath hitched, cold sweat dripping down her spine under her forest green dress.

"How many drops of rose water does the sleeping potion need again?" Allie asked.

Freya chuckled. "Stop stressing over this, you've got it. I'll be right next to you, and Marla and Aurora will be there too."

"Great," Allie muttered under her breath.

Marla and Aurora were two of the elder Witches in the coven

who had joined around the same time as her mom. Allie had hazy memories of the two visiting her mother when she was young and had expected them to welcome her into the coven with open arms. She quickly learned they had only disdain and scowls in store for her because she was a "disappointment" and a "waste of magic" compared to the exceptional Petra.

Allie and Freya reached the basement first, the elder Witches right behind them.

The potions room, dusty and dim, had an acrid smell from countless potions being spilled and never cleaned. Allie had once offered to deep-clean the basement, but Lydia had bitten her head off and snarled that this was what a potions room was supposed to smell like.

The Magistra was already there, enveloped in thick shadows, as if wrapped in a black velvet curtain. She sauntered toward one of the antique chests, pulled out a matchbox, and lit a couple of torches around the room.

Allie missed few things about Green Creek, but most of all, she longed for electricity, a coffee machine, and the other little luxuries that came with new magic. Unfortunately, Green Creek and new magic alike were tainted by Sam the idiot, and she would rather give it all up than think of him every time she turned the lights on.

"If Alecsandra would only master her fire, I wouldn't have to resort to this," Lydia said, loud enough for all of them to hear, but low enough so they would consider she might have been talking to herself. The Magistra had initially been thrilled to welcome a legacy in the circle, but she wore her feelings on her face, and with each time Allie's powers erupted out of control, her sneers of distaste and disapproval grew increasingly obvious.

Allie said nothing as she stepped to the heavy oak table in the middle of the room, the wood dented from erosive potion splatters. Empty tins and mortars were scattered on the surface next to bottles filled with colored liquids, herbs, stones, and some things Allie preferred to look away from. The other Witches assessed the elements and smiled wickedly, even Freya.

It had always been like this, and Allie's heart squeezed with a silent pain. She wished she'd had more time with her mother, so she could have learned from her why she was supposed to smile now. Yet she was left confused, alone, and feeling like she didn't belong. Sometimes, on her lowest days, Allie truly hated that she was a Witch.

"Today we are making sleeping potions and love potions to fulfill a couple of orders," Lydia announced, drawing Allie's attention to her. In the dim light, Lydia looked older than she was, with her red hair pulled back in a ponytail so tight that her eyebrows were lifted far from her brown eyes and a dark, glossy burgundy painted on her lips. "You will work in pairs, as always, and I will supervise."

Lydia had never supervised potion-making since Allie had joined the coven. Everyone knew the Magistra was here because of her. Because she expected her to make a mess out of this assignment. Allie couldn't blame her; she hadn't proven Lydia wrong yet. But Allie knew that with a bit of guidance and more time to practice, she would get her fire under control. She felt it in her bones. It wasn't supposed to burn her; it was supposed to burn for her. With her.

Allie and Freya worked on the sleeping potions while the elder Witches prepared the love potions, both the coven's bestselling products at the weekly market—a place for Pearls Fields' residents to shop, sell, and gossip. The room smelled like rose water and burnt sage, and Allie felt an itching sensation behind her nose and forehead.

Panic gripped her, the memory of almost burning down her old house with a simple sneeze slamming to the forefront of her mind. Her body went taut like a pulled bowstring. She held her breath and counted down from ten, wrinkling her nose in all directions to make the sensation go away. Allie stilled her movements, one hand grasping the edge of the table and the other tightening her grip on the mortar where she and Freya were mixing the ingredients.

As the stinging sensation subsided, Allie swallowed and inhaled, feeling it decrease to a tingle. She exhaled with quiet relief and picked up the rose water bottle. She could do this. The ingredients mixture was almost done, and then she would only have to infuse the potion with her magic. Allie had practiced this so much, she was confident nothing would go wrong. Thankfully, she could use these other branches of magic well enough without having mastered her untamed fire.

A spark drew her attention to the mortar where several herbs were mixed and crushed together. She blinked aggressively to clear her vision, but the spark still flickered in the herbs.

Her body felt warm. Not with a fever, but as if she was heating from the inside out like a furnace. She released her death grip on the mortar and took a step back.

"What's wrong?" Freya frowned.

The last thing Allie saw before the fire ignited was the curse-filled look that Lydia threw her. And knowing Lydia as well as she did now, it could have indeed been a curse.

The huge oak table burst into flames, tall and wild and sizzling hot. They reached for Allie as if they recognized her, as if they danced to a song she was wordlessly singing.

"Fire!" someone yelled. The Witches screamed and rushed to the door, racing up the stairs. The screams blared throughout the manor, and the entire coven hurried to bring buckets of water to the basement, cursing their lack of other elemental Witches.

Allie gaped at the fire until the first bucket of water diminished its flames. She flinched as if the water drenched her, the shock spurring her into action.

As she ran to fill a bucket of her own, she thought how wonderful it would have been to have a sister with power over water. Allie could have learned from her, and none of this would have happened. And if incidents still occurred, at least she'd have a sister to put out her fires.

But she didn't.

She was alone, destined to burn until there were only ashes left in her wake.

꙰

The Silverbarks stood around the dining table in the parlor, twenty pairs of damning eyes fixed on her. Lydia braced the heel of her palms against the table on the opposite side of Allie.

"I have few words for today," she said with an exaggerated sigh. "You do not excel in anything pertaining to Witchcraft. Your partaking in rituals is shameful, your flying is subpar, and you don't even have a knack for spells." Lydia listed Allie's shortcomings without blinking. She grimaced an ugly scowl, dark burgundy gloss dripping from the corners of her mouth. "I could have overlooked all of that, Alecsandra."

Allie hated how her name sounded from Lydia's mouth, entangled with her lie. The Magistra overlooked nothing. Allie just wanted to get this scolding over with, get her punishment, and go to bed.

"But you have put the lives of all your sisters in danger. You are incapable of controlling your power, and we cannot live safely around you."

Allie's breath froze in her throat.

"What?" she croaked.

"I'm sorry, Alecsandra, but I cannot allow you to be part of the Silverbarks any longer. All those in favor—"

"No, please, wait," Allie said, her eyes desperately roving

between her sisters. "I will do better. I can do better. Please, please don't kick me out!"

Nineteen arms shot up in an instant, with the twentieth only raising to Freya's shoulder. She mouthed something to Allie that could have been an apology or another curse. Allie couldn't tell; her vision was foggy and heavy, tears taking form in her eyes.

"Wait, please," she insisted. "Can you give me one more chance? I know I can do better. Please. Please, Lydia." Desperation was unbecoming, but it was Allie's last resort. She could not get kicked out of the coven that Petra had so proudly been part of. There was nothing else for her outside of this place. Nothing, and no one.

The Magistra's eyes turned to slits as she regarded Allie. Lydia's pause was met with contempt from most of the Witches in the room. But they all fell silent at once, and Allie knew that Lydia was using her unparalleled gift of telepathy to communicate with the coven.

It could have been a minute or a day before she spoke again.

"All right. You have until Hallows Eve to prove that you can master your power. You can be part of the Silverbarks if you can show us that we are safe around you." Allie felt a glimmer of hope bloom in her chest. "But you cannot live here until then. And we'll keep your broom as insurance that you will be back once you control this wild fire. Don't dare betray us for another coven."

"But—"

"This is our final offer, Alecsandra. Do we have a deal?"

Allie had to think on her feet. Hallows Eve was in seven weeks. If she found a safe place to practice, or maybe even someone to help her, she could do it. She knew she could do it. She had to be a Silverbark, just like Petra.

The life of a Witch with no family amounted to nothing unless she was part of a coven. People were wary of Witches outside of procuring potions or other services from them, and they hated any display of power, especially from elemental Witches, as Allie had learned in Green Creek.

She had no one, and nowhere to go.

So Allie was left with only one choice.

"Deal," she agreed on a watery breath.

Chapter 2

WELCOME TO SYCAMORE FALLS

Freya leaned in the doorframe of their small shared room, arms crossed over her chest. Her short red hair was tousled and ruffled by the commotion and gave her a boyish look. Gaze down and shoulders slumped, she had apologized twice already while Allie packed her bag.

"It's fine," Allie said. What else could she say? Witches who joined a coven wanted to remain part of it for as long as possible. She couldn't have jeopardized her position with the Silverbarks by siding with Allie. As much as the silent admission gnawed at her heart, Allie knew that if their places were reversed, she would have done the same. She wouldn't have been better. And maybe that showed most Witches, even those from the same coven, were not meant to be friends. Just friendly.

Allie had few things to pack, which would all fit in a duffel bag. Pearls Fields, her hometown and the Silverbarks' territory, was an unbearably hot place year-round, where even the thinnest dresses felt stifling. But this place had two things going for it. It made her feel closer to Petra, and it was a haven for old magic. Deep down, Allie knew there was no harm in new magic, and it came with so many opportunities, but Sam had tainted her experience, and...

No. He didn't deserve her thinking about him at all.

She wanted to stay in Pearls Fields. But if Lydia kicked her out, then with no other covens sharing the territory, her choice to stay here meant a life by herself. The thought of such a lonely life, one her mother had so often warned her against, filled her chest with crumpled paper.

Allie wanted the sisterhood and friendship that her mother had had with the coven. Petra had left the coven's manor for a small cottage in the same town when Allie grew up. She remembered her mother visiting the manor often, as well as Witches coming to visit them all the time. Petra and her friends would sit around the fire laughing, telling stories, and drinking weird, pungent liquids that tickled Allie's nose.

So she had tried to be one of them, and she would keep trying. Maybe they would never befriend her, but accepting her would be enough.

Allie grabbed her dresses and personal items from the wardrobe she and Freya shared, gathered the objects from her side of the bathroom sink, and shoved everything into a lavender-patterned duffel bag. She packed her potion powders and stones, along with a few candles, tucked the crescent moon necklace inside the neckline of her dress, and checked her rings. Her mother had gifted her a stone ring for every five years of life, and Allie wore the amethyst and ruby ones on her left hand and the sapphire and emerald ones on her right. Petra had passed away four years ago, a year before she could gift Allie her fifth ring. But she'd left her the crescent moon necklace, which she had inherited from Allie's grandmother. It hung around Allie's neck like an iron weight, reminding her often that she had no one to pass it on to.

She zipped the bag and turned to leave, abandoning her thoughts with the movement. Freya was still blocking the doorframe.

"I really am sorry," she said for the third time. Allie believed her. She would miss the only sister who had shown her a modicum of kindness. She gave her a side hug while slipping out of the room.

"I'll see you in seven weeks," Allie promised, more to herself than to Freya. The Witch accompanied her down the stairs and outside the manor and waved as Allie put distance between her and the place she had been reluctantly calling home for the past few months.

The dirt road was dry, and the sun would be fully out in about an hour. Allie dreaded walking through the heat, and she had no idea where to go, but she knew she wouldn't be going south. South was hotter than here, and...Sam was south. Or at least that's where they'd parted ways before she came to the Silverbarks' manor.

She would go north, in search of cooler temperatures. Allie had never been anywhere other than Pearls Fields and Green Creek, so now it felt like a great opportunity for her to learn more about this world. As much as she could in the next seven weeks, anyway.

Her heart broke to leave her sycamore broom behind. She hadn't earned one made of silverbark yet, but she had loved her broom. Allie and Petra had crafted it from a wild sycamore tree that grew behind their cottage. Strange for these parts, and all the more special because of it. They loved spending afternoons under that tree, reading stories and eating fresh plums and strawberries. As a little girl, Allie thought the tree was lonely, and Petra accompanied her daughter outside to spend time with it. In some ways, Allie was just like the sycamore tree.

Allie decided to take a detour and visit her old cottage and the lonely tree one more time. She had sold it to a lumberjack and his wife, and though they had been nice and polite to her, Allie hadn't missed the wariness in their eyes or the sharpness in their voices. Most people in Pearls Fields feared Witches and gave them a wide berth every time their paths crossed, unless they sought them out at the market. Or for other ungodly purposes.

The fiery red hair gave them away, and young Allie had tried many tricks to dye her hair a different color so other children would play with her. But it would never stick, her long red curls coming out victorious every time. The magic in her was strong enough not to allow her red hair to change, yet it had taken her twenty-eight years to manifest fire.

Allie walked down the winding path under the heating sunlight, through the river birches and the magnolia trees that scented the air with a sweet fragrance. She decided to pass by the cottage on the main road and keep to the far side, so no one would become suspicious of her lingering around.

She needed a plan if she were to master her fire in time to prove herself to Lydia. Her heart spasmed weirdly at the thought of returning to the manor, and Allie chided the silly organ. Joining the Silverbarks was her only option. If they didn't accept her where she was a legacy, no other coven would take her in.

For the next seven weeks, Allie would have to find a way to earn her keep. Her pouch was half-full from selling potions at the market, but it would empty quickly if she had to pay for lodgings and food for almost two months. Allie didn't dare hope that it would take her less than Lydia's deadline to control her power, so she had to plan for the entire period the Magistra had granted her. So, she would look for work to earn some money and a place to stay, preferably close to a hidden clearing in the forest or an isolated meadow where she could practice without putting anyone else in danger.

Allie strolled down the path to the right, keeping on that side of the road, knowing that in a few steps her old cottage would come into view. Witches lived removed from the towns and villages, although they often visited their shops and markets.

Witches were and weren't a part of society, so they created communities for themselves within covens that would accept and support them through life.

Except her.

But Allie didn't want to be bitter about it. She inhaled the floral scent in the breeze, the air hot enough to chafe her throat even with the early morning hours. The cottage came into sight on the left, but Allie almost didn't recognize it. The walls were bare without the ivy vines she and Petra had grown and trimmed for years, and the warm yellow brick was now painted a striking white. The roof was new, the garden was free of weeds, and there was a brown, boring door where the old blue one used to be.

Allie sighed as she passed by the house, a heavy glumness settling over her. She expected the new owners to make changes to the cottage, but it was as if her life with Petra had been erased with a white, meticulous sponge. Their happy, colorful life would always live in her memories, and that would have to do.

Allie turned to look at the house one more time, and from this farther angle she could see part of the backyard, too. Her breath caught when she noticed the patch of grass basking in the sunlight now where a familiar round shade had kept it cool before. The sycamore tree was gone.

Tears prickled her eyes as she regarded the place that had been her home, a peaceful slice of heaven where she grew up and became the woman she was today. Sadness pressed hot against her chest at the view she didn't recognize, but it still hurt to leave behind the only home she'd ever known. She had to look forward, had to practice and become better, so she could go back to her coven and live her life, just like her mother had done. So Allie wiped her eyes with the back of her hand and walked away.

And walked. And walked.

&.

Allie walked until the sky turned pink and the moon came out. None of the wheeled wagons stopped to take her, and she didn't even bother to ask for a ride in Pearls Fields before she left. Allie knew the villagers well enough, and they had never agreed to help a Witch.

She'd passed by two inns which had both been fully occupied but were looking for help. It had taken the owners only a quick glance at her red hair to come up with the excuse that the position had been filled, and the "Help Wanted" sign was old.

Allie had been walking for almost twelve hours. Her legs begged her to stop, but that was not an option. She had to end up *somewhere*. At the second inn, she exchanged a coin for a plate of nearly-spoiled vegetable stew and a cup of mint tea, which she gulped down before setting on her way again.

The road got darker with every step, and Allie feared she'd have to camp outside in the fields if she didn't find a room soon. A cot would do, too, or even a spot on someone's floor. Anything that would give her a remote sense of safety for the night.

A faint rumbling sound interrupted her thoughts. She stopped and strained to listen; it came from the road she left behind with each step, growing louder and louder.

The ground appeared clearer under her feet, and she watched as two round lights looking like tiny moons headed toward her. Allie took a few steps back as the object of the weird light and roaring sound came into view and stopped next to her.

"You all right, miss?" a thick voice asked from inside the vehicle. Cars were objects of new magic, and in Green Creek, almost everyone drove one. They weren't as popular in this area, where old magic dwelled, so Allie guessed the man was not a local.

A mix of fear and intrigue traveled through her body. The driver could be dangerous, but so could sleeping under the stars. Allie sent a tendril of her magic to Read the stranger's aura and intentions. This she was capable of as a Witch, and it had never failed her. Allie felt nothing malicious or reckless about him. Instead, a genuine warmth welcomed her magic from a resounding empty place; the man had no magic.

This discovery gave Allie the courage to approach the open window. The seat next to him was empty, but the backseat was packed with boxes and bags.

"Good evening." She forced a cheerful voice. "I'm looking for accommodation for tonight, do you happen to know a place nearby?"

"You passed the Hungry Chestnut?"

Allie told him about both inns she'd visited.

"Where are you headed?" the man asked. A simple question that rendered her speechless.

"I don't know." Allie told the truth with an awkward smile. Who wandered this earth with no direction or target?

"I'm going north, to Sycamore Falls." The man paused for a moment, looking over her and her duffel bag. "Do you want a ride?" he asked and leaned over to open the door on her side. Allie considered for the length of a breath, but was there anything to consider? This was her only option, and it gave her a destination. Something about having a place to go to made Allie feel better, more confident, and she opened the door wider and slipped inside the car.

"Thank you. I'm Alecsandra," she said on instinct. He regarded her for a long moment, his eyes resting on her red curls. Allie expected to hear an excuse masking his sudden change of heart, like a prior engagement, or that he didn't have room for her because he had someone else to pick up. He wouldn't be the first person to run fast and far away from her, or at least to refuse helping her after he noticed she was a Witch.

"I'm Brandon," the man said and started the engine. Closer to him now, with the clear moonlight trickling through the windows, she could see him better: a tall man with short dark hair and sharp features, maybe a few years older than she was. Brandon wore a wide smile that brightened his brown eyes, and Allie's instinct was that she would be safe with him. In any case, she had a hidden weapon of her own.

If anything went wrong, she could just sneeze and set his car on fire.

They traveled in silence, and Allie fought the urge to doze off. Being asleep was being vulnerable, and as kind as Brandon seemed, she was still in an enclosed space with a stranger. The vehicle tilted back for a long portion of the road, climbing hills upon hills. The temperature dropped, and Allie wished her only sweater wasn't at the bottom of the bag.

"We're almost there," Brandon said after a bit over an hour, according to the digital clock on the board. "Have you ever been to Sycamore Falls?" She shook her head. "You'll love it there. It's new magic," he said proudly.

"Wonderful," Allie mumbled. Sam's blue eyes and ruffled blond hair came to her mind. Allie winced, shaking the image away. She had loved living in a place with new magic, and this was the perfect moment to separate it from her ex.

"Where are you from?" Brandon asked her.

"Pearls Fields."

"Ah, I see. It makes sense now." Allie threw him an inquisitive look. "Pearls Fields is old magic, right? I've never been, but I hear it's one of the places where people refuse to let new magic in." Allie remembered how the villagers and her coven sisters had protested loudly and violently the last time the mayor brought the idea of allowing new magic up for discussion.

"I've lived there most of my life," she explained, conveniently leaving out her time south with Sam, "so I'm not bothered by old magic." Even if new magic made life easier, and made her feel...stronger, somehow.

"Then what made you leave Pearls Fields?"

Allie thought about how to answer this best and decided on: "A learning experience."

Brandon nodded, as if he agreed this journey would be exactly that for Allie. As if it sounded familiar.

"Do you know of any places in Sycamore Falls where I can work for a little while?"

"There might be a place," Brandon said as he turned the wheel. They descended the last hill, and Allie could see a town taking form in the shadows of the night. Twinkling lights vibrated in the woolly darkness, surrounded by pure black. The teeming, intense lights fought the night bravely, and Allie thought this might be a town like Green Creek. Maybe bigger.

"You can't see it now, but Sycamore Falls is bordered by mountains covered in dense forests and hidden waterfalls. It's breathtaking during the day," Brandon said in a dreamy voice.

"I can't wait to see it," Allie replied and was surprised to note it was true.

Brandon drove the car closer and closer to the city, where a myriad of lampposts lit the paved road. They crossed a bridge over a wide river—Dahlia River, Brandon told her—and Allie could see houses and buildings lining both sides of the street. So close together it seemed crowded, just like Green Creek, but so much better than living isolated. Allie had loved having neighbors, restaurants and shops that she could walk to, lots of light at night, movies and television, fairs and carnivals on the weekends. Activities that people in old magic towns did not want to engage in, as they preferred to keep to themselves and their families.

Her life in Green Creek with Sam had been like a dream, until he'd jolted her awake.

Brandon stopped the vehicle on a paved street, where people were eating and drinking, music was pouring out of buildings, and the crisp air was filled with laughter and the smell of delicious foods.

"Welcome to Sycamore Falls."

Chapter 3

I PROMISE HE HAS MANNERS

It was a little past ten at night and the town was still alive, celebrating the last day before the work week started. In Green Creek, some people worked the entire week, and some had the weekends off. Here, it looked like almost everyone was enjoying their weekend.

Allie gawked at the wide street with shops on both sides, restaurants with tables outside, and people having fun. The townspeople were a mix of those with and without magic, which was common in cities with new magic, and she felt a wave of relief settle over her pounding heart. There was a small chance that she could meet another Witch.

"Come this way," Brandon said as he walked down the vibrant street. Allie followed him, taking in the clothing boutiques, book shops, flower stores, beauty salons, and other enterprises lining the street. "This is Maple Street," Brandon told her. "It's the main street in town where you'll find most businesses, and the market is at the other end of it. Some business owners prefer to keep to narrower streets, but everything you need is here."

"Seems like it," Allie said, delight sneaking into her voice.

"I live on the other side of the river, earmarked for residences and farms. But most business owners reside on the top floor of the townhomes here."

The buildings were separated from the sidewalk by small gardens lined with low, white fences. Brandon entered the footpath of one of these spaces, and Allie noticed the wooden sign hanging above the entrance read "Dom's Sweets." A bakery?

The porch light went on as Brandon approached the door, but the place was dark inside, and the "Closed" sign hung in the window. Allie stayed behind on the sidewalk while Brandon knocked hard enough to rattle the door off its hinges.

"Hey! Hey, D! Open up!" he shouted.

"I think the bakery is closed," Allie dared. She put her bag on the sidewalk and hugged herself as shiver after shiver traveled through her bones, carried by the cold night wind through the thin material of her summer dress.

"It's fine. Don't just stand there, come here," Brandon urged her. She did what she was told, and when she reached the space next to Brandon, she saw the "Help Wanted. Room Included" sign in the window.

Oh.

"Let's meet your future boss." Brandon grinned.

A boss, right. Sam used to have a boss, and he always complained about him. But this was Sam, and after everything Allie had learned about him, she considered he might have been at fault. Nevertheless, Brandon was using unorthodox means for her to apply for this job. Who would want to hire some stranger in the middle of the night, when the business was clearly closed?

"I can wait until tomorrow," she voiced her concerns. In a town as big as Sycamore Falls seemed to be, she would for sure find an inn, or maybe even a hotel.

"D, wake up!" Brandon shouted louder, ignoring her.

The top floor lit up. And in two long, shallow breaths, a faint light went on inside the bakery as well. Allie didn't know what to expect, *who* to expect, and her heart galloped with anticipation.

A tall figure strolled from the back of the bakery to the door where she and Brandon had been waiting. A man, she realized as he came closer. He unlocked the door and stepped into the porch light.

🍩

Dominic had been fast asleep when his room's walls shook with heavy pounding and his friend's voice pierced his blissful silence. What a friend, he thought, if Brandon had nothing better to do than wake him up before a working day. The people of Sycamore Falls prolonged their days with the coming of fall. Why, exactly, he didn't understand, since the sun was setting earlier, and the weather was cooler. Yet his neighbors engaged in late-night walks, movie nights, late dinners, and other events that came alive only when the leaves started to turn, as if the moon shone brighter this season than the rest of the year.

There was indeed something about fall nights in Sycamore Falls, and it was Dom's favorite time of the year in this town, but he didn't like it enough to sacrifice his sleep for it. Running a bakery meant he was up before dawn to warm up the ovens, prepare the doughs, fillings, breads, and pastries of the day, clean the space, check his orders, and perform many other tasks.

Dominic had a hard time admitting it, but the truth was, he needed help. Desperately. He was used to being on his own, something that came with his other, secret job. And he had come here because of that: to fulfill his mission, then go back to the Order and start his next. Dominic had been here for three long, unsuccessful months, and after the first one, he thought he might like to stay even after his mission ended.

It wasn't the first time he'd made a home out of a mission, but it was the first time doing so in his hometown. He had loved growing up in Sycamore Falls, and when his mission led him here, it felt like an opportunity for him to...set roots, maybe? He had gotten used to being on the road, traveling from one assignment to the next, but it was time to settle. Get a job, be part of a community, and all that. How hard could it be?

Damn hard.

Because the people of Sycamore Falls collectively decided they needed bread with everything, always had a sweet tooth, and had established the bakery as their favorite gathering place in town. Things he didn't know when he bought the place. But he worked hard to keep the business going and not raise any suspicions while completing his mission. Which took fucking forever.

Dominic enjoyed his peace and alone time and made sure everybody was aware of that. He considered ignoring Brandon, but couldn't dismiss the urgency in his voice. Begrudgingly, he went downstairs and opened the door to find Brandon and a stranger—a Witch, he noticed by her bright red hair—crowding his doorstep.

He swept his eyes over the Witch's long legs and bare arms. She wore thin leather flats and a flimsy green dress that did nothing against the chill night. Rich red hair framed a freckled, round face and brushed her waist in lush, wild curls.

"What?" Dominic barked at Brandon, his voice heavy with sleep. The Witch flinched and took half a step back. Her big brown eyes went wide, and her rosy mouth parted.

"Glad to see you're in good spirits, Dom," Brandon said and clapped him forcefully on the shoulder. "I found someone to help you at the bakery. This is Alecsandra," his friend said and pointed to the beautiful Witch.

A tall, broad man stepped outside the bakery wearing nothing but black pajama pants. Immediately, Allie tried to Read him as she did Brandon, throwing her magic at him like a pointy arrow. She was met with an invisible wall of steel, making it impossible for her magic to reach him. Did he also not have magic? But still... She should have Read that.

The bothered man stared at her, his eyes falling and staying on her hair. Maybe he didn't want to work with a Witch; not many people did, and Allie couldn't blame him.

But she stared right back at his sleep-ruffled chestnut hair that swept his shoulders, his huge figure, his bare chest. Sharp jaw, handsome face. She bet his green eyes were breathtaking in daylight and hoped they were kinder when he wasn't annoyed.

"She's looking for a place to stay and a job," Brandon described in her stead.

"And you thought bringing her here in the middle of the night was a good idea?" the man asked Brandon, who rolled his eyes in response.

"You're looking for help, and she's looking for work," Brandon repeated and gestured through his words with open palms. They were quiet for a long moment, the tension building and growing like a creature between them. Allie tried to keep her eyes off the man's naked chest, off his tense and well-defined muscles, off the tattoo around his left arm she couldn't discern. She did a poor job of it, her eyes flicking back and forth between his skin and the doorframe.

Brandon groaned and sighed loudly before placing his hand on Allie's arm. "This is Dominic Ranford, the owner of Dom's Sweets. I promise he has manners," he added, throwing a pointed look at the bakery owner as if daring him to prove him wrong.

"Hi, I'm Allie," she rushed to say. "Allie Wells." But judging by the way his mouth pursed and his brows furrowed into a sharp scowl...he was never going to call her Allie.

Dominic crossed his arms over his chest, the movement straining the muscles she strived not to stare at. He studied Allie as if he wanted to extract everything there was to know about her onto a piece of paper and read it rather than talk to her. His jaw clenched and his green eyes turned to slits.

"Do you have any experience baking?"

Allie knew there was only one answer she could give Dominic if she wanted to get this job. And she desperately wanted this job. At least for tonight, and for a couple of days, she had to work for him. If things didn't work out, Sycamore Falls seemed big enough for her to find another place. Brandon had said there were mountains and forests around, which sounded like the perfect place for her to practice controlling her fire. She *had* to stay in Sycamore Falls.

"Yes," Allie answered with fake confidence. "I used to bake with my mom." Partially true, as Petra used to do all the baking, and Allie used to do all the eating. But Dominic didn't need to know that.

"You would also be in charge of cleaning. Sometimes deliveries," Dominic added, his scrutinizing look burning hot patches into her cold skin. His scowl remained intact, but he raised a challenging eyebrow. Did he expect her to refuse the additional tasks? Ha.

"That's perfectly fine." Cleaning and deliveries were part of her chores in the coven; cleaning was a daily duty, and she would deliver potions and other orders to the villagers two times per week. Granted, she knew Pearls Fields like the back of her hand, and Sycamore Falls was a few times bigger than her old village. But she would manage. She had to. She had to practice and master her fire, so she could go back to her coven and her life, and this was the perfect place.

"Why don't you try to work together for a few days and see how it goes?" Brandon suggested, obviously out of patience. He took two steps back and saluted Dominic as the owner opened his mouth to argue. "Have a good night!"

And then he ran away from the bakery's garden, leaving Allie alone with Dominic.

The mountainous man said nothing and continued to stare at her, as if she was an object of great confusion to him. Allie realized it was up to her to convince him to hire her through any means necessary. She wasn't below begging, but she held a tiny flicker of hope that it wouldn't get there.

"Look, Mr. Ranford," she started and straightened her back, looking him in the eyes. "I'm a great worker, I never complain, and I will do my best to help you with anything you need." All of these things were true. "Give me a chance, at least for a couple of days, and if you cannot make use of me, I will leave," she promised.

Dominic didn't bat an eye, didn't even breathe for all she knew. And how was he standing half-naked in this cold without flinching, when Allie barely kept her teeth from chattering?

The fact that she couldn't Read him didn't give her peace. And with every second spent in his presence, Allie leaned toward him being a mean boss rather than a kind one. Nothing new under the sun—Lydia hadn't exactly been the picture of kindness toward Allie in the months she'd spent with the Silverbarks. She could endure anything for the seven weeks before she went back to her coven and the familiar meanness of her Magistra.

"Please," Allie added in her last attempt before resorting to begging on her knees. She held his scrutinizing look, although it chilled her more than the crisp night wind. After what felt like days with no end, Dominic exhaled and uncrossed his arms.

"The wage is one hundred per week, work starts at five every morning, and the bakery is open every day from half past eight to five in the afternoon with shorter weekend hours. Any questions?" Dominic asked as he turned his back on her, walking back into the dimly lit bakery.

"No!" Allie shrieked. Even if she didn't know where she was going to stay, or what her early morning tasks were, or a bunch of other things. Instead, she squealed from the doorway, "Thank you, Mr. Ranford!"

Dominic stopped somewhere in the middle of the bakery and turned his head enough to grunt over his shoulder.

"Are you coming?"

Chapter 4

OUCH

Allie picked up her duffel bag and followed her boss into her new workplace, closing the door behind her. She stopped for a second to take in the cozy space, the light beige floors, and the ivory wallpaper patterned with wide flower petals. The front of the bakery and the right-side wall hosted five square wooden tables painted a creamy white, surrounded by velvet azure chairs. In the back of the bakery was a marble counter with a register and a shelved display case for the baked goods, and behind it, a smaller counter with a fancy coffee machine on top of it. Allie had used Sam's coffee machine every day, but this one looked much more complicated than the one with two buttons. For the Silverbarks, she had ground the coffee beans freshly every morning using a mortar and pestle, then poured boiled water over the powder, wishing she had Sam's coffee machine.

"This way." Dominic's thick voice hurried her steps. She followed him past the counters, down a narrow hallway with an open door on the right, revealing a huge kitchen space. A few steps farther, a wooden staircase curled to her right, a small door under it labeled "Storage Room," opposite the last door on the left.

Dominic opened this door and turned the lights on. "This is your room."

Allie stepped inside but turned around instantly.

"Thank you again, Mr. Ranford. I promise I won't let you down," she declared enthusiastically.

Dominic grunted and headed for the stairs, with no further instructions for her job. A problem for tomorrow. Allie closed the door and noticed the lock wasn't working. Panic grew hot inside her, but she gripped it by the neck and shoved it away. Everything would be fine, and she was not defenseless. Although it would be such a pity to set this cozy bakery on fire. Allie started a mental list, with a door lock at the top.

The space was more like a studio than just a simple room. The kitchen was immediately to her right, a narrow island with two bar chairs separating it from the rest of the room. She had everything she needed: a stove and oven, a small fridge, and a counter next to the sink. Two cupboards were nailed against the wall, and a big window—the only window—revealed the bright moonlight above the sink. She pulled the deep green curtains and decided firmly that the color did not make her think about Dominic's eyes.

On the other side of the room, a wooden desk lined the left wall, and a plushy yellow sofa sat opposite the kitchen. It looked like a sofa bed, like the one in Green Creek, and more comfortable than her single bed at the manor. Suddenly, Allie wished Sam had let her handle more things around his house, but she would figure out how to expand it.

The bathroom was next to a closet where she found sheets, a pillow, a duvet, and enough space for her clothes.

All right.

This was great. She could do this. She would wake up early, clean, bake, deliver, and do anything else Dominic would ask. And come evening, when the bakery was closed, she would explore the town's surroundings and find her perfect place to practice.

She could do this. After all, she'd just left the Silverbarks this morning and already found a place to stay and a job. More like Brandon had found her on the brink of despair, but what did it matter now? Allie would forever be grateful to him and thought the first thing she baked should be for Brandon.

Maybe not exactly the *first* thing; she had a strong feeling that her baking might not be edible anytime soon. The thought that she lied to her boss about her baking skills sent shivers down her spine, his scrutinizing eyes coming to the forefront of her mind. Or maybe it was the cold. Yes, definitely the cold, so different from the sticky heat of Pearls Fields.

Allie drew a bath and made another plan, since the one she'd made this morning was successfully completed. Mainly by Brandon. She needed to buy warm clothes and to learn about baking. And about her magic. She added the clothing store and a bookstore to her list, deciding to leave the outside exploration for the next day.

Freshly out of the hot bath, Allie felt the chill in the air worse than before. The cold seeped through her skin and clung to her bones with pointed claws as she fumbled to get her blue camisole nightgown on. She wished that the duvet was as warm as it looked.

Allie shivered in front of the yellow sofa, pondering whether she really needed a bed for tonight. It looked as if she could squeeze in on the sofa if she slept with her knees pressed against her chest.

No.

She could figure it out. She had found a job and a place to stay on the same day. There was nothing much she couldn't do. Except bake or master her power. But she refused to let an inanimate object best her, even if she was known as the clumsiest Witch in the world.

Allie kneeled in front of the sofa like Sam used to do. She looked under it and behind it for a mechanism or a button to turn the cursed thing into a bed. With new magic, there was a button for everything. If only she had been paying attention to his actions instead of gawking at his face like a lovesick idiot.

A loose string was tucked in a crevice at the front, and her memories of Sam's movements clicked into place. Allie stood up and pulled on the string, but nothing happened. She pulled harder, certain the thing was stuck, and even jiggled it left and right. Unsuccessful, Allie decided she would try one more time before giving up. Sticking her heels into the floor, she grabbed the stubborn string and put her entire strength into this last pull. The string slipped from her hand, and that force worked against her.

She went stumbling back, tripped over one of the bar chairs, and plunged down with it.

"Ouch," she hissed and rubbed her hip. She glowered at the sofa, dubbed it her worst enemy, and resolved to sleep on the floor rather than try to convert it into a bed.

Loud footsteps drew her attention as the sound grew closer and closer and turned into an urgent knock on her door.

"What's going on?" Dominic's voice carried through the wall, thick and low and drastically annoyed.

"Nothing!" Allie shouted and heard the nerves in her voice. Her skin heated, as if Dominic could see her sitting on her ass in nothing but a see-through nightgown. Allie hurried to stand up and, in her rush, hit the fallen chair with her ankle. She sat back and suppressed her groan of pain, but the clattering noise echoed loudly through the room.

"I'm coming in," Dominic announced.

"No—" But the doorknob turned before she could protest further.

❦

Dominic knew he was going to regret hiring the Witch first thing in the morning, as soon as the daylight cleared the fog that had clouded his mind when he agreed to take her in. He was so damn tired he would have left a fire-spitting dragon in just to go back to sleep. He imagined the long string of colorful phrases he'd throw at Brandon the first time his friend dared show his face.

Why did he put that sign in the bakery's window in the first place? Did he *really* need help? Dominic should have known better and found a way to make it work on his own, like everything else in his life. No help needed, no one to crowd his space.

And definitely no one to wake him up in the middle of the night, for the second time, with a banging noise so loud it rattled his walls. It took a moment for his brain to connect the dots—Brandon, the Witch, hiring her, her living right under him—before he jumped out of bed and stormed down the stairs.

The manners Brandon had promised were the only thing that kept him from barging into her room without knocking first. But he could hardly be expected to act the gentleman after a certain time of the night.

The room was warm and dewy, wrapped in tangerine soap smell. Dominic took in the image before him: the Witch was sitting on the floor, one hand clasped on her ankle, the bar chair tipped over next to her. He ran various scenarios through his mind, but nothing made sense of the scene before him.

"What happened?" he snapped, glowering at Alecsandra.

"Nothing," she said again, as if he couldn't see the aftermath of whatever had occurred. She averted her gaze, gathering her ankle close to her body. "I just tripped," she admitted in such a low voice, it was almost a whisper. She brought her knees to her chest, stuffing them under her chin, and curled into a ball on the floor.

It was then that Dominic realized she was trying to hide from him.

Because she was in a thin, see-through nightgown.

A soft blue, gauzy camisole that offered Dom an unobstructed

31

view of the skin underneath. If her knees weren't covering her breasts... Fuck.

He noticed her blushed ivory skin, freshly out of a hot bath. The specks of water that pooled around her chest from the loose wet locks. The freckles that stood out so much more under the light than they did in the darkness. A flash of chocolate brown eyes she was trying to keep to herself.

Dom noticed all the things he had no business noticing. His brain switched into employer gear, and he bent down to grab the fallen chair, wanting to keep his hands busy.

Dominic picked up the bar stool as if it was made of feathers. Allie was glad he had found something to do other than stare at her pathetic self. But then her boss stretched his ink-covered arm to her, his crystal-green eyes fixed on her face. She gaped at his hand as if it put her life in danger.

It kind of did, though, as she wore this damned flimsy camisole, and taking Dominic's hand to stand up meant showing him much more than any employee should show their boss. Not only was this highly unprofessional, but she'd known the man for all of five minutes. And the last man who had seen her in this camisole was Sam, and that was...different. So, so different. She should have just burned the thing and wrapped herself in a rug.

Allie's breaths came in faster and hotter, the freezing cold long forgotten. She couldn't think of a reason to refuse Dominic's help and remain sitting on the floor.

"You fine?" he asked with a low grumble, his voice thicker than before.

"Great!" she spat the word before thinking better of it. "I'm fine, thank you, Mr. Ranford."

"What happened?" He sighed through his nose and finally took his hand away, but only to pull his fingers through his hair.

Allie thought about lying to him. The truth was stupid, and she was embarrassed. But nothing came to mind, and she was tired, and getting cold again, and her ankle hurt. With her clumsy skills in life, it was likely not the last time she would embarrass herself in front of him.

"I lost the fight with the sofa," she admitted, still avoiding his eyes. Dominic was quiet for a few breaths. She didn't know if he still watched her. Then his feet went out of sight, and Allie looked up to see Dominic bend down in front of the sofa. He tugged hard at that string and pulled out the extra piece that would make the sofa into a bed. Allie absolutely did not notice how his muscles flexed with the move. Not at all.

"That sticks sometimes. I'll fix it tomorrow," Dominic said.

"Thank you," Allie breathed. She dared a glance at him, but her boss bid her a hurried good night and left the room.

She sat there for another moment, waiting to make sure he wasn't going to come back. He had no reason to return because he didn't barge in here randomly. Allie cursed her clumsiness ten times over and made it a point in her plan to buy very soft slippers. And another carpet. And anything else that would stifle sounds, so she wouldn't bother him again.

Allie crawled to her feet, desperate for the bed's warmth. Before jumping under the soft duvet, she took the alarm clock from her desk and set it to four thirty in the morning, counting her few hours of sleep.

She fell into a restless slumber, nightmares of green-eyed monsters in the forms of cakes and croissants haunting her through the night.

Chapter 5

START THE OVENS, ALLIE

I f she had even a modicum of control over her power, Allie would have set the alarm clock on fire.

Smashing it until the ungodly noise stopped had to do. She was used to waking up early, but not *that* early. Lydia had her start the day's chores around dawn. Allie always spent a few moments by herself in the early mornings, watching as the dark world was painted over in warm colors, enjoying the last breathable moments before the scorching heat in Pearls Fields took its rightful place.

Now she watched the dark world stay dark, the thick night draping over her window like a velvet blanket. The urge to pull the duvet over her head and go back to sleep was strong. Her bones felt heavy like lead, confining her to the warm bed.

Dominic's scrutinizing green eyes haunted her, and she pictured him coming downstairs into the bakery only to find she was still asleep.

Allie jolted up and ran to the bathroom.

She splashed freezing cold water on her face and tamed her wild bed head. Dominic's eyes returned to the center of her mind, and an image of one of her hairs on the bakery counter took form.

Allie gathered her red mane and styled it quickly into a tight low bun. While she was at that, she stored her four stone rings on the bathroom shelf and tucked her crescent moon necklace tightly into her dress.

Dominic had enough reasons to sack her without Allie contributing her own. She had to make up for the fact that she couldn't bake to save her life, so everything else needed to be perfect. Allie donned her only long-sleeved purple dress and leather flats, looking forward to that evening when she got some warmer clothes.

Five minutes before five in the morning, Allie exited her room and nearly knocked over her boss as he came downstairs.

"Good morning," she chirped, taking a step back to make room for him. He wore a black T-shirt, dark jeans, and laced boots. His chestnut brown locks were pulled into a neat bun on the top of his head. Allie was thankful for whatever instinct that had coaxed her into doing the same.

Dominic sized her up, flats to bundled hair, and grunted, "Morning," as he switched on a bunch of lights around the shop. Allie followed the trail of crisp cedarwood scent with a tinge of leather her boss left behind him, wondering if he wasn't an early riser, or if he was still annoyed from last night. Or maybe grumpy and monosyllabic was his entire personality.

Allie went down the hallway into the bakery floor. The place was even more stylish and cozy than it had appeared in the dim light last night, the dark blue chairs elegant against the warm-colored floors and walls, sophisticated but homey. A few abstract paintings hung on the walls, splattering them with dark violet and burnt orange shades.

Dominic shuffled between the kitchen and the storage room before coming to the front, a notebook in one hand, and an apron he offered Allie in the other. The all-black intricate tattoo on his left arm was right under her nose—a thick tree trunk covered his forearm, and leafless branches stretched up and wrapped around his upper arm, hiding beneath the T-shirt sleeve. Delicate details were woven through the ink, but she needed to be much closer to Dominic to distinguish and inspect them.

"What should I start with, Mr. Ranford?" she asked, tying the apron.

"Start the ovens and clean the kitchen counters. The cleaning supplies are in the cupboard under the sink." He slapped the notebook on the front counter, picked up a pen, and glanced at Allie over his shoulder.

Dismissed.

"Right," she said to herself and left for the kitchen.

The space was predominantly white, with a huge working table in the middle and walls lined with two sinks on the left, three different refrigerators on the right, shelves, counters, and multiple types of ovens.

Start the ovens, Allie.

She stood helplessly in front of the oven that resembled the one from the coven's manor. Resembled in appearance only, as this one had infinitely more buttons and knobs. Not even the one she had used in Green Creek was similar. The next oven was identical, while the last two were tall, vertical ovens Allie had never seen before. And they had *a lot* of buttons.

Start one oven, Allie.

But which one? And how?

Perhaps she should clean first.

Yes, that was a great idea. After all, it was part of her tasks. She opened the cupboard under the sink and pulled out cloths and a cleaning spray. Allie scrubbed the surfaces in the kitchen as if her life depended on it.

She didn't know how much time had passed until her boss sauntered into the kitchen to check on her work. He walked in casually, hands in his jeans' pockets, and surveyed the shining space. Allie smiled broadly, waiting for him to find anything wrong with her work, knowing he would find nothing.

Dominic stopped in the middle of the room, his green eyes turning to wide saucers. Allie followed his gaze and gulped, her heart thudding in her ears. Okay, there was *one* wrong thing to find. Or four.

"Why are the ovens off, Alecsandra?" he asked in a low voice. When she didn't answer instantly, he went on. "Did you know a bakery cannot bake anything if the ovens are not turned on?" Dominic's voice raised with each word, his rage-filled eyes turning to her. He hurried from one oven to the next, pressing and turning dozens of buttons and knobs in a sequence that she would have to write down to remember.

Allie wanted to make herself small and hide under the table at the clear disappointment etched on his features.

"You cannot tell me you forgot," he stated.

She couldn't. Forgetting one of the two tasks she had been assigned was far more embarrassing than admitting she didn't know how to turn on the fancy ovens. Dominic's nostrils flared as he waited for her to say something. The truth was her only option, and she cleared her throat of the orange-sized lump stuck there and straightened her spine. She had faced Lydia's wrath countless times, and each time she did it with dignity. So why should she cower now?

"I'm sorry, Mr. Ranford." As humbling as it was, she held his gaze. "I don't know how to turn on these ovens."

Dominic closed his eyes for a long inhale and pinched the bridge of his nose.

"Why didn't you tell me?" he asked in a calmer but colder

voice. She'd said she was familiar with baking, but maybe not commercially. Dominic had been too sleepy and annoyed to inquire about all the necessary details last night, *before* hiring the Witch. It wouldn't really be a problem if she had only baked at home. He could show her how to turn on the damn ovens. Dom realized he had missed other important details, like where she was from and *why* she came to Sycamore Falls. "Where did you say you were from?" His eyes snapped open and fixed on her, waiting. Bracing for whatever answer she would give him.

"Pearls Fields?" she asked more than answered, fidgeting with her apron.

"What?"

"But I lived in Green Creek for a while," she added quickly, taking a step toward him. "I've been around new magic before, I promise."

In a poor attempt to hide his irritation, Dominic gritted his teeth so hard they were on the edge of cracking. He deserved this. He had hired a stranger in the middle of the night under pressure from his friend without knowing anything about her. A Witch who had been living with old magic for her entire life. He didn't even know what power she'd mastered. Lucky for him, she had no way to learn about his own.

"What, exactly, do you know about baking?" he asked, his left hand cupping his chin and rubbing it to relieve the tension in his jaw.

He saw the answer in her deep brown eyes, when fear mixed with embarrassment coated the beautiful color with thin glass. She swallowed, keeping the obvious answer to herself but, to her credit, didn't drop his gaze.

Of course she knew nothing about baking.

He deserved this.

Dom couldn't look at her struggling to answer him, so he

turned on his heel and barked an order to clean the tables and front counters before storming out of the bakery. He should address the problem at the root, which meant paying a quick visit to his idiot friend.

Dominic jumped into his black coupe and drove away from Maple Street, crossing the bridge to the other side of the town and winding through the forested hills to the farmlands area. The night was still strong, a couple of hours away from thinning, hiding the beauty of Sycamore Falls. Dom drove through the light of the lamp posts, pondering what he should yell about first when he met his friend.

Brandon owned and managed the Riverbend Farm, one of the best-known and in-demand farms in Sycamore Falls. He had customers from many neighboring towns and an entire team of employees living on the premises to get all the work done. The place was huge, and one time, when they were young and he went looking for Brandon, he ended up getting lost in the spinach fields.

As the road twisted to the right and the inky river came back into view, so did the red sign with gold writing and the farm's name on it. Dominic entered the driveway to Brandon's place, hoping he wasn't already away doing chores. But his friend stood on the porch of his green-roofed, white brick house, mug in hand, and waved with a smile when he noticed the black car approaching. Dom's first thought was to wipe that carefree smile off Brandon's face. He got out of the car and slammed the door, heading for the porch.

"Morning, D," Brandon greeted him cheerfully.

"What the hell is wrong with you?"

"I take it you didn't have coffee yet?" Brandon offered him the coffee mug, which Dom considered pouring over his head.

"Why did you bring her to me?" Dominic berated him.

Brandon pulled his fingers through his short black hair,

averting his dark eyes. "Come on, Dom," he started, and Dominic knew this wasn't going to end in his favor. Every time Brandon said those three words, Dominic ended up doing his friend's bidding.

"Why?" he pressed. He needed a reason, at the very least.

"She was alone at nighttime on the side of a rarely circulated road. I happened to be on my way back from the Sanders." The elderly couple living in a secluded forest area, far away from Sycamore Falls. Brandon had learned about them from one of his customers and took it upon himself to visit and bring them fresh produce once a month. Dom had often baked extra goods when he knew Brandon's visit was approaching, and sometimes, they went together. "Honestly, she was lucky I found her, and not someone else." The meaning behind Brandon's words sent a cold chill down Dom's spine. "I couldn't just pass by and leave her there, Dom. What if it was Mia?"

The question hit Dominic in the middle of his chest like a cement brick, and hot panic gripped him as if the words were true.

"Don't talk about my sister," he warned Brandon, who rolled his eyes in reply. His friend played dirty, putting that thought in his head. The idea that Alecsandra had no one to look out for her, as he looked out for his sister, didn't sit well with him.

It pained him to admit that Brandon was right. Not that he'd ever, *ever*, let Mia put herself in a situation like that. But if it ever happened—after he was dead, of course—he would be a grateful ghost if his sister stumbled upon people with good intentions. Like freaking Brandon.

Dom didn't know if he should hug him or punch him in the face.

Brandon watched the realization set into his friend's face and offered his coffee mug again. Dom snatched it and took two big gulps, the hot, bitter liquid warming him up.

"How bad is it?" Brandon asked him. Dom scoffed.

"She doesn't know the first thing about baking, she comes from a place of old magic, and for all I know, she is a master of tripping over her own feet." That was and wasn't the case, but Brandon didn't need to know that. Dom took a note to borrow his tool kit and fix the yellow sofa. And get a new lock for the room.

Brandon chuckled and scratched his head awkwardly, again avoiding Dom's eyes. He immediately knew why.

"You knew about Pearls Fields?" he shouted. "And you still brought her to me?"

"Yours was the only business in town that I knew was looking for help," he said, raising his palms defensively, almost as if he knew he was one word away from having coffee thrown in his face.

"What else did she tell you? Why did she agree to come with you?"

"Probably because the alternative was to sleep under the stars and pray nothing and no one would endanger her life?" Brandon asked sarcastically.

"What if you were the dangerous one?" Dom asked, trying to make sense of all of this. Was she reckless? She must have at least used her Reading magic before climbing into Brandon's car.

"You know I'm not!" Brandon said defensively. "But that just tells us how desperate she was." Dominic sighed through his nose and shook his head. "She said she left Pearls Fields for a learning experience." Great. A wandering Witch with no clear goal, no connections, and probably no money. "What are you going to do about her?"

Dom had no clue how to answer that. It would be an immense pain to train her to help him at the bakery. She would make a thousand mistakes and drive him crazy, when he could very well hire someone capable. Someone who knew how to turn on the damn ovens, who knew the difference between wheat flour and rice flour, and who lessened his burden around the bakery so he could focus on completing his mission.

But could he turn her away, send her roaming the streets looking for another place? Dom was unpleasant and grumpy, but at least his place and this job were safe.

What if it was Mia?

He handed the empty coffee mug back to Brandon and asked after a long sigh, "Can I borrow your tool kit?"

Chapter 6

YOU LOOK MORE BOTHERED THAN USUAL

Allie scrubbed the kitchen again, then the tables and counters in the front. She even moved that fancy coffee machine and wiped the area behind and under it, and cleaned the display case as well. With a soft brush, she dusted the blue velvet chairs, then wiped the front door's window. She found a broom, a mop, and a bucket in the supply closet and used them vigorously. When the place smelled too much of chemicals, she opened the door and the windows, letting the chill morning air flow in and ignoring the chattering of her teeth.

She had earned her shivers.

Why, *why* hadn't she told her boss from the start that she didn't know how to turn on the ovens? In the end, she'd had to admit it anyway, with the added horror of Dominic knowing she intentionally hid this from him. Why she'd thought that a good idea was beyond her now. Dominic had every right to bite her head off.

Allie wanted to keep her job while she strove to get her crazy fire under control by Hallows Eve. There was no other acceptable outcome. Looking for another place was a waste of time when Sycamore Falls, and more specifically, Dom's Sweets, was everything she needed. But she had to get her silly act together in front of her boss and find a way to clear the fog that clouded her brain whenever Dominic spoke to her. She had to do better and be honest, even when it was embarrassing.

No more lying or keeping things hidden. The bookstore climbed up her list of priorities, since she desperately needed to learn basic baking skills to help Dominic. More like be able to do her job.

A revving engine drew her attention to the street. She closed the bakery windows and stood in the doorframe, watching as the darkness surrendered to the first rays of light. The auburn colors of the sycamores lining the street came to life with shimmering shades of red and yellow, and the mountaintops surrounding the town basked proudly in the sunlight. Pearls Fields held its evergreen beauty, but this was the most beautiful landscape she had ever seen.

Dominic climbed out of the car and crossed the sidewalk and small front yard in long strides, a toolbox in his hand. She took him in, tall, dark, and broad, oozing confidence and annoyance. She couldn't help but notice the stark contrast between Dominic and, well, all other men she had met. There was something about him that drew her in, and she wished she could Read him. Did he have any magic? What kind? What if he was a Wizard? Would he help her if she asked?

Probably not.

Allie stepped away to make room for him to enter the bakery and closed the door behind them. She cleared her throat and started on the speech she had prepared while scrubbing the place clean.

"Mr. Ranford, I'm really sorry about earlier." Dominic stopped in his tracks with his wide back to her and didn't turn around as she spoke. "I should have told you the truth. I don't have any baking experience, not even domestically, but I am a quick learner, and I promise I'll bridge the gaps in no time." She hoped she could keep this promise. "This evening after work, I'll stop by the bookstore. Are there any books about baking I should start with?"

Dominic was quiet, and Allie would've given anything to see the look on his face. After a while, she heard him sigh, the muscles on his back shifting under his shirt.

"Do you know how to separate eggs?" he muttered.

Separate eggs, separate eggs, separ—yes! Separating eggs was one of the few tasks Petra had entrusted her with.

"I do!"

"For real this time?"

Allie couldn't fault him for doubting her.

"For real. I need to put the yolks in a bowl, and the whites in another bowl," she explained, waving her hands. He nodded once, still not turning around to face her.

"Take bowls from the shelf on the left and twenty eggs from the middle fridge," he said and walked away, down the narrow hallway. Toward her room.

"Is there anything you need?" she asked when Dominic stopped in front of her room. Allie had nothing to hide, and last night proved her boss would respect her privacy. Kind of. He *had* knocked first.

"I'm going to fix the sofa," he grumbled as he slipped through the door. "And put in a new lock."

Allie stared dumbfounded at the empty hallway. Not only was she still employed, but her boss would go through the trouble of fixing stuff around her room. All the more reason she had to prove to Dominic that she could be useful and not a pain. "Thank you!" she shouted after him and sprinted to the kitchen.

Allie put the bowls and the eggs on the table and washed her hands thoroughly. Focused on not messing up yet another task today, she cracked and opened the first egg gently, trying to keep the shells intact to separate the whites from the yolks without any shell pieces falling in. With each egg, she gained confidence, her hands became steadier, and she caught herself smiling. Maybe she should not have felt that pang of pride for accomplishing such a small feat when she couldn't even start the ovens.

The eggs' cracking sounds were occasionally accompanied by hammering and drilling noises coming from the back of the bakery. Dominic fixing the sofa instead of firing her made a spark of hope bloom in her chest. Getting rid of her might be a peripheral idea in his mind, given all her shortcomings, but she could lean into this safety for a while. She hoped for at least two weeks before his patience ran out, so she would be able to explore the town and save some money.

When she was done with the eggs, Allie put the shells in the bin and cleaned the table. Dominic walked in as she was wiping it, wearing a black apron just like hers over his all-black clothes.

A muscly vision in black.

She whisked the thought away, shaking her head.

"You okay?" Dominic asked.

"I'm fine, thank you!" she shrieked. "And thank you for the sofa. And for the new lock." Allie paused for a second but added quickly, "And for taking me in."

Dominic grunted and started working around the kitchen.

Every time he took out a new utensil or ingredient, Allie tried to remember their place. He gave her small tasks: hand him this and that, sprinkle flour or sugar over a dough he was mixing, tape the oven trays with baking paper. She paid meticulous attention to each detail, and between tasks, she paid meticulous attention to her handsome boss.

Which she scolded herself for, over and over. Then proceeded to do it again.

Her eyes traveled over his straining muscles as he kneaded the dough with ease and mastery. She could have been fooled about the difficulty of this task if it weren't for memories of Petra sweating and cursing every time she kneaded dough.

Dominic looked so much in his element, focused but content with each task, and when he tasted something he approved of, Allie saw a hint of pride take form on his handsome face. Never enough to turn into a smile, though. Her traitorous eyes moved over his arms and broad chest, up to his neck, and short of pulling them out of their sockets, she was helpless.

The man was attractive. And that was all there was to it, Allie decided, as she broke her gaze from him for the hundredth time.

That was how the early hours of the morning passed. The place smelled divine, and when some cakes and pastries were ready, Dominic showed her how to arrange them in the display case. He'd made ham and cheese croissants and kept two slices of apple pie for them to eat for breakfast. The croissants were buttery and soft, the pie was warm and not too sweet, and Allie fought to keep the moan lodged in her throat from escaping. She had never eaten anything more delicious in her life.

Sorry, Mom.

Close to opening time, there was already a line outside the bakery.

"Is it this busy every day?" she asked, surprised to see so many people waiting this early in the morning.

"Yeah. Most folks in town stop by before work to get coffee and stuff," Dominic said in one of the longest sentences he'd spoken to her.

Coffee, too. Great. Of course, coffee, too; why else would that machine be there? Allie prayed to whatever gods were listening that he wouldn't ask her to make coffee using the fancy, overly-complicated machine in the front.

Dominic wiped his hands on the apron, which was now peppered with flour marks and dough smudges. A lock of hair had pulled free from his bun and hung loose over his cheek. His emerald eyes were sparkling, as if he'd come alive together with his pastries. Allie wondered how a wide, genuine smile would look on him.

Her boss checked the time and gave Allie a short nod before he went to unlock the door and flip the sign to "Open."

⁂

Dominic was used to the morning rush. He was also used to most people's daily orders, so when he served them out of habit, he noticed Alecsandra's puzzled looks.

What he wasn't used to was the townsfolk's sneers and suspicious looks. Their usual smiling faces turned into glaring grimaces when they noticed the Witch behind the counter. The people of Sycamore Falls were a tight, wary community with all the dangers looming over their lands, part of the real reason Dom was here. They weren't particularly friendly to any newcomers, but he didn't remember them glaring collectively like that. Sure, there was a valid reason people here grew to hate Witches in the last year, but that didn't mean they were all the same. They didn't even know Alecsandra.

The hypocrisy of that thought hit him in the head like a hammer when he realized he might have given her the exact same look last night. He didn't know the Witch either, but she was his employee now. And didn't he deserve the benefit of the doubt, as a born and bred citizen of Sycamore Falls? Dom hiring someone should be a vetting card. If people were suspicious of his employee, weren't they suspicious of him?

All this time, Alecsandra served the bags and packages he handed her with a smile on her face. He didn't know if it was genuine or fake, but he leaned toward the latter because surely she noticed the long, rude looks aimed at her. Yet she greeted everyone politely, asked if they needed anything else, and wished them a good day, that smile not faltering once.

His fourth customer was the first to alert him to his behavior.

"Is everything okay, Dominic?" Anna O'Brien asked, batting her eyelashes at him with exaggerated worry in her blue eyes. She wore her long, black hair in a sleek ponytail and visited the bakery every morning without exception, making her Dom's Sweets' most loyal customer. Anna had had an obvious crush on him since before he'd left Sycamore Falls to join the Order, and he tried to be polite while keeping his distance. The last thing he was interested in was a relationship, especially with one of the town's sweethearts.

"Yes," he barked.

"Are you sure? You look more bothered than usual." Anna chuckled. The scrutinizing look she fixed on the Witch was different than the others, and Dom did his best not to roll his eyes to the back of his head.

"I'm fine," he said and heard the bite in his tone. The people in line behind Anna made faces at him. Had he been glaring back at his customers? Dominic cleared his throat awkwardly, then asked, "Do you need anything else, Anna?"

"Ah, yes. Coffee to go, please. Also..." She twirled the end of her ponytail. "Are you free tonight?"

"Not tonight."

Dominic turned to Alecsandra, who was packing Anna's order of croissants and blueberry scones. "Can you make—" Her terror-filled eyes shot up, as if he punched her in the stomach.

So the coffee machine was off limits, too. Great. Dominic needed to sit her down and figure out what he had to teach her. And while he was at that, he should ask a couple hundred questions that he didn't get to ask in the middle of the night.

Why was she here? Why did she leave Pearls Fields? How long was she here for? What was her power? Were the people in Sycamore Falls right to be so wary and unwelcoming? He hadn't spent much time around Witches during his thirty-five years of life, and the ones he'd met had been…all right. Not dangerous, but not exactly innocent either. Except the one that made Witches the sworn enemy of the town.

Maybe he should get some answers before glaring at his customers on her behalf.

"Never mind, I'll do it," he mumbled. Dom noticed the coffee machine was almost empty. "One second, Anna," he addressed the customer before running to the back to get a coffee pack.

When he returned, he found Alecsandra standing in front of the coffee machine, two different-sized to-go cups in her hands, a wide smile on her face. A *very different* smile from the one she used with his customers. Her brown eyes were hopeful and expectant, and as much as Dom didn't know about her, he couldn't deny that she seemed willing to do the work, to learn.

What if it was Mia?

Fucking Brandon. He'd messed with his head, and now Dom couldn't get rid of the made-up version of his baby sister being in the Witch's place. What if Alecsandra also had a brother? He should find him and kick his ass for letting her roam the world by herself. The simple thought made his blood boil, and he sighed through his nose as he snatched the cups from the Witch's hands.

"Give me those."

Allie felt her smile melt. Did she pick the wrong cups? She thought the morning was going well. Ever since the oven debacle, she hadn't made another mistake. Except for the fact that she didn't know how to operate the coffee machine, which wasn't *exactly* a mistake, she did everything Dominic asked. She worked quickly and carefully, and even smiled at all the customers who scowled at her in return. Not the first or last time she would get this treatment as a Witch; Allie was used to it. People had a hard time trusting Witches, and for valid reasons. Besides their usual devious powers that let them into people's minds, they'd had a reputation for being cunning and manipulative for centuries. Allie couldn't break that belief with a simple smile.

But she wasn't here to make friends or to change the folks' minds about Witches. She was focused on her goal, on practicing her magic and going back to her coven in a few weeks. The bakery job was a means to an end, and she needed to treat it that way. And if this "means" was to last up until the very end, she needed to become good at it.

Packing and serving was easy, as she had to pick between a paper bag or a box based on the order's size. Or plates for eat-in customers, which they'd had none of so far. The prices were listed on the inside of the display case under each product, and she had always been good with math. Allie made no mistakes with the totals, even when an order contained multiple products.

What had pissed her boss off in his short trip to the storage room? She wanted to watch him make the coffee, but she had a tingling sense running along her spine that she should move away and give him space. After all, she was a stranger who came to him in the middle of the night looking for work and a place to stay, and couldn't even make coffee. They didn't know each other, and he owed her no kindness or courtesy.

Allie stepped out of Dominic's way and let him handle the to-go coffee while she took the next customer's order, plastering that fake smile back on her face.

Chapter 7

HOW DO YOU KNOW DOMINIC?

The rest of Allie's first day of work was fortunately uneventful. She stuck to the tasks of packaging, serving, and cleaning tables between customers. After the lunch hour rush, Dominic elbowed her and pointed to a sandwich and an apple on the kitchen table. She thanked him and made a mental note to go to the market as well, to be responsible for her meals starting tomorrow.

In the late afternoon, after Dominic flipped the sign to "Closed," she noticed there wasn't much left of the goods baked today. Dominic had baked several batches throughout the day to serve them warm and fresh. He said he'd rather have people wait longer than sell them stale pastry. It was also his strategy so that at the end of the day, he wouldn't be left with a lot of unsold pastries and loaves of bread. Dominic said all of this in very few words, most of which were grumbled and forced out with invisible pliers.

He told Allie she could have anything left at the end of the day if she wanted. She kept a loaf of bread for later, then picked the last piece of strawberry chocolate cake and one of the croissants, which she gobbled down while her boss counted the money. They had agreed on payment at the end of every week, which worked for Allie, as the money she had was enough for the next few days.

Now that she knew the bakery cleaning was done before the day started, Allie was taking her apron off when she noticed Dominic pulling out a stack of boxes and packaging the goods that hadn't been sold.

"Can I help you, Mr. Ranford?"

"I'm good," he said with a deep rumble inside his chest, not taking his eyes off the boxes. She waited until he was done anyway, just in case. Dominic must have felt her intense gaze, as he said, "I'm taking these across town."

"Okay." That meant nothing to Allie, so she dared ask, "Where are you taking them?"

Dominic's hesitation was obvious, his green eyes moving swiftly over the five boxes he'd filled with the baked goods.

"Each day to a different place. Orphanage, nursing home, library, if they have a community event." He spoke as if this meant nothing, as if he was just driving around town for pleasure. But this gesture told Allie so much about him, about the kind of man he was. A man who took a stranger in need into his home without *much* resistance.

"That's incredibly kind, Mr. Ranford. Do you need any—"

"I'm good, Alecsandra," he rushed the words out. "You can go." All this time, he never looked at her once, his glare focused on the bakery boxes as if they had wronged him.

Allie gave her boss a short nod that went unseen, took her apron off, and left to explore the town. She had a list to complete: clothes, books, and food. Brandon had said Maple Street was the place where she could find anything, and he had been right.

Across from Dom's Sweets was a bookstore, and two doors down, past a hardware store and a pharmacy, was a clothing store. Allie kept walking up to the other end of the street, where she saw the green, wooden sign that read "Sycamore Falls Market." In

Pearls Fields, the market closed at dusk, earlier than all shops, so she decided to start there.

The market was devised as two rows of stalls facing each other under a sort of pavilion: a single long, wooden roof held up by multiple tall pillars set into the ground. It was open on all sides but covered against the elements. Did it snow in Sycamore Falls in the winter? She'd never seen snow with the constant summery weather of Pearls Fields, and Green Creek had been even hotter.

Allie strolled through the market stalls, gathering wary looks from the vendors, who kept glaring at her red hair. She smiled shyly, but that warm, pressing feeling of not belonging that had built in her stomach when she was younger didn't come now. With every year and every time she came across rude strangers, her skin had grown thicker, and she had stopped taking the apprehensive looks personally. Now she focused on her shopping task and purchased all kinds of vegetables for soup and stews, honey-baked ham, chicken, a piece of beef, three different types of cheese, apples, pears, dates, and fresh plums that made her think of her mother. All vendors had served her tight-lipped and with deep frowns on their faces. No reason to be upset over that. At least they didn't refuse her.

After dropping her full bags from the market in her room—and noticing but not caring that Dominic had left—Allie crossed the street and walked down to the clothing store. The door opened with a loud bell that drew the shop owner's attention.

"Welcome," the woman said on instinct before her blue eyes fell on Allie. She recognized the vendor as one of the customers from this morning who'd addressed her boss in a friendly way, asking him if he was fine.

Allie said, "Thank you," knowing that she wasn't welcome in the true sense of the greeting. She quickly perused the shelves and hangers in the store and set her eyes on the sweaters and jeans section. She was running her fingers over the materials and checking their sizes when a form shadowed her from behind.

"May I help you?" the woman asked in an icy tone, as if "yes" would not be an acceptable response. Allie shook her head.

"I'm good, thank you." She sounded like Dominic.

With this, she hoped to regain some privacy, but the shadow lingered, and when Allie turned to face her, she found the woman's eyes squeezed to slits, arms crossed over her chest, watching her.

"How do you know Dominic?" the shopkeeper asked. Allie's brows shot up.

"Excuse me?"

"How do you know Dominic?" she repeated, her tone growing impatient.

In general, Allie was a kind, mild-tempered woman. She'd had her moments, of course, but they were rare and more than well justified, in her opinion. The reply shocked her as it came out of her mouth.

"How do *you* know Dominic?" Allie hadn't spoken his name until now. It tasted sweet and warm and dangerous. Would she ever get to call him that?

The woman's brows rode her hairline, wide blue eyes gazing dumbfounded at Allie.

"I'm Anna O'Brien," she said matter-of-factly, like it meant something. When Allie didn't react to her very common name, she added, "Dom and I grew up together," in a tone of voice that was a challenge more than anything else. Allie's heart squeezed on a beat when she realized this woman had known Dominic for so long. Unreasonable jealousy sparked inside her, but Allie crushed it with the heel of her mind.

It didn't matter. She was here only for a short while, so she glued a smile on her face and returned the fake politeness.

"I'm Alecsandra Wells," she said, mimicking the Anna's

iciness, not wanting to introduce herself as Allie. When Anna's glare didn't move from her face, Allie ordered herself not to roll her eyes. "I'll be working at the bakery for a while." The woman looked down her nose, a look of superiority very familiar to Allie. She turned on her heel and went back to the counter, her slim ponytail swinging with the movement.

Allie gave some serious thought to freezing her ass off in Sycamore Falls. What if she wore multiple dresses in layers? Or she could sew new clothes. Was there another clothing store in town? Maybe she could find a kinder shopkeeper, or at least one that would ignore her and glare from a distance.

Ugh. It was already late, and she wanted to stop by the bookstore too. Allie sighed, her shoulders slumping as she gathered some weather-appropriate items.

She picked jeans and a purple plaid skirt, a pair of comfortable black boots, a few sweaters and long-sleeved shirts, fleece-lined PJs, and a jacket. Anna wore her feelings on her face too well, and Allie noticed she was torn between being grateful for her business and kicking her out empty-handed. Anna decided on the former, so Allie left the store with two large shopping bags.

She stepped outside into the fully darkened street, where all the lampposts were lit now, looking like cocky fireflies guarding the town. The temperature had dropped even lower with the loss of sunlight, and Allie looked forward to breaking into her new clothes. Even so, she enjoyed breathing in the crisp, cold air and was excited to live in a place where the fall season was thriving, all the more since this was only for a short time.

Bookstores were her favorite places, and in Green Creek, Allie visited one every couple of weeks. She went in eager to see the selection and purchase some books on baking and elemental Witchcraft in a quiet, chill place.

But she was welcomed into a loud and chaotic space.

The books were scattered all over the place, on the floor, on all the shelves, on the counter. Some were laughing, some were crying, all chittering in a collective warble that made her want to cover her ears. The shop was narrow and long, similar to all the other businesses here, and filled with dark red, wooden shelves that smelled like a wet forest. Allie looked around for the shopkeeper but found no one. She checked the sign again to make sure it said "Open." Searching through all this chaos and finding what she needed would be impossible.

"Hey, knock it off!" a voice shouted from the back of the store, followed by a clapping sound. The books flew back to their shelves and quieted in an instant.

A petite brunette with long, wavy hair and brown eyes hurried to the front but stopped abruptly when she saw Allie, her long, red wool dress pooling at her feet. She smiled at Allie, fleetingly pausing on her red bun, then asked in a chirpy voice, "May I help you?"

"I didn't know there was old magic in Sycamore Falls," she said instead of answering. "I was told this was a place of new magic."

"It is, at large. But I've always preferred old magic when it comes to books. There's something special about letting them be alive before they find forever homes," the woman said. A book on the left shelf made a cooing sound, and the petite woman slapped it hard on the spine. "Naughty," she chided it. Allie couldn't help but chuckle, which drew the vendor's attention back to her. "Are you just passing through?"

"I'm here for a while," Allie said, trying to hide the hope from her words. "I'm working with Mr. Ranford at the bakery."

The woman's cackle resounded in the now quiet space.

"Pfft. Mr. Ranford." She scoffed with a smile. It appeared everyone here had an opinion or other about her boss. "How did you end up at Dom's Sweets?" she asked, and Allie detected curiosity only. She told her about Brandon and the previous night, and briefly about her first day of work. When she was done, the woman looked at her with a grin that stretched her brown skin. "I'm Mia," she said, and extended her hand. "Welcome to Sycamore Falls."

Allie took her hand and smiled, genuinely this time. "It's nice to meet you. I'm Allie."

"Can I help you find anything today?"

"I'm looking for books on baking." The women stared at each other for a moment before Mia burst into laughter.

"He hired you with no experience. Yeah, that sounds like Brandon's doing," she said more to herself. "Let's see what we can find." Mia waved her hand, twirling her wrist, and several books flew off the bookshelves and came floating in front of her. She flipped through them as if they were all pages in one book.

"You're an Archivist," Allie said, wonder in her voice. She'd never met one but had heard about them in school. Mia beamed proudly.

"I am. And if you know enough about Archivists, you know we prefer old magic to new magic," she stated, raising her brows in question. Allie nodded, and Mia resumed her search. After flipping through dozens of books, she finally grabbed one out of thin air and handed it to Allie. "I think you can start with this one."

Baking for Dummies.

How suitable.

"I'll take it," Allie agreed. "And..." How could she ask about a book to help with her power? It meant admitting that she didn't have it under control. That she didn't know enough about it. Would the people of Sycamore Falls feel threatened by her lack of control, as her coven sisters did?

"And?" Mia looked intently at her for a moment, her hazel eyes kind and patient. She must have felt Allie's hesitation as a corner of her mouth lifted just a tad. "I'm very discreet. I promise." Allie held her steady gaze and sent a quick wisp of Reading magic around the lovely shopkeeper, looking for any signs of malice or evil intent. She found none and felt that the Archivist's magic was warm and soft, like velvet or honey. So far, her intuition and Readings hadn't failed her, so Allie decided to trust Mia with this piece of herself.

"I need a book on Witchcraft." Mia blinked slowly once, twice, and Allie knew she expected at least one other crucial detail. She exhaled through her nose and added, "Elemental Witchcraft."

Mia nodded and repeated the hand wave motion, bringing forth several books from which to pick. She frowned and grimaced at them until she found one she deemed worthy for her client.

"Here you go," she said and handed Allie the second book.

Insights into Elemental Witchcraft.

"Thank you."

Both headed to the counter, where Mia packaged the books and pocketed the money casually, disregarding the register. She must be the business owner.

"Have a good night," Allie said and headed to the door.

"Allie." Mia's voice came rushed. She stopped and turned to look Mia's way. "If anyone here is giving you trouble, don't read too much into it. There was an...incident," she spent a moment picking the right word, "about a year ago, with a Witch who had been living here for a while. I'll tell you about it another day, but I guess she is mostly the reason for all the wariness." Mia gave her a soft smile, but there was no trace of pity in it.

"Are there any other Witches in Sycamore Falls?" Mia shook her head, lips pressed in a straight line. "Thank you for the heads up," Allie said and exited the store.

A precedent was highly inconvenient, especially because she didn't know what had happened, but based on how she'd been treated her first day, she knew it had been something bad. As long as that Witch wasn't a clumsy one like her with no control over her power, Allie was ready to prove to the people here that she was better.

She crossed the street to the bakery and noticed the lights were on. The sign on the door read "Closed," but as she approached the entrance, she saw Dominic sitting at one of the tables, hands clasped under his chin, brown hair let loose atop his shoulders.

"Good evening, Mr. Ranford," she said as she entered the store. Her boss didn't move an inch, except for his mossy green eyes that moved over her so swiftly she paused in the middle of the bakery. He took her and her shopping bags in before leaning back in his chair, pointing to the one opposite him.

"Have a seat, Alecsandra."

Chapter 8

MEN DON'T MAKE FAMILIES WITH WITCHES

Allie sat down facing her boss and shoved the bags under the table, trying not to crowd Dominic, and ended up rustling the paper for a solid minute. When she was finally situated, she smiled at her boss, unsure of what to say or do.

"Tea?" he asked, pointing at the pot and cups on the table.

"Thank you." She picked one of the cups, and Dominic poured the amber liquid into it, steam curling up and caressing her cheeks. "How was your night, Mr. Ranford?" she attempted. His eyes had been glued to her ever since she walked in, and it was a long moment before he shifted on the chair and leaned forward, clasping his hands on the table. He didn't waste any time getting to the subject of this impromptu meeting.

"Brandon told me how you two met last night," he started. "Why did you leave Pearls Fields?"

His question didn't offend her or take her by surprise, but she took a sip of tea to gather her thoughts. The man had taken her in, so he deserved to know more about the woman living and working under his roof. Allie pondered weaving some white lies into her story but decided against it. She had nothing to hide, although she wasn't thrilled to admit her biggest shortcoming out loud.

To her boss.

Who could fire her.

Allie's heart pounded, and she wished the tea had a magical calming effect.

"Well?" he demanded.

"I was living with my coven in Pearls Fields, the Silverbarks. They sent me away for a few weeks so I could learn more about my magic."

"I thought covens were supposed to...teach you." Dominic frowned and leaned back in his chair, crossing his arms over his chest. Allie peeked at the intricate tree tattoo that stretched over the tense muscles.

"There's no other Witch with power like mine in the coven," she admitted, looking straight into his teal-colored eyes. "They don't know how to help me." As she spoke the excuse she'd heard for months on end from her sisters, Allie *heard* it. Truly heard how ridiculous it sounded, so the puzzled look on Dominic's face made sense. Allie shrugged and picked up the cup of tea, as if her statement meant nothing. Deep down, it meant a bunch of things, but her boss didn't need to know that.

"I've met Witches before and never heard of this," he stated. Allie saw the question brewing in his mind, and she had no idea why he chose not to ask her about it.

What kind of magic do you have?

She should tell him without being asked. That would have been the honest thing to do. Instead, she said, "Each coven is different." To this, the man raised his brows, so Allie continued, "My mom was a Silverbark," hoping this detail would be enough. Her boss nodded once, then took his first sip of tea. They sat in silence, sipping, glancing at each other only accidentally. At least, Dominic's peeks seemed like an accident, whereas Allie was outright staring at the handsome man in front of her.

She had questions of her own, things she wanted to know about him and the town—mostly about him—but this moment here was about her. It needed to be about her, to give her boss the reassurance he needed to let her live and work here.

"What about your father?" Dominic asked. Unlike before, this question had taken her by surprise, and she struggled to reel it in, forcing her eyes not to turn into saucers. In her world, no one would have asked a Witch this question. Her boss must have met other Witches only fleetingly, then.

"I never knew my father." This never made her feel one way or another. It was almost an unwritten law of nature concerning her kind. "Men don't make families with Witches."

Alecsandra gave him a soft smile, like she wasn't bothered by what she revealed. Dominic, on the other hand, had an intense urge to strangle any man who would fall into the "men who don't make families with Witches" category. The reason was beyond absurd to him, and he tried to calm his angry heartbeat before he spoke again. He steered clear of family matters, as he recognized it was too personal to share with...practically a stranger.

"How long are you here for?"

"Until Hallows Eve. If you'll have me," she added quickly, that soft smile melting as she parted her rosy lips, her eyes filling with hope.

Just a little under two months. That wasn't such a long time. And he did need help around the bakery, not that she knew much about it. Or anything about it.

What if it was Mia?

And what was the alternative? Send her back to wander the streets and towns until she found someone else who would take her in for this short period? People didn't always have the best intentions, especially when it came to Witches, and he didn't want to have Alecsandra's misfortune on his conscience. If anything, he was being selfish for letting her stay; he would keep his conscience clean while getting help at the bakery. She just wanted to learn more about her magic, whatever that meant. He knew Pearls Fields was a small village of pure old magic, and nothing would compare to the knowledge she'd find in a town of new magic. He sighed through his nose and spoke on the exhale.

"Fine."

Alecsandra smiled at him again, this time big and wide like she had done in the morning with the coffee cups, what he gathered was her genuine smile. She lacked that Witch-like sneer, and she looked at him as if he had found the remedy for an incurable ailment.

"Thank you, Mr. Ranford!"

She was about to say something else, but he cut her off. "Tell me your limits with new magic." He needed to know what he was working with here.

"I spent a few years in Green Creek." A town a bit smaller than Sycamore Falls, but a new magic town nonetheless. "I was around new magic there, and in the small apartment where I lived, but never in a place like this." Her eyes scanned the room, and she chuckled, fixing them on the cup between her hands. "I don't know how to use professional equipment like the ovens and the coffee machine here. But I can learn." He read the unspoken challenge: *if someone shows me.*

In all truth, he had been kind of a jerk that morning. True to his nature, Dominic just nodded once and repeated, "Fine."

The conversation with her boss went better than she'd expected. Besides him being mostly monosyllabic and constantly surly, which seemed like just the type of person he was, it had gone really well. He'd agreed to let her stay until Hallows Eve, provided she could help him around the bakery. And she was determined to do everything in her power to make that happen.

Back in her room, Allie laundered her new clothes, grateful that the machines were similar to the ones in Sam's apartment.

In her *old* apartment.

Allie was famished and excited to cook something delicious with all the ingredients she had bought earlier from the market. She spent the night in the kitchen, cooking vegetable soup and beef stew, and preparing breakfast and lunch for tomorrow. She'd settled on the honey-smoked ham and cheese sandwiches and a fruit salad for lunch.

After stuffing herself with two bowls of soup, she showered, snuggled in her new PJs, and spent the last hours before sleep stole her with *Baking for Dummies* in her arms. On the sofa that was so, so easy to expand.

In the early morning when the alarm of hell rang, Allie wondered how many mornings it would survive until she smashed it against the wall. She growled into her pillow, her limbs heavy as she rolled over and pushed the hair out of her face. She lifted the clock in front of her face to stop the alarm. Allie fumbled with the button and stopped the horrible noise, blinking away the sleep from her eyes.

Only to see that it was fifteen minutes to five in the morning.

"This isn't happening," she groaned, jolting up and running around the room like a headless chicken. She picked the first items of clothing her hands fell on—a navy-blue sweater and jeans—put on her boots, and had the presence of mind to brush her teeth.

At two minutes to five, Allie unlocked her door while

gathering her hair in a bun, the scrunchie between her lips. She walked into the bakery, hoping to be there first, only to find all the lights on and her boss looking over his notebook in the kitchen. He was dressed just like yesterday, except for his shirt, which was a deep green today, so much like the color of his eyes, and his brown locks were up in a tight bun.

Her hands were still up on her head, gathering her hair, and the scrunchie was still in her mouth when Dominic looked at her and said, "Morning."

She must have looked like a crazy person. With trembling fingers, she managed to tie her hair and say, "Good morning, Mr. Ranford," hoping her bun looked half-decent. She noticed he wasn't wearing an apron, so she went to the storage room and picked two, putting hers on.

Dominic flipped the notebook closed and took the apron from her hand with a grunt. He came to stand in front of the ovens as he tied it behind his back.

"Watch."

Allie stood one step behind him, paying close attention to the buttons and knobs her boss pressed and turned. The ovens that resembled the one from the manor only had two extra buttons that needed to be pressed before turning the final knob, and Allie also took note of the temperature that Dominic had set on them both.

The tall, vertical ovens with eight to ten trays in them were the real challenge. She asked Dominic if she could take a piece of paper from his notebook to write the details down, to which he huffed and nodded once. While she took notes, Dominic turned on the first oven, then had her start the second one to make sure she wrote everything down correctly.

Allie hadn't been this nervous since showing up at the Silverbarks' door, demanding they take her in. She went through each step on the paper carefully, and when she was done, she looked to her boss for confirmation. Her heart was in her throat, beats pulsating in her ears, and she squeezed the piece of paper to her chest like it was her most precious possession.

"Good" was all Dominic said. It was more than enough, and Allie released a long breath, pushing her heart back down to its place.

They moved to the coffee machine in the front, which was less complicated than the ovens. Compared to the one she had used in Green Creek, this machine was larger and had multiple options, including one to foam the milk. But Dominic gave her a list of coffee orders they served and the measurements of coffee and milk in each one of them, which made things easier for her. She watched as he made a large cappuccino that filled the air with her favorite smell of ground coffee beans. Getting her hands on the machine was now a personal mission, as she was desperate for coffee this morning.

"Want this?" her boss asked, handing her the cup of coffee.

"Me?" she blurted out, then bit her lip.

Of course, you, who else is here?

Allie chuckled awkwardly and took the cup with both hands. "Thank you." The coffee was a bit sweet for her taste because of the foamed milk, but it was still delicious. "Can I try to make one?"

Dominic jerked his head at the machine, arms crossed, watching her. A man of very few words, indeed. She put down the cup and picked an empty one, looking over the list for the measurements. Allie clicked on the coffee options and placed the cup in its designated slot. While the fresh coffee dripped, she picked up the milk carton and poured some into the special steel recipient used for foaming.

Allie tried to imitate the motion Dominic made and circle the steel cup.

"Like this?" she asked, not taking her eyes off the task.

"Smaller circles." She heard footsteps before Dominic's

shadow crowded her from behind. He stretched his arm along hers but pulled it back immediately. "A bit smaller."

She followed his instructions and finished foaming the milk, then poured it over the coffee and offered the cup to her boss, who tasted it and nodded with a grunt. Allie took it as approval and smiled widely.

"Thank you for taking the time to teach me, Mr. Ranford." It might have sounded more backhanded than she wanted, but if Dominic got that hint, he didn't say anything. "I'm going to start cleaning the kitchen." She took her cappuccino and went around her boss, who looked like he'd grown roots in that spot.

Allie followed the routine she'd established yesterday, thoroughly cleaning the kitchen while Dominic scribbled over and crossed things out in the notebook. When she was done, Dominic stopped her in the hallway to the bakery and said, "Help me in here first."

She remembered where half of the things were from yesterday, and for the other half, her boss had pointed to the right place. He didn't seem annoyed that she didn't remember all of them. Progress.

"I need a batch measuring cup full of cold milk. Don't spill it," he warned her.

Allie opened the fridge, got the milk out, and filled one of the biggest cups—which she had learned yesterday morning was a batch measuring cup—almost to the brim. She took the cup with both hands and turned to set it on the table. Some bubbles clung to the cup's edges as Dominic reached for it and hissed, jerking his hand back.

"This is boiling hot!" he yelled. Dominic's eyes grew impossibly wide, the green turning to a threatening shade as he stared into her soul.

Allie froze.

Her breaths came in labored as she looked between her palms

and the cup, shaking her head. She took a step back, clasping her hands behind her back.

Dominic's scrutinizing glare turned into realization, the angry frown smoothing into utter shock.

"Is that... Is that your power?"

Chapter 9

PROMISE ME

"Alecsandra." The name was charged with meaning, but his still expression was like the eerie calm before a storm that ravaged lands and blew off roofs. Allie felt her knees go weak. She kept her hands hidden behind her back as if she could make them disappear, the skin damp and cold even after the spontaneous heating she had channeled.

Dominic had a right to know the truth; in fact, she should have told him about her power last night, when he had, indirectly, asked about it. But she couldn't ignore the part of her that feared he would let her go after discovering her uncontrollable fire. Allie had hoped to stay for as long as she could at Dom's Sweets.

Which, with her crazy power and bad luck, had been only two days.

"Alecsandra." A warning, his tone louder and more urgent.

"Yes," she relented, fighting the urge to squeeze her eyes shut. She held Dominic's deeply green, deeply shocked eyes against her every instinct. "It's fire."

Dominic flinched as if she'd slapped him. He regarded her in a way that could mean so many different things, but she didn't know this man. He could be thinking about firing her or murdering her. When he finally spoke, it was barely above a whisper.

"Fire?" The low sound was coated in shock and despair, and Allie wished he'd yelled at her instead.

Her breath hitched in her throat, but she nodded. Dominic was still as a statue, as if afraid that if he moved, she would set him on fire. That could very well be the case with her unpredictable power, but Allie pushed the thought away. She would never hurt anybody. Intentionally.

"And what, exactly, are you looking to learn about it here?" he hissed through his teeth. Allie swallowed once, twice, trying to shove that lump from her throat to make room for the words that would determine her fate in Sycamore Falls. Because if Dominic chose to kick her out, no way in hell anyone else in this town would take her in.

She didn't get to be a coward now. Well, she was a coward, but she didn't get to act like one. It was just a matter of time until the truth came out, and with her luck, it so happened that she'd only had a day to prepare for it. Time she hadn't used to prepare for it.

"I need to learn how to control it."

❦

Dominic must have heard her wrong.

"What?" he barked, breaking his carefully built restraint. The Witch didn't cower from him, but fear took charge of her features. He couldn't tell if she was afraid of him or afraid to lose her place in Sycamore Falls.

"I don't have it under control," she repeated, and this only made Dom's rage flare through his veins as if someone set him on fire. *Ironically.*

Dozens of scenarios flew through his head like a flock of

uncoordinated geese. The bakery could spontaneously burn. *His home* could burn. His customers were in danger, and—

Mia.

He had seen some books in the bags Alecsandra had carried last night, meaning she'd already met his sister. The Witch had been at his sister's business, *a bookstore*, a place full of paper and wood. He couldn't suppress the shivers crawling down his spine at the thought.

But she was fine; Mia was fine. All of them were fine.

"I'll go pack." The hushed, small voice broke Dom's spiraling, and he focused on the woman before him.

Dominic rarely used his magic to Read people. He simply did not care enough to know about them, or understand them, or be around them. He had few friends and was more than content that way. Growing up, this strong sense of justice was instilled into him as soon as the nature of his magic came to light. Most times, he had an unfair advantage using his magic, so he didn't use it often. But now was the time to make an exception.

He grabbed at that silken tendril of power hidden inside him, just enough to toss it at the Witch and see what answered. The power left him on a swift wind, and he felt it swirl around her, poking at her magic.

Dom picked up a sizzling heat, a restless energy, giddy to be let out. His magic caressed a strong but gentle power. Under all that tension, a pure kindness welcomed him, undeniably soft and warm. Did her random channeling happen only because she didn't know how to control this fire?

He remembered the time when he had no idea what to do with the power outbursts, the strength he didn't feel he was ready for. But he'd had his father's guidance and his mother's words of encouragement. Alecsandra clearly had no one, if her own coven had sent her away instead of trying to help her.

What if it was Mia?

He'd punch Brandon in the face for branding that thought into his brain with a hot iron. Just once, he'd punch him one time for this. Hard.

Dom realized he had been silent for too long when Alecsandra passed by him on the way out of the kitchen. The last thing she had said was about packing, and he'd said nothing. She must have taken his lack of response as a dismissal, although he hadn't meant it like that.

Had he?

Living alone and not having to worry that everything he held dear could end up in flames sounded pretty sweet. But he still needed help around the bakery so he could focus more on his mission. And it would just be for a few weeks. He could endure it, but... Could his bakery?

"Don't." He was surprised at the command in his voice. He turned around, and it took a second for the feminine figure with the cherry-red bun to come back into view.

She kept quiet, but her eyes brimmed with water. He was uncomfortable around people crying, more so knowing he was the reason for it.

"Does this happen often?" he asked. She seemed confused before Dom fixed his gaze on her hands, but then she answered him in an even voice.

"Not very often."

So he might be right, and the power might just need release. People who were blessed with magic had to use it; otherwise, it consumed them. Now that he had a moment to think about it, the fact that she was just now going through these unplanned fire bursts told him her power was fairly new.

Huh.

Most Witches manifested at young ages, just like everyone else.

"When did you manifest?" Dominic acknowledged how personal this question was, and under normal circumstances, he would never have dreamed of asking this of a stranger. Yet these were not normal circumstances, and if she was going to live with him and around the people he cared about, he needed to know more.

Alecsandra wasn't taken by surprise, as if she'd expected his question, and she replied without reserve but with an obvious and considerable amount of shame that made her cheeks turn rose pink under her freckles.

"Six months ago."

Forget fairly new, this was brand-new power. But she was—

"I'm twenty-eight," she admitted, the color spreading to her neck.

A dam broke in Dom's mind, flooding it with questions, but one look at her slumped shoulders and bright red skin made him think twice before asking anything else. He placed his hands on his hips and took a long breath in.

"Promise me you'll tell me if this happens again." He made sure there was no room for negotiation in his voice.

Alecsandra was taken aback, her eyes going wide, her lips parting just a sliver.

"I can stay?" she asked, not even trying to conceal the surprise and happiness in her voice.

"Promise me," he warned her.

"I promise."

Dominic hoped to hell he wasn't going to regret this.

"Go to the front and get the bakery ready for customers."

❧

Allie cleaned every surface in the bakery, mopped the floors, and aired the place out, happy to take in the crisp morning breeze instead of having her teeth chatter until her jaw hurt. She resolved to split her reading time better between baking and Witchcraft. Now that the truth was out, she felt lighter and scolded herself for waiting until that uncomfortable moment to tell Dominic everything.

He didn't call her for help in the kitchen that morning, and she made it her business to give him space and avoid the kitchen at all costs. Even if she couldn't Read him, there was no question that he was upset. And who wouldn't be? Allie was beyond grateful to stay at Dom's Sweets, but she understood how hard it was for a stranger to accept her into his space with all the risks she posed. Hell, not even her coven sisters had wanted her around until she got the hang of her power. So if Dominic had shown her the door, she would have walked out without argument.

But he hadn't.

He'd stopped talking to her, though, even after he flipped the bakery sign and they welcomed customers for the day. They worked around each other in silence, and he didn't ask her for help at all. Allie picked up on tasks around him, trying to be useful while not getting in his way.

And if he stopped speaking to her for the rest of the day, or the week, or until she left, and even if he'd only bark orders at her and nothing more... She was still grateful. Call her a model, silent employee while she practiced her magic. Allie truly hoped no other spontaneous release of power would occur, but if it did, she would tell her boss. She didn't intend to break the promise she made, as much as just thinking about it made her want to crawl underground with embarrassment for being so weak and untrained at her age. Why did she have to manifest so late, and with so little control?

Fate was a cruel, wicked bitch. But she had a place to stay and work at while she practiced, and her sisters to return to when she was ready. Fate was a bitch, but it had dealt her a decent hand.

The place quieted for the first time that day with two more hours left in the shift. Allie cleaned the front and rearranged the display case before going to the kitchen to get the freshly baked pies she smelled. Her stomach protested, but she ignored it, feeding it images of devouring the food in her fridge later that night.

Dominic stood by the large kitchen table, fork in hand, tasting one of the pies freshly out of the oven. Allie's mouth watered, but she swallowed her craving and went to the tray with the cut slices.

The plate on the table moved.

Allie looked at the finger that pushed it toward her, her eyes sliding up his wrist and tattooed arm until she met her boss's green gaze.

Was he offering her pie?

Maybe her imagination was playing tricks on her because of the hunger. She must have started seeing things. She should ask Dominic for a five-minute break to get her sandwiches or fruit salad.

The plate moved again.

Dominic articulated his first words to her since that morning.

"Want some?"

Some? How about the whole thing? It smelled divine, and everything Dominic made was delicious. But Allie didn't think her boss wanted to eat with her and chat about their day.

"No, thank you." Her stomach chose that moment to growl like a drowning ape.

Yeah. She was certain she could fit under the table and hide there until her skin changed back to its normal color. So, until next week. Her cheeks heated, and she chuckled nervously under Dominic's unwavering stare. Allie cleared her throat, eager to come up with anything to fill the pressing silence.

But Dominic beat her to it.

"Eat." He shoved the plate closer to Allie, and the sweet smell flooded her senses, her stomach rumbling in response. She hesitated before picking up a fork and digging into the pie, barely suppressing a moan.

&.

Dominic was used to witnessing people enjoy his baking. He'd gotten his fair share of compliments and delighted stares, but never one that made him feel...like this. Uncomfortable. Strained. Bewitched.

And that's exactly how he felt watching Alecsandra's lids flutter closed and hearing the soft moan she involuntarily let out in response to the huge bite. The table groaned under the weight of his grip, and he quickly shoved his hands in his pockets, clearing his throat loudly. The Witch's eyes snapped open at the sound.

"This is so good," she said around a mouthful, pointing with her fork to the plate. "Thank you."

Dom needed to remember that very few people were accustomed to his crazy schedule, and most would need food before the bakery closed for the day. He had remembered this yesterday, so when he'd heard her stomach growl, he felt a twinge of guilt pass through him.

Yes, he was still toying with the idea of firing her, although he'd already agreed to let her stay. And yes, he was excruciatingly annoyed and on edge, thinking of what could happen. But that didn't mean he would treat her badly, and not letting his employee eat during the workday was inconsiderate.

Alecsandra ate almost half of the pumpkin pie before she gave a happy sigh and licked her lips. Dominic's body went taut as her tongue swirled around the fork once, twice, on the front and back. He couldn't look away. The Witch had put him under a spell that sewed him to that spot, his eyes glued to her mouth.

What the hell was he doing?

"I'll be out front," he grunted and sprinted out of the kitchen with his glass of ice water.

Dom had a sudden urge to pour that water over his head.

Chapter 10

DON'T GIVE IT ANOTHER THOUGHT

After feeding her the most delicious pumpkin pie in what she could only describe as a religious experience, Dominic stopped talking to her again, and Allie had no intention of infringing on his space. After closing up, she went to her studio room and wolfed down the sandwiches and fruit salad as a quick dinner. Then she let her hair down, put on her jacket, grabbed the book on Witchcraft, and left, no sign of her boss on her way out.

It was her second time walking around Sycamore Falls, and with the appropriate clothing, she appreciated the feeling of cold air on her skin and in her lungs. Taking a deep inhale felt like breathing for the first time in a long time, as Pearls Fields's heat left her wearied and drenched in sweat.

Dusk set over the tree-covered mountains that guarded the town, the beautiful, amber fall colors shimmering under the pink hue. Leaves lined the sidewalk and the street like chocolate shavings on top of a pie. How beautiful was Hallows Eve in this town? Allie dreamed of the townhouses decorated with pumpkins and webs, the smell of apple cider donuts and cinnamon buns wafting through the streets. She bet the moon was more powerful here that night. With her power finally manifested, maybe she could try to carry on her mother's Hallows Eve tradition of charging it with the moonlight.

Allie exhaled and wiped away those silly dreams from her mind. She'd be back with the Silverbarks by then, and they would perform the coven's traditions and midnight rituals. Allie made a mental note to charge her stones in the moonlight before that night.

The road snaked closer to the river and the woods at the end of Maple Street. Allie was searching for a secluded place close to the river so she could practice without an audience and within a safe distance of some water. She did not want to hurt anybody. There was no doubt in her mind that she would be failing for a while before using her power with confidence. Besides, even her coven sisters feared getting close to her during practice, and on the few times they stayed, she'd heard them mutter rude comments—unfortunately, most of them accurate—under their breath. Petra had taught her that other people's opinions didn't define who she was.

Her mother had been right, but that didn't make it easier to feel left out.

Allie followed the paved road long after she passed by the last building. In moments like this she missed her broom dearly, so she let the thought of getting it back be a match for her motivation. She just had to light it. Literally.

Allie carved away from the path and into the forest, following the gurgle of the river, the moon lighting her steps. She stumbled upon a small clearing on the edge of the flowing water, spacious enough to double as a sports field.

Perfect.

She sat cross-legged on the cold ground, close enough to the river to run the tips of her fingers through the water. Shivers wriggled up her arm at the contact with the freezing cold water, and she pulled her hand away. Good enough to put out any fire she might ignite.

Allie opened the book and read a few pages on power categories and manifestation—like she needed to be reminded that she'd manifested about twenty years later than the average Witch—and skipped the other elements until she got to fire.

She learned quickly that unused power tended to implode and cause impromptu flares through the Witch's body. These could only be controlled once the Witch's power was mastered. Which, in Allie's case, it wasn't, but now all her previous mishaps with randomly setting things on fire or excessive heating made sense. She found solace in this explanation, knowing that what had happened to her was expected and that nothing was wrong with her. The wave of relief at gaining this knowledge washed over her, lifting an invisible weight she carried in her soul. She had no one to teach her, but her power was like anybody else's.

A few pages later, she found the section on power control and was ready to dedicate a couple of days to each page under it.

"Find the source of power within your body. This is different for every Witch, and one can find it in the head, heart, core, or maybe someplace else in the body. Once identified, draw from it..." Allie muttered to herself, but stopped when she realized there was no point in going forward.

She had to find the source of the power in her body.

All right.

She could do that.

Allie closed the book and pushed it far enough away to make sure it wouldn't become collateral damage. She scooted closer to the river, took a deep breath, and closed her eyes.

The power in my body. The power in my body. The power in my body.

Allie mentally scanned herself from head to toe, searching for...

something. For the way this source of power would feel inside her. Hot, probably.

But she felt nothing.

She squeezed her eyes shut and tried harder. Head, heart, core. Arms. Legs. Even toes. Eyebrows?

Nothing.

Allie tried and tried until she felt a headache coming on after looking for something she didn't know how to find. Why didn't the freaking book tell her exactly how to find this power source? It was mentioned as if it was a piece of cake, something that was probably innate for other Witches.

Not for her.

She growled and got to her feet, seeking revenge on the book, and angled it toward the river. Ugh. She would need the damn thing again.

"Fine. Keep your secrets." She dropped it and scowled at the inanimate object, wondering if there was any spark of life hidden in it after Mia had sold it to her. Allie stuck her tongue out at the book in case there was.

A rustling sound halted her frustration, her senses perking up, ears straining to listen. It came from the opposite side of the path that led her here, and Allie concluded this was enough for her first day of solo practice. She snatched the traitorous book from the ground, tucked it under her arm, and dashed through the tall sycamores that she'd come through.

If she was in full control of her power, she would not have run away. But in her current state, she didn't want to risk anyone, or anything, finding her alone in the middle of the woods. Allie raced back to the main road, lit up by the firefly soldiers, and only then did she pace herself. She looked back every three steps to make sure she was alone until she reached the left turn onto Maple Street.

And knocked into someone in the middle of it.

"I'm so sorry," she babbled, pressing the book to her chest over her galloping heart. She took in the tall man who stood there, hands in his pockets, not a bother in the world. The nearby lampposts shed eerie light over his sharp features and sandy blond hair. Something about him reminded her of Sam.

"Is everything all right?" he asked in a grave voice that sounded like soft thunder. A wickedness shone in his eyes, and Allie quickly Read him to confirm the malevolent intent that hung around him like an obscure coat. This would have been a great moment to have her broom and fly far, far away.

"Yeah. Sorry for running into you," Allie said and walked around him. She took two steps away from him before he spoke again.

"Are you lost?"

"I'm all right!" she shouted and sped up.

Fortunately, the man didn't follow her, and when she worked up the courage to look back, Allie saw his retreating form. Maybe she was a bit paranoid, and that little bit of magic she controlled with Reading people was off. She should consider that, given how *off* everything else about her magic was.

Allie made it back to the bakery in record time.

The lights were off inside when she arrived, but the first-floor windows were lit up. She slipped quietly into her room, tossed the book on the kitchen counter, and plopped down onto one of the bar stools. The disappointment of her first practice day settled in, and she allowed herself a minute of wallowing. A minute of wondering why she was the way she was, why her sisters didn't help her, why her mother had left her alone, and why in the world she had wasted three years of her life with an idiot like Sam.

Allie shook off all the negative feelings, sighing loudly and pushing them out with the air. It was a coping mechanism her mom had shared when Allie was a young teen, and everything in the world was always wrong, hard, and against her. Not unlike now.

She fixed herself a bowl of warm soup, showered, and slipped under the covers with no book tonight.

Tomorrow will be better.

Dom woke up that morning with a pain in his shoulder, preventing him from lifting his arm. He hissed while pulling a white T-shirt over his head and swore through his teeth when he wasn't able to gather his hair into a bun. Jeans had been fun to put on, too.

"Fucking hell," he cussed under his breath. This muscle blockage happened sometimes, but it usually didn't make him feel like he wanted to strangle somebody. Today was going to be a fun day dealing with so many people.

And with his new employee.

Alecsandra had stolen his secluded place in the forest last night. He'd seen her sit so close to the river that he wondered how she hadn't just slid in. She'd been out there alone with a book, at night, in the middle of an unfamiliar place. Sycamore Falls was safe—especially because Dom was there—but she had no way of knowing that. Her frustrated reaction told him she had unsuccessfully tried to practice her magic.

Was that the reason she sat so close to the river? What had she gone through to make her so cautious?

The sycamores were calm in her presence, confirming that he'd Read the Witch well. She had a good heart and no bad intentions, just a load of bad luck with manifesting this late, with no help during these times. Dom knew the later one manifested, the harder it was to control the power, and he'd never heard of anyone who had manifested later than fifteen.

He couldn't speak from experience, as his power had manifested when he was six, and now he was considered one of the most powerful in his lot. This came with long missions that had him leave Sycamore Falls when he was young, and this current assignment was the first one to bring him back home.

And he didn't plan on leaving again.

Dominic gave up on tying his hair and placed the band on his wrist. He'd try the bun later, when the pain lessened.

He went downstairs, stretching and massaging his shoulder, and stopped dead in the narrow hallway at the end of the staircase. A strong, warm coffee smell enveloped him, together with a faint scent of cleaning products. Dom went into the kitchen.

Two freshly made cups of coffee sat on the table. All of the ovens were on, and the Witch was rubbing the fridge door as if it had insulted her profusely.

"Morning," he grumbled, still holding onto his shoulder.

Alecsandra spun around and flashed him a wide smile.

"Good morning, Mr. Ranford." Her brown eyes locked on him and stayed a long moment around his face, on his loose hair, before a soft frown creased her forehead. "Is everything okay?" she asked, looking pointedly at the hand clasped over his shoulder.

"Fine," he lied.

"You're clearly not fine."

Huh.

Uncharacteristic of the tame and obedient Witch he'd come to know for the past two days. Not that you could truly know anyone in two days.

"Slept weird" was everything he was going to say about the matter. She nodded, but her chocolate eyes turned to slits.

"Do you need help in here or should I clean out front first?"

"Let's start here." The sooner he'd be done mixing and kneading, the better.

Dominic had blown the hair out of his face about twenty times before Alecsandra asked if she should tie his hair back. To that, he barked an instant "No," as if that was the thing of his nightmares.

He regretted his outburst the tiniest bit. Just because he slept poorly and was in terrible pain didn't mean he could lash out at his employee. The Witch didn't seem to take offense at his behavior though, instead bringing him the vanilla sugar bag he'd asked for.

He kneaded and mixed with one hand, which made everything twice as hard and infinitely more irritating. The vein in his temple took life and was moments away from bursting. Alecsandra asked repeatedly if she could take over, but he refused while blowing the hair out of his face. Again.

By the time the croissants, pies, and macarons were in the oven, he was already exhausted. While Alecsandra got the bakery ready for opening, Dom plopped on one of the blue velvet chairs. This morning was the first time he was truly, honest to gods grateful to have help around the shop, be it a Witch who could set the place on fire. He looked over the orders notebook and...

"Ah, shit," he grunted. Two of the pages had stuck together, and he'd missed the important notes he'd left for today.

Flour delivery at 1:30 p.m.

Meeting at 2 p.m. with H&T for wedding prep.

The wedding was a couple of weeks away, but he had to place some orders that would take a longer time to get to Sycamore Falls. Because the brides had wanted some special type of marzipan for the cake, and some special type of chocolate fondue for the fountain, and some special type of everything.

Harper and Tina were lucky they were Mia's best friends.

Dominic flipped the notebook closed and would have stood up, had it not been for two slender hands falling on his shoulders. He swore low through his teeth when he attempted to turn, and the stiff shoulder blade kept his neck in place.

"Sit still," Alecsandra said as her fingers combed through his hair.

"What are you doing?"

She dragged the tips of her fingers from his forehead to the back of his head once, twice, pulling the locks tight behind his ears and gathering his hair in a ponytail.

"You'll scare our customers if you keep huffing and puffing." Dom heard the smirk in her voice.

Our customers?

Dominic knew he was capable of scaring his customers just by being in a bad mood. That was feedback he'd gotten ever since he was young. The simple act of him blowing the hair out of his face wouldn't scare them, but the rage it would provoke inside him for hours on end certainly would.

It would also be highly unprofessional to walk around the bakery with his hair let loose, so he didn't argue any further. That was the only reason he allowed the Witch to touch him, to pull her soft fingers across his scalp. And he did not lean into that touch at all.

"Give me your band," she ordered as her palm came into view. He placed the elastic in her hand, and she twisted it around his ponytail, forming a bun. "All done." The Witch stepped away and came into sight, all tall and lean and annoyingly smiley.

Beautiful.

"Thanks," Dominic mumbled, not embarrassed but not comfortable either. She waved a hand in dismissal.

"Don't give it another thought."

He wouldn't. He shouldn't. He really, *really* should just forget about it. Not another thought of her touch. Just an employee helping her boss with another task. That was it.

But Dom knew that if he'd let his guard down, the memory of her hands on him might seize him completely.

Chapter 11

YOU AND ME BOTH

"So if you have to stay there, let's meet another day," Dominic snapped into the bakery's telephone. "No. No. Because I can't. And also, I don't want to." He'd ended up huffing and puffing anyway, and Allie couldn't tame her smile. "Fine!" he shouted and slammed the phone on the receiver.

Allie did her best to distract the elderly couple of customers in front of her, but they shot nervous glances at her boss. She made quick work of packaging their baguettes and slices of apple pie and sent them on their way before Dominic noticed he had an audience.

Allie didn't get much sleep the night before, and she'd gotten a head start on the day. It was about time she took responsibility for her tasks, and she was happy to do that instead of sulking around her room. She'd also resolved to be more like herself around her boss, now that he had agreed to let her stay. Less reserved, more... bubbly, her mother used to say. She had nothing to lose and wanted to make the most of the time in Sycamore Falls. Her nights would be entirely dedicated to magic practice, but she could enjoy her job and a few hours of strolling through the town here and there. In a few weeks, she would be back with the Silverbarks, back to the rest of her life.

Her mature Witch life.

The thought sat wrong with her and made her feel like she'd swallowed a cactus. Yet, once she mastered her power, she was sure the joy of being part of a coven, the sisterhood she had craved ever since she was young, would come more naturally. She'd be accepted and acknowledged by her peers and would dedicate her life to Witchcraft.

A frustrated grunt grabbed her attention.

"Is everything okay, Mr. Ranford?" she asked loud enough for him to hear only if he wanted to.

Dominic threw exasperated looks around the bakery as if searching for the cause of his irritation, but found nothing and no one besides Allie.

"I have to go meet the brides on the other side of town," he spat through his teeth, like that was a death sentence.

"I thought they were supposed to come here," Allie offered pointlessly.

"They were, but—you know what, I don't even want to get into that. I need to have words with my sister," he muttered.

She had learned this morning about the upcoming wedding of Harper and Tina, who were apparently close friends of Dominic's sister. Allie loved weddings, and as an official employee of Dom's Sweets—as official as one could get—she was excited to cater this event.

It came as no surprise that her grumpy boss displayed zero feelings about this wedding. And now, it seemed he either hated leaving the bakery during open hours, or moving meeting places without enough notice, or both. Most likely both.

"I'll cover the bakery while you're away," Allie offered with confidence. Everything on the menu for the day was in stock, the lunch hour rush was almost over, and she was ready to take charge if it meant Dominic could go to the meeting without worrying about things here.

He crossed his arms over his chest and assessed her with those shining green eyes, narrowing them slightly. Allie saw the wheels spinning in his head, going through various scenarios of her being here alone. She waited patiently, willing some confidence into her pose, and glanced at his tense arms only once.

Twice.

"I guess I don't have another choice." He deflated, letting his arms hang and hissing at the sudden movement. It seemed like the pain in his shoulder wasn't completely gone. Dominic checked his watch and mumbled something to himself. "I have to leave now to make it in time."

"Okay." Allie nodded.

"There's a flour delivery coming in about twenty minutes. It's already paid for. If you're busy when it gets here, tell John to leave it on a table."

"Got it."

Dominic looked her over, as if reconsidering his plans, but he ended up picking up the car keys and heading out of the bakery.

Allie spent some time wiping tables and rearranging the goods in the display case. She noticed one too many lemon-flavored macarons lying on the tray in the kitchen and popped one into her mouth. A few customers came and went, all of them pinning her with hostile looks in exchange for their orders. But she smiled and served them, understanding that their prejudice was based on what Mia had mentioned.

She liked Mia. The Archivist had been the only person to treat her with kindness. Allie didn't dare hope to make friends, but she would like to spend more time with Mia while she was in Sycamore Falls. Could she ask her to have tea or coffee together?

Hm.

After twenty minutes on the dot, a middle-aged man with

thick, round glasses and a red puffer jacket entered the bakery with a box in his arms. Allie had three customers in line then, so she followed her boss's orders.

"Hello! Please leave the box on the table there." She pointed to the one closest to the window. The man nodded and did just that, then bid her goodbye and walked out.

See? She got this. She could cover for her boss for a couple of hours whenever he needed. Her pride inflated to the size of a hot air balloon.

When the last customer left, Allie wiped her hands on her apron and went around the counter to pick up the box and take it to the storage room.

The box moved.

Allie stopped in her tracks, gluing her eyes to the package to check if she had hallucinations. She really should spend her nights sleeping rather than overthinking magic practice.

The box moved again.

Right then, the bell at the door rang, and a young man with bright brown eyes and a clean shave came in, a box in his hands.

"Hi there," he said in a chirpy voice. "I'm John, I'm looking for Dominic."

"The...flour delivery?" Allie asked, feeling her heart climb into her throat. The boy nodded. "I'll take that, thanks." He placed the package in Allie's hands and left quietly.

Allie dropped it on the nearest table and turned to the moving box. It shook again, and a chittering sound came from it. She hurried to it and opened the lid without checking the label, thinking there was *something* in there looking for air.

A creature jumped on her, claws and wings digging into her sweater.

"Whoa, whoa." She grasped the thing with both hands around its belly and brought it to eye level.

A purple baby dragon stared back at her with wide, curious eyes.

"Hello." She hadn't seen one in so many years, since the time her mom took her to see street performers in a bigger village close to Pearls Fields. The dragon fluttered its tiny wings in response, not fighting to get away from Allie's grip.

"Let's see who you are." Allie wanted to put the baby dragon back inside the box to check the label, but as soon as she set it down, it flew up and perched on her shoulder. The dragon was the size of a cantaloupe, so it couldn't have been older than ten years.

Allie fumbled with the box and found a paper inside. She took it out to read it and noticed the dragon leaned forward, as if wanting to read it too. The document had just a few details about its...contents.

Name: -
Age: 7 years
Type: Male
Breed: Tree dragon
Color: Purple
Diet: Fruits, vegetables, seeds, leaves
Notes: Rejected by its kind. Cannot spit fire.

"How come you don't have a name?" Allie asked, frowning at the paper. How did it—he—end up here? No way Dominic had just, what? Adopted him? Allie scoffed, and her eyes fell on the last line again.

Cannot spit fire.

"You and me both," she whispered. A strong feeling of pity blossomed in her chest, but she reigned it in. Allie hated being pitied for her shortcomings. Why wouldn't the dragon feel the same way?

She took the dragon back to her room after popping by the

kitchen and slicing an apple and a banana. The creature wanted to fly around and inspect his surroundings, but Allie warned him that would only land him back in the box. He deflated but stayed quietly on her shoulder.

She put the plate of fruits on her desk, and the dragon flew over and sat next to it. He looked between Allie and the plate with large, hopeful eyes.

"You can eat everything on the plate," she chuckled. "Just don't ruin anything around the room, okay?" To her surprise, the dragon nodded. So he *could* understand her. Interesting. "I should give you a name. Everyone should have a name," she muttered. The creature watched her expectantly, her wish to name him echoing in his beady, dark eyes. Echo... "How about Ekko?" The dragon's eyes sparkled, and he flew up and around Allie, briefly brushing her cheek with his wings. "Ekko it is." She laughed.

Allie went back to the bakery, hoping her new friend would not ruin anything while left alone. Ekko was too tiny to do much damage, but his claws were sharp enough.

She took the box full of flour bags to the storage room and spent the next two hours serving, packaging, and cleaning. Mercifully, no noise came from her room, and she could only hope Ekko was behaving. She didn't know much about dragons, only that some of them were friendly, and some enjoyed human company.

But what about her boss? Allie doubted he would welcome the presence of a mystical creature under his roof. She hoped he would allow her to keep Ekko for a few days until she figured out what to do with him.

The door swung open as Dominic came inside. The bun she'd tied for him had loosened a bit, wild strands of hair framing his face. Allie suspected he wasn't going to let her near him again anytime soon by the way he had stiffened like a board on that chair. But she could not *not* help him, or force him to accept her help, even with the risk of making him more testy than usual.

"How did the meeting go?" Allie jumped into the conversation, pointlessly prolonging when she'd tell her boss she was hiding a baby dragon in her room.

"We need more of everything," he grumbled.

"And how is your shoulder?"

Dominic narrowed his emerald eyes at her. "Fine. What's wrong?"

The man wasted no time.

"Everything is fine," Allie said, clasping her hands behind her back. "Except..."

Dominic tensed, his back going ramrod straight. He stopped by the counter and raised his brows, bracing his hands on the edge. Allie chuckled awkwardly, considering how to go about the unusual news.

"Except?" Dominic demanded.

"We got two deliveries today." He frowned, jerking his head back. "I put the flour box in the storage room," Allie went on slowly, as if she was approaching a freezing lake and was about to jump into it headfirst. Naked.

"What was the other delivery?" he asked in that low, thick, alarmingly calm voice.

Allie gave him a big smile, wanting to say this casually, like it was just two boxes of flour instead of one.

Except it wasn't.

"A baby dragon?" She shrugged.

"A baby dragon," Dom parroted the words Alecsandra had uttered. "You let a fire-spitting creature inside the bakery?" The

Witch winced, and the weight of his words hit him in his idiot head. "I didn't mean—"

"He can't spit fire," she interrupted him with unexpected force. "It says so on the document." She glanced at something behind him: an empty box on the table by the door.

Dominic crossed the distance in long strides and grabbed the open box, putting the lid together. He read the address and—

"This says 73 *Mable* Street." Alecsandra was right behind him, reading the label with a lot of interest for someone who was supposed to know what it said. Dom didn't feel like he needed to voice that the bakery was on 73 *Maple* Street. "It's also addressed to the Mystical Creatures Institute." A puff of air that could have been a sigh or a chuckle tickled his ear.

"I didn't exactly read the label," she declared. Dom set the box on the table and turned to fully face her.

"What?"

"The box was moving as if there was something inside it, and I guessed it could be something alive, and I was scared it wasn't getting enough air, so I just went and opened the box, and then the dragon jumped on me and I didn't get to read the label and—"

"Whoa." Dom put his hands up. Her eyes were wide, her breathing labored from the intense speech she sputtered. She bit her lip and fixed him with expectant brown eyes. Waiting for him to say something. Anything.

Dom didn't know what to say. Honest to the gods, he had no idea what he would have done if he had received a moving box. Well, he would have at least checked the label. But he wasn't heartless, or so he liked to think. Unpleasant, grumpy, and easily inconvenienced, sure. But not heartless.

And it was impossible to blame the beautiful Witch when she licked her dry lips before speaking again.

"Please let me keep him for a few days," she sputtered. A boy?

"I'll go to the Institute and ask them about him. I promise Ekko will not bother you once."

"You named him?" Somehow, Dom found this was the most natural outcome, and he had to fight the smirk that tried to crawl on his face.

"Everyone should have a name." Alecsandra said this with so much poise and conviction that he was embarrassed he'd asked. He took in her determination, the soft pink flush under her freckled cheeks, and the lock of hair that had broken free from her bun and hung by her ear.

"Keep him for a few days," Dominic agreed on a long breath.

What else would this woman convince him to agree to? He was afraid of that answer.

Then again, what was one more fire hazard under his roof?

Chapter 12

BE FRIENDLY ON YOUR OWN TIME

Watching Dominic and Ekko get acquainted must have been one of the most endearing moments Allie had ever witnessed. Dominic stood still, arms crossed at his chest, feet apart, while Ekko flew tentative, curious circles around him, getting closer and closer with each lap. When the dragon was within arm's reach of the unpredictable, broody man, he flew away and hopped on Allie's shoulder.

"See? He's harmless," she said, scratching his soft belly. Her boss huffed and turned around, heading for the kitchen.

"Keep him in your room," he shouted across the hall.

Allie snickered and ran back to her studio room, setting Ekko down on the sofa.

"Be good, okay?" He nodded and plopped down on his butt. The other day Allie hadn't found anything wrecked or misplaced, so she trusted Ekko to continue to behave himself, especially now after meeting Dominic. "I'll bring you something to munch on later," she said, and left the creature alone.

Allie and Dominic fell into a comfortable rhythm after that. She felt relieved now that her boss knew the truth about her power, and her dragon, and seemed to accept both. He made it clear he wasn't happy about it, but he had accepted them, and it was more than Allie could have asked for.

So for the next couple of days, she woke up and turned on the ovens, made coffee for herself and Dominic, cleaned the bakery, and helped him whenever he asked. Ekko was a delight when he wasn't crowding her pillow at night, and he kept her room intact, with the exception of a potted plant he'd knocked over on the desk.

Allie had conflicting feelings about the weekend when it finally rolled around, which came after what felt more like a month than just a working week. The bakery closed after lunch, and she was excited to explore the town during the day, but she dreaded going to the Institute to ask about Ekko. She'd heard both good and bad things about Mystical Creatures Institutes and she would have loved to postpone this visit for as long as possible.

But she'd promised Dominic.

And Allie quickly found out that she wasn't willing to threaten the trust she was beginning to build with him. Even if she was only here for a short time, she would be eternally grateful to him.

"Morning." A thick voice halted Allie's train of thought. She looked up to find Brandon, who she hadn't seen ever since the night he had saved her from sleeping under the stars. He leaned over the counter in a worn, brown leather jacket, his short black hair tousled from the wind, the same kindness she remembered from almost a week ago lining his dark eyes.

"Brandon, hi!" She gave him a wide smile. "I didn't get a chance to say thank you for helping me. I truly appreciate it," she babbled.

"Nah, don't worry about it." He waved her off, looking around the bakery. "Are you sure you're thankful?" He laughed.

"Why wouldn't I be?"

"Have you *met* Dom?" he teased her. Allie couldn't help but laugh.

"I have—"

"Are you getting anything or just distracting my staff?" Dominic's gruff voice came from behind her. Allie shifted to the left to make room for her boss in front of the register, and in front of his friend.

"Morning, D. Cheerful as always, I see." Brandon smirked. Her boss managed to raise his eyebrows without disturbing his scowl. "I'm just chatting with my friend," Brandon said defensively. "We're friends now, right, Allie?"

She was taken aback by the statement, mainly because she didn't have many friends. Or any friends, outside of her coven, at least, but only Freya had been remotely friendly to her. She made friends when she had been with Sam, but had abandoned that life together with him. Allie hadn't held many friendships, but someone going out of their way to help a stranger was definitely friend material.

"Of course we are." She grinned. Brandon grinned right back.

And Dominic... Well, nothing changed on his face. He turned around and muttered, "Be friendly on your own time."

If not for Brandon's snicker and head shake, Allie might have thought she'd done something wrong.

"Don't mind him. I'm here for my bread order." His dark brown eyes moved to the display case. "And maybe a couple of the lemon macarons. And a slice of pumpkin pie."

"Coming right up," Allie said. She packaged the pie and macarons, then slid a copper in the register and added two extra macarons to the bag. "For helping me. I still can't bake," she admitted.

Brandon took the bags from her with a smile. It seemed like he was always smiling. Or it was just easier for her to notice because she'd been dealing with her ever-scowling, never-smiling boss.

"Thanks, Allie."

She turned to go retrieve the bread order and hit her shoulder against a sharp corner. The box in question was not floating but was in Dominic's arms, who balanced it in time to keep all the bread from falling to the floor.

"Sorry, Mr. Ranford." Allie took a few steps away, making more room than necessary around the counter.

"Here." The man practically shoved the box into the customer's arms. They were good friends; they must be.

"Always a pleasure, D. I'll call you later," Brandon said.

The store's bell rang and another familiar face walked in. Mia, the Archivist, entered the bakery and stopped abruptly at the door when she noticed Brandon. Her sweet smile melted, Brandon's steps slowed as they came face to face and stood there for a silent moment. They exchanged some mutters and glances potent with unnatural awkwardness, yet likely full of meaning.

Because Mia's face was flushed as she came up to the counter.

"Allie!" She tucked her hair the color of wet roots behind her ears. Today she was wearing jeans, a green sweater, and brown leather boots up to her knees.

"Hi Mia!"

"So you did meet," her boss grumbled. The Archivist threw him a bored and unimpressed look.

"Were you hoping we didn't?" she provoked him, but didn't let him answer. "I'm here for one of your weekend specials." Mia eyed the display case with big, hopeful eyes. Her face fell when she noticed the empty space behind the "Weekend Special" label.

Allie had learned that morning there was a different dessert every week that Dom made only during the weekend. This week it was chocolate brownies filled with raspberry cream, and they were divine. No surprises there.

"I saved you some in the back," her boss said and waved Mia in behind the counter.

Oh.

Oh.

Allie busied herself around the front despite the lack of customers, straining to *not* listen to the voices coming from the kitchen. She didn't want to intrude and suddenly felt like she should sweep the bakery's entryway. Fortunately, she'd left the broom out earlier instead of taking it back to the storage room, so she went outside and closed the door behind her.

It wasn't long before Mia and her boss came out, Dominic... not scowling for a change.

Huh.

In the very long week she'd been here, Allie had never seen her boss act so comfortably around anyone. Not even around Brandon, and they were supposed to be friends. He was polite—most of the time—to the customers, and to her, but he was generally snappy and almost always glaring.

"Didn't you sweep earlier this morning?" Dominic asked, that familiar frown taking its rightful place. Allie made a noise in the back of her throat.

"I did, yes," she blurted, "but it looked as if it was dusty again." She glanced between him and Mia, feeling her cheeks heat. Mia must have noticed and put her out of her misery.

"I'm going to sign up for the Harvest Festival. Do you want me to sign the bakery too?" Mia asked Dominic, hand on his arm. He nodded reluctantly and patted her hand once. "Allie, would you like to come with me? I can show you around town," she offered.

Allie checked the time and saw there was one hour left before the bakery closed.

"Sorry, I can't right now."

"Dom, you can spare Allie for one hour today, right?" she asked in a sweet voice, batting her eyelashes at him. Dominic held her gaze for a moment before speaking.

"Fine," he huffed.

Allie had the feeling there was possibly nothing Dominic would deny Mia.

"Are you sure, Mr. Ranford?" Allie asked, and Mia scoffed and rolled her eyes, a smirk across her face. "I can stay and finish—"

"Go," he said in that tone that didn't leave room for conversation.

"All right. One second," she told Mia. She ran inside to take her apron off and put on her jacket. She also threw a bunch of pumpkin seeds in a bowl and left it with Ekko while she grabbed the document that came with him.

Allie rushed down the hallway while pulling at her hair band to let her hair loose.

"Ready," she said when she was back outside. Dominic watched her closely, his deep green eyes fluttering to her curls. His jaw clenched, and Allie messed with her hair and instinctively asked him, "Do I have flour in my hair again?"

"You're good," Mia answered instead, her eyes moving between her and Dominic before she took Allie's arm and dragged her through the small yard onto the sidewalk. Allie turned and waved at her boss, who stood rooted in the same spot, following them with that burning gaze. "What's that?" Mia looked at the paper in her hand.

"I need to stop by the Mystical Creatures Institute. Did Mr. Ranford tell you about Ekko?" Mia shook her head, so Allie told her in a few words how she'd ended up with a pet dragon for the past couple of days.

"And Dom agreed?" she asked with raised eyebrows. "To keep the dragon?"

"Only until I had time to go by the Institute and check with them about the misunderstanding," Allie assured her. "And I promised Mr. Ranford that—"

"Okay, hold on." Mia interrupted her with a laugh. "What is it with you and Mr. Ranford?" At Allie's confused look, Mia added, "Why don't you call him Dominic?"

"Because he's my boss." And he'd never corrected her, and he kept calling her Alecsandra, and as much as she wanted to correct him every time, she didn't.

Mia tsked. "I had no idea my brother was one for honorifics," she muttered more to herself.

Allie stopped in the middle of the sidewalk, and Mia halted with her.

"Brother?"

"Yes," Mia said as if it was as obvious as the sun in the sky. "Dom's my brother. He didn't tell you?" Allie shook her head, and Mia laughed. "Wait, did you think—is that why you left the bakery earlier? You thought—"

"I didn't think anything!" Allie blurted out, but Mia was still laughing.

"Come on." Mia motioned for Allie to keep walking.

They strolled to the end of Maple Street and where Allie usually made a right to go to her secluded space in the forest, now they made a left, heading around the market, and in a couple of minutes they stopped in front of a blue-painted building.

"The Mystical Creatures Institute" was written in large, white letters on top of the double wooden doors. Allie and Mia walked inside, the receiving hall empty save for a cherry-red wood desk at the end. Behind it sat a petite lady with gray hair and elongated eyes, who Allie recognized from the bakery as Mrs. Chen. She'd come in every two days to get fresh bread and was one of Allie's chief scowlers.

"Hi Mrs. Chen!" Mia chirped.

"Hello, dear." The elderly lady offered her a smile, which quickly wilted when she noticed Allie approaching the desk as well.

"Good afternoon, Mrs. Chen." The woman made a gruff sound and looked through her round glasses at the paper in Allie's hand. "I think there was a mistake with a delivery this week. A baby dragon was delivered to the bakery instead of here," she explained.

Mrs. Chen took the paper from her and studied it at arm's length.

"It says here the delivery was three days ago. Why did you only bring it today?"

"The Institute was closed during the time I was not working," Allie said, keeping her voice even. Mrs. Chen scoffed and shoved the paper back at her.

"You can bring the creature back here during the week."

Okay. All right. She could do that. She would tell Dominic she needed some time to take care of this.

"But what will happen to him here?" Allie couldn't help the question that bubbled out from inside her.

The lady rolled her eyes as if it took her immense effort to answer. "We'll store him with the others and put him up for adoption."

Allie knew she was trying her luck with another question, but if she were to bring Ekko here, she needed to know what his fate would be.

"Are dragons adopted often?"

"Girl, I'm busy. Go." She gestured for them to leave.

Mia and Allie muttered their goodbyes and went back outside.

"For what it's worth, I helped around the Institute last summer when they catalogued all the creatures, and I remember there were more than fifty dragons already housed." Mia squeezed her arm.

"Thanks," Allie whispered.

She didn't want to leave Ekko in a cage for gods knew how many years. She thought about keeping him, but what would Dominic say?

A problem for later today, Allie decided as she took a long breath of chilly air. She loved the cooler temperatures more with each day and didn't miss the sweat and stickiness of Pearls Fields. Or Pearls Fields at all.

They walked down the wide street lined with sycamores on both sides. The huge, coppery trees had trunks so thick that three or four people could embrace them.

"So all the trees here are sycamores?" Allie asked, watching the amber giants flutter their leaves in the chill midday breeze.

"Indeed. Sycamore Falls is rooted in old magic, and there was a spell placed on the land here long before the town came to exist. Before humans settled here, it was known as the Land of the Sycamores. Most of them are hundreds, if not thousands of years old. They're wise and their magic is pure, and they keep this place safe and sheltered from any calamities. Well, at least until last year."

"What happened last year?"

Mia studied Allie's face for a while, and she wondered if the Archivist was Reading her. She didn't know if Archivists had that type of magic, but she had nothing to hide, so she waited patiently until something settled on Mia's face, and she spoke again.

"A terrible tornado wrecked the town," she said on a long sigh. "There were a couple of casualties too, and many people injured. We rebuilt quickly using a lot of new magic, and that was when the town officially became a 'new magic' place. Still, no one expected it. The land here and surrounding the town should have been protected by the sycamores' magic."

"Does this mean that the sycamores are...sick?" Allie asked.

"Something like that." Mia's cheery demeanor was diminished by a sadness clinging to the corners of her eyes, and Allie thought of giving her a moment of silence to process the pain that wreckage must have caused.

Petra had taught Allie when she was little that magic breaks sometimes, or it sickens. They had read books together on this, and Allie knew that happened when something or someone interfered with a spell. Unfortunately, there were rarely cures for broken magic, and the few that existed could be performed only by a special class of magic wielders: Mages.

Mages were Wizards or Witches who had immense power, elemental or not, that allowed them to weave magic and spells to their will, making them the only wielders who could cure broken magic. But they were also rare and precious, very few of them born in a generation. The Diviners' Order, an organization Mages were signed up to just by virtue of being born, protected the Mages and dictated their lives by assigning them missions. It was a job one was born with.

"Were any Mages assigned here to investigate the magic on the sycamores?" Allie broke the silence.

Mia looked at her again as she had a few moments ago, but it seemed like this time she decided against sharing more with Allie.

"Here we are," she said instead as they came to the entrance of an enormous park.

The park was right at the foot of the mountain, an open field with scattered wooden benches and light posts. People walked their pets, some were running, or just enjoying the warm sunlight. On the far-right side was a tent with a sign that read "Harvest Festival Registrations."

Mia headed toward the tent and Allie trailed her silently, wondering if she shouldn't have asked about the Mages. Maybe it was a sensitive subject around the town because the Order hadn't sent anybody. If that was the case, and the incident already happened one year ago... It was just a matter of time until something happened again.

After Mia signed some papers and picked the best available locations for her storytelling booth and for Dom's Sweets as well, they went back to Maple Street the same way they came.

A question brewed in Allie's mind and heart, and she wished her instincts were wrong, although they rarely were.

"Hey, Mia." The Archivist turned her brown eyes on her.

"That Witch you mentioned on the night we met... Did she have anything to do with the spell on the sycamores?"

Mia's mouth pressed into a line as she nodded. "She's the one who broke it."

Allie wanted nothing more than to have been wrong about this. Her heart squeezed thinking about all the pain this one person had caused. Even after all her life as a Witch, she didn't understand how most of them were so selfish and...evil. But she understood completely why people here were on edge around her.

This was one of those days when she really, really wished she wasn't a Witch.

Chapter 13

I'LL TRY

"I want to keep Ekko," Allie blabbered as soon as she laid eyes on her boss, so she didn't have time to talk herself out of it. Which was as soon as she flung the door open to the bakery and stormed inside to find him sitting at a table, going over the books.

He didn't bother to raise that incredible pair of emerald eyes, ignoring the hurricane that smothered his space. He said nothing, his head hanging down, fully focused on the books before him and following a trail of numbers with a pen.

"Please, Mr. Ranford. I promise he won't bother you. I went by the Institute, and they would take him, but Mia told me there are already so many dragons there, and it would be years before someone took him. I'll take care of him, and you won't even know he's here." Allie exhaled, her heart pounding against her chest, hands fisted in the pockets of her jacket.

In the short time she'd spent with Ekko, they had grown fond of each other. Allie realized how much she'd missed having someone, be it a baby creature, to come back to every day. Ekko snuggled with her at night, and when she read, he kept the book open by holding one side of it up because she hated cracking the spine.

He'd be welcome with the coven, or at least tolerated. One of her sisters had a cat, and another one a chimera. No one had complained about them before. And even though it broke her heart that he could not spit fire, it was an advantage in keeping him in enclosed spaces. Fate was funny this way, and Allie believed it brought them together, a Witch and a dragon born with fire they could not wield.

Dominic finally raised his gaze from the documents and scanned Allie from head to toe, his eyes again spending more time on and around her face. She moved her curls behind her ears and smoothed them over with her fingers, taming the crazy hair ruffled by the wind.

"Fine," he said and went back to his files.

And that was that.

Allie whispered a thank you and reeled in the urge to jump up and down in excitement. She went to her room and told the good news to Ekko, who flew around her in circles and stopped on her shoulder to nuzzle her jaw.

She took Ekko shopping at the market to get more fruits, vegetables, and seeds for him. He picked pumpkin and chia seeds, grapes, grapefruits, apples, and a cabbage almost his size that he insisted on carrying. Ekko nearly fell from midair a few times, but did not relinquish carrying his cabbage.

Allie spent the rest of the day cooking, ate an early dinner, and grabbed her Witchcraft book while the sun was still out for her daily practice session. Ekko accompanied her to the forest and tried to cheer her up by doing air tricks after endless hours of failure upon failure to find the core of her power. Or a clue to grasping her power. Or anything, *anything* related to the damn fire inside her.

And that was their every-night routine for the next few days, until the second half of the next week. Allie was exhausted after the bakery closed because, for the first time, Dominic had given her more tasks than usual around the kitchen.

Prepare the butter for the croissant dough. Chop the apples for the pies and strudels. Mix the filling for the pumpkin pies. Fill the cupcake pans with batter and top them with frozen fruit.

It took Allie a little longer than it should have to understand that her boss was testing her power by putting her under pressure. For each task, she needed to deal with something specifically not meant to be warm. When she understood his intentions, Allie strained herself, mind and body, to keep everything under control. Exhaustion built inside her gradually as she tried to contain a power she couldn't grasp. She still had no idea where the core was, or how it felt to experience her power and not just witness it popping out at inappropriate times.

That night, Allie wanted to give up. At least for one night, she wanted to give up. She didn't want to practice or think about the Silverbarks and how each day was taking her closer and closer to their deadline with no progress made. Let her rot in bed for the night until the daylight claimed her for work.

But Ekko didn't let her.

He flew incessantly around her, pulled at her sweater, pushed at her back, and huffed smoky breaths that broke her heart. If the dragon knew how to stomp his feet, he would have done so in her pathetic face.

"I'm tired, Ekko," Allie said, defeated. She didn't like the weakness in her voice and knew she shouldn't waste any spare moment, but every inch of her body protested the thought of going to practice. She slumped on her bar stool and picked up a knife to slice an apple, appetite lacking, but Ekko landed in front of it and huffed at her again, unwavering determination shining in his dark, beady eyes.

You can try. Of the two of us, you can still try. Guilt grew in her core and overpowered the exhaustion by a hair's breadth.

"All right, all right," she ceded. "I'll try."

Ekko made happy laps around her as she grabbed her jacket and the book, and they went to that secluded spot in the forest, following the path that had become familiar.

Allie sat as close to the river as possible, and Ekko perched on the closed book, watching her patiently, his violet scales almost black in the dark.

The power in my body. The power in my body. The power in my body.

Where in gods' names was it? Why couldn't she locate it? Her power was fire, for crying out loud. She shouldn't have difficulty finding or feeling fire. It should *burn*. Somewhere, someplace inside her should burn. Where was that smoldering piece, that source of power that was so natural for all other Witches to find?

Allie only felt frustration build up inside her. *Failure, failure, failure.* The disgusted looks on people's faces haunted her, the disapproval on her sisters' faces haunted her, the betrayal and heartbreak in Green Creek haunted her. She fisted her hands in the dry grass and felt a tear drip down her cheek. Ghosts crowded her soul and her mind, and maybe that was why she couldn't find her power. Maybe it was hidden under all of them, these wicked and twisted and malevolent ghosts. They painted her memories red, clung to her like a second skin, and she felt suffocated, *hot—*

Ekko chittered and pulled at her sweater, nudging her cheek urgently until she opened her eyes.

Oh no.

Dominic was running out of time. Each day that crept by increased Dom's fear that another calamity could hit their vulnerable town. A full year had passed since the tornado, and he wasn't any closer to discovering how to fix the broken spell. Magic was picky like that, and he could not just weave a new spell between the land and the sycamores. No. He had to find a way to repair what was broken to restore the balance, and he was out of patience.

He had to search everywhere but felt like it would take a lifetime. Each day, he scanned another portion of the land, every nook and cranny of every tree, and still didn't find the rupture in the magic. All pieces he had tested had been intact. The sycamores were humming every time he touched them, the earth was singing every time he sent his magic through it in search of the sickness.

Nothing cried. Nothing withered. Nothing was rotten.

And he was damn frustrated. He never imagined one of the hardest missions of his life would be in his hometown.

After yet another failed attempt to find the rupture in the magic, Dom was heading home on a longer path than usual. Ever since the Witch had stolen his favorite spot—the one place where he could access the most remote parts of the land from a distance —he had to venture farther and farther away to send his magic all the way to the edges, where the last sycamores bordered the area.

The night was chilly when he had left the forest, and now a strong wind blew through the streets, rustling dry leaves and branches, sweeping his hair over his eyes. Dom used a bit of magic to keep the air at bay, a privilege he always enjoyed in the colder months when he was not stationed in a warm town. He hated the endless heat and couldn't imagine living with a constant coat of sweat on his skin. The thought made him shudder, and he stepped up his pace, as if the imaginary sweat was chasing him.

A flicker caught his attention. Through the naturally dark forest, he noticed a throbbing red glimmer lighting the thick tree trunks.

Fire?

Dom mapped the area quickly in his head and concluded that

it might be around the secluded spot he used to go to every night before—

Alecsandra.

Dom ran.

He cut through the forest on a shortcut he hoped to remember well from his childhood. Dom sprinted through the darkness, through sharp branches and dry leaves fighting to grip him. But as the red flare grew and grew in his line of vision, he put his full strength in his strides, molding the wind with his magic to push him from behind. The cold air scratched his throat with every breath, and his muscles protested, but he didn't slow down.

Had this forest always been so fucking big?

Dom felt like he'd been running forever when he entered the clearing that he knew like the back of his hand and halted in front of angry flames taller than him. They licked furiously at the ground, forming a perfect circle on the edge of the river.

But he heard nothing else than the horrific crackle of the scorching fire.

"Hello?" he yelled, coming as close as possible to the heat. Through the dancing inferno, he made out a figure curled into herself on the ground. "Alecsandra!"

Nothing.

Why wasn't she screaming for help?

His chest caved in under an invisible weight. She couldn't be... No. Unconscious, maybe, but nothing more. Dom refused to admit it to himself, but he felt responsible for her. What if anything happened to the Witch while in his care?

Ekko flew up from within the circle of flames, diving to him and chittering with desperation in his black eyes, claws pulling at his jacket.

"I know, I know," Dom said. "Alecsandra!" he yelled again, louder, hands cupped around his mouth.

The shadow behind the flames moved. If she said anything,

Dom didn't hear her past the flames' hisses. He readied his magic to put out the bloody fire when one of the flames broke from the blaze, grew taller and longer than the others, then plunged toward the middle of the burning circle.

She screamed then, a sound so raw and dire that it cracked something in Dom's heart.

"No!" he screamed with her and threw his arms out, shoving all his power to put out the godsforsaken flames.

ॐ

Am I dead?

No, wait.

Allie felt the horrified thud of her heart in her chest, and she snapped her eyes open to the quiet, dark clearing, the gurgle of the flowing river and the faint whooshing of the leaves the only sounds around her. She coughed heavily, her lungs rejecting all the smoke she'd inhaled.

The absolute fear for her life that had sunk its sharp talons into her faded just a fraction, and Allie tried to let it go with every breath and cough.

She was *alive.*

She unclenched her fists, feeling the bite her nails took out of her palms' skin, then stretched her legs, unfurling from hugging her knees to her chest. The pain was real, and she tried to shift her focus to it and away from the excruciating prospect of being burned alive and turned into ash, her pieces scattered through the solemn sycamores.

Alive.

How was she alive? Where was the fire? Had it just been in her head? No. The air had been so hot, the blaze so close to her, so real...

Allie flinched when Ekko crashed into her from the side, his claws and wings hanging onto her hair, making a mess of her curls. She scratched him between his wings and untangled him carefully from her hair. Her cough had eased, and she took her first full breath, in and out.

The book hadn't made it through the fire; its black ash slumped in a sad pile. Was this a sign that she shouldn't strive to learn more about her power?

A loud thump behind her drew her attention, and she turned to see the last person she expected to see at that moment.

Her boss knelt on the ground, hands on his thighs, his shoulders rising and falling rapidly. His head was hanging, hair forming a curtain around his handsome face. Allie shoved aside her pain and fright and ran to him.

"Mr. Ranford!" she shouted, falling on her knees next to him. "Mr. Ranford, are you okay? What are you doing here?"

His breaths came in fast and loud, and she didn't expect him to answer right away. But he did, and he raised those clover-green eyes to her, a trace of anger shadowing them. They roamed urgently over her body, head to toe. What was he looking for?

"Why weren't you calling for help?" he growled through his labored breaths, that scowl that seemed to be part of him deeper than she'd ever seen it.

"I... Well... Because I was trying to fix it," she said in a small voice. She had been trying to get it under control *somehow*. Dominic stayed quiet, instead focusing on evening his breathing. Allie had no idea what to do, how to help him, so she just stood there watching him, Ekko propped on her shoulder.

Was he the last person she expected to see, though?

If not him, who else? Who else in Sycamore Falls would care enough not to let her burn? The people here had a personal vendetta against Witches. If anything, they'd have happily ignited the flames that almost killed her.

Alive.

Had Dominic been the one who put out the fire?

Allie for sure wasn't, or at least she didn't think she was. Gods, this was embarrassing, not even knowing if she did or did not stop the fire she ignited. She felt nothing but useless, and so, so terrified. No way she was the one to masterfully control the blaze that had taken form and tried to attack her.

Her own power had tried to attack her.

"Were you... Were you the one who put out the flames?" she asked when she no longer heard him struggle to breathe.

Dominic gave her a curt nod and stood up, not breaking their stare. Allie followed.

Right. That made infinitely more sense.

It also meant Dominic had magic, too.

"Thank you, Mr. Ranford. I don't know what would have happened if—"

"Don't." A muscle ticked in his jaw, his lips pressing into a straight line. That frown deepened even more, and his hands fisted at his sides.

Okay. All right. It's not like Allie wanted to think about what would have happened if he hadn't gotten here in time.

"So..." Allie said, desperate to find a way to soothe the tension out of her boss's features, afraid his muscles might pop from the strain. "You have magic?" Another curt nod, his eyes never leaving hers. "Fire?" She didn't want to assume, but she had seen no water, and what other power could have put out the inferno she'd inadvertently started?

"Air."

Her brows rose in surprise. Then...

He'd used his power to suck the air out of the flames, putting them out. An elemental Wizard?

But why couldn't she Read him? Why did it feel like her magic knocked against an adamant wall, when—

Oh.

Ohhhh.

Oh gods.

Allie gasped, her hand flying over her mouth. She studied the man in front of her, all tall and broad and broody, sharp jaw covered with the beginning of stubble, soft curls framing his face. Deep green eyes staring at her, searching, waiting.

"You're the Mage who's investigating the magic rupture on the sycamores."

Chapter 14

THOUGHT THERE WAS A SPLINTER

"How do you know about that?"

"Your sister told me."

His eyes narrowed, and Allie wasn't sure if it was because she referred to Mia as his sister or because Mia had told her about the town's history.

"What else did she tell you?" he rasped.

Allie swallowed and broke his intense gaze, her eyes finding an interesting patch of dark grass under her boots.

"She told me about the Witch who broke the spell on the sycamores." She fidgeted with the sleeves of her jacket, then crossed her arms tightly against her chest.

A pair of bigger boots came into her view. She felt more than heard Dominic's long sigh, hot air brushing the skin on her forehead. His warm fingers gripped her chin, and he tilted her head up, drawing her gaze back into his shimmering emeralds.

"That has nothing to do with you." A fierce strength commanded his tone, and Allie wanted to accept the truth in his words more than anything. But she couldn't. The hatred toward Witches she grew up with, the isolation she fought, the prejudice she tried to overcome—these were all justified when Witches kept proving their vileness.

Allie wasn't foolish enough to think she was any different when her lack of control put the people around her in danger. Sure, she never did it on purpose, but did that truly matter in the end?

She stepped back from the Mage's touch and offered him a weak smile, shoving her fisted hands back in her pockets.

"Thank you for saving my life, Mr. Ranford. I don't know how I'll ever be able to repay you."

"You have nothing to thank me for."

Allie didn't have enough energy left to protest. She felt empty and dry, as if the flames that had exploded out of her took her essence with them.

Tomorrow would be better. Even though it would bring her one day closer to Lydia's deadline. With almost two weeks having passed and no progress, maybe tomorrow wouldn't be better. Maybe it would be worse.

But tomorrow was tomorrow's problem.

"Let's go." Dominic's voice was so uncharacteristically soft, Allie didn't know what to do with it.

She followed him and was shocked when Ekko flew from her shoulder to Dominic's, nuzzling his cheek. Dominic did not react, but he didn't shoo the dragon away either.

They walked back to the bakery in silence. The temperatures had dropped each hour into the inky night, and Allie expected the crisp, cold wind to gnaw at her cheeks. She was surprised that not one lock of her hair fluttered when the sycamore branches were waving lazily against the starry night sky, like she was shielded against it.

Dominic unlocked the door and turned on the lights, the white hurting Allie's eyes. All she wanted to do was plop into bed and forget about today. She was alive, and that was all that mattered.

At the end of the small hallway, Allie made a left to her studio room while Dominic made a right to the stairs, Ekko flying next to her by the door. She stopped with her hand on the doorknob and turned abruptly.

"Mr. Ranford." He halted at the foot of the stairs and turned, his broad frame sagging with exhaustion. Allie had scraped the bottom of her soul for a wisp of energy during the walk and thought of sharing a few words of gratitude. But when she looked at Dominic now, at his ruffled chestnut hair and tired eyes, she decided against it. She would babble all the words she thought of tomorrow. "Thank you."

Dominic opened his mouth to object again, but something made him decide against it.

"Let's start at six tomorrow," he said, then turned around and climbed up the stairs, leaving no room for debate.

The next morning, Allie was up and ready to start at fifteen minutes before six. She turned on the ovens, made coffee for her and Dominic, and took hers out to enjoy a quiet moment in the cool, fresh air that smelled like rain. She resisted going inside for all of five minutes until she shuddered enough to spill her coffee. Allie needed more time for her body to get accustomed to the cold temperatures in Sycamore Falls, and it would do her good to be outside more during the hours the sun was out.

She went inside and headed for the kitchen, intent on cleaning the space.

"Morning." Dominic nursed his coffee, leaning against the kitchen table. He wore a soft green turtleneck sweater and dark gray jeans, his hair secured in a tight high bun.

"Good morning, Mr. Ranford." Allie watched her boss with awe, processing everything that had happened last night. After they had returned to the bakery, Allie had no brain power left to *truly* comprehend the importance of what she had learned.

Dominic was a Mage.

A. MAGE.

Allie had never met a Mage. When she had tried to Read him and couldn't, it didn't cross her mind that this was the reason. Mages were highly valued and protected amongst magic wielders, and they were bestowed shields by the Diviners' Order to protect their identities.

When she woke up this morning, the first and only thought that ran through her mind was that her boss, a Mage, had saved her life last night. She'd spent time crafting the perfect speech to express her gratitude, so she set down her coffee mug and cleared her throat.

"Mr. Ranford, I can't thank you enough—"

"Stop," he hissed, and Allie bit her tongue. "I don't want to hear it." Dominic busied himself with pans and trays, setting up the table to start baking. He took eggs and butter out of the fridge and sugar and baking powder from the cupboard, then lined them on the counter.

Allie didn't know what to do. She waited patiently by the door in case he needed something but after a few minutes decided to get the cleaning supplies and start in the front.

"No one knows," Dominic said. He stopped what he was doing and faced her, clasping the table's edges until his knuckles were white. "Besides Mia and Brandon," he clarified, but the look in his eyes told her what he meant by that.

"I would never," Allie said in a steady voice. She wasn't surprised to learn people in Sycamore Falls didn't know a Mage lived among them. The townsfolk might expect one to be here investigating the magic rupture, but as far as Allie knew, Mages usually kept ridiculously low profiles, away from the public eye. Not exactly running a bakery in the middle of the town.

Allie was brimming with curiosity, but she kept her questions to herself. It was not her business, as much as she wanted to make it her business to learn more about Dominic. But she would never reveal his secret, not even under the threat of a burning fire.

The irony wasn't lost on her.

Dominic nodded once, and Allie saw the appreciation in his eyes. She offered him a smile and a nod of her own.

"If you ever need help..." he stopped as if the rest of the sentence was supposed to be obvious. Allie threw him a confused look. Help with... Baking? Orders?

"What do you mean?"

"With your power. Let me know."

Allie was sure of the dumbfounded look on her face without needing to check a mirror. A Mage, helping her? With her power?

Was he mocking her?

She didn't know if she should laugh or focus her efforts so her skin didn't turn the shade of a ripe strawberry. Allie stood there watching him for a long moment, waiting for the other shoe to drop. For him to say he was joking, or that he meant something totally different. But his gaze was genuine, his green eyes unwavering, and that scowl she had become so familiar with was... smaller. Barely a crease.

Did he really mean it?

Insulting him was the last thing she wanted to do, so Allie considered he was offering his help when she said, "I will. Thank you, Mr. Ranford."

They stood in silence for a while, and Allie couldn't help but think that she needed to find a way to properly thank him for saving her last night. She understood he did not, for some reason, want to hear the words, but maybe he would take another form of gratitude.

Food!

Allie's exceptional cooking skills made up for her lack of baking skills. In fact, she was convinced that she had been in charge of cooking for the Silverbarks not only because she was their newest member, but because her food was the most delicious. She had tasted some of her sisters' cooking, and, ugh. Her stomach recoiled at the memory of watery stew and undercooked vegetables.

Allie could cook for her Mage boss as her token of gratitude.

"Mr. Ranford," she said before she lost her courage. "If you're free this weekend after the bakery closes, I would like to invite you to lunch." She stared intently at him, trusting that the words he didn't want to hear were evident in her eyes.

His features were set in stone and didn't betray any thought he might have about her invitation. Allie waited, her heart pounding in her chest like a lunatic. She had no reason to be nervous about *lunch*.

Dominic put her out of her misery when he said, "I'm free."

"Great!" Allie cheered. She smiled at him and could have sworn his cheek ticked up the tiniest bit.

Dominic turned his back on her, grabbed one of the bowls, and started mixing the ingredients. He always used the whisk at first, then his strong hands to knead the perfect dough. Allie leaned against the doorframe, ogling the muscles on his back as they tensed with every movement. She realized in the almost two weeks she'd been here that watching Dominic had become one of her favorite activities.

"Can you bring me—" Dominic turned swiftly, and Allie bounced from the frame like it burned her. She faced it and rubbed the wood with her thumb, fixing an imaginary issue.

"Thought there was a splinter," she muttered as if she had been utterly occupied by the task of assessing the doorframe. She turned fake-innocent eyes to her boss, hoping to all the gods he *did not* just catch her gawking at him. "What do you need, Mr. Ranford?"

Was her voice too high? It sounded pitchy. And why was she rocking on her heels?

"Apron," Dominic said, narrowing his eyes at her.

Allie marched to the storage room and took a moment in the hallway to catch her breath. What was wrong with her?

Don't answer that.

She took one of the clean aprons and returned to the kitchen after taking five—seven—deep breaths.

"Here you go," she said and extended it out to her boss.

Dominic looked from her to his hands, wrist deep into the dough. He lifted his hands to his sides and leaned down, facing her. She stared at him like an idiot with the apron in her hands until her boss spelled out the obvious.

"Can you put it on?" he said, dragging the words out.

Allie blinked.

"Yes?"

"Are you asking me?" Dominic's patience slipped. "I don't have all day." He gestured with his raw-dough-covered hands.

Right.

Allie stepped closer to him and hung the string over his head, careful not to disturb the perfectly tied bun. Then Dominic stood to his full height and turned around. This close, the smell of spicy cedarwood with a faint scent of leather enveloped her, and she fought against taking a full breath in. Allie cleared her throat and stretched her arms to grab the apron string and tie them around his back. She avoided hugging her boss from behind, but her arms grazed against his waist as she pulled at the ropes.

Knotting the damn things was hard with trembling hands, but mercifully she managed a lopsided bow and stepped back.

"Thanks," Dominic said.

Allie nodded and left the kitchen, her coffee forgotten. This was the perfect moment to go back out into the cold air.

✦

After their lunch break, Dominic left Alecsandra to handle the customers while he worked on perfecting his dulce de leche recipe. This was Mia's favorite dessert, and he didn't make it for the bakery anymore since everyone complained it was "too sweet." Dom couldn't argue; it *was* too sweet. But Mia loved it, and he hadn't made it in a while, and now with Alecsandra's help, he had a bit more time on his hands.

Dominic wiped his palms on the apron and was immediately reminded of this morning, of Alecsandra's fingers brushing his sides, the goosebumps that blossomed all over his skin. He should have washed his hands and put the damn apron on by himself, or risk getting his sweater dirty.

He was a fool.

A fool who could bake a mean dulce de leche, but a fool nonetheless. The dessert was cool enough to taste now. It was as sweet as he remembered, and Dom couldn't suppress a shudder. He scooped a bit onto a small plate and went to the front to have Alecsandra taste it too.

Dom had come to appreciate having the Witch help around the bakery, not that he'd ever admit it out loud, especially not to Brandon. The smugness that would fill him would be eternal, and Dom would never hear the end of it. But it was nice to have someone else taste what he baked and give him feedback, even if her feedback was always the same: "Everything is delicious, Mr. Ranford."

From the small hallway that led to the front, Dominic saw Alecsandra standing in front of the register. But her posture was rigid, her arms wrapped around her. He stepped behind the counter and met one of the few men he loathed from the bottom of his heart.

"Afternoon, Dom," Jared Finn said in an overfriendly tone, as always. They were not friends, they would never be friends, and every time he crossed the bakery's threshold, Dom fought the urge to shove a "We reserve the right to select our customers" sign in his face and kick him out. But that was not the image he wanted to create for Dom's Sweets, and he wouldn't let the asshole ruin it.

Hopefully.

"Jared," he spat through his teeth. His eyes went to Alecsandra, who stood there staring at the man, back ramrod straight and lips pressed into a thin line. Jared was the first customer she didn't smile at. Dominic had witnessed his customers treat her with contempt, with ugly sneers and not-so-much-whispered comments, yet she had always smiled at them.

The jerk made her feel uncomfortable.

"Take this and go to the back." Dom shoved the plate to her. Alecsandra flinched as if she just noticed him standing there, and her big brown eyes watched Dom with an intensity he couldn't understand. But she took the plate and left for the kitchen without another word.

The moron looked after her like she was something he wanted, and that rubbed Dominic the wrong fucking way.

"What do you want?"

"Just getting to know the newest resident of our small town here," Jared said with a sleazy smile that made Dom want to knock his teeth out. He didn't need to Read him to know what was going on in that sick mind of his. He'd been the same ever since they were kids.

"Don't even think about it," Dominic growled. Hot anger traveled through him, pushing his breaths in and out faster. He gripped the edge of the counter and hoped to not break a piece off it.

"Are you gonna have at it?" The smirk on Jared's face grew bigger. Dom locked his jaw, teeth clenched so hard his head hurt.

"Get out."

"I thought you wanted to keep the appearances up, *friend*," he pressed on the word.

Everything he wanted to do was keeping Jared-fucking-Finn out of his place.

"Out," he snarled and wasted no time rounding the counter.

Jared took a few steps back, putting distance between himself and Dominic. He raised his arms in a fake peaceful gesture and left without another word.

Dom didn't know what to do with all this pent-up anger. He felt like punching a hole in the wall, but he'd regret it later when he had to fix it. His nostrils flared, and his breathing was still loud when Alecsandra returned from the kitchen, a glass of water at her mouth.

She looked around the bakery and her features relaxed into her casual smile when she didn't find the man that had made her shy away. For Jared's sake, Dom hoped she had only felt uncomfortable and nothing else. When her eyes met Dom's, her smile grew and turned genuine and warm, a smile she didn't share with many people.

"I don't want to upset you, Mr. Ranford, but I don't want to lie to you either." That had Dom's heart standing at attention, his brain going through wild scenarios about what that fucker could have said to her. Or worse, done to her. If he laid a hand anywhere near her, or hell, looked at her the wrong way...

At least Alecsandra wasn't willing to lie to him about it.

"What is it?" he asked, trying to keep the rage from his voice and not quite succeeding at it.

"That thing in the kitchen... I don't know what it is, but it's really, *really* sweet," she said and chugged the rest of the water.

Dom felt the anger evaporate from his body.

Chapter 15

CALL ME DOMINIC

Allie was buzzing with excitement on the first morning of the weekend. She had found everything she wanted at the market the night before for her lunch with Dominic today. After hours of deliberation, she'd settled on a spinach salad with smoked duck, figs, cherries, and red onion, and a cream of mushroom soup with shallots and fresh portobellos. She had prepared all the ingredients last night and agreed with Dominic that she needed about half an hour today for the food to be ready.

Three hours into the day, Allie felt like time was mocking her. She could have sworn at least five hours had passed since she had woken up, yet they were still not open for customers. Dominic was busy baking the weekend special, salted caramel apple pie, and had shooed her away from the kitchen twice after she finished helping him set up. He said all his weekend specials were secret recipes, which only made her more curious. Allie hovered by the kitchen entrance and tried to peek until she caught one of her boss's glares that pierced through her soul. She bolted to the front and decided to make a second coffee to calm her nerves.

Tea might have done the trick better.

She picked up the hot coffee cup and started for the door,

hoping the morning chill would help her get a grip on her agitation. It was just lunch. Food, and nothing more.

With her handsome, protective boss, who was also a powerful Mage.

She decided to channel all her thoughts on the "boss" part to avoid her mind slipping in other directions. Which happened more and more often. Midway to the door, Allie felt the cup in her hand grow hotter, so much so that the skin on her palms was burning.

Allie dropped the cup on the closest table and looked at her hands when the pain did not subside. The skin was red and swollen, but not blistering.

"What..." A glimmering thread of light lined one wrist through her fingers. Another one appeared on her other palm, and then more and more threads came to life, lighting her skin up. The fire web brightened until the pain became impossible to bear, the throbbing climbing up her arms to her elbows.

The fire was out of control, and it burned her alive.

Her hands trembled, and with each breath her body shuddered harder, pain searing through her muscles and bones.

"Mr. Ranford!" Allie screamed without another thought, suffocated by sheer panic. Not only had she promised to tell him if this happened again, but the fear that she could ruin something or harm someone shoved its ugly claws into her heart, sending her into a frenzy.

Dominic came out of the kitchen like a hurricane and was next to her in a second, another type of panic shining through his green eyes.

"What's—" He stopped when he saw Allie's upturned palms, the strings of live fire digging into her flesh. Dominic grabbed her wrists, and she hissed when the movement intensified the pulsating pain. Even her own breathing made the pain worse. He dropped her hands, his eyes moving from her to her palms, brows furrowed. "Come with me."

Allie followed him blindly to the kitchen, her vision clouded by unshed tears gathered there from the sizzling pain. Dominic pushed his palms out and sent a strong current of air to the sink that turned on the cold water while he grabbed ice from the freezer and poured it into a bowl.

"Put your hands here," he said in a painfully gentle voice. She placed her hands in the ice bowl, cold water pouring over them. A whimper escaped through her clenched teeth, her tears now free to streak her cheeks. Allie hid her face into her shoulder, embarrassment making its way through the stream of emotions drowning her.

A warm, wide palm came to rest on her back, and Allie hoped she had suppressed her flinch of shock in time. Dominic kept his hand there and drew lazy circles between her shoulder blades. His touch was strong and comforting, and she leaned into it, shifting her focus away from the excruciating pain and into the steady movement of his hand.

She had no idea how much time passed before she was able to take a breath in and not feel like her flesh would split. Slowly turning her hands, she saw the fiery threads on her palms had faded, leaving behind reddened and swollen skin. She pulled her hands out of the bowl, and Dominic leaned in to turn off the water, his hand still on her back.

He watched her with raw intensity, his green eyes roving around her face, waiting, searching. She wondered if he was Reading her, magic that was just another thought for a Mage, and she hoped he did. Allie found it impossible to put into words what was going on with her or what was in her heart.

"I know you've been practicing. What did you learn?" he asked. Allie scoffed.

"Not much. I only got to the part where I'm looking for the

source of the power in my body, but I couldn't even do that," she confessed.

Dominic went quiet. His green eyes trembled, a hidden conflict brewing behind them. Allie let him gather his thoughts, wondering what sent him into a spiral.

"Do you trust me?" His voice was hoarse, like the words were thorns in his throat.

"Yes," Allie answered on instinct, not surprised to discover it was true. "I trust you."

Dominic's eyes softened and his features relaxed as he exhaled a long breath.

"Let me take a look."

Allie had no idea what he was talking about. She nodded, too exhausted to question him. He took a step closer, his cedarwood scent wrapping around her like a soft blanket, grounding her. Dominic had saved her life and helped her now without the slightest hint of hesitation, so whatever he wanted to take a look at, he was more than welcome to do so.

Allie tipped her chin up to watch her boss, one of his hands still on her back, the other one coming to rest on her belly. His long fingers splayed around her core, and Allie held her breath. Dominic's hands were on her, still and wide and warm. Her heartbeat jumped to a frantic rhythm, and she hoped her boss couldn't feel it under her skin.

His eyes closed, and he frowned deeper and deeper, while doing...whatever he was doing. Allie had no idea about the limitations of a Mage's power, but she was confident she was in good hands.

Literally.

Dominic's eyes snapped open, and he rushed out the words, "I'll be right back," before fleeing from the kitchen, leaving Allie with a dumbfounded look on her face, running hot for various, unrelated reasons.

Dominic stormed out of the bakery and crossed the street in long strides, ignoring the "Closed" sign and barging into his sister's bookstore. The door flew open and hit the wall, sending some of the chatting books back into their place.

Mia stood at the register, flipping through a catalogue, unfazed by his intrusion. She raised her big brown eyes to her brother, not even slightly bothered by his state of uneasiness.

"Yes?" she said in a calm voice that irked him, half a smile tilting her cheek up.

"I need a book on power seals," he barked. Mia studied him for a moment, taking in his rushed breathing and the look of concern that twisted his features. She rounded the counter and went looking through the shelves without a question.

Dominic waited by the door, calming his breathing and his galloping heart. He wished he was wrong more than anything, but his Assessments had never failed him before, and he doubted they would start now.

Mia's hissing at the naughty, loud books filled the space while she looked for the one he needed. It was lucky the bookstore was still closed to customers, not that Dom would have cared enough to alter his behavior.

"This is the only one I could find on the floor," Mia said and handed him a book titled *Sealing: The Line Between Right and Wrong*. Dom kept the comment about sealing never being right to himself and nodded at his sister. "Let me know if you can't find what you need, and I'll look through the storage, too."

"Thanks, Mia." He turned to leave but stopped with his hand on the doorknob at the sound of his sister's voice.

"Is this about Allie?"

Allie.

The feeling of his magic hitting a scorching hot brick wall that tried to suck the power out of him came back rushing and made his head spin. Dom looked at Mia over his shoulder.

"Yeah."

"Is she going to be okay?" Mia asked with deep concern in her voice. One of the many reasons Dom loved her was this pure heart of hers. She barely knew the Witch, and yet she was worried about her. Dom wanted to reassure her, wanted to reassure himself, but he couldn't be sure, so he settled for the best he could offer without lying.

"I hope so." His knuckles went white gripping the book. "Do me a favor, will you?" His sister agreed without blinking as he detailed what he needed.

Dom flipped the book open and skimmed through the first pages on his way back to the bakery. With his eyes glued to the text, he knocked into someone on the sidewalk.

"Sorry," he muttered, not bothering to lift his eyes.

"Morning, Dom," a chirping voice greeted him. Anna smiled at him, ponytail swishing, her hands on his arms to steady herself. "I haven't seen you in a while. Let's have coffee together," Anna suggested, although she saw him every time she walked into the bakery, which was...every day.

Dom avoided seeing her alone. He didn't want to give her any false hope as he did not share her feelings. He had not felt like that about anyone in a very long time.

"Maybe another time." He nodded and went around her, his mind reeling over the details about power seals.

"Dominic." He halted at the sound of his full name and faced her. "Are you sure you're keeping the best company at the bakery?"

"What?"

"I mean, no one knows anything about this Witch. For all we know, she may be here to continue what the other one—"

"Stop." Anna flinched at the snarl in his voice.

"*I trust you.*" Words he had been hungry for for so long,

coming from the most unexpected person in his life. Words that made his aching heart feel like it was dipped in warm honey.

"You don't know anything about her."

"I don't want anything to happen to you, or your bakery," Anna plowed on with her biased concerns.

Concerns about one of the kindest souls he had ever met. A Witch who kept her promise, no matter how embarrassed it made her feel. A Witch who loved an orphaned baby dragon as if she had been raising him for years. A Witch who smiled at everyone who sneered at her, who struggled to learn as much as she could about this temporary job. Who put herself through literal fire to learn how to control her power, with no one to help her. Yet.

"Don't you worry about me," Dom warned her, then left.

He crossed the street and entered the bakery, holding the book to his side, title hidden. Allie was sitting at a table, her fingers drawing patterns on the rim of the coffee cup. She welcomed him with a small smile, her chocolate-brown eyes wary, fear still clinging to their corners, making them wide and glassy.

"How are you feeling?" he asked just when she opened her mouth to say something foolish like thanking him for helping her.

"I'm all right. I wanted to—"

"Thank you," Dom interrupted her, more than likely stealing her words. Allie watched him with the same wide eyes as he went on. "For telling me. Thank you for keeping your promise." He did not want to think about what would have happened if she hadn't called for him in time. And he was truly grateful there was someone in his life—besides Mia—who did not break their promises. Dom inhaled and gathered his courage to utter the words that dug a knife into his heart and twisted it endlessly. "And for trusting me."

Allie, frozen in place, watched him with her pink lips parted like he'd said the silliest thing ever.

"Cover the front for me for a while, will you?"

Dominic left her standing in that spot, her mouth likely still open. He heard a scraping chair and knew she snapped out of her endearing shock.

"Of course, Mr. Ranford," she called after him.

He stopped in the doorframe to the hallway and turned to face the beautiful Witch. Her eyes were on him, flashing one of those full smiles that he preferred to think were only for him.

"Call me Dominic."

Allie was lucky the bakery was packed with customers today. She did not want a spare moment to think about what had happened in the morning. Later, she would be consumed by all of it. She would be consumed by Dominic's kindness, by the way he'd looked at her burning skin as if he could feel the heat on his own. She hated that she had endangered the one person in her life whom she desperately didn't want to hurt. She never wanted to hurt anyone, but Dominic...

Call me Dominic.

Her heart quivered at the memory, and she mentally slapped the stupid thing. There was nothing to quiver about, as everyone else called him by his name. It had only been a matter of time for them to get to know each other and become...closer.

I should have told him to call me Allie.

Dominic had been hiding in the kitchen all day under the pretense of the weekend special. Allie was selling the last tray in stock, so she saw through his innocent lie. She guessed it had something to do with the book he had returned with and hidden from her.

"Miss!" A somewhat familiar voice brought her back behind the register. She greeted Mrs. Chen, the lady wearing her usual long yellow coat, gray hair up in a bun like Allie's. "Where is your dragon?" she asked with a glare.

"In my room. Dominic asked me to keep him away from the bakery, but he's doing really well." Allie spoke his name as if she had done it hundreds of times, and it just felt right.

"I'd like to see for myself," Mrs. Chen huffed. "It was not a traditional adoption that you did, but I still need to make sure the creature is cared for."

"Of course." Allie went back and stopped by the kitchen, laying her eyes on her Mage boss, whom she could call by his first name. "Can I bring Ekko out front for a bit? Mrs. Chen is here to make sure he's okay."

"Sure," Dominic answered without raising his eyes from the book that held him captive.

"I thought you were working on the weekend special," Allie teased him.

"I am." The man jerked his head at a simmering pot on the stove, still not moving his gaze away from the pages.

Allie allowed herself one more moment to look at him, tense arms crossed over his chest, feet spread wide, frowning at that book as if it was his worst enemy. Under all this broodiness and grumpiness was an incredibly beautiful soul that she was lucky to have glimpsed.

Allie grabbed Ekko from the room, the dragon overly excited to get out of that space. He was behaving himself, but Allie knew he got bored while she was gone. Ekko flew in laps around her three or four times before he settled on her shoulder, after Allie warned him not to leave her side.

They went to the front without stopping by the kitchen, but Ekko turned his small head and looked wistfully at Dominic while they passed by.

"Mrs. Chen, this is Ekko," Allie said and tickled his belly. The baby dragon chittered but stayed on her shoulder, then watched the elderly woman with quizzical eyes. She studied him, cocking her head left and right before she concluded that he looked healthy.

Mrs. Chen left with two slices of the weekend special, and Allie went about rearranging the display case and cleaning the tables that were just vacated. She kept Ekko with her for a little while longer since there was no one else in—

"Allie!" Mia's voice carried from the entrance together with the bell. She came in smiling, wearing a pink knitted dress with a denim jacket on top and tall leather boots. Her dark caramel hair was braided over her shoulder. "This must be Ekko," she said as she approached them. Ekko made big eyes at her, and Mia didn't hold back and grabbed him from under his wings, crushing him to her chest. "*Que cariño!*"

Allie chuckled as Ekko struggled to breathe. When he was finally free, he flew away from them to the back of the bakery.

"I wanted to see if you had plans for lunch," Mia told her. "The girls and I are going out for butternut squash pasta at Rogelio's. Come with us," she said.

Allie looked from Mia to the counter area, worried about Ekko's whereabouts. She had promised lunch to Dominic, and she was so, *so* looking forward to it.

"I'm sorry, I—"

"She's free," a deep, thick voice came from behind her. Allie turned, and her heart flipped at the image before her. Dominic stood behind the counter, arms still crossed, Ekko proudly perched on his shoulder like it was his greatest achievement. She looked back at Mia and gave her an awkward smile, then turned and crossed the distance to her boss, stretching her hands to pick Ekko up.

"I thought we were having lunch today," she whispered. The dragon evaded her and flew around Dominic to his other shoulder.

"We can have lunch tomorrow," Dominic said in an end-of-the-conversation tone and left, Ekko still on his shoulder.

What was happening?

"So?" Mia asked.

Allie didn't feel like she had much of a choice. It would be nice to meet more people, and if they were Mia's friends, there was a smaller chance they would sneer at her.

"I'm in," Allie agreed with a smile that didn't quite reach her eyes.

Chapter 16

I WILL HELP YOU

Allie quickly changed into another sweater and let her hair down before she left the bakery with Mia. Dominic was absorbed by the book, and when Allie called for Ekko, the dragon faked sleeping on the floor by Dominic's feet.

The fall day was the coldest Allie had experienced so far in Sycamore Falls, no sun in sight, thick, dark clouds covering the sky. The biting wind moved the tree branches that lined the streets, rustling leaves filling the otherwise quiet area.

"Is everything okay?" Allie threw Mia a confused look, so she clarified, "Dom almost ripped my door off its hinges this morning looking for a book. I assumed you might know why." Mia smiled weakly.

"I don't know about the book, but..." Allie considered for a moment. Dominic might have told Mia about her power struggles. He seemed like a man who would not share what wasn't his, but would he make an exception for his sister? "Did he tell you anything about my power?" Mia shook her head, so Allie took a deep breath and told Mia about her embarrassingly late manifestation and the way she still struggled with her power.

"That's tough." Mia rested a hand on Allie's arm. "And you

really need to get back to the coven before Hallows Eve? Will they kick you out if you don't get your power under control by then?" Allie nodded, though hearing someone else say it out loud sounded unreasonable. "Can't you join another coven? They sound...mean." Both of them chuckled.

"My mom was a Silverbark. It's tradition to follow in your family's footsteps as a Witch, especially since we don't have much of that. The coven becomes your family, and this way, you are not alone. I guess it's a bit pathetic," she said, moving some curls behind her ears.

"There is nothing pathetic about not wanting to be alone," Mia said in a strong tone that reminded Allie of Dominic. The first resemblance she'd noticed between the two.

They walked in silence to the end of Maple Street opposite the market. Rogelio's was buzzing with people talking and laughing around their plates and glasses. A hand flew up from one of the tables by the window, a grinning woman with bright blue eyes and strawberry blonde short hair hovering over her shoulders motioning them over.

"That's Harper. She's the funny one," Mia explained. "Tina, her fiancée, is the wise one."

"Which one are you?"

"I guess you'll have to stick around long enough to find out," Mia challenged her. If Allie had to guess now, she would pick "witty."

Allie followed Mia to the table, keeping two steps behind her.

"Mia!" The blonde threw her arms around Mia's neck.

"We saw each other last week, Harper," Mia laughed. She leaned down to hug the tall, brown-eyed brunette in the wheelchair. "Hi, Tina." She gave her a peck on the cheek, then straightened and said, "Girls, this is Allie. She's working with my brother at the bakery. Allie, this is Harper"—she pointed to the grinning blonde—"and Tina."

"Nice to meet you," Allie said with a smile. Tina and Harper smiled back, widely and warmly, their eyes barely moving over her red curls. The three of them sat down and ordered the famous butternut squash pasta and a pitcher of lavender lemonade.

"So, Allie," Tina said and clasped her hands over the table, "how is it living with our town's most eligible bachelor?" She wiggled her brows, and Allie felt her cheeks warm at the insinuation.

"We're just working together." She nervously played with her napkin, the memory of Dominic's hands splayed on her back and abdomen flashing to the center of her mind. Allie changed the subject before she heated from the inside out. "I'm really grateful to him for taking me in. Brandon, too," Allie rushed the words, and Mia found something interesting under the table at the mention of Brandon's name. "If it weren't for them, I'm not sure where I would have ended up."

"They are great guys," Harper said, and Allie noticed the look she exchanged with Tina before they glanced at Mia. Allie was missing some pieces and was curious to learn more about the meaning behind those looks.

"How long are you staying in Sycamore Falls?" Harper asked, sipping her lemonade.

"Just until Hallows Eve." Allie was thankful they didn't ask for other details, even though she had made up her mind not to lie in case anyone asked.

Everyone knew she was a Witch, so there was no point in keeping her power a secret. However, she would not willingly advertise to the entire town her lack of control and that she was under a strict time limit from her coven to get the hang of it. For now, it was enough that Mia and Dominic knew about it. But she would tell the truth if questioned about it because the people living here deserved to know, and she wanted to show them Witches could choose to be different.

Even more so after Tina had shared that the reason for her injury was the tornado a year ago, which wouldn't have happened if that Witch hadn't broken the spell on the sycamores. She said it would be years of recovery, but she and Harper were both hopeful and taking it one day at a time.

The four of them spent the rest of lunch talking about Harper and Tina's wedding next week. Allie learned the ceremony was outdoors with a tent party afterward, both happening at Brandon's Riverbend Farm. She put Harper's nerves at ease, assuring her the bakery would be ready with everything they had ordered.

They cracked jokes and laughed about the silliest things until Mia snorted her lemonade, and Allie wished it would be like this with her coven sisters, too. Experiencing this closeness made her all the more aware of how much she wanted this in her life. Maybe things would change once she mastered her fire. Lydia would accept her, and all the others would fall in line.

"Do you think Brandon would mind if we wanted to have the wedding on the other side of the farm?" Harper asked around a mouthful of pasta.

"Yes," Mia and Tina answered together.

"He already flipped when we told him we wanted to change the lights, Harps," Tina said in a sweet voice, squeezing Harper's hand.

"But the other ones were really small!" she pouted.

Mia withdrew from the conversation and became preoccupied with some invisible lint on her sleeves.

Interesting.

They parted ways outside the restaurant, the brides-to-be getting into the car to cross the bridge over to the residential area.

"Thank you for letting me tag along," Allie told Mia on their way back. "Harper and Tina seem really nice."

"They are. We grew up together, as with most people in this

town, but the three of us have always been really close. They were my first friends when I came here, and the only ones who didn't treat me differently because I was adopted."

Allie stopped in her tracks. Her chest filled with conflicting feelings, but she was happy that she had earned Mia's trust enough for her to share that.

"If you ever want to talk about it, I'm here to listen," Allie said, continuing her stroll.

"Not much to talk about. I lost my parents when I was five. Dom's parents were their closest friends, and they took me in, as my parents had stated in their will." Mia smiled softly, and Allie didn't press her on the subject. She was thankful for this piece of trust Mia showed her, and she didn't want to upset her friend by prying.

Friend.

They were becoming friends. A warmth filled Allie's chest at the thought. Someone befriended her because she was herself, not because she was a Witch, or her mother's daughter, or Sam's fi— nothing. In Sycamore Falls, she was just Allie, and Mia was her friend.

"Can I stop by the bookstore to pick up another book? I sort of turned the other one into ash."

"Sure," Mia chuckled, and Allie saw the sparkle of gratitude in her brown eyes that she didn't question her more about her family.

Dominic paced in front of the bookstore entrance, wearing a path in the dry grass. He wore his black jeans and a brown leather jacket that stretched over the muscles on his arms, hands in his pockets. His hair was loose, the dark chestnut strands tickling the collar of his deep green turtleneck sweater.

"What's up, Dom?" He paused his pacing at the sound of his sister's voice, and his emerald green eyes snapped up.

"Allie."

Dominic said her name like a statement, like something that

was precious. Allie's heart melted like butter into a puddle at her feet, hearing her name the way she loved it from the powerful Mage's lips. She didn't think it would make any difference what he called her, but the swirl of butterflies she felt in her stomach disagreed.

"I need to talk to you."

Allie saw Mia's grin grow the size of a banana before she said, "Go. I'll look for another book and bring it to the bakery tomorrow."

"What book?" Dominic asked.

"Another book on Witchcraft." He looked at Allie like her words made absolutely no sense. "The other one burned, remember?"

"You don't need that anymore. I will help you," he declared in that boss-like voice.

Mia giggled. Loudly.

"I'll see you later, Allie." She squeezed her arm, and Allie thanked her again for inviting her to lunch.

Alone with the mountain of a broody man, Allie put her hands on her hips. Then dropped them. Then crossed them across her chest.

"So, what did you want to talk to me about?" she asked.

"Not here. Let's go." Dominic picked up a blanket that Allie hadn't noticed was by her boss's feet.

She followed him down the familiar path through town to the forest clearing she used for practice. The same place he'd found her that week, almost burning alive from her own power.

Dusk had fallen over the bronze leaves dancing softly in the chill breeze. The forest drowned in dark orange and purple hues as if it had been dipped in lavender honey. Allie zipped her jacket all the way up, suppressing a shiver.

"Sit." Dominic spread the blanket farthest from the river, close to the trees. "Here, by the tree." He motioned for Allie to lean against the sycamore trunk.

Dominic sat facing her, leaning back on his arms in the most casual and relaxed way Allie had seen from him. He even closed his eyes for a moment, taking in the fresh air and peace that surrounded them. And when his green eyes opened and noticed her obvious shivers, he flicked his wrist once, twice, and warm air bound them in a comfortable bubble.

But Allie was sure she could have gotten warm just from sitting so close to him.

He had not been wrong. He knew he wouldn't be but had still hoped that the book Mia gave him would prove him wrong. Dominic had read the section on elemental seals at least four times lest he miss a keyword that would turn everything around.

He didn't.

He spent the rest of the day pondering how to tell Allie the truth. Dom doubted she knew, given her clumsiness with the power and her relentless practice that almost led to a tragedy. He didn't want to be the one to break her heart, but he couldn't keep this to himself. She'd trusted him that morning to make the Assessment, and now he had to trust her with the results. To trust that she wouldn't hold this against him.

She trusted him.

For years, Dominic thought his heart had healed. He thought he didn't need anyone to prove that he was trustworthy, but he couldn't deny the wave of relief that smothered him when Allie said those three words.

Now she waited patiently, knees hugged to her chest, her thick red hair framing her round, freckled face in a mess of tangled curls. Her big hazelnut-colored eyes were warm and kind, and she watched him as if he was fascinating, with a soft smile on her pink lips.

He really, *really* hated this.

"How was lunch with the girls?" he started, intent on putting it off for as long as possible. Allie looked at him as if he'd grown another head. He never asked about her day. But she humored him.

"The food was delicious, and Harper and Tina are really nice. They were worried about some stuff for the wedding next week, but I told them we have everything under control," she stated with confidence.

We. We have everything under control.

An itching sensation climbed through Dom's chest, and he coughed to make it go away.

"I doubt this is what you wanted to talk to me about, Mr. R— Dominic." Allie averted her eyes but smiled, as if she tried his name and liked how it fit on her tongue. That thing tickled his chest again, and he cleared his throat.

"Right." Dom shifted on the blanket to face the beautiful Witch. "Do you know what I did this morning?" Allie shook her head, her smile fading, and Dom felt like a cold wind had broken through his warm air shield. "It was an Assessment." He waited to see if Allie knew what he was talking about, but she just stared at him, waiting. "Mages have access to a kind of Reading magic that goes deeper than the average one."

Allie stiffened, her back straightening away from the tree trunk. "How much deeper?"

"You can Read intentions and the general spirit of a person, right?" She nodded. "More than Reading someone, Mages can perform an Assessment. If the person is a magic wielder, the Assessment gives us access to their power source and nature." Allie's eyes grew wide, but she remained silent. Dominic wanted her to ask him a thousand questions about this magic, only so he could delay telling her what he had learned during her Assessment. "We can understand a lot about someone's power through these deep Readings. The way your magic acts seemed strange to me, ever since that day you overheated the milk." A corner of her mouth jumped up for the shortest moment. Dominic desperately wanted to turn it into a full smile, but knew he might do the opposite. "I wanted to ask you to let me do it this weekend. But this morning—" Dom sighed.

"I understand," she said. "And what did you...find?"

She looked at him with fearful anticipation, hoping for good news. Dominic felt a frown taking form on his face, his jaw clenching, hand fisting into the blanket. He had to tell her. He had to be the one to break the sweet, soft heart of a woman just trying to find herself, and hope to hell she wouldn't hate him for it. The thought gave Dom pause, but hate or not, he couldn't keep it to himself. Allie had no one besides her coven sisters, and he doubted the good intent of those Witches who'd sent her away instead of helping her.

He had to tell her.

Dom took a deep breath and held her gaze as he said, "There is a seal on your power."

Chapter 17

THERE IS NOTHING WRONG WITH YOU

Allie's heart skipped a beat.

"A...seal?"

The powerful Mage looked stricken as soon as the words left her lips. He sighed, reeling in the rage in his eyes that Allie thought was not directed at her.

"A seal is a magic-suppressing technique. It's quite advanced and meant to dull a wielder's powers. It is likely the reason why your power is so out of control. Because the seal started to break." Dominic paused for a moment, that rage slipping and filling his green eyes. "The seal could be the reason you manifested late."

Allie froze with shock, a thousand questions swarming through her mind.

"Manif—you mean I could have had my power twenty years ago?" she shrieked.

Dominic shook his head.

"Most seals last up to a few years before they start breaking. And when they do, the power has been suppressed for so long that it..."

"Goes crazy." Allie finished his thought. She could have had her power for a while now, even if still much later than other

Witches. The questions of who had done this to her, when, or how were muffled by one thought.

It was not her fault that she couldn't control her fire.

Allie felt a weight lifted off her shoulders after spending so much time blaming herself.

"Why are you smiling?" Dominic's forehead creased with confusion.

"I'm sorry." Allie chuckled nervously. "It just feels so good to know that this is not completely my fault, and that something is only partly wrong with me."

"There is *nothing* wrong with you."

Allie swallowed her smile at the sound of his growl. Dominic looked like her words had ravaged him somehow, like he shared some of her pain.

It was painful to learn that she had manifested her power years ago, but it had been kept hidden until recently because of this seal. This seal that was now breaking and making her life a living hell.

And someone had put it on her. Who? Who in this world had loathed her enough to do that? None of the Silverbarks could have done it, as Allie's seal was breaking when she joined them. She had no other friends and no other people crossing through her life, except for Sam, who didn't have magic anyway.

"What can I do about it?" she asked as steadily as she could.

"If it breaks on its own, the stream of power that has been suppressed runs the risk of...exploding inside you," Dominic ground out. "But if it's broken by magic in a controlled environment, you should be safe. That suppressed power would be released gradually, so you might feel some discomfort." Allie didn't have to think too much to understand that her only option was the second one. "We have to take it off," her boss declared.

We.

Like they were a team. The simple thought filled Allie's heart with warm joy that threatened to overpower her building dread.

"How?"

Dominic scoffed. "I am a Mage."

Allie didn't expect him to ever be cocky about it, and it was almost playful and definitely endearing.

"Ah. Of course," she said and nodded solemnly. No need for further explanation, since Mages sat at the top of the magic wielders' hierarchy when it came to power and skills. As a Witch in her situation, certainly it wasn't for her to question her Mage boss. She trusted him.

The prospect of having a power she could control was both exhilarating and terrifying. Allie hadn't grasped the fact that over the years, she had made peace with things as they were. She had never resolved to give up, but deep inside her heart, she acknowledged that she wouldn't be a great Witch. Maybe not even an average one. But for the last few months, ever since she joined the Silverbarks, she had been living with the hope that she could at least control her fire enough not to be kicked out of the coven.

Her future could look so different now, with the possibility of becoming a great Witch. She had a lot to make up for in a very short time, especially because of Lydia's deadline, but Allie felt like she had a chance. A *real* one.

Dominic kept quiet at her side, moving his green eyes from her to the trees a few times. He gave her space to understand and organize her feelings, and she was grateful for it. Yet no matter how much time she mulled over this, the conclusion was plain and simple.

Allie cleared her throat, drawing his emeralds back to her.

"So how do we take it off?" she asked with a smile.

Dominic straightened, surprised she was ready to tackle this already. He expected her to take a few days to think about it, but he also understood her excitement to be rid of the fucking seal.

He wouldn't get into *who* the hell had done that to her just because he didn't want to put Allie through an even more emotional turmoil. But if he ever found out...

"It's tricky, but it won't take long," he started, one hand scratching his temple, as if to make those thoughts shrink. "Seals are woven in a way that hides their magic until a spell is cast to break them, so I can't know what kind of seal it is before I start working on it. I've always hated seals." Dom grimaced. "And because we both have elemental magic, I'll need to draw power from nature. From the sycamores, to make sure we don't tip the power balance one way or the other." The beautiful Witch frowned. "Once the seal is broken, and your power is free, there is a risk that it might be drawn to me, or draw my power to it."

Her mouth formed a silent "Oh." Dom knew this would be the most difficult part, to ensure their powers wouldn't get intertwined. Maybe he should get another Mage to—no. The thought repulsed him, and he didn't trust anyone else with Allie.

More importantly, *she* trusted *him*.

But shouldn't it be her choice? Dom cursed this voice that sowed doubt in his heart, but it was too late. Now he couldn't avoid giving Allie the option without hating himself.

Even if he could live with hating himself.

"I can find another Mage to do it for you, if you want. Someone who doesn't possess an eleme—"

"What? No!" She leaned forward on her hands into his space, bringing those big, round, chocolate eyes close enough that Dom wondered if she could see into his soul. They trembled and sparkled with determination as the setting sun basked them into soft light. "I don't want anyone else. I trust you." Again, those three words he'd longed for came to Allie's lips so naturally. His heart did a strange quivering thing in his chest. "Unless you don't want to..."

What?

"I want to." The last thing Dominic had wanted this badly was to find a cure for the sycamores.

"Then it's settled," Allie said and leaned back. "But how can you draw from the sycamores if they're sick?"

"The magic is still there, I can feel it. It's strong enough to resist this rupture for a while." As if on cue, a chill wind swept against the warm air shield Dom had put up, bending the sycamores' branches downward. They had been listening to him ever since he was a child, and Dom always felt like he borrowed their power at times. "The sycamores' magic is disconnected from the earth. They cannot act to protect the land as they did before, at least not until the connection is restored. But the sycamores still have their magic."

"Makes sense," Allie said, her gaze wandering over the dancing auburn crowns surrounding them. "I'm sorry that happened," Allie whispered, and before Dom could brush it off she went on. "I promise not all Witches are like that. Unfortunately, most of them are and have this wild behavior of biting anyone who tries to get close. I guess it's because we live lonely lives unless a coven chooses to accept us. And even if they do..."

Dominic waited, but she didn't finish her thought. It wasn't hard for him to guess at the ending. Allie had left her coven to learn about her power because they refused to help her. Didn't accept her. His hand flexed on the blanket.

"About the seal." She changed the subject suddenly. "Can we do it now?"

Dom nodded. He came prepared to do it if Allie wanted to.

"Whenever you're ready."

"I'm ready."

All right. He could do this. He had performed spells much

more difficult than breaking a seal. He'd also broken his fair share of seals while working and learning under the Diviners' Order.

"Lie down close to the tree." Dominic guided Allie so he could reach both her and the tree. She obeyed, that trust she'd offered him shining through her relaxed features. "Close your eyes," he urged her, fearing he might lose focus from the spell if he met her gaze. "I'll make it as painless as possible."

The corners of her mouth went up, crinkling the freckles on her cheeks.

"I know you will."

Dominic did his best not to let her words overwhelm him as he placed one hand on the tree trunk and the other on Allie's abdomen and focused on his magic.

A warmth built inside Allie's core that wasn't caused only by Dominic's touch. She was heating steadily, like a pot on the stove. It wasn't painful, but it was uncomfortable, like he had warned her.

Allie wanted to open her eyes and watch the powerful Mage at work, but she wouldn't move an inch until he told her so. She didn't want to risk messing up the spell or breaking his focus, so she lay there patiently, heating up.

More and more.

Sweat beads gathered on her forehead, her palms, the back of her neck. Allie felt like she was running a high fever, one that kept rising with every breath. Her skin was scorching, from the top of her head to the tip of her toes, her muscles pulling taut under it. The pain came in waves, pulsating through her body faster than her heartbeats. She squeezed her eyes, forcing her body to sit still and to not writhe on the cool ground.

"Dom," she whispered when the pain became unbearable.

"Don't move," he hissed, voice strained through uneven, loud breaths.

She wouldn't. She would not move even if it killed her. Which it might, Allie thought as she swallowed a whimper and pressed her lips together.

"Almost done," Dominic panted.

The heat drained from her limbs into her heart like a flowing stream. She wiggled her fingers and felt the blanket under her skin. Her lungs took in the cool air and didn't burn anymore. Allie was left with a comfortable warmth in her chest, like a quiet light vibrating inside her.

The source of power in my body.

It was in her heart, so easy to point out, so natural, as if she had known it her entire life.

Dominic's hand slid off her body in a gentle caress.

"You can open your eyes now," he said through soft pants. Allie did, and she sat up on the blanket, watching her boss lean against the tree trunk, catching his breath. Sweat dripped along his temples, down to his jaw, messy strands of hair sticking to his face.

Had he burned himself?

"Are you all right?" Allie blurted, her hand going to rest on his arm.

"Me?" Dominic scoffed. "You're asking *me* if I'm all right?" She nodded, scanning him for any signs of injury, especially around his hands. "You almost burned from the inside out, and you're worried about me?"

"Yes." Dominic looked at her and shook his head.

"You have much more power than I expected to find. It flooded out once the seal was removed, and it was hard to keep under control."

"I can feel it now." Allie put her hand over her heart, feeling a grin stretch her cheeks. "It's all here." It was within her reach now, but her smile faltered watching the disheveled state of the man who had made it happen. "Did it hurt you?"

"Stop worrying about me." He put his hand briefly on hers and pinned her with a determined look. "I'm sorry it hurt more than—"

"Don't even finish that sentence." Allie threw him a look of warning mixed with amusement, wondering if he understood she was taking a page from his book.

She stood up and offered him a hand, at which Dominic rolled his eyes.

They walked in silence out of the forest and onto the lit-up road. The beautiful trees became dark shadows lining their path, the cold wind rustling their branches and leaves. Allie stopped in the middle of Maple Street, just by the market entrance, where multiple lights brightened the street.

"Thank you," she said, and Dominic stopped and turned to her. "Thank you so much for doing this. If you hadn't discovered this, I—"

"Allie." Dominic shook his head.

"Let me help you, too," she said eagerly. "With your...task." He frowned. "I might not know much about my power yet, and I definitely know nothing about yours, but I am a Witch. I can think like a Witch, and maybe I can find something helpful. Please."

"Let's have dinner." He shoved his hands in the jeans pockets, the blanket squeezed under one arm. "Since we were supposed to have lunch," he clarified.

Dinner.

With her boss.

When she had just convinced herself that lunch wasn't a big deal. Just lunch.

It wasn't dinner.

And now it would be.

"Sure," Allie agreed before her long pause became suspicious. "But I only have stuff for soup and salads."

"Great. I'll bring dessert." Dominic resumed walking, and she jogged to catch up with him.

"Bring?" she asked. Dominic raised his brows at her.

"You invited me over."

Right. She had done that. Which meant he would come over. To her place.

"Of course. I'll need some time to get everything ready."

"I'll be there in two hours."

Allie slammed the door to her studio room and woke Ekko up from a deep nap. She told him everything that had happened with the seal, and the creature nuzzled her jaw and flew in circles around her until she finished the whole story. Allie steered clear of the drilling thoughts about who had done this to her. It made little to no difference now, although she'd love to fry them once she learned how to work with her fire.

"We need to get cooking," she told her dragon, choosing to focus on the time she had to spend with Dominic. Ekko flew through the cupboards and brought Allie everything she asked for. She chopped all the ingredients for the salad and made the dressing, then focused on the soup. Allie tasted the food multiple times while preparing it, adjusting the flavor with condiments and spices. Ekko stole a couple of figs when he thought Allie wasn't looking, and she caught him with his cheeks round and full.

"Here." She laughed, piling some figs and cherries on a plate. The dragon munched on them while Allie finished cooking, then helped bring everything to the sink.

She was relieved to have enough time to shower. Once the water flowed over her, Allie took a moment to breathe, to grasp what had happened today. She felt that buzzing light in her chest, and there was no hint of rebellion to it. The power was waiting for her to beckon it one way or another. She felt safe and in control, and it was all thanks to Dominic.

What would have happened if Brandon hadn't found her on the side of the road that day? If she had wound up anywhere else than here? With Dom?

Allie shooed those fleeting thoughts away.

She dried her hair, putting half of it up with a wooden pin. Then she chose her new plaid skirt and a white sweater and was out of the bathroom just when there was a knock at her door.

"Come in," she said with a smile, opening the door wide.

Dominic entered and placed a tray with chocolate brownies and a baguette on the kitchen isle.

"For the soup." He pointed at the bread.

His eyes roamed over her, stopping at her legs, then moving up to her face, her pinned hair. In turn, Allie was fascinated by the black button-up shirt that stretched over his upper arms, the sleeves rolled up to his elbows, revealing the dark branches on his forearm.

"Thanks," she muttered on instinct.

Dominic's hair was loose but tame, and the black ink of his tattoo was so much richer under the warm and dim light.

Allie set the table and poured two tall glasses of lemonade, topping them off with fresh mint leaves.

"Fine," Dominic spoke all of a sudden, confusing her. "You can help me with my mission here in Sycamore Falls." Allie grinned and clapped her hands. "But only if you promise to come to me if you have trouble controlling your power," he added, his intense green gaze burning her with a smooth fire. "Just don't get another book."

Chapter 18

IMPERFECT THINGS HAVE A BEAUTY OF THEIR OWN

Allie had agreed to Dominic's terms last night. She hoped to manage the fire on her own now that the seal was broken, but it made more sense to ask someone with Dom's experience wielding elemental magic rather than reading about it in a book.

Throughout the rest of dinner, Allie had told him about Pearls Fields and a bit about Petra. They spent a nice evening together, with her doing most of the talking and him doing most of the grunting.

This morning, she woke up feeling free and refreshed, that newly discovered light humming in her chest. Being in control, knowing that her fire wouldn't act without her permission anymore, made Allie's heart somersault with joy.

With this newfound confidence and the fuel of two cups of coffee on an empty stomach, Allie entered the kitchen, hands on her hips, and made a loud demand.

"Let me help you."

"I thought that was decided last night," Dominic mumbled. He bent over the table, piping bag in his hands, decorating apple cider cupcakes.

"Not that. Here." She waved her hands around, but his

attention was on the buttercream swirls. "I want more responsibility at the bakery, especially with the wedding coming up. I'm less of a fire risk now, and I promise to let you know if I feel something is off." That made him stop with the decorating pipe midair. "It's not even me helping you, it's me doing my job," she insisted.

Dominic straightened and focused his green gaze on her. His bun was in perfect morning condition, and he wore a black T-shirt under his apron that allowed Allie to gawk at his tattoo. He looked between her and the table a couple of times before he spoke.

"Come here."

Allie held back the urge to skip across the kitchen. Dominic wordlessly taught her how to hold the bag by positioning his hands on it and pointing the thing at her.

"Squeeze lightly until you learn the pressure." In a swift move that Allie might have missed if she blinked, he drew a perfect swirl on top of a cupcake. "Try it."

She took the piping bag and held it over a fresh cupcake. Her first attempt was a failure, as she hadn't moved fast enough, and the buttercream dripped in a big splotch.

"Quicker," Dominic told her as he stuffed the pitiful cupcake in his mouth.

The cream didn't drip the second time, but the swirl was tilted and uneven.

"You eat this one." He replaced it with another cupcake, then came to stand next to her, taking hold of the bag over Allie's hands as if he did this every morning. Dominic's skin was warm over her fingers, and his leathery cedarwood scent filled her senses.

Allie stared at his profile, but his attention was dedicated to the pastry, positioning the icing bag in the correct spot to start the buttercream swirl.

Was she jealous of a cupcake?

Allie forced her eyes away from Dominic's handsome face.

They decorated this cupcake together, and she tried to memorize every move and the pressure he held over the piping bag. An impossible task, given her attention to said pressure was *not* about the bag.

"Try again," he said, crossing his arms over his chest. She wished she had his poise. But then again, he was just teaching her to decorate cupcakes. That was it.

This time, the swirl of frosting stood on top of the cupcake, more symmetrical than before. It wasn't as perfect as Dominic's, but it was better than the other ones.

"Keep going. I'm going to start on the croissants," he said and rounded the table.

"But it doesn't look like yours."

"Yet." Dominic turned to her, empty bowls in his hands. "And I'm not running a bakery for the queen, Allie. Imperfect things have a beauty of their own." His words echoed into her heart, making her chest feel stuffed with feathers. Dominic was probably just talking about cupcakes, but his words meant so much to her. "Finish those." He jerked his head toward the five trays of cupcakes waiting on the counter.

Allie got to work. Each cupcake was less wonky than the one before, and after she decorated about thirty of them, she managed to do one that looked almost like her boss's.

In the time it took her to finish all the cupcakes, Dominic had finished everything else needed for today. Multiple types of bread, croissants, pies, five flavors of macarons, and two cakes of the day. Part of them were already out cooling, while the others were still in the oven, filling the space with a savory smell that left her mouth watering.

Allie surveyed the cupcake trays, noticing how each row looked a bit better than the previous one. She sprinkled them proudly with the pumpkin spice mix Dominic had left out for her.

Then she took each tray and arranged them one by one in the display case and the tiered serving tray in the front.

Their first customer was Brandon, who came to get his weekly bread order. He flashed his signature warm, wide smile, walking in with that cheery air about him.

"What's up with the cupcakes?" he said, tilting his head to the tiered tray on the counter. Allie pouted for a moment, but Brandon's look was kind and playful. Teasing.

"I decorated them."

"The door's right behind you, Brandon." Dominic's voice carried from the kitchen.

Brandon snickered then said, "I'll take two." Allie packed the two ugliest cupcakes she could find and brought his bread order from the back.

"Are you all set for the wedding this weekend?" she asked him.

"I want to say yes, but last time I did, I got a call from Harper asking me to position the chairs the other way around. For the third time. So I'm going to say, maybe." He shook his head, still with a smile. "How about you? I heard they had a lot of special requests for the cake and the other sweets. Do you need a hand?"

"We're fine, Brandon," Dominic yelled from the back again. Allie smothered a laugh.

"Everything's under control," she assured him, handing over his order and putting the money in the register.

"You're staying for the wedding, right, Allie? As a guest, after you're done setting up for the bakery."

Allie nodded. The girls had officially invited her yesterday during lunch, when they had mentioned that everyone working for the wedding was their guest. "Sycamore Falls is just one big family," Tina had said, and while Allie yearned for a thread of this feeling, her time here was limited. Not enough to become part of their family. But she had happily accepted the invitation, which reminded her that she didn't have a dress to wear.

"Great! Do you have a date for the wedding then?" Brandon smirked.

A blaring, clattering noise of bowls and pans followed by a string of curses carried from the kitchen through the entire bakery. Allie motioned for Brandon to wait a second while she checked on Dominic.

"Is everything all right?" Allie asked, stepping into the kitchen.

She found Dominic kneeling among an array of bowls, pans, and trays scattered on the floor.

"Fine," he grumbled.

Allie helped gather all the items and noticed a hint of fresh anger shadowing his features. She knew better than to pry, so Allie went back to the storefront only to find it empty.

Huh.

"Allie," Dominic called from the hallway, and she turned to face him. "I'll be upstairs going over everything we need for the wedding prep next week. Can you handle the front?" He muttered something else that sounded like he didn't want to be bothered.

"Of course, leave it to me."

Dominic settled into the hallway den upstairs that served as his office. He could still hear everything going on in the bakery downstairs if he strained to listen, but he focused on the checklist for next week. The orders he had placed were delivered on time, and nothing was missing from the ingredients list. All that was left was for him to schedule daily tasks to ensure everything was ready on time.

No, not him. *Them.*

Because Allie wanted more responsibility around the bakery.

Dominic had ignored the heat that had climbed up his neck in the morning when she came in and demanded to be given more work. He shouldn't get used to having her around, as she would return to Pearls Fields soon.

He'd have to hang the "Help Wanted" sign back up. The thought of someone else doing Allie's job filled his heart with dread, but he tried to ignore it, too, shoving it deep, somewhere under his lungs.

In the long list of things he was trying to ignore, he added Brandon's audacity, and told himself the kitchen mess was because he was distracted by the timer on the oven.

No other reason.

"...unavailable." The raised tone coming from downstairs had Dom stand up from the desk and take a few steps toward the stairs.

"What do you mean he's unavailable?" He recognized Anna's voice, getting louder with each word. Whatever the reason, she had no right to yell at Allie. Meaning, at his employee. He took two steps down before another female voice pierced the air.

"I mean, he is not available," Allie said in a no-nonsense tone steeped in that Witch-like sneer she never displayed. "You can either sit down and wait for him or come back later." There was a moment of silence before he heard Allie's voice again. "If you're not ordering anything, please step aside as there is a line behind you."

Dominic heard stomps followed by the doorbell. He couldn't control the half-smile that ticked his cheek up at Allie's display of fierce protectiveness.

Fool.

What protectiveness? She was just doing her job, doing what he asked her to do. As her boss.

But Dominic could count on her. He was learning that with every day, and the dread he'd tried to bury resurfaced with the thought that maybe he shouldn't. He should not count on her as she would be leaving, but...

He did.

§♠

The week before the wedding, Dominic was laser-focused on having everything ready for Tina and Harper. Allie didn't want to risk jeopardizing anything for their special day, so she took up more tasks around the bakery. She followed Dominic's instructions to the dot and had him taste everything she made, but he was the one to tackle the more complicated doughs and pastries. They were so busy that Dominic even allowed Ekko to help them. The dragon was beyond excited to be out of the boring studio, and he executed each order with adorable pride and care, making sure to stay out of their way—mostly Dominic's—when they didn't need anything.

Every night after dinner, disregarding her exhaustion, Allie dragged herself to the secluded area in the forest to practice her magic. She started by focusing on the source of power in her heart, and each time she found it ready, waiting for her to pull on its threads. The first time Allie tried to summon a flame, only tiny, colorful sparks ignited at her fingertips. The second night, she had summoned a flame so big she was lucky it floated and landed on the river, putting itself out. Clearly, she had to learn how to calibrate the power, but even with all the mishaps, she felt much closer to her goal. Soon, she would be ready to prove to Lydia and her coven sisters that she had her power under control. They would feel safe around her, and she could go back to her life.

A thought that used to bring her more hope and joy than it did now.

Mia came by one evening, three days before the wedding, when the bakery was closed. She brought a pot roast, caramelized carrots, and mashed potatoes, and the three of them had dinner together.

Allie had told them a dozen times she didn't want to intrude. She also wanted to eat quickly and sneak out to practice because every minute counted, but the siblings had none of it.

"Can I borrow your car tomorrow? Mine's not back from the shop," Mia asked Dominic over dessert. He'd made dulce de leche again because it was Mia's favorite, but Allie still couldn't stomach the sweetness. So Dominic had offered her a piece of pear and lemon tart, which she hopefully devoured with poise and restraint, and not like she had never tasted a fruit tart.

"Sure," he answered around a mouthful of tart.

"I'm going to a shop in Rocky Hills to pick a dress for the wedding. You should come with me," Mia said, looking at Allie over the clasped hands under her chin.

"Really?" She'd rather wear jeans than visit Anna's store again anytime soon.

"Really." Mia chuckled. A meaningful glance passed between brother and sister, leaving Dominic narrow-eyed and Mia grinning. "It's a date," Mia declared, and Dominic choked on his tart.

Allie smiled at Mia and pushed a water glass to her boss, which he gulped before getting up and rounding the table. He stopped behind Mia's chair and faked gripping his arm around her neck, but leaned down and kissed her on the top of her head.

"Bye, menace." Allie watched his retreating broad back as he headed toward the stairs. She and Mia got up and tidied the table.

"Sometimes I don't know if I want to shake him or squeeze him into a hug, you know?"

You and me both.

Chapter 19

READY WHENEVER YOU ARE

The next day, Mia drove them a couple of towns away to a charming place hidden in the mountains. The evening air was frigid and harsher than in Sycamore Falls when they stopped in front of a boutique and entered quickly, running from the wind.

The owner greeted Mia and welcomed them to look around the store. They had their backs to each other, perusing opposite racks, when Mia cleared her throat and drew Allie's attention.

"So, are you getting along with my brother?" she asked as if talking about the weather.

"He hasn't fired me yet." Allie chuckled halfheartedly. If Dominic had let her stay through all the previous trouble, he would likely let her stay until Hallows Eve.

"Dom is all bark, no bite, I can promise you that." Allie felt Mia shift closer, their shoulder blades touching. She whispered, "The nature of his magic can lead to a lonely life. He'd murder me if he knew I'm telling you this, but many years ago, he had... someone." Allie's heart snapped to attention, and she was grateful Mia couldn't see the curious look on her face. "They had been together for a while, and Dom... He was always on the road with his assignments, but he wanted a life outside of that. A family. She didn't trust him to be around enough to do that, so she left him."

"Why?" Allie breathed.

She didn't trust him.

How could anyone not trust someone like Dominic?

"I don't know, and I don't want to remember that traitorous bitc—" Mia inhaled. "The thing is, under all the thorns and grumbles, my brother is a good man, Allie. I just wanted you to know that."

Allie held back the sharp agreement bubbling inside her, thinking Mia would interpret it in her sneaky way. She had been a stranger to Dominic, and he had been there for her more than the people who knew her. People who were supposed to be her friends. He'd helped her not only by offering her temporary work and a place to stay, but he went so far as to get involved with her power control issues, uprooting something that could have ended her life. The seal that could have destroyed her.

Dominic was not just a good man; he was a great man with a huge, beautiful soul. He hid it under a spiky demeanor, grunts, and scowls, but if you looked past them, it was right there. Allie found it endearing.

How could someone have Dominic and decide to leave him? The thought terrified her. *She* had to leave him in about a month.

But she didn't *have* him. Which, funnily enough, did not make it easier at all.

"Do you have a date for the wedding?" Allie asked, wanting to distance herself from the dangerous subject that was Mia's brother. She didn't wait for her friend to answer before she added, "What about Brandon?"

"What about Brandon?" Mia parroted defensively. Allie turned around and faked interest in a dress next to Mia, knowing she had struck a chord.

"What's going on with you two?" Allie dared ask. After all,

Mia had asked her about Dominic, and even if she had ignored it, Allie heard the not-so-subtle implication in Mia's voice.

"Nothing's going on." Mia picked up a hanger from the rack, studying a bright pink taffeta dress that would look terrible on her. Allie slowly took it from her and put it back, raising her brows in a silent challenge. Mia sighed and said, "We're just friends."

"Aha."

"Do *you* have a date for the wedding?" Mia shot back, a flirty grin stretching her beautiful tawny skin.

"Brandon asked me the same thing the other day," Allie said with her own cocky grin. Something passed over Mia's features that turned her smirk into a thin line. She didn't want to play any games with her friend, so Allie told her she was going alone.

They shifted their focus to the task at hand, and Mia found a dress she deemed perfect for Allie: a forest green velvet dress with a thin cord around the waist that could be tied into a bow, with a deep V-neckline and a skirt two palms over her knees.

"Isn't it too short?" Allie turned around in the tall mirror. The dress was beautiful and sexy while still appropriate, and very much within her price range.

"It's not too short. It'll go perfectly with these." Mia handed her a pair of knee-high soft leather boots with a block heel in a brown so deep it was almost black. "I'm tall enough as it is," Allie said as she reluctantly put them on. Of course, they went perfectly with the dress.

"Some people are still taller than you," Mia muttered under a smirk.

"It's too cold for a dress like this," Allie tried her last argument. She wanted but didn't want to be convinced to get the dress. If Mia wasn't here, Allie might have mooned over it, but for sure wouldn't have tried it on, let alone left with it. Now that she had...

"Trust me, it won't be cold." A wordless challenge lit up Mia's eyes, and Allie didn't have time to question her before she scurried back to look for her own dress.

They found an equally short dress for Mia in a soft, elegant pink with a square neckline and short sleeves that fit her like a glove. She paired it with red high heels, and Allie was suddenly curious what Brandon's face would look like when he saw Mia. Her unruly mind also wondered what Dominic would think about her green dress, and her fickle heart went galloping at the thought of his emerald eyes scanning her from top to bottom.

Walking out of the store, she was grateful for the strong wind that knocked some sense into her.

Dominic decided to close the bakery early the day before the wedding. He had planned to tell Allie last night, but she and Mia came back pretty late from their dress shopping, giggling and shoving each other when they entered the bakery, craving sugar.

He had gone upstairs but watched them from behind the curtain to make sure they made it back safely. And maybe also heard them because he lingered by his den like a creep. They raided the fridge where he had left half a pumpkin pie and two caramel brownies he absolutely did not make for them. Dominic made them for himself, and there were leftovers. He knew Mia would come over and snoop into his fridge; it wasn't the first time and certainly wouldn't be the last.

The next morning, the bittersweet coffee smell filled the space up the stairs, beckoning him to start the day. He descended into the bakery with the plan to post the schedule for today on the door, triple-check everything for tomorrow's event, then get on with the morning's baking duties.

His plan went to hell when he walked down the narrow

hallway leading into the bakery and found Allie bent over the counter.

She was wiping down the surface, her body aligned with the entryway, those dark, tight jeans hugging her form perfectly right in front of his face.

Dominic swallowed, his hands forming fists at his sides.

He should look away. It was inappropriate to stare like that. What if she turned around and found him gawking? Allie was his employee. He was her boss.

He was an inappropriate, drooling moron because he didn't look away.

Dominic had never denied that Allie was an attractive woman. Extremely attractive, with her long legs, soft curves, and sensual lips. He always noticed things he wasn't supposed to be noticing and, more than once, sent silent thanks to whatever gods were listening that no magic in the world gave anyone access to his thoughts.

A flash of pain snapped him to attention. The knuckle of his fist was caught in a strong bite in his mouth, as Allie stretched on her tiptoes to reach the farthest corner. Her soft blue sweater traveled up, revealing a sliver of her ivory skin.

Dominic felt hot, as if a fever was coming over him, and swallowed the sound that was building in his throat.

"Allie!" he shouted instead. She turned around, alarm coating her features, looking from left to right as if trying to identify the threat that made him shout like that.

"What's wrong?" She dropped the cloth and approached him. Dominic thought he'd scared her before his eyes moved to her freckled face. Allie was frowning, some shadows he'd never seen hanging around her eyes, as if she was ready to torch anything or anyone he would point at.

Literally.

His heart might give out.

"I need help in the kitchen." Dominic pivoted and left, desperate to put some distance between them so he could clear his head. Except he did not stop in the kitchen but went back upstairs, straight to the bathroom to splash cold water on his face.

Dominic was acting strangely. He said he forgot something upstairs but carried nothing back with him except a weird look on his face and a couple of water droplets hanging from his jaw. Allie thought he might not be feeling well, but every time she asked him, he grunted a "Fine." She made him mint tea at lunch, which he drank only after it had cooled down.

The short shift was more than welcome today as it gave Allie enough time to prepare for tomorrow's event. She laid out her outfit, styled her hair into tame curls, and had an early dinner. Tina and Harper had told her their two chimera pets would be present, and all others were allowed as it was an outdoor event. Allie gave Ekko a bath, his purple scales shining under the soap bubbles, and prepared a white bowtie for him for tomorrow. Besides sometimes acting like a clumsy creature, Ekko was a great companion. If anything, his being clumsy made Allie feel closer to the dragon.

"Let's get some practice in, too, shall we?" she told Ekko, who flew in happy circles around her, then plopped on her shoulder before Allie opened the door.

"Everyone is worried."

A voice she didn't recognize carried from the bakery. Allie turned around to stay in her room and give Dominic privacy, but stopped and cracked the door a bit more instead when she heard him say, "She's not like that."

"How do you know for sure?"

"Because I do." Dominic fixed the chairs in the bakery with

more force than necessary. "Has anything happened since she's been here?"

"No, but—"

"Then I don't want to hear it. Thanks for stopping by." The bell at the door rang, and it was quickly followed by the slam of the door.

There was an extremely low, almost nonexistent chance that it wasn't about her. Allie contemplated staying back in her room instead of going out to practice, but Ekko flew around and tugged urgently at the sleeve of her jacket.

"You're right," she whispered. Why should she pout in her room because of people who didn't really know her? Dominic had gotten to know her a little, certainly more than anyone else in this town, and he was on her side. Adamantly. Allie leaned into the gratitude and joy she had felt hearing him defend her. Even if no one else would ever accept her, Dom having her back meant the world to her.

"It only takes one person to see you for who you are, and your heart will be content."

Words her mother had said to her time and again. They had meant nothing then but now rang true, leaving her chest feeling heavy.

Allie waited until the sound of footsteps up the stairs echoed from the hallway before she left her room and went out in the crisp night, down Maple Street, and into the forest.

She felt most at peace under the moonlight, unobstructed by clouds, with her now quiet power humming inside her. Her mother used to say the moon was a Witch's best friend, and Allie wished she knew why. Maybe it was just this feeling of comfort it gave her, or maybe there was more about her power that she could learn from the moon's magic.

Another time. For starters, she must learn to work with what she had. Allie sat by the river and reached for her fire, unsuccessfully, while Ekko sat back and watched her with suspense in his eyes. As if he was waiting for her to succeed for them both.

One hour into it and no flame in sight, Allie got up to walk along the river and warm herself up. She went from not being able to control the fire bursting out of her to not being able to summon a measly spark. This was due to her lack of experience, but...

An obsessive thought prevented her from focusing completely on her power.

Should she leave Dom's Sweets before Hallows Eve?

If her presence made it hard for Dominic to deal with the townspeople, she would leave early. The trouble she had with her power now was more manageable than before. Lydia should accept her after she learned about the seal, and maybe some of her sisters would agree to help her. Even if none of them were elemental Witches, at least they wouldn't be scared to live with her anymore. Freya might assist her under these new circumstances.

Allie hated the Witch who had broken the spell on the sycamores. Witches didn't care to establish a good reputation for themselves, but this one had gone too far. Allie groaned in frustration and crossed her arms.

Heat crawled up her arm, and she turned her palms up to find a tiny flame flickering on its surface. Allie stared at it, feeling a grin bloom on her face.

"I did it."

Ekko chittered and nuzzled her hair, puffing hot steam that clung to her cold cheeks.

Allie focused on making the flame bigger, and it grew to the size of a peach. She made it small again. Big, small. Then she willed it to move to her fingertip. It didn't hurt her, that comfortable heat only tickling her skin as the flame burned. With the next thought, she snuffed it out, turning her hand up and down to check for marks—there were none.

"Yes!" Allie clapped her hands once before she was on her way back to the bakery with a very loud and excited baby dragon who kept flying and jumping around her from one shoulder to the other.

The morning of the wedding, Dominic loaded the refrigerated van he'd borrowed from a bigger bakery in Rocky Hills by himself. He gave Allie more time to primp and preen, knowing how long it took his sister to get ready for events. There was an hour left before the wedding started when he was done, which gave him plenty of time to shower and get dressed.

Unsurprisingly, Mia had stopped by the other night and gifted him a crisp white button-up shirt and a green tie and warned him to wear them or risk her wrath. Dom knew better than to cross his sister, so he donned the new shirt but rolled its sleeves up to his elbows, leaving part of his sycamore tattoo out. He tied his hair back, knowing he was going to handle the cake and pastries for the sweets bar.

Mia had also told him that any time he wanted to stop being an idiot and notice what was in front of him was a good time. He had kept quiet, but her words drilled into his brain and sent him on a trip to the flower shop.

He picked up the box he'd spent an embarrassingly long amount of time picking and went down the stairs. The familiar tangerine scent softened his senses as he filled his lungs with it, this time with a subtle vanilla fragrance.

"Ready whenever you are," Dominic yelled as he walked down the hallway, hoping Allie heard him with her door closed. Ekko flew to him and barely stopped in time not to crash his snout into Dom's face. The baby dragon proudly wore a white bowtie, his scales shining in the early morning light as the creature circled him once, twice, as if to check he was dressed appropriately for the day.

"I'm ready."

Allie stood in the middle of the bakery wearing one of the most beautiful smiles he'd ever seen. Her lips were pinker than usual, and he wondered if the red stains in her cheeks were natural or if she was wearing makeup.

His eyes roamed over her body, down her green dress that ended too soon, to her long legs and her tall, sexy boots. His heart pounded frantically, and he cleared his throat of the tumbleweed that had stuck there to make room for words.

"You look..." The mane of her red hair was clipped half-up, leaving part of her long curls cascading down her shoulders and back, along her exposed neck. Dom's gaze swung to that deep neckline where the crescent moon locket hung on her bare skin. "Beautiful."

"Thank you. You look handsome, too." Her cheeks colored a brighter shade. She looked between her dress and his tie and smiled, softly shaking her head. "I like your tie."

Mia.

"My sister—" Dominic stopped before spitting out any excuse that Mia had been the one who had matched him with Allie. The box in his hands clearly stated he had thought about her. He got it *for her.*

Dom shook himself from the spell Allie had cast on him with her beauty and closed the distance between them. The vanilla fragrance was stronger this close, and he resisted a much-desired deep inhale into his lungs.

"This is for you." He opened the box and pulled out the corsage made with a pearl bracelet, so it was less itchy around her wrist. Her features morphed into admiration and disbelief, and Dom got ready to fight any argument she might make against wearing it.

But then her full smile came back, and she extended her left hand, watching him with wide, delighted eyes that melted his heart. Allie was wearing her gold rings, the amethyst and ruby stones glinting in the light. He slipped the corsage on carefully, his fingers brushing her soft skin in the process.

"It's beautiful," she said, turning her hand in the light. "Thank you."

She swept a glance over his chest and arms that left a hot trail in its wake, biting her lower lip.

Today was going to be a long fucking day, in the best or worst way possible.

Chapter 20

LET'S PUT IT TO THE TEST

The moment they went out the door, a strong gust of wind swept Allie's skirt up, raising Dominic's heartbeat to impossible levels. He threw an air shield around them, a warm one, to keep her from shivering.

"I told Mia this dress was too short," the Witch hissed to herself. But Dom knew that arguing against Mia's stubborn opinion was in vain.

"There will be air shields over the farm, too." Dom opened the passenger door of the van, and Allie climbed inside, smoothing the skirt of her dress. Ekko followed her and plopped on the back seat, while Dom went around and climbed into the driver's seat. "Tom and Andrew are also air Wizards, and between the three of us, it's going to be a piece of cake to keep the place warm." Allie laughed at his silly cake reference, her chuckle one of his favorite sounds.

"Is Tom the owner of the pharmacy?" she asked, struggling to grab the seatbelt, which was positioned farther back in this type of van.

"Yes." Dominic leaned over to help her with the seatbelt after her next failed attempt.

Allie gasped and froze with her hand over her shoulder. He

came so close he could count her freckles, could see the amber sparks in her eyes, the unruly red hairs over her forehead. Her shallow breaths tickled his skin, her chest heaving up and down rapidly, rubbing the inside of his arm.

Dominic made quick work of the belt, the closeness making knots in his stomach, then cleared his throat as he started the engine.

"And Andrew is the owner of Rogelio's."

"Not Rogelio?" she asked, a little out of breath.

"Rogelio was Andrew's husband. He passed away a couple of years ago."

"Oh." Her expression saddened, and Dom didn't like it one bit. He racked his brain in search of a change of subject, but the damn thing failed him. "I lost my mom four years ago," Allie confessed in a low voice.

"I'm sorry, Allie." He wanted to offer her more comfort than these words, but could he just touch her? Should he? He refrained from squeezing her bare knee and kept his eyes on the road.

So she had been entirely alone, struggling with her power. Although there must have been someone close enough to her to put that seal on. Maybe another Witch from the coven?

"Thank you." She smiled softly, then asked him questions about the people coming to the wedding, Brandon's farm, and the brides' families. Dominic didn't know if she had changed the subject for his or her benefit, but he was thankful not to see that sad look on her pretty face anymore.

When they arrived at the farm, Allie shifted in her seat to unclasp the belt. Her skirt rode up her thighs, and his eyes fell on a spot way higher than it was his business seeing.

Was that... Could it be...

Dominic frowned at the dark smudge, but Allie followed his gaze and pulled urgently at the skirt. He heard her mutter something about the freaking dress as she got out of the van, only to be welcomed by another gust of wind. He slammed an air shield around her just in time before she could offer the best view of the day to the guests that had already gathered.

A long fucking day.

❦

Dominic abandoned all bakery duties and went to find Tom and Andrew to get the wind shield in place. Everyone else seemed content with the chill wind, even if Allie had spotted skirts shorter than hers. But without Dom's shield, she would be freezing. With enough time, she might get accustomed to the cold weather, but there was little time left in Sycamore Falls for her.

This morning, she had decided to tell Dominic that she could leave the bakery earlier than Hallows Eve. But then he gifted her the corsage and made her heart flutter and knees weaken.

No, Allie.

The gift felt like it was directed by Mia, together with coordinating Dominic's tie and her dress. Her boss had almost admitted to the tie. She sighed and stared at the corsage, the beautiful white rose sitting on a sycamore leaf, with small bits of pine leaves stuck under the flower, tied together with a white lace bow. The pearl bracelet was elegant and very comfortable to wear.

"Hey, you!" Mia put her arm around Allie's shoulders. "You look great." She looked her up and down, so Allie did the same. Mia had put her caramel hair in a high ponytail and more daring makeup than Allie's pale lipstick.

"You too, Mia. Do you know what else is great? Dom's tie," Allie challenged, waving the corsage in front of her in case the jab was not obvious enough.

"I don't know what you're talking about," Mia said, then acted as if someone called her and bailed, although no other guests were around.

Allie stood by the van, waiting for Dominic to be done with shield duty so they could set up the sweets bar. Ekko hovered impatiently next to Allie until she gave him the go-ahead to roam around the place, but only after she fixed his bow tie. Brandon's farm was huge, and her boss had told her it was vaster than the field set up for the wedding, stretching over the hills to the base of the mountains. On the other side of a fence, she saw a private driveway leading to a white house with a green roof that looked homey and welcoming.

On this side of the fence, where the wedding was taking place, white satin-covered chairs had been placed on each side of a red carpet leading to a flower arch. To the left was a huge tent for the reception, where they would install the sweets bar.

Dominic and Brandon, together with the other two air Wizards, headed to her and stopped at the back of the van. Tom and Andrew didn't smile at her but didn't sneer either, so she called that a win. Allie was in for a lot of sneers for the rest of the day.

"Allie, hi!" Brandon greeted her with his usual charming grin, wearing a white button-up shirt with dress pants, and his dark hair less unruly than usual. His heavy arm came around her shoulders in a side hug, and he surprised her by pressing a kiss on her cheek.

"Hi, Brandon." The chuckle stuck in her throat at the sight of her boss, who glared at them with an intensity that made her hot around the neck. Dominic's jaw ticked, and he punched the van's door open.

"It sticks," he growled in explanation. "Can you go get the table ready? It's the long one on the right side of the tent," Dom asked her.

Allie nodded and left. Tom might have said something about looks that could murder, but Allie heard nothing past Brandon's howl of laughter.

She made quick work of the table, setting the cream white

covers over it just in time before the four men came in carrying boxes and trays. They made two trips, and Allie had already started to arrange the display for the macarons, candy, and cupcakes before they returned with the second load. Dominic would take care of the chocolate fountain, and the cake would stay in the refrigerated van until it was time to cut it.

"Save me a dance, Allie," Brandon told her with a wink.

Dominic put his arms on Brandon's shoulders and turned his body around, shoving him away from the sweets table.

"Thanks for the help. Don't let us keep you from your host activities." His friend guffawed, and Allie wondered if there was some sort of inside joke she was missing.

They worked around the table in silence, Dominic focusing on setting up the chocolate fountain, and Allie focusing on the way his veiny arms tensed as he strained them, or how closely she could inspect that fascinating tree tattoo, or how tight that white shirt was around his shoulders and back.

Safe to say, Allie was focused on lots of things she should not be focused on. Her boss caught her staring once and did the most unexpected thing that twisted Allie's heart into a knot: he *smirked*. A half smirk, to be more specific, but a smirk nonetheless. The closest thing to a smile she'd glimpsed on him. The temperature in the tent must have been raised with magic.

They finished with the sweets bar a couple of minutes before the ceremony started, so Dominic and Allie rushed to take the seats Mia had saved. Allie had expected to find her next to Brandon, but he was sitting on the other side, looking a lot less cheerful than earlier.

Harper and Tina walked down the aisle hand in hand, Tina's brother pushing her wheelchair, her mother on the other side, and Harper's dad proudly holding his daughter's arm. They both wore cream white satin dresses, and while Tina's had long lace sleeves, Harper's was off-the-shoulder sleeveless, revealing her collarbone.

They were incredibly beautiful and wore blinding smiles during the entire ceremony.

As soon as it was over, everyone flocked to congratulate the happy couple. When it was Allie's turn, she didn't get to say anything before Harper spoke.

"Your dress matches Dom's tie. Are you here together?" she asked with unreasonably wide eyes while Tina wiggled her brows.

"No—that's—Mia." Allie settled on the simplest explanation. The brides exchanged a look before Harper's eyes darted somewhere behind Allie.

"I wouldn't say that if I were you," she said, her eyes still trailing behind Allie. "I mean, just let everyone believe you're here together. It's for the best." Allie glanced behind and only saw a trail of a blue skirt before it disappeared inside the tent.

"I'm not so sure," Allie said with a small smile. She didn't think Dominic should be seen with her outside their business, given how the people here felt about her. If anything, she should stay away to prove to them Dominic had nothing to do with her. A sharp claw of painful disappointment gripped her heart, but this wasn't about her. This was about Dominic, the man who had helped her and who would stay in Sycamore Falls and deal with the townspeople long after she was gone.

"We promise Dominic is a really good guy," Tina said, tugging at her hand. "He just takes a bit to warm up to."

What was with everyone trying to convince her that Dominic was a good guy? She knew that. Allie was one comment away from shouting it at the top of her lungs.

"Congratulations. I wish you great happiness," she said instead, kissing both of them on their cheeks.

Allie left for the tent, where the guests started to gather. She spotted Dominic by the sweets table, inspecting everything and moving the trays one inch to the left or right. The corners of her mouth turned up in an honest smile, one she rarely got to share, as she headed to him.

Her smile faded, and she stopped in her tracks when Anna approached Dominic from the other side. She wore a long, elegant marine blue dress that split around her thigh, and her hair was loose for the first time, flowing around her in a rich dark curtain. Anna leaned in and kissed him on the cheek, resting her hand on his arm. She moved it to his chest as if she was picking lint off his most likely lint-free shirt, then back to his arm.

Allie wished she could touch him like that. It didn't have to be in public; she'd be content to have this privilege in private. Heat crawled from her spine up to her neck at the thought of her hands on him, and she was sure about the red stains coloring her cheeks. She needed to get a grip, lest someone think she was sick and running a fever. Her breathing labored, and... Was this jealousy? Was she jealous of Anna?

Allie watched her laugh at something Dom had said and guessed that it was a fake laugh. Her boss was not that funny. But why did it bother her?

You need to get a grip!

And she needed something else, too.

Needed to admit it to herself.

Allie had a big, fat crush on her boss.

"You like her." Brandon sipped whiskey out of his glass and raised his brows at Dominic, who was seconds away from pouring the amber liquid on his friend's head.

"I don't know what you're talking about." Dom sipped from his own glass, scanning the room and avoiding Brandon's eyes.

"Oh, okay." His friend put the drink down and fully turned to him. "I'm talking about Allie, the Witch who's been working with you and living under your roof for the past three weeks. You like her."

"Mind your business, Brandon." He didn't want to confirm or deny, as Brandon would find a way to pester him about both answers.

"You know she's nothing like the Witch who—"

"I know."

"I mean, you weren't here when it happened, and while she lived here, but I can tell you, Dom, she's nothing like Miranda." Dominic hated hearing the name of the Witch who'd brought trouble to his hometown, and even more so since he'd met Allie. She was good and kind, yet everyone insisted on holding a grudge against her for a sin that she didn't commit.

"I know," Dom repeated. He didn't have to meet this Miranda to know that someone like Allie would never do what she'd done to Sycamore Falls. And out of pure revenge, no less.

"And she's certainly not Sheila," Brandon scoffed.

"Don't." Dominic inhaled, letting the wave of rage and betrayal pass through him, weathering it so it didn't flood onto his innocent, big-mouthed friend. "Don't speak her name in my presence," he snarled.

"Sorry." Brandon raised his palms in a peaceful gesture.

The depth of his pain from so long ago was now just an unpleasant memory, but five years ago, that pain had consumed him. He had been stupid and believed the woman who had loved him for seven years would keep loving him regardless of where his job sent him. Dominic had been so sure she knew he would always come back to her.

Instead, she chose a man named Gordon from a couple of towns over, who ran a farm and never had to leave it. Because she didn't trust Dom enough to always come back.

The easiest way for someone to put a knife in your back is when they're hugging you.

"Admit it," Brandon said and pulled him from the dark trail his thoughts had taken.

"What?"

"You like Allie. Or have a little crush on her, at the least."

Dominic moved his eyes to his friend slowly, making sure the threat was clear in them in an attempt to make him drop the subject. Because there were only so many ways he could avoid saying "Maybe." Or just "Yes."

Allie was... She was... She trusted him. Even without his Reading magic, he knew how to recognize a beautiful soul when he found one. But he wasn't ready to share these thoughts with anyone else.

"Let's put it to the test." Brandon grinned. He downed the remaining whiskey in his glass, stood up, and walked pointedly toward a tall, lean form hiding in the shadows.

Allie.

She smiled at Brandon as he approached her, and when he extended his hand, she took it and followed him to the dance floor. The melody changed to a slow waltz, and Brandon snaked his arm around her middle, lifting her left hand and holding it firmly in his palm. The white rose at her wrist caught his eye, the corsage *he* had put on her—

Dominic jumped up and almost toppled the table in the process.

He strolled as if he owned the place to the pair he couldn't wait to break up. Allie had noticed him, her eyes growing wide. Once he was behind Brandon, he cleared his throat loudly and said, "May I?"

Brandon turned around and offered a polite, "Of course," but the prick flashed Dominic the biggest smirk of the century as he backed away.

Dom couldn't care less about Brandon being right once his hands got hold of Allie's waist. He pulled her close to him. Her arms wrapped around his neck on instinct, like it was their rightful place. He noticed the glimmer of shock at her own bravery and felt her hands slip away like she wanted to take it back, her freckled cheeks blushing a beautiful pink. Dom did not want to lose her touch, so he did something he had rarely done and only for the people who had earned it.

He offered her a smile. Or half of a smile, enough to encourage her to keep her hands in place.

It worked.

Allie settled her arms better around his neck, her fingers gently playing with the short hair at the base of his nape. Her touch was gentle and curious, and it rivaled his attention for the look in her eyes. A look that said so much if he allowed himself to read into it. Instead, he chose to lean into her touch and step even closer to her body.

Allie must have been dreaming. She discreetly pinched her finger behind Dominic's neck, and the spell wasn't broken. This was real.

She was dancing with her boss, her body nearly flush against his. Goosebumps erupted across her skin as his thumbs moved lazily up and down her back. His cologne held a hint of delicious mint, and Allie inhaled deeply and tried to ground herself in it. The desire to move her hands across his arms and chest as Anna had done so leisurely was strong, and Allie almost gave in before Dominic spoke.

"I need to ask you something," Dom said, his teal-colored eyes drilling into her. *Need to*, not *want to*. She was curious about the thought that had his features change from that perfect half-smile he'd just shown her into this dark curiosity, so she nodded. "Do you..." A muscle ticked in his jaw. He cleared his throat and looked away from her for a second before his eyes came back to hers. "Do you have a tattoo?"

Allie paused her rhythmic swaying and stared open-mouthed at her boss. He *had* seen something when the cursed dress lifted up her thigh in the van. She thought she might have seen his eyes wander, but wrote it off as her imagination running wild.

But why did he look...at her legs? Enough to notice the black edges of her thigh tattoo. Did he...

No.

But what if...

Hm.

This would be a great opportunity for her to test the waters. There was no reason for her to lie about her tattoo, so she resumed dancing as she came up with a strategy to check if Dominic had even the slightest interest in her. Allie had nothing to lose since she'd already decided to tell him she could be leaving the town early. And if this was one-sided, she would stomp on her crush before it grew into something else.

She inched closer to him and tilted her head up to whisper in his ear.

"I have...more than one." She stepped back, but Dominic's hands gripped her waist harder, keeping her in place. This time, he stopped their slow dance, his emerald eyes scanning her body up and down, as if he was searching for the tattoos. The music came to a crescendo, signaling that the end of the song was near. His jaw clenched so hard that Allie feared it would snap.

But then he pulled her against him in a swift movement and bent her back at the waist on the last notes of the melody. Her curls fell back, leaving her neck exposed, and Dominic leaned over her until his lips breathed hot air on the skin of her neck.

"I'd like to see them."

Chapter 21

WE'RE...COMFORTABLE

If Dominic hadn't been holding her, Allie would have slumped to the floor from the shock of his reply. While the words were innocent, she could have sworn his tone had a flirty flavor, but the music had been too loud over his voice. It was also possible he had an artistic curiosity about tattoos, given that he had one, or more, not that Allie knew or ever thought about what hid under Dominic's clothes.

Three days later, she was still spiraling over his words.

"I'd like to see them."

After their eventful dance, Tina and Harper had asked them to bring the cake out. Allie had stumbled on the way to the van twice and told Dominic she felt a bit dizzy from the wine—lie, she only had one glass—so Brandon or someone else should help him. She wanted to protect the cake from her clumsiness, which she had, but her dragon made up for her lack of destruction. Ekko had stolen a piece of cake and flew away with it, smudging chocolate all over his snout and his white bowtie.

Dominic had seemed unfazed by her not helping with the cake.

In fact, he'd acted normal for the past three days, too. If Dominic's words held more meaning, he would have said something by now. Her feelings were silly in the first place, given her limited time in Sycamore Falls. Limited time with him. Likely Dom knew better than her, knew better than to get attached to someone who was leaving sooner or later.

Sooner. Sooner would be good. The distance would allow her to forget about any fluttering feelings blossoming for her Mage boss. Not only that, but it would give Dominic his peace back.

Allie struggled to ignore all the gossip and whispers she'd caught wind of during the wedding.

"Why did Dominic dance with her?"

"Why did Brandon dance with her?"

"Out of pity, of course, but were they safe? Should we have done something about it?"

"Why did they allow her to attend the wedding?"

It would not be the first nor the last time Allie heard words like these. They hurt, but she had grown thick skin and trained herself to overlook them. What didn't sit well with her was all of these people pestering Dominic for the remainder of the event. Was he fine? Did he need anything? Maybe this or that person should help him at the bakery while he looked for permanent help. While he still had a bakery.

If Allie left, it would get the townspeople off Dominic's case, and they would cease with the surprised looks they tossed his way when they found the bakery still standing.

Today. She would tell him today. This way, she had a couple of days before the weekend to make travel plans and leave everything in order at Dom's Sweets.

They were getting ready to close for the day, Dominic packaging the unsold inventory to take over to Mia's for today's toddler story time at the book shop. Allie wished that at least once she could have gone with him on one of these volunteer deliveries, but she didn't want to take away from people's enjoyment and

Dominic's kindness. Which seemed to happen every time she breathed.

"I'll be right back," her boss muttered, running out the door holding two boxes in his muscular arms.

They're just arms, Allie.

Today he wore his standard black T-shirt, dark jeans, and boots, and she'd chanced fugitive looks at the tree tattoo on his arm that was a work of art. The tattoo, that was.

He rushed back in, since he'd left in just his T-shirt, cold clinging to his body and clothes. Dominic rubbed his hands and headed to the back, passing by her.

"Dominic." Allie's voice made him stop. "Can I talk to you?" He turned on his heels and his eyes narrowed to slits, as if he wanted to determine if this was serious, or if she just wanted to eat an extra cupcake. But Allie schooled her features into something serious—or so she hoped.

"Sure." Dominic pointed to the table closest to them and took a seat. She sat down facing him and clasped her hands on the table, holding his gaze. She was reminded of the first time they sat here like this, coincidentally at the same table, on her first day in Sycamore Falls. When they had tea, and he'd agreed to let her stay.

Allie had done her fair share of overthinking since the wedding about how this conversation was going to go. She remembered all the times she had tried to thank him and Dominic cut her off, so she decided to save that for the end and start boldly. Overthinking about it did not make it easier, though. Unfair. Allie took a deep breath and exhaled the words.

"I'm thinking about leaving Sycamore Falls early and heading for Pearls Fields this weekend." She paused to check his reaction, but he had none. Dominic stared back at her like he was frozen, like he wasn't breathing. "I don't pose a threat to my sisters anymore, so I think they will take me back. They might even help me learn about my power," she explained, trying to convince herself as well. Lydia had said she needed to prove she was in control, and she was...in a way. Dominic's green eyes moved over her face, and the familiar frown took its rightful place between his eyebrows.

"No."

"What?" Allie's head jerked back in surprise.

"You're not leaving early."

"Why not?" It was her turn to frown at him. "I'll get everything in order by then, I promise. I'll get the room cleaned—"

"No." Her boss slammed his hands on the table as he stood up and left, heading up the stairs.

Dominic left Allie to close the shop as he wore a path on the carpet in his living room. He pulled at the band in his hair and threw it on the floor. His nails dug into the heels of his palms, anger making his breaths come out hot and fast. Anger with himself and his fucking lack of restraint. He was sure his comment had put Allie off, and now she wanted to leave early. For a man who had lived his life with his mouth mostly shut, he wondered what the hell was wrong with him that he opened it then.

Why did he have to act like a flirty ass at the wedding? He'd let Brandon get in his head, and now Allie wanted to leave because he had hit on her and made her uncomfortable. And his acting like a child earlier for sure didn't help, either.

He'd always known she would leave Sycamore Falls, so why was it an issue now that she wanted to leave early? Why?

Because Brandon had been fucking right, and if what had happened at the wedding didn't prove it, his present rage did. Dominic kicked the edge of the couch.

He liked Allie.

He liked that she was kind, patient, and willing to learn. He liked that she smiled at him sincerely. That she trusted him. That she was beautiful, soul and body, and she made him a better person. He liked who he became when she was around.

Having her around the bakery had been a blessing. With her here, Dom had more time to spend on his mission. This week, he'd left after the lunch rush for two to three hours, which helped cover more ground around the area. He was still unsuccessful, but he needed to search every piece of land to find where the magic was broken. And he could do this faster now, having Allie at the bakery.

Selfishly, he liked having her around. He stopped his annoying pacing and pinched the bridge of his nose. He had no right to be selfish. Ultimately, it was Allie's choice, and he had to respect it, even if he wished it was different.

Now that he was coming back to his senses, he had to find her, apologize, and maybe *ask* her why she decided to leave early instead of acting like a jerk and yelling like a caveman.

Dominic went downstairs and knocked on Allie's door. He waited for a beat, then knocked again. No answer. The lights were off in the bakery, too. If she wasn't here...

Dom grabbed his jacket and went out into the cold night, zipping it to his chin. Fall was great and all that, but he hated the darkness that set in at four in the afternoon. It had been dark for a couple of hours already, and he didn't keep the time he'd spent brooding by himself.

How long ago had Allie left? She practiced by herself at night almost every day, but today the thought of her alone in the middle of the forest made him more restless than any other day. He rushed along Maple Street, down the winding path to the secluded clearing he knew too well.

Barely a couple of moon rays escaped through the immense crowns of the sycamores to light his path. But once a glimmer of red light caught his eye through the thick darkness, Dominic sped toward it, his chest growing heavy with the panic that had seized him the night he found Allie surrounded by fire.

Now she stood by the river with her back to him, her long, big curls loose, brushing the small of her back. Her right palm was up, and above it burned a fire the size of a wine bottle. Dominic slowed his pace, seeing that she wasn't in any danger.

A soft purple smudge flew up and nudged her jaw toward him. Allie turned abruptly, her brown eyes wide, and the fire exploded into a tall, campfire-sized one.

"Whoa, whoa, whoa," she uttered, stepping away, but the flame followed her on her palm. Dominic fought the urge to clench his fist and put the fire out with his magic. He should teach her, as he'd promised to do.

"Stop!" he shouted. "It's yours, it's not going to burn you." Allie obeyed, fresh fear lining her gaze, her chest rising and falling rapidly. Dominic talked as he approached her. "You are in control, Allie. Pull it back."

"How?" She looked befuddled between him and the fire, still keeping it as far away as she could. Dom thought to share something he had learned in school, and if it didn't work immediately, he'd put the fire out. His magic was ready, buzzing through his veins. He wouldn't let anything happen to Allie. Did she know that?

"Think of your power like a ball of yarn. You pull on the thread, and the fire ignites. The more you pull, the brighter it burns. And when you want to put it out, you roll the thread back in."

"But..." she started, panic in her voice.

"Come on, Allie. Roll the thread back," he encouraged her

through clenched teeth, power at the ready. Her eyes stopped moving between him and the fire and squeezed shut. On the next breath, the flame decreased the slightest bit. "That's good, keep going." The flame dulled until it was the size of a peach, then Allie clamped her fist shut and snuffed it out.

Dom heard the loud breaths grazing her parted lips. He walked to her—

"Move," he hissed as Ekko planted himself in Dom's face, blowing warm steam at him through his nostrils. The creature looked irritated and bared his teeth at Dominic, as if warning him not to approach the Witch.

Cute.

He stepped around the tiny dragon, only for him to fly into his face again.

"Come here," Allie said.

"I'm trying," Dom argued, his eyes narrowing at Ekko. He considered summoning a gust of air to keep him at bay, but that would not sit well with Allie.

"Oh. I was talking to Ekko." She stifled a laugh with the back of her hand while her dragon flew to her and sat on her shoulder, tucking his tail with more sass than necessary. "What are you doing here?"

Dominic finished crossing the distance between them. Finally.

"Why do you want to leave early?" he asked softly.

"I..." Allie paused and studied him with her chocolate brown eyes, scrunching her freckled nose. She sighed and put her hands in the jacket's pockets. "I don't want to lie to you."

"Then don't."

She scoffed and bit her lip, averting her gaze. But Dominic's dropped to her mouth, and hell. How was he supposed to focus on anything else than her lips?

"I don't want the people here to keep holding you responsible for me anymore." That was enough to break the spell Dom had fallen under.

"What?"

"I hear all the whispers, Dom," she said in a defeated voice that cracked something in his heart. "I'm used to people sneering at me, being wary of me, avoiding me on the street. I'm used to gossip and theories they have about Witches that are not true about me, not only due to the nature of my power, but also due to the nature of my soul. I'm not like that."

"I know!" he blurted.

"I'm used to living with the burden of being a Witch, and I'm fine with that. It is my life. But I cannot stand watching the people here question *you* about it. If anything happens, they'll hold you accountable, and maybe I didn't understand that well enough at first, but it's clear as day to me now. And I can't have that. I won't have that. You are not responsible for my actions or lack of control over my power, yet everyone is ready to make you take that responsibility." Allie's breath was ragged, her eyes covered with a translucent sheen. "I don't want that to happen. You have been incredibly kind to take a stranger in, and so patient with me through my power struggles. Now they're mostly contained, I can go back to my coven and keep learning with them. I'm really grateful, Dom. If it wasn't for you, I would have never known about the seal. I know I can never repay you for this, but at least if I go, everyone here will be at ease, and they'll stop bothering you."

Allie's voice cracked on the last word. Dominic had wanted to cut her off at the end of every sentence, but he bit his tongue to let her get everything out. She would go back to people who hadn't wanted her when she was struggling, to a place where she had no friends, just so the people in this town left him alone?

To spare *him*?

Fuck that.

"Allie." He stepped closer to her and tipped her chin up,

ignoring Ekko's throaty growl. "The people of Sycamore Falls will be on my case for the rest of my life. It's how the community here is built, and as much as it annoys me, it also...comforts me. At times." He'd never said these words out loud and doubted he would ever repeat them. "So if you go, they will find something else to pester me about. I don't care about any of that."

"I care," she whispered. Determination was clear in her watery eyes, and Dom knew this was not an argument he could make in his favor. There was one last thing he could say to make her stay until Hallows Eve. One thing he really did not want to use, but he had no choice.

Dominic wanted her to stay. At least a little longer. And if it worked, he would clear any confusion about the wedding, too. Anything to keep her from leaving early.

"You can't leave yet." Dominic took a step back and schooled his features into that no-nonsense look that Brandon said would forever help Dom get his way. For this rare moment, he hoped his friend was right. He watched Allie's sadness transform into shock as he said, "You promised to help me with my task."

Allie felt her eyes go wide, a goose egg sticking in her throat.

"You can help me with my task here in Sycamore Falls. But only if you promise to come to me if you have trouble controlling your power."

Dominic had offered her this bargain, and Allie had been so excited when he had agreed to let her help. But she had been overwhelmed by everything else that had happened and selfishly focused only on her practice. Dominic hadn't asked her for help, but she hadn't offered either.

Not only that. When she was adamant about getting more responsibility at the bakery, Dom offered to teach her with such gentleness... Just so she would leave now. Guilt curdled in her chest for the things she had asked for and was ready to give up because of other people.

Selfishly, she wanted to stay. To soak in every minute in this beautiful place that offered her so many opportunities, with people who were starting to mean so much to her.

"You're right," Allie breathed. "I'm sorry." She rolled her lips once and took a step closer to her boss. "Let's start tomorrow."

"So you'll stay?" he asked, and Allie didn't want to read too much into his rushed words, or the shade of hope that seemed to light his emerald eyes.

"Until Hallows Eve." They both nodded once in silent agreement, then Ekko flew from Allie's shoulder and circled Dominic twice with clear suspicion in his dark coal eyes. The Mage ignored the adorable creature and bore his green gaze into Allie's.

"About the wedding."

Allie straightened at his words, her heart pounding ten times faster than three seconds ago. Dominic could be upset that she hadn't helped him with the cake. He could also be referring to the tattoo remark, and the simple memory of Allie's daring flirtation made her cheeks warm.

"I have...more than one."

Why, Allie?

"Yes?" she asked, a little out of breath.

"I'm sorry if I made you feel uncomfortable."

"What?" Allie blurted. *He* made *her* feel uncomfortable? Not the other way around? "You have not," she added quickly, shaking her head. "I made you uncomfortable, didn't I?"

"No." Genuine surprise took over Dominic's features. Allie chuckled.

"Then if neither of us is uncomfortable...are we... Are we fine?" Allie knew this approach was cowardly and avoiding the subject, but it was the safest bet if she were to stay here until Hallows Eve. With Dom.

Dominic looked her over just like he had done the night of the wedding, top to bottom, leaving a trail of heat crawling over her body. His frown softened just before he turned around and started for the path out of the forest.

"We're...comfortable," he muttered.

Chapter 22

WE'RE FRIENDS, RIGHT?

Dom and Allie fell back into their routine the next morning: she made coffee, turned on the ovens, and cleaned while he reviewed orders and prepared the kitchen for the day. Allie felt better about staying until Hallows Eve after the conversation last night. It wasn't lost on her that they did not, in fact, set the record straight about what had happened at the wedding. However, she was more than happy to go with the "comfortable" Dom had defined at the end of that conversation. No reason to insist on hashing out a subject that could upturn this...comfort.

Now, the only thing left was to snuff out her crush as she did her fire. Allie should focus on helping Dominic, both with his mission and in the bakery, instead of dreaming of pulling her fingers through his chestnut hair.

She entered the kitchen with that in mind and put her hands on her hips.

"Teach me something new today."

Dominic stood by the large table, sipping his coffee and flipping through the pages of his notebook. He looked at her over the rim of the coffee cup, a glimmer of amusement in his green eyes. The rich brown turtleneck he wore under the bakery's apron made his eyes pop even more.

"All right." He placed the cup on the table and gave Allie a look full of challenge. "Butter, sugar, yeast, salt, flour, and milk. Cold milk," Dominic clarified, a corner of his mouth ticking up. A smile stretched her lips as she gathered the ingredients Dominic had rattled off. The morning she'd accidentally heated the milk seemed so far away, with her power now warm and calm in her chest.

Allie spread the ingredients on the table and frowned.

"Croissants?"

"Good." Dominic looked through the end of his notebook and pushed it open to Allie. The quantities list was there, with no other instructions on the recipe. "Mix the dry ingredients in a bowl, then whisk the milk in bit by bit until the dough thickens. Hand me the butter." Dominic rolled the sleeves of his sweater to his elbows in two smooth moves, revealing the dark ink of his tattoo. Her eyes rested on it, studying the intricate details of the branches, and how they wove around the muscle—

"Allie?"

"Yes. Butter." Allie did as instructed, embarrassed to be caught gawking. She had seen Dominic roll butter into sheets with extra care and skill dozens of times and was happy he didn't deem her ready for that step.

Her focus went into the bowl in front of her, but there was movement around her, and the rolling pin kept coming into view. She forced herself to keep her eyes on the mixing task, *knowing* how Dominic's muscles strained when he used the rolling pin.

"Start kneading," her boss said when the dough got too thick for the whisk. Allie raised her eyes to him and nodded. She sprinkled flour on the table and spilled the dough over it. Cautiously, she squished it in her hand, but unlike the times she'd watched Dominic knead dough, this one trickled through her fingers.

"I think I did something wrong." Allie raised her hand, dough sliding off it.

"Nothing's wrong. It needs more flour." Her boss rounded the table and stood beside her, sprinkling flour over the dough. Dominic's presence was distracting, with his clean cedarwood scent and his muscular arms right there in her face. "Try again." She did, but had the same result. "Keep your fingers together and use the heel of your palm. Like this."

Dominic kneaded the soft dough into a ball with skilled ease, but Allie's eyes wandered from his fingers up to the arms flexing with the movement.

"Allie?" She shook her head and looked at him. Dominic paused and frowned, worry etching lines on his forehead. "You seem off. Is there something wrong with your power?" he asked, that worry seeping into his gruff voice.

Embarrassment heated her cheeks and neck, and her heart thudded in her ears.

Pull yourself together, Allie.

"Nothing's wrong, I promise. I'm just a bit...distracted," she admitted, keeping the reason for the distraction to herself.

"Hm." His frown didn't lessen, but Dominic didn't press further and tipped his chin back to the dough. Allie followed his lead and managed to knead it slowly into a ball. They let it rest while Dominic took care of the bread and cupcake batter, and Allie tidied the space.

Allie had learned what her boss needed at every step of the baking process. She handed him ingredients and utensils, and since he had agreed to give her more difficult tasks—and had already caught her staring at him—Allie paid more attention to measurements and the order of mixing the ingredients than normal.

Dominic had filled all the ovens and set the timers while Allie took out the croissant dough and stared at it, rolling pin in hand.

How hard could it be? Dom did this every day. Allie grabbed the tool with both hands and pressed it against the dough slightly.

She hardly made a dent in it. Okay, so more pressu—

"You need to apply more pressure." Her boss's voice broke through her thoughts. "Here."

Dominic came behind her and grabbed her hands, moving the rolling pin over the dough. Allie swallowed a gasp at the overload of sensations provoked in her body. Her heart stopped for a moment then went galloping, raising her blood pressure and pounding in her ears. Dominic's arms draped around hers, his front lined against her back in a hard, hot wall of muscles. She felt his breath on her neck, turning her skin into goosebumps.

This was much more intimate than the time they'd decorated cupcakes. Then, he merely stood next to her and held her hands over the piping bag, and even that had made her weak in the knees.

Now... Now...

Allie turned abruptly, thinking her boss would step away and put distance between them so her body could cool down. But Dominic held on to the rolling pin over the dough and caught her between the edge of the table...and him.

Dominic picked croissants for Allie to keep himself away from her. There was no decorating to be done, and he even rolled the butter sheets himself.

Watching Allie around the kitchen bewitched him, with her unnecessarily careful movements and the cute line that formed between her eyebrows. He knew he should stay away, but he couldn't, and frankly didn't want to. Ever since she confirmed his flirty reply didn't make her uncomfortable, Dominic had strayed away from thoughts of leaving her alone and closer to dangerous ideas.

Was there a chance she had flirted with him at the wedding? The possibility filled him with a fool's courage, and after he had convinced her to stay until Hallows Eve, Dominic decided to shoot his shot. And even if he hadn't, it only took him looking her over once, roaming around his kitchen in her tight jeans and pastel sweater, to know he had to at least try. It wasn't like him to waver from one feeling to the other, but the pull he felt toward Allie was too strong to deny anymore.

So when she strained to flatten the dough, Dominic took advantage of the moment like the greedy man he was. Could he have helped her by giving her instructions from a distance? Maybe. But he liked the scenario where he touched her so much better.

He practically draped himself over her, inhaling the tangerine scent on her skin, feeling her soft body against his. Allie's bun left her neck exposed, together with a sliver of her shoulder and collarbone. Dom hungrily stared at her ivory skin and noticed the necklace she always wore tucked under her sweater. His traitorous eyes followed it, and he wished—

"Dom," Allie breathed urgently, turning around in his arms. Her freckled cheeks were flushed, her plump lips parted, and Dominic's desire flared through his body like a shock wave. Wide brown eyes stared at him with surprise and something else, something urgent. She squirmed between him and the table, and the move sent delicious jolts of yearning through his body.

You are driving me crazy.

He wanted to kiss her. Everywhere. To unravel her red mane of hair and get lost in it. He wanted to be much closer to her than he was, and didn't remember when he'd last wanted something this badly.

"Mhm?" he growled, incapable of forming words through his lips that only wanted her. Dom squeezed the rolling pin so hard the wood groaned under his grip.

Allie's labored breathing calmed down, and her lips pursed as her dark caramel eyes gazed at him with newfound determination, like she had made a decision.

"We're friends, right?"

The rolling pin clattered against the table with a sharp sound that tore through the kitchen like claws on a chalkboard. Dominic took *many* steps away from her, something like hurt flashing in his deep green eyes. A muscle ticked in his jaw, and his fists clenched at his sides.

Maybe he didn't consider her a friend?

Either way, Allie could not take offense. All she wanted to do was fist Dom's shirt and kiss him senseless, but Allie couldn't risk their remaining time together only to fulfill her hot desire. Stronger feelings had taken hold of her, and she had to weather them.

Want. Need.

She seriously marveled that she was still standing and hadn't melted into a puddle at his feet.

But she was leaving, and Dom was staying, and Allie feared that if she started something with him... She might not be able to leave.

"We're friends, Allie," Dominic ground out before storming from the kitchen like a tornado, leaving her gripping the edge of the table for support. He said it like an accusation, like the words tasted sour. If she were honest with herself, she would agree.

Because she wanted *more*.

Dominic finished turning the discarded dough into croissants with his ever-present frown in place. He was back to his silent and broody self, but Allie could deal with that. She'd dealt with it ever since she arrived at Dom's Sweets, so while he worked on the pastries, Allie gave them both space from each other.

She slipped into her room and whipped up two omelet sandwiches with goat cheese and red bell peppers. She ate hers while the other one was cooking, then put the second sandwich on a plate and went back to the kitchen.

"I'll do that while you eat," Allie said, placing the dish on the table. She took the icing bag from Dominic's hands and continued filling the macaron shells as her boss stood there, unmoving. "Eat it while it's warm," she urged him without taking her eyes off the macarons.

The air shifted around her, and steps filled the room together with a grumbled "Thanks."

They finished getting the bakery ready in silence. If Allie didn't know any better, she might have thought Dominic was ignoring her. As much as you can ignore someone you work with. But his mood was no different than on any other broody day.

They got through the morning rush, and Allie thought everything was mercifully back to normal.

"Hi, Allie," Brandon shouted as he came in, his grin so big she could see it from across the bakery. Allie waved him over to the counter. "What's good today?"

She almost said "croissants," then thought better of it and recommended the apple pie.

"I'll take a slice to go." Brandon leaned over the counter as she packaged the pie. "Do you have any plans tonight?" Allie shook her head. "I'd like to show you the other side of the farm," he offered with a sneaky smile.

"That would be—"

"Outside. Now." Dominic's voice carried from the small hallway into the bakery before his tall form came into view. He grabbed his friend by the elbow as Brandon made a "one second" gesture to Allie. She stared after them helplessly with the apple pie box in her hands.

Since there were no other customers, Allie had a clear view of the outside through the tall, wide windows. Dominic stood with his arms crossed while Brandon cackled so loudly, the sound reached Allie through the closed door. Her boss looked like he was part of a heated exchange, but his friend seemed more entertained than ever.

Dominic almost tore the door off its hinges when he came in, surrounded by a cloud of rage that was taking form around him. Brandon followed him leisurely as if he was having the time of his life.

"Here's your pie," she said, offering the box to him in exchange for a bill.

"Thanks, Allie. As I was saying before we were rudely interrupted," he raised his voice on the last two words, "I'd love to show you around the farm. How about tonight?"

"I—"

"Great. I'll pick you up after closing time," he said with a wink and left.

Shortly after that, Dominic walked out of the kitchen without his apron and barked orders about the timers he'd set, saying he was taking the afternoon off to take care of his other work. Allie wanted to go with him, but they couldn't both leave during business hours. If only he'd told her more about his power and how he was using it to look for a cure, she could have spent this time thinking of a plan.

Think like a Witch, Allie.

She still had no idea *why* anyone would do what that Witch did, but she didn't need to know the reason behind it to consider the method employed by the Witch to break the spell.

Dominic had said the magic between the earth and the sycamores was severed. Allie guessed there must be a piece of land where this detachment occurred. It was one of the few times Allie wished she was more like her sisters, more like Lydia, who was smart and cunning and cruel.

Allie racked her brain trying to think of something, anything that could be useful to Dominic. It was difficult since she wasn't like the other Witches, but also because her mind flew to what had happened that morning in the kitchen. To Dominic's body lined up with hers.

Again, and again, and again. And every time her thoughts wandered, Allie wished she had kissed her boss, risks be damned.

Chapter 23

ARE YOU HAPPY NOW?

A silver car was parked outside when Allie came out of the bakery, after she had changed into a different sweater and grabbed her jacket. And her dragon. Ekko had filled her studio room with happy puffs of steam when she told him they were visiting Brandon's farm, where he could fly freely. Allie hadn't asked Brandon if her baby dragon was welcome on this visit, but the first thing the ever-grinning man did was scratch Ekko under his chin and say, "Hey, buddy." The creature stretched and purred from Allie's shoulder, more house cat than dragon.

"Ready?" Brandon said and held open the passenger door.

Allie took advantage of the last rays of daylight to soak in the scenery. Once they crossed over the bridge to the residential and farming area of the town, they were lost between auburn hills and snaking bronze paths. It was breathtaking, and peaceful, and somehow comforting to live in a place with changing seasons. Pearls Fields was forever bound to summer by the old magic in the land, and while Allie had enjoyed the endless sunny days when she was little, now she found herself running from the scorching sun more often than not.

"How do you like it here so far?" Brandon asked her as he pulled the car into the driveway of the house with the green roof.

"It's beautiful."

Ekko started to chitter and nudge her jaw urgently. They got out of the car, and Allie asked, "Is it okay if I let Ekko fly around here?" Brandon nodded, and Ekko took flight, making a mess of Allie's curls.

"What kind is he?" Brandon asked.

"Tree dragon. Don't worry, he can't spit fire. Unless you have an orchard growing any types of fruits, everything else is safe."

"I have multiple orchards." Allie froze, but Brandon continued with a laugh, "He's welcome to anything he can find. Yes, I'm sure," he said once he noticed the look of dread on Allie's face.

They walked from his house on a path to the right, away from the land where the wedding had taken place. The sky became thick with darkness by the time Brandon showed her around the vegetable crops. The place was enormous. It would take Allie forever not to get lost here, but she got drunk on the freedom, the refreshing air, even the cold. Her body had grown used to lower temperatures, and Allie found she enjoyed the chill that made her snuggle under a blanket with a hot drink.

"I should've known we won't see much with the sun setting so early," Brandon said as they made their way back to the house. He stopped and pointed to some lit barns on the other side of the hill, telling her that was the cattle's residence.

"How many do you have?"

He rattled off a string of animals and their quantities, much higher than Allie expected. Riverbend Farm was truly a big deal.

"Wait." Brandon felt his jeans' pockets, then his jacket. "I forgot the flashlight."

"Do we need one?" Allie looked around, and some low lights were on already around the field, through the vegetable rows.

Brandon put his hands on her shoulders and turned her around to a darkness so thick, Allie felt like she could grab it and spin it into a yarn.

Yarn.

Well, it was about time Brandon learned a bit about her, too. Allie held her palm up and focused on the warmth in her chest. She unspooled a thread of power and let it flow through her until it took form over her fingers.

"Wow." Brandon looked from her to the fire and back, his mouth open. "You're an elemental Witch." Allie nodded, a proud smile escaping her lips, only because she was managing to control her power so well right now. "Does Dom know?" The wariness in his voice shoved that smile away, deep inside her.

"He knows."

"Good," Brandon said, visibly relaxing.

Allie told him her story, keeping everything related to her boss to herself. They had been friends for so long—"basically our whole lives," Brandon told her—so it was Dominic's choice to tell him about the seal or about the other issues he had helped her with. If he wanted to. Allie stuck to her own life, her mom, and her coven, steering clear of Green Creek, and confessed that she had manifested late and came here to learn per her coven's request.

"That's shitty," Brandon scoffed. "They should have helped you, not sent you away." Allie didn't argue, but asked him for a favor.

"The people in Sycamore Falls don't know about my power, and I think it's best to keep it that way."

"Yeah, you bet. The last thing people here need to know is that the town's Witch can burn it to the ground." He'd clearly meant it as a joke, but it struck too close to the truth for comfort.

Back at the house, they sat outside and drank hot chocolate. Brandon insisted they go in, but she was enjoying the quiet and the misty air too much. The moon was out, looking over them from the top of the hills, and Allie felt best under the moonlight. Safest. Strongest.

"Do you know who the Witch was who broke the spell on the sycamores?" Allie asked, and when she saw Brandon's confused look, she added, "Mia told me about it." Something passed over his features at the sound of Mia's name, and Allie was itching to ask him about her, but decided against it. For now.

"Jared's ex." He looked at Allie with raised brows until she placed the name to the person. The man with the gross and disturbing aura and intentions that kept popping into her life. Allie shivered at the thought. "Exactly. They had been together for a few years when she found out that Jared was cheating on her." Oh, no. "Witches are kind of..."

"Vengeful? Grudge-holders?"

"Right." Brandon chuckled. "They had been living together in a southern town far away, but when they split up, Jared came back. He's the mayor's only child, who hopes to leave the business to Jared." Allie grimaced as if the drink had turned sour. "The Witch came here soon after he'd returned and...you know the rest. No one wants him here, and he doesn't even want to be here, but all he can do is follow in his father's steps."

Allie tried to muster a drop of pity for him, yet nothing came but a full-body shiver. The cold was getting to her.

"I'll get a blanket," Brandon said, and handed her his cup.

Dominic pulled up his car by the gate and walked the length of the farm's driveway to cool...whatever it was that came over him when he returned to the bakery and found it locked. Earlier, he'd overheard Brandon asking Allie to come visit the farm, but

Dominic wrote it off as one of the annoying skits his friend attempted to get him to admit his feelings. Yet when he found no trace of Allie or Ekko, a weird feeling snuck into him and gripped his chest with vulture-like claws.

Allie must have left with Brandon, and Dominic hated it with everything he was. Even if Brandon had been his friend ever since he could remember, it didn't sit well with Dom for Allie to be alone with any man but him.

His boots crunched on the dry path, and with every step through the dark driveway, Dominic realized the feeling that had made him jump into his car and race here was jealousy. He was jealous of Brandon.

"Idiot," he muttered under his breath. The logical part of his brain told him Brandon would never make a move on Allie after all the time he spent getting Dom to admit his crush on her. Unfortunately, the part that told him the exact opposite was louder. Dominic rushed his steps into a jog and only slowed down when the house lights came into view.

A lean figure sat on the porch swing, drowning in an ocean of red hair, holding two cups in her hands. Dominic walked to her like a moth drawn to light, and he could swear the air was warmer as he got closer to her.

"Dom," Allie said when she noticed him climbing the porch stairs.

His name like that on her lips made his heart somersault inside his chest. Dominic didn't remember why he had angrily rushed out of the bakery earlier, leaving her behind. How could he be angry with her?

Allie had said they were only friends, but if she didn't want anything else, wasn't friends better than nothing?

"What are you doing here?" A smile spread on her face, one of those large and genuine ones. Was she happy to see him?

"I came to pick you up." During the drive, Dom had

considered inventing a reason to come to Riverbend, then coincidentally leave with Allie. Then he had thought better about it and decided on the truth: he just wanted to take her home. No lies, no games.

The door slammed open and missed hitting Dominic in the face by a hair's breadth.

"I found the—oh. Hey, D," Brandon greeted him with a shit-eating grin. He *knew* he had gotten under Dom's skin. By coming here, Dominic had just proved his friend right. Admitted he had gotten under his skin.

"Brandon," Dom said with a slight tip of his chin. He scowled at his friend, whose smile only grew. Then he noticed the blanket under his arm, and Allie holding two cups...

It wasn't hard to put two and two together, and hell would freeze over before Dominic let Brandon get all cozy next to Allie. Without another thought, Dom grabbed the cups from Allie's hands and handed them to Brandon as he snatched the blanket, fluffed it up, and draped it over Allie's shoulders.

"Let me know when you're ready to go." He sat next to her and held his arm around her longer than needed. Allie leaned closer to him, a sparkle in her chocolate eyes that had Dominic thinking it was more than just the lamplight reflection.

"Ekko's not back yet. He's roaming around the farm, probably in the orchards." She chuckled softly and shook her head. Dominic wanted to swallow that breathy sound.

"I can bring him back."

"I bet you can," Brandon mumbled, barely containing his laughter. Dom turned murderous eyes on his friend, who had the audacity to say, "I would have driven Allie back. You can spend the night here, too, if you want," he addressed the beautiful Witch.

Dominic wanted to punch him. He wanted to punch him so damn much.

He replaced that urge with a flare of his power, flicking his wrist and sending a gust of wind through the farm to find Allie's dragon. It blasted to life more powerfully than Dom had anticipated, and he positioned himself in front of Allie to take the brunt of it. Brandon swore and moved his arms in front of his face, spilling hot chocolate on his shirt.

"Was that necessary?" his friend complained.

"I'm bringing Ekko back so we can go home." Dominic didn't leave Allie with the choice to accept or reject Brandon's offer. He knew it was a jerk move, but he'd rather suck the air out of his own lungs than hear Allie say she wanted to stay here. Away from him.

"Good," she said in a sweet voice that brought his eyes back to her.

Good.

A chittering chaos of purple flew to them from the darkness as Ekko fought the gale with his head upside down. Dominic slowed the wind and placed the creature in Allie's lap. His snout was smudged with dark purple, and his cheeks were rounder than usual.

"Ah, he found the winery," Brandon said.

"I'm sorry." Allie laughed as she struggled to clean the baby dragon with the end of her sleeve. "He really likes grapes."

"You can bring him here any time." Although Brandon was talking to Allie, he threw Dom a look full of meaning, and he answered with one full of menace.

"Thanks, Brandon. Your farm is really lovely." Allie gave him one of her radiant smiles, then cupped her palm up and lit a fire in her hand. "Ready?" she asked Dom. He looked pointedly from her hand to Brandon and back. The Witch inched closer to him, her tangerine smell wrapping around his senses. "You trust Brandon, right?"

With my life.

The simple question made Dom reconsider his childish

behavior. He placed the car keys in Allie's other hand and said, "The car is just outside the front gate. Get in. I'll be right there."

Allie nodded, then smiled and waved at Brandon before leaving. Ekko flew to him and nuzzled his jaw while Brandon scratched under his chin and said, "You're welcome."

Alone with his friend, Dominic crossed his arms and glared in what Brandon had always called his "signature move."

"Fine," he barked. "I like her. Are you happy now?" He felt as if someone dragged needles through his throat.

"Overjoyed." Brandon slapped him across the arm in acknowledgement. "But will she be okay?"

Now Dom could take his friend's worry and be grateful for it.

"What did she tell you?"

Dominic discovered that Allie had left out anything connected to him. He'd never kept secrets from Brandon, so he told him about the seal.

"Who the hell did that to her?"

"I don't know." Sizzling rage ignited inside him at the memory. "But if I ever find them..."

"I'll help," his friend grunted. Dominic nodded, then his eyes moved to the darkness along the driveway. "Go." Brandon made a shooing motion.

They shook hands, and Dom made to leave but stopped abruptly where the light still reached.

"Brandon?" His friend raised his brows, putting his hands in his pockets. "Thanks."

"Don't go soft on me now, Ranford."

"Not a chance, Peterson."

❧

Ekko fell asleep in Allie's lap as she dragged her fingers over his purple wings. His soft snores were the only sounds she could hear, and Allie found the quiet less peaceful now in this dense darkness that clung to the car windows. She thought she should have waited for Dominic in the driveway, let him have a moment with his friend, then walk together to the car guided by the light of her fire. Now...

Shadows moved around the car, and despite trying to convince her heart and brain that it was probably just Dominic, the loud beating in her chest echoed in her ears with alarm. When the driver's door opened, Allie jolted and woke up Ekko, who snarled in defense at her door. With his tail facing Dominic, who had just climbed inside the car.

"What's that about?" he asked. Ekko turned and blew hot steam Dominic's way before he curled back into Allie's lap.

"Nothing." She chuckled, her heartbeats slowing down. "Let's get to work."

"Work?"

"Yes. Didn't we make plans to start today? I'll help you with your task, then I can practice my power. Sorry you had to come all the way here, but I couldn't say no to Brandon. After all, he's the reason I'm here. And I really wanted to see more of the farm. It's beautiful out here. When there's light outside, at least."

Dominic looked at her as if she'd grown another head. Allie was sure she'd rambled like this before countless times in his presence. What fazed him now?

He started the engine and drove in silence until they crossed the bridge and reached a familiar paved road with a side path through the forest. Dominic parked the car there and got out while Allie carefully gathered her sleeping dragon into her arms.

Her door opened, and Dominic's extended hand came into view.

"Can I leave Ekko on your seat?" Her boss grumbled a half-hearted agreement, and Allie placed the ball that Ekko had become onto the chair.

Allie took Dominic's hand and got out of the car. He pulled her close to him, conflict lighting up his green eyes.

"Would you have stayed?" He grimaced, like the question was causing him pain. "At Riverbend?"

"No," Allie answered immediately. His brows knitted, and she shared a piece of the truth that she had wanted to keep to herself. "I wanted to be here, with you."

Chapter 24

EYES ON ME

"Tell me more about your power. How do you use it, for this task specifically?" Allie started as they walked down the forested path to the secluded clearing. "I only know basic things about Mages."

"There's not much public knowledge about us," Dominic sighed. They both had their hands in their pockets and walked within arm's length of each other. "For this mission, the only power tactic I can use is to imbue the earth with my magic and search for the rupture." Allie tried to imagine that but came up blank.

"How does that work?"

"I send waves of my magic through the earth's magic, which is connected to the sycamores everywhere but where the spell is broken. I must check every inch and every sycamore on this land. It's taking forever," Dominic grumbled.

"Do you need to be in different places each time?"

"Not really. I can search as far as my magic can reach. The clearing here is a central spot in the land, allowing me to reach the furthest." And she'd stolen his spot.

"How much have you searched already?"

"Not nearly enough. Not even half, and I've been at it for months."

Oh. Allie heard the words he didn't say, that he didn't have much time until another calamity hit. She had read in books that magic didn't survive long after a spell like this was broken. The sycamores and the magic here were in real danger.

It also sounded like Dominic was using tremendous amounts of power every time, and so far, with no results. His overall grumbly self made more sense to Allie now.

"Can I see?" she asked.

"You won't be able to see anything, but maybe you could feel the power."

Dominic crouched down and laid his palm on the ground. He closed his eyes, and the next moment, Allie felt a soft vibration underneath, barely strong enough to register if she wasn't paying attention to her surroundings. She watched her boss's expression turn into a frown, his breathing intensifying. His splayed hand shook, beads of sweat forming around his temples. It was impossible for her to imagine the extent of a Mage's power, but it sure looked difficult and tiresome.

The tremor stopped abruptly as Dominic rose to his feet and heaved a sigh.

"That was just searching around here and past the river," he panted. Allie's eyes widened, her jaw dropping between her ankles.

"So much power for covering only this small area?" she asked with disbelief. Her boss nodded solemnly, jaw clenching under his chestnut stubble. "You can't get anyone else to help?"

"There are very few Mages, and so many places that need our help. It would be selfish to pull one of my peers away from their tasks to help with mine. Besides, Sycamore Falls is my home. It's my duty to protect it." He said this with ease, as if it was the most natural thing to bear so much responsibility. Allie smiled sadly, wishing she loved something—or someone—so much that she would give anything to protect them.

She had hoped her coven sisters would become those people for her. Even only one of her sisters would have sufficed, but beyond being grateful for having a place to stay and some sense of community, Allie didn't feel much toward the Silverbarks. They certainly felt nothing good toward her. Now that she had summoned fire and woven it to her will, Allie was starting to lose the desire for them to accept her. Allie could finally be herself, an elemental Witch playing with fire. And maybe it was enough that she accepted herself.

So what else was out there for her? She could return to the coven and live her predictable life, just like her mother. There were worse fates for Witches, but...

Would it be enough?

She had another month before Lydia expected her to come back, power mastered. And she was confident she would learn to command it expertly before then.

Allie watched the man in front of her deep in thought, as if he'd tear the world apart to find a cure for the magic that protected his home, and she decided she would adopt his dream until it came true. She couldn't pretend to love Sycamore Falls, but she cared about Dominic, this strong Mage who had taken her in and helped her without batting an eye. Allie didn't want to help Dom because they had made a deal. She just wanted to help *him*, plain and simple.

From a two-month deadline to master her power to a one-month timeline to find a cure for the sycamores, Allie felt like she had a purpose. A goal. She didn't want to think about going back to Pearls Fields. Not yet.

"Do you know the areas you've already searched?" Dominic told Allie how far he'd reached in each direction. Going back and forth to Riverbend gave her a bit more knowledge about the town, so she registered every place her boss listed. "Give me some time to think about this, maybe I can come up with a plan."

"Thanks, Allie." His lips rolled in a straight line that made it clear Dominic was uncomfortable getting help, yet sufficiently annoyed with the issue to accept it. "Your turn." He crossed his arms across his chest, muscles bulging under the leather jacket.

"Okay."

Allie concentrated on the warmth in her chest, hot and buzzing, like the power had heard Dom and was at the ready. Thread by thread, she unspooled power from the core until a flame ignited at her fingertips. This way of molding power had become easier with every summoning, and it gave Allie peace of mind to work with her magic in these defined steps.

"How did you come up with the ball of yarn analogy?"

"Learned it in school," the Mage said, narrowing his eyes on her upturned palm. "Make it bigger."

Allie rolled the thread and expanded the fire to a melon-sized flame. Instinctively, she took a step back, together with the fire that was attached to her. She chuckled at her silly fear, straightening her spine and mustering the courage not to budge from a fire that was not hurting her and would never hurt her.

"Bigger." Allie shifted her gaze from the flame to Dominic to see if he was messing with her.

He wasn't. Determination mixed with silent challenge simmered in his eyes, and Allie wanted to rise to his expectations.

She unspooled the warm thread of magic and fed the fire until it was as big as the time Dominic had taught her the yarn trick. This time, she kept her breathing in check, her arm steady, and her power completely in control. The feeling that her magic would never betray her was present now more than ever and made her grin with pride. Just a month ago, she had been a danger to the people around her, and now she could use her power safely. She could *enjoy* being a Witch, having magic, and using it whenever and however she liked.

"Bigger."

"What?"

"Bigger."

"I heard you the first time." Allie sounded snarkier than she'd intended, but what did he mean *bigger*? The flame was about four feet tall. Any bigger than that and it would swallow her. Dominic looked at her with an "If you heard me, then do it" expression on his face. The fear she was so proud of *not* feeling reared its ugly head and caused Allie's heart rate to grow to a strong, quick pounding. Telling this powerful Mage she was scared was equally terrifying. Allie didn't want to disappoint him. Curiosity raced for a place in her mix of emotions: how much farther could she take it? How much power could she handle? Allie wanted to tell him everything and nothing at the same time.

"Dom."

That summed it up.

Dominic got closer than anyone not controlling a huge wall of fire had business getting. The sparks danced in his green eyes as he fixed them on her, then extended his arm and grabbed her free hand.

"What—"

"Allie," he said in that commanding voice of his. Dom interlaced their fingers as if he had always done that, his cold skin cooling her fiery one. He squeezed her hand as his brows furrowed, that notorious frown reigning over his features. "I would never let anything happen to you."

Allie was sure of two things in that moment: one, she'd squeezed Dominic's hand harder than he had hers, and two, her mouth hung open in a big, stupid O.

"You trust me, right?"

"I do!" Allie answered way too fast, too enthusiastically. But she didn't want there to be any doubt about how much she trusted this man. "I do."

"Good." Dom settled his hand better in hers, then said something that ignited Allie's heart more than any magic ever could. "Don't be afraid to burn bright. I will put out all your fires."

The Mage used his free hand to create a bubble of air in his palm, ready to extinguish anything she set aflame. And this reassurance, this safety net he created for her, made Allie's crush deepen. Grow. He cradled her heart in a way she would never be able to put into words, and the thing only pumped blood like crazy and spun feelings into her.

But now was not the time to focus on that.

Allie frowned at the flame in her hand, threatening to reduce it to smoke if it dared hurt the man holding her hand. In this moment, with him so close to her, Allie didn't fear for herself anymore; she feared for him. For she would not be able to live knowing she'd hurt the one who meant so much to her. The one her heart fluttered over.

The flame smoldered in her hand in a threat of its own, but Allie was determined to win this silent war. She tugged at the string of power, and the fire exploded. Hot sparks danced and crackled through the cold air, and Allie looked up, up, noticing the fire was as tall as her.

"Set it down," Dominic ordered.

"Do you want me to set the forest on fire?"

"You won't. Set it down."

When she made no move to lower the fire, Dominic inched closer to her, closer to the fire. Allie shifted it away from him, but the Mage moved closer still. At this rhythm, they would end up turning in circles.

"Down."

"Fine!" she ceded.

Allie crouched down, and Dominic followed, never letting go of her hand.

You won't burn the forest, you won't burn the forest, you won't burn the forest.

The chant went on and on in Allie's mind as she spilled the fire onto the ground like it was liquid. She resisted the urge to shut her eyes and wait for Dom to put it out before it spread.

But the flame crunched and sparkled in a still dance, not extending more than they had in her hand. Allie laughed.

"How?"

"Your power is your will, Allie. Unless you sic it on this earth intentionally, it won't hurt anything or anyone. It's an extension of you. It answers to you." Dominic's words were slow and gentle, and so doubtless that Allie believed him. It was easy to believe him, with the proof that she willed her fire not to burn the place to the ground, and it worked. She was awestruck. Her life had gone from fearing a simple sneeze to being able to summon fire and mold it as she wished. All due to the man *still* holding her hand.

"One more thing," Dominic said, pulling them to their feet. Allie regarded him curiously; what else was there? "Step into it."

"Excuse me?" Allie looked between the fire and Dominic, huffing with disbelief. Touching it was one thing, setting it down was another, but...stepping into it with her entire body? Allie wasn't that comfortable with her power yet. "No, thank you."

"You already know it won't hurt you," Dominic argued.

"My brain cannot conceive stepping into a burning fire, Mr. Ranford." Allie bristled.

"Yet that fire is an extension of you, Miss Wells," Dominic countered her banter, and her heart quivered. "You are stepping into yourself."

"If you put it like that..." Allie eyed the flickering flame and changed her internal chanting to "You won't burn me."

You won't burn me. You won't burn me. You won't burn me.

Her breath hitched, and the anticipation of stepping into a live fire made her feel like she'd swallowed glass. The flames were still, yet daring her to come close.

See what happens.

"Eyes on me."

Dominic tugged at her hand until she was close enough to brush her nose against his chin. He wrapped their clasped hands into a vortex of air and said, "So it doesn't burn me."

"I thought you said it was my will." Allie raised one brow. "I would never want to hurt you."

"You don't look like I'm your favorite person right now," he said, and then he did something that Allie had given up thinking was possible.

He smiled.

Widely.

Not just half of a smile, or a withering smirk.

A full-on, stunning, blinding grin that crinkled the skin around the corners of his eyes, stretching up to his cheekbones. A different type of light shimmered in his eyes, one that came from within, from his soul.

Allie was a goner. Her crush exploded into a cascade of feelings that she'd bottled up because "he was her boss," and "she would leave soon," and "he wasn't interested in her." None of these mattered anymore in front of the force that was Dominic Ranford *smiling*. And Allie didn't think too much before she squeezed his hand and opened her mouth.

"You might just be my favorite person, Dom."

Then she stepped into the fire.

Dominic would spend the rest of his life trying to find something more beautiful than this woman coming into her power, and he already knew he'd fall short.

Watching Allie conquer her fears and take charge of the fire inside her filled him with inexplicable joy. Maybe the reason was that she had trusted him implicitly, blindly, to guide her through this. Maybe it was because he knew firsthand how hard it was to come to terms with the magic inside you for the first time. Or maybe it was because...because he felt something for her. Because she was dear to him, and her smile lit up every room despite all odds being against her. Because she was beautiful, and she didn't give up on herself, even when she hadn't known it was a seal messing with her power.

Having someone like Allie in his corner was a glorious victory. She'd lodged herself into his heart, despite all the thorns and ice covering the organ.

Dom watched her step into the fire and stand there before she moved her free hand around, testing the flame with her fingers. She smiled brightly at him and stepped out, fisting her hand and snuffing the fire out.

He wanted to kiss that smile of hers. Her cheeks. Her jaw. Her neck. Her everything.

He wanted to kiss her so badly that his knees might give out, and he would fall at her feet.

Selfishly, he wanted to at least pull her into his arms.

But when Allie jumped up and down with delight about what she'd just done, when she looked at him as if this win was as much his as it was hers, Dom bit his tongue and nodded his encouragement. He didn't want to take this moment away from her. So he watched her, mesmerized by the pure happiness she exuded, and thought...

Maybe next time.

Chapter 25

YOU'RE NEVER SMILING, BUT YOU'RE SMILING NOW?

Allie and Dominic spent the rest of the week buzzing around the bakery during the day and roaming around the forests at night, baby dragon in tow. Her baking skills had improved compared to one month ago, but she still had so much to learn. Two bad batches of pie filling later, Allie finally got the correct ratio between the fruits and the sugar and added this to the list of her daily tasks. Between cleaning, decorating cupcakes, preparing the croissant dough—which Dominic had insisted on rolling himself—and now mixing the pie fillings, Allie found a lot of joy in such full days. After they closed the bakery, she fed Ekko and cleaned the space while Dom went on the end-of-day volunteer deliveries. He had asked Allie to join him one night, and as excited as she was at the prospect of being a part of the community, the sneers that still followed her around town came front and center into her mind and kept her away.

But she decided to let nothing take away from the weekend's festivities. Mia had told Allie that the town businesses and residents were going to put up Hallows Eve decorations during the next couple of days. Allie loved decorating for Hallows Eve, but doing it in Pearls Fields or Green Creek had lacked a certain charm, with all the crude greens, the bright colors, and the heat. Of course, she had never noticed these shortcomings before coming to Sycamore Falls and being surrounded by the auburns, the reds and oranges, the sycamores with their burnt colors that painted the perfect Hallows Eve atmosphere. So when the weekend finally came, she and Ekko sprinted out of the studio room into the bakery fifteen minutes earlier than usual.

Allie made two cups of coffee, fixed the hair she'd hurriedly pinned into a sloppy bun, and started cleaning. Ekko brought her cloths and anything else he could carry between his claws while Allie hopped between tables, humming a song she vaguely remembered hearing during her time in Green Creek. She was so focused on her task that she didn't notice until an hour later that, well, her boss was an hour late.

"Wait here," she told Ekko after she peeled a pear for him and tossed a bunch of almonds and raisins in a bowl.

Allie stood in front of the staircase that led to Dominic's floor. There had been no reason for her to go upstairs so far, and now she considered whether she was crossing any boundaries by climbing up uninvited. She perched on the third step and shouted, "Dominic?"

Silence was her only answer, so Allie jumped up a few more steps and tried again. "Dom?"

Nothing. Maybe he wasn't home? But Allie had been up for a while, and that would mean her boss had left in the middle of the night. Not impossible, but highly unlikely.

Worry trickled into her heart, and Allie gripped the wooden stair railing until her knuckles went white. She called for him one more time, and when the same quiet echoed back to her, she damned all protocol and climbed up to the end of the stairs.

The floor was open plan, with a den on the left that hosted a surprisingly tidy desk, the mostly empty living room except for a blue sofa and a floor-to-ceiling bookshelf, and a small kitchen identical to Allie's by the window. Between the living room and kitchen space was a closed white door. Allie walked to it and knocked softly, her heart pounding in her fist's rhythm.

"Dom?" Nothing. Allie knocked again, louder this time. "Dom, are you in there?"

A muffled groan.

That did *not* sound good. Allie shouted again, but no other sounds followed. By now, she was filled with dread thick as molasses, so she pounded at the door and yelled, "I'm coming in!"

As she turned the doorknob, Allie remembered Dominic had uttered the same words during her first night here, when she'd lost the fight with her sofa bed. The time when they were strangers seemed so long ago, and Allie didn't miss it one bit.

The bedroom was dark with the curtains drawn and the sunrise an hour away. Allie made out the form of the bed between two low nightstands, but she accidentally kicked the dresser next to the door. A standing lamp swung on top of it, and she caught it and turned it on. The warm light revealed a messy bed with a tall and broad form in it.

Dominic was still asleep.

That didn't seem right. In the mornings, he was energetic in his own broody way; for sure, he did *not* sleep in.

"Dom?" Allie said softly. The cover shifted with the weight under it, and Dominic groaned again. If it was her name, or a plea to the gods, Allie couldn't tell. She inched closer to his bed until she distinguished his face.

Sweat trickled on his forehead down his neck, messy locks of chestnut hair plastered to his temples and cheeks. Dominic had a mild frown, nothing like the one Allie was used to, the serious and threatening one that was seared into her memory. She called his name again, undoubtedly close enough for him to hear her now. When Dom made no sign that he'd heard her, Allie kneeled next to the bed and touched his skin with the back of her palm.

"You're burning up," she whispered. Allie went into caretaker mode as if she had flipped a switch. Sam was a sickly person, and she'd taken care of him during their years together. With the Silverbarks, it was considered part of her chores to attend to her sisters who had fallen ill. Allie's mind raced, already lined up with ingredients she needed for the medicine potions and the healing food Petra had taught her to make for these times.

She propped her hand on the edge of the bed to hoist herself up, but stopped when Dominic grabbed her by the wrist. His skin was scorching hot, yet his grip was firm, desperate. Allie used her free hand to remove Dom's hair from his face.

"I'll be right back, I promise." She caressed his spiky, unshaven cheeks for a moment longer, a selfish moment, then gently loosened her wrist from his fingers. This time, he didn't resist, his hand falling limp over the blanket.

"Hello?" Allie recognized Mia's voice coming from downstairs and rushed out of the room, back into the bakery. She found Dom's sister scratching Ekko between his wings as he lay sprawled on his chubby belly, looking as if he was in dragon heaven.

"Hi, Mia," Allie said, a little out of breath.

"Allie—what's wrong?"

"I think Dom's sick."

Mia's brows furrowed. "Sick how? He never gets sick."

"He's running a fever, and he's not exactly...lucid," Allie described. Mia's head jerked back.

"That has never happened before. At least, not that I know of. Dom's healthy as a horse, and the only times he gets sick it's just a mild cold."

Huh. That *was* strange, indeed. Allie inventoried their last couple of days, went through every moment that could have led to this, and found nothing.

Except...

"Mia, how much do you know about Dominic's power?"

"I only know he's a Mage. Every time I tried to pry details out of him, Dom came up with an excuse to leave," she said, and raised her arms in defeat.

"I think...I think he might have used too much power lately." It was a bold assumption, given that Allie knew as much as Mia did about a Mage's power. Yet she couldn't dismiss that during their practice last night, he looked...off. Spent. Allie hadn't thought too much about it at the time, but now...

Dominic hadn't looked *off*, he had looked exhausted.

"I don't know how his other missions as a Mage have gone, but I think he's trying too hard. Giving too much."

"Why?" Mia asked, perplexed. "Why would he consume himself so much?"

Allie offered her a sympathetic smile. "Because Sycamore Falls is his home, and he wants it to be safe." Even if no one else knows why he's back, Dom is putting pressure on himself more than the town would.

"*Que tonto*," Mia muttered. "What do you want to do?"

"I'll run to the market to get ingredients for medicine potions, and for soup too," Allie answered mechanically, then realized she might have overstepped assuming she'd be the one to take care of Mia's *brother*. "Unless you want to—"

"You're obviously more qualified than I am to take care of him," Mia said with a vulpine smile that Allie decided to log in her memory and dissect later. "How can I help?" Allie looked at her awkwardly, not feeling like bossing around Dom's sister. "Really, Allie. Don't overthink it. Just tell me."

"Okay." She nodded once, mentally listing everything that needed to be taken care of today. "What should we do about the bakery?"

"Closed," Mia declared. "The people of Sycamore Falls could do with a sweets and pastries break." Allie chortled.

"Can you put a sign on the door—"

"Done."

"Ekko—"

"You're coming with me today, you spoiled creature." The baby dragon flew to Mia's shoulder and nuzzled her jaw. Allie bopped his nose and warned him to be on his best behavior. "What else?"

"Oh. Brandon has his weekly pick-up." It was Allie's turn to smirk at her friend. "Please let him know we can't make it today."

Mia looked as if she'd asked her to run around the town naked. Allie didn't want to give her time to find an excuse not to talk to Brandon, so she grabbed Ekko's food from the kitchen and shoved it into Mia's arms as she guided her out of the bakery.

"You can bring the sign later!"

Mia mumbled something that made Ekko fly up and around her with loud chitters.

Allie grabbed a bowl of cold water from the kitchen and a clean cloth and rushed back upstairs. She sat by Dom's side for the next hour before the market opened, dabbing the skin on his face with the cold material until that unfamiliar frown disappeared and his features relaxed. Dominic fell into a calm sleep, and Allie left the cold cloth on his forehead before running to buy all the ingredients she needed.

The market was quiet this early in the morning, filled with heavy-lidded vendors who still found the energy to scowl at her. Allie was unfazed, her entire focus on Dominic and getting him better.

"What do you need so many herbs for, anyway?" the tall, gangly man with a thick red beard asked her. Allie had seen him around town a few times, mostly at the market, but he was one of the people who sneered at her less. Occasionally, only.

"Just tea," Allie said and offered him a strained smile as she took the bags from him. The last thing she wanted was to say the word *potions* and watch the townsfolk gather to run her out of the bakery and their town once and for all. The man harrumphed with a fake air of disinterest, and Allie took that as her sign to walk away.

Back at Dom's Sweets, Allie made ginger tea with honey and lemon, chicken broth with vegetables and semolina dumplings, and two different medicine potions which she infused with the purest of magic she could find in her heart. Still unsure if Dominic's illness was caused by him straining his power, Allie made one potion with echinacea and dried elderberries and the other with peppermint leaves, rose hips, and chamomile flowers. She added a pinch of salt together with the purple healing powder she'd brought from Pearls Fields.

Allie used a large wooden cutting board as a makeshift tray, placed a bowl of soup, a cup of tea, and two shots of the medicine potions on it, and prayed to whatever deities were listening that she wouldn't trip on the stairs.

She didn't, but it took her forever to climb up. Allie pushed the door open with her elbow, thanking her past self that she had had the common sense to leave it cracked.

"Knock, knock," she said softly, and was welcomed with a groan and the sound of rustling sheets. Finally, she placed the tray of hell on top of the dresser, next to the lamp, and went to check on her patient.

Big green eyes stared back at her.

"How are you feeling, Dom?" Allie asked, kneeling next to his bed. His eyes followed her until the angle made him drop her caring gaze, so he gathered the little energy he had and rolled on his side. A cloth fell on the bed, and Dominic grabbed it and rubbed his face with heavy, lazy moves.

"Like I've been run over by a truck. Twice." Dominic cleared the glass from his aching throat. "Did you..." He fluttered the material, and Allie snatched it and discarded it on the nightstand.

"I did. I also made tea, and soup, and some medicine potions you might not like, and I'm not leaving here until you eat and drink everything."

Dom's initial instinct was to argue. But he was so damn tired, and she was so damn beautiful, with that soft pout that made him want to grab her by the neck and kiss her senseless. If only he wasn't fucking sick—he'd get into the how and why of that later. Now this amazing woman stared at him with such determination in her eyes that he was glad to be lying down. He clutched the sheets to keep himself from twirling his finger around the red strand of hair that had escaped Allie's bun and fell freely over her cheek.

Such a lucky strand of hair.

"Fine," Dom uttered as he pushed himself up into a seating position. Even if his first reaction was to argue, Dominic quickly realized there were fewer and fewer things he would not do if Allie was the one to ask.

Especially when she smiled like *that*, wide and fully and only for him, and so bright that the sunrise had nothing on her.

He was gone for her. And he would not fight it a minute longer.

"Great!"

Allie roamed around the room in her tight jeans, and he ogled her shamelessly because he was just sick, not dead. Her pastel green sweater had a V-neckline that hid the crescent moon locket in a warm place that he had an intense urge to explore.

"Is your fever high again? You're flushed." Allie dropped a bowl of soup in his hands and felt his forehead with her cool, soft fingers. Dominic leaned into her touch like a greedy cat, fully aware of the reason he was flushed, and that it had little to do with his fever.

Despite his infatuated brain, he felt lightheaded and weak, so Dom leaned against the headboard and gobbled down the hot and tasty chicken soup, which had some weird puffy dumplings he hadn't tried before.

"Ginger tea," Allie said as she exchanged his empty bowl for a steamy cup of the tea he hated most in this world. But she smiled at his empty bowl, then at him, and Dominic was powerless. He'd bathe in the damn tea if it meant keeping that expression full of light on her face.

"This is horrible," he confessed, coughing through an entire cup. Allie grimaced.

"I know. I don't like it either, but it's helpful, I promise." She went to the dresser where she'd set up her mobile nursing station in his bedroom, then came back holding two shots of suspicious-looking liquids: one pink and one green. "Why are you sick?" There was an edge in her question, almost like she was scolding him.

"I—"

"Is it because you're overdoing it? Using too much of your power?" Again, that edgy, irritated voice. Dom hadn't thought about it, but he *never* got sick, so... She might have been right. He had stretched his power too much yesterday, but wrote it off as a mere busy, tiresome day that a night of sleep would fix. Apparently, he was wrong. When he didn't answer, Allie muttered, "I thought so," and shoved the green shot into his face. "That tastes horrible," she warned him and lifted her nose. Like she was a bit happy he was being punished for getting sick.

Beside himself, Dom smiled.

Allie cared about him.

"You're never smiling, but you're smiling now?" She dropped the pink shot on the nightstand, looking downright outraged. He couldn't help himself.

Dominic laughed. Loud and full, a belly laugh of joy provoked by the woman glowering at him. She watched him as if he was new and strange, and Dom supposed that wasn't far from the truth.

Allie turned on her heels, but he caught her wrist just in time.

"Allie, wait." He tugged at her hand until she sat down on the edge of his bed. "Don't leave." If the simple request wouldn't work, he wasn't above pleading like a child. Or holding her hostage, whatever worked.

The beautiful Witch scoffed and made a poor attempt to hide the smile playing at her lips.

"I'll get some food for myself and be right back," she assured him.

Reluctantly, he let her go, even if keeping her captive in his bedroom sounded like the best idea he had ever had.

But then she squeezed his fingers and smiled at him, and all was good in the world again.

Chapter 26

DO I HAVE SOMETHING ON MY FACE?

Allie decided to eat her turkey sandwiches downstairs, as there was no place to sit in Dom's room besides his bed. And she didn't know if her heart could take that crazy, deafening pounding again anytime soon. He'd just...*pulled* her to him, and it took Allie everything not to lean in and kiss him. Just a peck. At least on the forehead, or on his cheek, anywhere on him would really—

"Here's your sign." Mia stomped into the bakery and plastered a piece of paper on the glass door with a loud thump. She'd changed into one of her dark red sweater dresses that fit her like a glove and now matched the blush on her skin.

"What's up with you?" Allie asked with her mouth full.

"Nothing." Her friend looked at Allie until her scowl smoothed and turned into a pout. "Brandon."

"Oh?" Allie couldn't mask her surprise, her eyes the size of grapefruits. It was the first time Mia brought up Brandon on her own. "Do you want to...talk about it?" Allie asked slowly, keeping the food in her mouth still, as if the chewing sounds might scare Mia.

The Archivist studied her friend for a long moment, blinked

more than the average person, and opened and closed her mouth a few times.

"I'm good." She waved awkwardly and left the store in a hurry, almost tripping over the long skirt of her dress.

Allie wasn't hurt by it. After all, they were only recently friends, and—

The bakery door slammed open.

"He's just such a... Ugh!" Mia paced around the floor like a lion in a cage, gesticulating with her hands and yelling in a language Allie didn't speak. She had no idea how to console her friend, much less when she didn't really understand the problem, so Allie did what she knew best.

She snuck a cookie between her fingers and approached her friend with careful steps, stopping whenever Mia's eyes fell on her. When she was close enough, Allie gently grabbed her by the elbow and stuffed the cookie in her mouth.

Mia chewed with wide eyes, a faint smile shadowing her full lips. Allie grabbed her by the arms and fixed her most intense gaze on her.

"Do you want to talk about it?"

"No?" She deflated, then her brown eyes followed the narrow hallway to the staircase. "How's Dom?"

Allie's mind was flooded with his rich laugh, a sound so whole and genuine, and so precious from someone like him. How the skin around his eyes had crinkled, and how his lips had parted with the large grin, how his cheeks stretched and crowded his eyes.

"He's surprisingly energetic for a magically depleted Mage."

Mia wiggled her eyebrows, a smirk wiping the grimace off her face. "I might have an idea why."

"So did you want to tell me about Brandon?" Allie countered, feeling her face heat. Mia's smirk died a swift death.

"Mean." She hugged Allie and left, promising to return later to check on her brother and eat more of her cookies.

Allie felt a little bad for feeding Dominic only tea and soup, so she plated two cookies and took them with her after tidying the place up.

When she returned to Dominic's room, she found him sound asleep. Between standing by the door and sitting on the floor, Allie didn't know where to place herself in *her boss's bedroom*. After awkwardly looking around for a moment, Allie decided to go to the living room and perch on the blue sofa.

"Hmm." The hoarse purr made Allie stop in her tracks.

"Dom?"

"Come here," he said in a thick, sleep-coated voice. Allie approached the bed, dropped the cookie plate on the nightstand, and sat down on the edge of the mattress, so far away from him that she was seconds from falling to the ground on her ass. She checked his fever, which had decreased but was still higher than healthy.

"I'm going to—" Dominic shifted and hauled her into his arms, snuggling her under the cover. A move too fast and sneaky for someone who was sick. "What's happening?" Allie asked, feeling her entire body solidify like a brick wall.

Dominic pulled her closer, lining the back of her body with his front, his big, heavy arm hugging her around her middle. He was hot like a furnace, and Allie wondered how much of it was from the fever, and how much was just...Dom.

"You smell so good," he drawled out, propping his chin in the crook of her neck. His prickly short beard sent shivers all over her body, and her heartbeat sprinted to the front of her chest.

Allie discreetly pinched the side of her arm, hard enough that she barely suppressed a hiss.

Wide awake.

"Was this your first medicine potion?" He hummed in response. "I think I made it too strong. Maybe it wasn't the best for you," she whispered and attempted to break free. Dominic's hold tightened, squishing her to him with no intention of letting her go.

"You are the best for me." His voice was deep and guttural, but it was the statement that made Allie's heart quiver and turn into mush. Her skin was on fire and not because of Dom's heat, but because of the way he drew lazy circles with his thumb on her abdomen, and the way he nuzzled her neck with his nose and chin, and the way he was *touching her everywhere*.

It was everything she ever wanted. And more.

Allie took a deep breath and relaxed, melting into him like clay into the perfect mold. And she fell asleep.

Allie spiraled into the middle of next week.

After she woke up in Dom's arms, specifically him lying on his back while she was sprawled over him, Allie quietly left the room before he woke up. She went outside to the forest clearing with practice on her mind, but ended up wearing a path in the grass by the river, shivering and gritting her teeth in the sunless, windy cold.

About two hours into her overthinking session, which she'd surely win a medal for if it ever became a sport, Allie went back to the bakery and found Dominic at the counter, flipping through his notebook, sweat covering his pale skin. It took little effort to coax him back into bed with the offer to read him next week's schedule aloud.

Allie swept their sleeping together under the rug, at least until Dominic felt better. She wanted and did not want to know his thoughts and feelings. If his brain had been hazy with the medicine potion, if his judgement had been inhibited, her heart might break. But if he wanted her there, if he meant the words he'd said that fed her soul...

"You are the best for me."

So Allie postponed the conversation until the next week.

Mia had come by that same night and teamed up with Allie to convince Dom to keep the bakery closed for the entire weekend. Brandon had brought a jar of honey and some fresh lemons, insisting his friend should rest longer. The three of them managed the feat, so Dom's Sweets had stayed closed for two days.

At the beginning of the week, Dominic was up and about in the morning as usual. He wasn't back to his full strength, but he had declared that, "There's no way in hell I'm keeping this place closed a minute longer."

The week was busier with the past weekend's deliveries and orders being rescheduled, and Dom and Allie barely had time to grab a bite, let alone talk about their feelings. On the one hand, by prolonging this, Allie's heart was *somewhat* safe. On the other hand, it killed her that she didn't know what Dom thought about the weekend's...activities.

At the end of their shift on the fourth day of the week, Allie resolved to talk to Dom. Her heart couldn't take any more uncertainty. She did about a dozen different pathetic pep talks in the mirror before she came looking for him.

"I'm leaving for the night to meet with my parents," he said in a rushed voice before Allie got to open her mouth.

"Is everything okay?"

Dom sighed. "Mia told them I got sick, and now they want live proof that I'm fine." He seemed to struggle reconciling the inconvenience of travel with the clear desire to visit his parents, who had recently moved to a small village a couple towns after Rocky Hills. Allie wished she knew such struggles. "Should be back tomorrow morning early enough to open together."

"No rush," she said, swallowing all of the words she'd prepared.

Dom came back the next day, an hour before opening time. Allie had baked and prepared everything she could before her boss stepped inside the kitchen.

"Everything okay with your parents?" she asked, giving him an involuntary once-over. Dom had nodded, back to his usual amount of grumpiness. A good sign.

He had paired his deep green turtleneck with dark jeans and black boots, the sweater material so tight that Allie discerned the form of his muscles when he gathered his hair in a bun. When he tied his apron. When he kneaded the croissant dough.

"I want to try a new filling today. For the croissants," he clarified. "My mother gave me an idea." That small smile that Allie had glimpsed once or twice twitched around his lips for half a second.

"Is she a baker, too?" A curt nod. "How can I help?" she asked enthusiastically.

"You can taste it when it's ready."

Allie fed Ekko a bowl of grapes and pistachios and sent him to their room, then made herself useful by handing Dom ingredients, cloths, and utensils.

He labored around the kitchen with an adorable frown, dedicated to getting this filling right. Ten dirty spoons were scattered around the table as Dominic tasted the cream at different steps in the process.

"I think it's ready," Dom said after what felt like an entire day, filling two croissants with the hazelnut cream that smelled divine and made Allie's mouth water. She had been busy cleaning the worktable when her boss shoved a croissant in her face. "Taste this."

"What?" Allie looked between his face and the pastry in his hand. She tried to grab it from him, but Dom evaded her, bringing the croissant to her mouth.

"Bite." It was a command, uttered in a thick, urgent tone.

"Bite?" she parroted, perplexed. Any other time Dom had her taste samples, he'd either offer her a plate, or a piece on a tray, or point to a fork or a spoon. Now he nodded once, narrowing his green eyes at her.

Allie bit into the pastry.

"Mmm," she moaned, the sweet and nutty cream wonderfully soft and rich in her mouth. Dominic's eyes were glued to her lips, as if they held a secret he had to uncover to save his life. He took a step closer to her. And another, until his leathery, manly scent enveloped her, and she tipped her chin up to keep his smoldering gaze. "Do I have something on my face?" Allie asked dumbly, incapable of forming another coherent thought.

Dominic scoffed. He lifted his arm and cupped Allie's cheek, brushing his thumb from the corner of her mouth to the middle of her lower lip, his calloused finger harsh against her soft skin. He was touching her like that again, intimately, setting her nerves on a fire she couldn't control.

"Dom…" Allie whispered, unsure what to say next. Her mind was blurry with heated emotions and the thousands of scenarios she'd spent all week overthinking.

"Allie," Dominic said like a plea. A prayer. His eyes darkened with something dangerous, watching her like she was something to eat.

Then he took his hazelnut cream-covered thumb to his mouth and licked it off in a luscious move, swirling his tongue around the finger without dropping Allie's gaze. Green fire burned in his eyes, his nostrils flared, and he moaned like he was tasting it for the first time. This image of him was hot-ironed into Allie's brain for eternity.

"Hello? Is anyone here?" A voice from the bakery carried to them, breaking whatever spell the powerful Mage had put her under. Allie fumbled with her apron, all too interested in the clean state of her fingers.

"Coming," Dominic growled, low and annoyed. He left the kitchen muttering words about locked doors and murder.

§◆

Dominic had been surprised at the amount of restraint he'd shown by not licking the cream off Allie's lips, especially as she parted them and fixed him with that innocent-but-secretly-naughty-for-the-right-man look. And he was. He was the right man for her, and she knew it by the glistening desire that sparked in her eyes. That look had been the confirmation he was waiting for, if sleeping together had not been enough of a sign.

But he wanted to be sure. Sure that she hadn't stayed with him the past weekend just because he was sick. Sure that when he kissed her, she'd let him.

Brandon leaned against the edge of the counter with his stupid grin and his arms crossed, creasing the old, brown leather jacket he wore.

"What."

"It's impossible you're already this broody," Brandon remarked. "You're not even open yet."

"Exactly," Dom snarled. "So why are you here?"

"Why is your face red?"

"It's not." Dominic rounded the counter and draped his arm over his friend's shoulders, guiding him back to the exit. "Thanks for stopping by."

Brandon dug his heels into the ground and stopped them in place. "As much as I love the warm welcome, I'm here for a reason." Dominic doubted it was important enough to interrupt his moment with Allie.

"Hey, Dom?" Both men turned to face the counter, where Allie stood holding his notebook and a pencil. Her face was still deliciously red, and her chest rose with uneven breaths that told him she was as affected as him. His smirk faded when she said, "Brandon. Good morning."

His friend looked between her and Dominic and gave him the smuggest look he'd ever seen on Brandon's face. He greeted Allie, eyes still on Dom. Allie raised her index finger and turned back to the kitchen.

"I see," Brandon said, the word longer than necessary.

"You see nothing. Why are you here?"

"Next weekend I'm going to visit the Sanders, and I want you to come with. Mrs. Sanders keeps asking about you, and she insists I'm the one who doesn't let you tag along." They scoffed in unison at the silliness of the thought.

"I'll come," Dom rushed the words out and urged Brandon to the door again.

"Wait!" Allie jogged from the kitchen. "Here." She offered Brandon a brown paper bag, then stepped closer to Dominic. Like her place was next to him.

Damn right it is.

Her scent curled around him, and he formed tight fists to keep from pulling her into his arms.

"Thanks, Allie." Brandon opened the bag and pulled out a croissant, biting greedily into it. "Hmm. What's in it?" he asked around the full bite.

"Hazelnut cream," Allie answered, then swept her gaze from Dominic's fist up his arm, to his lips and eyes. "My new favorite flavor."

Chapter 27

STAY AWAY FROM MY GIRL

Allie decided to open herself up to whatever was happening between her and Dom. No more excuses like her leaving, him being her boss, and the hundreds of others she'd conjured to fight this. His latest flirty actions gave her the courage to approach this as she deeply, truly wanted to: unafraid and unapologetically herself.

It had been different with Sam, and as much as Allie didn't want to think about him, she had to remember their time together to make sense of her growing feelings for Dom.

She'd met Sam as he was passing through the Pearls Fields market. They both reached for the same piece of rhubarb at the vegetable stall, and he smiled at her brightly, curiously. Unlike everyone else, who scowled at the sight of her red curls. His short blond hair was tousled by the warm wind, and he shook her hand with his tawny palm. Sam had been on his way back to Green Creek and was supposed to be in Pearls Fields only for two days.

But two days turned into two weeks, then two months, and Allie loved having someone close in her life. Ever since Petra had passed, and with her power still not manifested so she could join a coven, she'd been pretty much on her own. Solitude was not the worst curse, but it felt like it had been once there was another soul she could share her life with. Good food, walks in the forest, lying in the shade on a hot day... Everything was better shared. So when Sam asked Allie to come with him to Green Creek, she said yes without giving it another thought.

Allie loved everything about Green Creek except the heat, which was thicker than in Pearls Fields. It was the first time she experienced new magic, and Sam was there every step of the way, teaching her everything he'd learned while living with it, as someone without magic.

Most of all, she loved waking up next to Sam, his blue eyes kind and full of love. She loved his long fingers raking through her hair, the sweet words he murmured, and the fact that he made her laugh. Sam introduced her to his friends, found a few recurring clients for her potions. Offered her a life. One that had never been on Allie's mind, not even in her wildest dreams.

Then he asked her to marry him, and she said yes, thinking it was the easiest yes of her life.

The day her power manifested—now better known as the day the seal had started to break—Allie had been thrilled to share this with Sam. He knew she'd been struggling with her late manifestation, yet he was never keen on broaching the subject. Allie wrote this off as a man who didn't have magic and could not fully understand the importance of this. The magnitude of her pain. But that day came, and Allie laughed and cried and shivered with excitement and fear while she told him all about it.

Allie would never forget his grimace, the disappointment and disgust that took over his features. She'd never seen him like this, and it was... It was as if by succeeding at this, she had failed him.

Sam broke their engagement and kicked her out, appalled by the prospect of living with a Witch. Allie had argued that she had always been a Witch, would always be one, and why was he reacting as if she'd kept it a secret? He had always known, from the first day he met her, when he'd said, "I love your fiery hair."

Allie had never known betrayal like this, cold and bitter and disgusting. She joined the Silverbarks, and as much as she wanted to tell her sisters about Sam, she was glad she didn't. He didn't deserve to be brought into her life anymore, not even in conversation.

And Allie was even more sure of this after she met Dom.

Dom, who took her in without giving it another thought.

Dom, who treated her power outbursts with such care and interest that her heart had expanded like a hot air balloon.

Dom, who had been so invested into her struggles that he found the freaking seal on her power.

Dom, who was coming to her now, holding a tower of boxes and wearing the shadow of a smile she was slowly, steadily falling in love with.

❦

"Can you help me with some of these deliveries today?" Dom asked Allie reluctantly. They were busier than usual with the bakery being closed last weekend, and he couldn't manage everything by himself. And he didn't have to. He had Allie.

"Of course I can."

"Are you sure you know your way around town?" Dom tried to keep his worry out of his voice but failed.

"I have been here for five weeks now." Allie smirked with the confidence of someone who had lived here their entire life. Dom had a few ideas about what he could do to that sweet smirk, how he'd unravel her perfectly tied bun and pull his fingers through her red locks.

Instead, he cleared his throat and gave Allie three of the six boxes and said, "The addresses are on top of the lid. They're all on this side of the river. If you get lost, ask for directions." Allie nodded and took the boxes, but he didn't miss the flash of hurt and doubt that lit her brown eyes. He almost heard her thinking "Do you think anyone would help me?"

Dominic hated everybody in this town except the handful of people who had proved they lacked prejudice. How could anyone not see Allie for the kind, caring, selfless woman that she was? He knew the town had taken a hit and some people had gotten hurt because of a Witch, but Allie was nothing like her. Nothing at all.

Fate had a wicked sense of humor, and Dom had been left with deliveries to people he knew firsthand had a thing against Allie. He handled them with quick and rude grumbles, but no one seemed too fazed about his short fuse as it was on par with his normal temper.

His last delivery was to the mayor's townhouse, and Dom used the back entrance as usual. He was walking out from the side alley into the main street when a head of bright red hair caught his eye, attached to a shuddering form that hugged her jacket close to her body. Allie kept saying she liked fall in Sycamore Falls even when she was shivering, and Dom couldn't wait to be the one who warmed her up.

Dominic strolled to her but stopped at the edge of the house when he noticed a strange man approach Allie with a dumb smile on his face. The man went in for a hug, but Allie took two steps back and held her hand out. She looked shaken up, lips parted in a way that wasn't to his liking.

Dominic tried to quench the urge to suck the air out of the idiot's lungs and make him fall at her feet. What was the reason behind her trembling eyes? Fear? Aversion?

He didn't want to take any risks when it came to Allie, so Dom did the thing he usually avoided. He Read the tall, blond man facing the woman of his dreams, and when his magic curled and twisted around his aura, Dom had everything he needed.

It was the man's unlucky day, because Dominic's rage had been fueled since early in the morning. And he was on the wrong side of things.

❧

"Sam?" Allie asked pointlessly as her palm hit the middle of his chest. His name was like dry sand on her tongue. There was no doubt that Sam stood there, staring at her with those familiar blue eyes, daring to smile kindly at her. "What are you doing here?"

"I've been looking for you. I just want to talk, Als," he answered, like it was the simplest, most logical thing in the world. She hated being called "Als," but he loved it, and Allie had let it go because it hadn't been that important to her.

Now it was.

"Alecsandra," she corrected him icily, crossing her arms and taking another step away. "I have nothing to say to you."

"Don't be like that, Als."

"Don't call me that!"

"I made a mistake," he blurted out. "I shouldn't have let you go. I'm sorry."

"I don't care." Her voice was wobblier than she wanted, but she struggled to tamp down the stinging sensation behind her eyes and nose, the lump in her throat. She didn't want to give him the satisfaction of seeing her cry.

Actually, she did not want to cry at all, because Sam didn't deserve any more of her tears.

Sam's head jerked back, his brows furrowing in confusion. Did he expect her to obediently jump into his arms and thank him for saving her from a Sam-less life?

"Why are you being like this?"

"Why am I—" Sizzling hot anger overwhelmed her and quieted all other emotions Sam had stirred inside her. "You *discarded* me, Sam. As soon as my power manifested, you kicked me out because, and I quote, you 'won't make a family with a Witch.'" He flinched. "You knew I had nowhere else to go, but you didn't care because you were scared of something you couldn't control."

"I was not... I am not..." He reached for her again, and Allie backstepped. "Stop running away from me!" Sam shouted, an ugly, desperate sound paired with a crazy look in his bulging blue eyes. His predatory fingers would have grabbed her arm if not for the hand that grasped and bent his wrist at a painful angle before pushing him away with a force backed by magic.

"Dom?" Allie breathed. She traced his arm up to his handsome face, now twisted with wrath and revulsion.

"Don't touch her," Dominic growled.

"This is a private conversation," Sam barked, rubbing his wrist. Dominic took one threatening step toward him, and to his credit, Sam didn't back away.

"Is it?" he asked, his voice coated with malice. "A private conversation?" This time, Allie noticed his chin slightly tilted her way. She shook her head.

"Of course it is!" Sam bellowed.

"I am *not* talking to you." Dominic didn't take his eyes off Sam, his back ramrod straight, feet apart, forming a comforting wall between Allie and her stupid past.

She inched closer to him and took his hand shyly, but Dom wasted no time interlacing their fingers together. He squeezed her hand in his strong palm and pulled her closer to him.

"I'll take that as a no." Dom took another careful step forward, keeping Allie close to his side. Not behind him. Next to him.

Dominic's eyes turned to slits and he snarled the words, "It was you." The wind picked up around them, ruffling wild strands of hair around Sam's face. Allie's curls didn't move. "You're the one who put the seal on her."

Allie stopped breathing.

For a long, slow moment that stretched around her like hot glue, she felt like she was underwater and could not breathe. Sam had... He had...

"What?" she mouthed, unsure if any sounds came out.

The man who she had loved with her entire heart, who she had trusted, who had *allegedly* loved her back—he was the reason she went through that hell. He was the reason she endangered the people she cared about, he was the reason she had suffered, he was the reason for her pain, he, he, he...

Warm, calloused skin closed tighter around her fingers as Dom tugged at her hand. He pulled insistently until her side was plastered to his, until her brown eyes met his greens, until he pulled her out of the water.

Allie found enough rage and strength steeped into his eyes that she could borrow some. With every breath, she was letting go of the shock that had taken hold of her. When she moved her eyes to Sam's, he looked at her as if he was having a heart attack.

"Als—"

"How?" She didn't stutter. "How?" Allie moved her thumb over Dom's hand before letting it go, and took a step further. "You don't have any magic."

Sam looked anywhere but at her.

"I... I... I do have...magic," he muttered, scratching his head and taking a step back. Allie took another step toward him.

She felt that power behind her chest rattle, as if it recognized the hand that had suppressed it. It took half a thought for Allie to unspool that power and fill her hands with living fire. Out of the corner of her eye, she noticed Dom cross his arms across his chest, a wicked expression covering his face.

Sam's eyes almost popped out of their sockets as he put more distance between them.

"Whoa whoa whoa, wait a minute, Als, let me—"

"What?" she shouted, walking to him, the comfortable fire crawling up her arms. "Let you what? Live?" That intrinsic Witch hate Allie had never known, that malice her sisters seemed to be born with, blossomed in her chest. For the first time, Allie felt like an authentic Witch. "Why should I?"

Sam walked backward until he tripped and fell at her feet.

"Please. I love you." Allie scoffed. "I'm telling the truth. I did fall in love with you, and you were not like the other Witches, and I thought that maybe if you hadn't manifested... Maybe you never would be like them."

"Then why did you bother to seal my power?" she yelled.

"Because I was afraid! My father was poisoned by a Witch, and I..."

A dark laugh bubbled out of Allie's throat. Not the first or last time she had been judged because of her kind. She stopped and looked at the pitiful man as he rose to his feet, conflict and bitterness filling his blue eyes.

Heavy steps crunched on the pavement behind her as Dom came to stand at her side. He was close enough to tell her he did not fear her fire.

"Do you want to fry him, or can I suffocate him?" he asked nonchalantly.

Allie wanted to give the thought more consideration, but that would just make her one of the Witches she strived to be different from. She sighed long and loud and called her fire back into its place.

"It would be a waste of magic either way," Allie spit through her teeth.

"I don't mind," Dom said with a hint of irony that should have scared her. If anything, it thrilled her.

"Als..." Sam dared to reach for her again, but Dom stepped in his path, and the next thing she knew, Sam was back on his knees, clawing at his throat. Gasping for air.

"Stay away from my girl, you filthy piece of trash."

"Samuel!" A shout, followed by rushed footsteps. Then a man knelt next to her struggling ex.

Jared Finn grabbed Sam by the elbow and helped him up as Dom released his magic hold on him. The mayor's son threw them a reprimanding look that fell off his smug face once he met Dominic's eyes.

"I guess scum sticks together," Dom muttered. "If either of you come near her again, consider that your last moment on Earth."

Then he draped his arm around Allie's shoulders and guided her away. Away from her unfortunate past, from a man who had made her doubt her worth, and into the broad Maple Street that housed the bakery where she had found herself again.

❧

Dominic's blood boiled for the rest of the day. He should have just murdered the moron who threw away the best thing that had ever happened to him. The Diviners' Order did not forbid Mages from committing such actions, although it was frowned upon and viewed as a power trip. He couldn't care less. Let every damn person in this world frown upon him. As long as Allie smiled at him, he did not care.

Back at the bakery, Allie made coffee and sat him down.

"I owe you an explanation," she said, hand wrapped around the hot mug.

"You don't owe me anything," Dom argued. But she

countered that by saying she *wanted* to tell him, so he shut his mouth and listened.

At the end of her story, Dominic was pacing around the bakery, one step away from running out to find the scumbag and make him one with the ground.

"I can't believe it was him," Dom hissed.

"With every moment, I can believe it more and more." Allie chuckled. But it was dark and oily, and he hated it.

Dominic sat back down and took her hand in his, holding her warm gaze. He said nothing more and let everything he felt pour out of his eyes. He knew Allie would get it. She could read him like an open book, no magic involved.

"Thanks," she breathed. Dom nodded, pressing his lips together, grinding his jaw so hard his head hurt.

Allie let out a watery sigh. If she shed a single tear, he would kill him. Dominic allowed Allie a few moments to gather her thoughts, and no tears came into sight. Relief like never before overwhelmed him that she was not crying over that fucking clown.

"How did you know?"

"I Read him and recognized his magic, the one I found woven with the seal." He explained to Allie that she hadn't been able to Read her ex because he had a Mage place a shield around him. This practice was borderline illegal, and he couldn't wait to report it to the Order, so they could trace the Mage who had sullied their power with a lowlife like him.

"So he and Jared knew each other. Do you think he's the one who told Sam I was here?"

"Probably." Dom moved his thumb lazily over Allie's knuckles. "The Witch Jared was dating was from Green Creek, and he spent a lot of time there."

Fucking Jared. He'd find a way to run him out of town, back to whatever hole he'd crawled out of when he returned to Sycamore Falls. He would run for mayor, and make Brandon run for mayor, too, and threaten the townsfolk to permanently close the bakery and stop the farm supplies if they dared vote for Jared. As much as nepotism was a thing in small towns like Sycamore Falls, if Dom had put it in his mind to change that, he would.

Even if he had to reveal to the entire world that he was the Mage in charge of fixing the broken magic on the sycamores.

Chapter 28

YOU'RE SMITTEN

Allie refused to let Sam's presence mess with her mood more than it already had. She allowed herself to feel sad and process the pain and rage of her past for the next few days, even if her boss kept her occupied during the day, as well as at night.

Dominic had Allie practice jumping through fire hoops that turned smaller and narrower every night to help her deal with the fear of getting burned. The night she stepped into that huge fire had been a win for Allie, but not enough to casually put her hand in any nearby flames.

Recently, since she was quicker to finish her bakery tasks, Allie stole half an hour every morning to walk around town and guess at places a Witch would put her curses on. She suggested some isolated areas in Sycamore Falls for Dom to check the magic disruption, but they had all been frustrating dead ends.

Into the middle of the week, Dominic and Allie were hard at work decorating Dom's Sweets, inside and out. They had missed the weekend the entire town decorated for Hallows Eve, and last week they'd been crazy busy catching up on the piled-up orders. This week, they were out of excuses and both exasperated by every customer who came in and pointed at the lack of holiday spirit in the place. Allie knew it was just a matter of time before Dom exploded and kicked someone out, so that morning she waited for him, coffees ready, hands on her hips, and demanded they start decorating the place. Her boss halfheartedly agreed, less due to a secret love for Hallows Eve and more knowing that it would get everyone off his back.

Dom retrieved two boxes labeled "Hallows Eve stuff" from the storage room, and Allie dug through them curiously. She found fake spider webs, bones that formed tall skeletons, sticky bats and spiders, a couple of black cat statues, and strings of hanging candles.

"These are great!" She pulled the decorations out of the boxes, glancing at Dom, who scowled at one of the cat statues as if it hissed at him. "Can we also carve pumpkins and make jack-o'-lanterns?" Allie asked with the enthusiasm of a child, forgetting for a minute who she was talking to.

Dominic studied her with unblinking eyes. Allie should know better by now. He did not seem like a man who would *carve pumpkins*. Yet he surprised her by saying, "Sure. Whatever you want."

Allie's heart raced, and she clapped her hands with delight.

"So..." Dominic cleared his throat, looking uncomfortable. "Why do Witches like Hallows Eve this much?"

"Really?" Her eyes widened, immediately filled with joy to share this with Dom. Allie talked while they decorated the inside of the shop. "It's different for all of us, and it depends on the Witch's power. Some love it because it's the night when the veil between worlds is the thinnest." Allie shuddered at the thought. "Some love it because magic is at its strongest, and they get to experiment with spells made possible by this increased magic. Others love it because their visions are most clear during Hallows Eve night." Allie's voice was strained as she rose onto her tiptoes to reach the corner of a painting and hang a piece of web around it.

Strong hands grabbed her waist and lifted her in the air. Allie gasped, covering her mouth with her free hand.

"Why do you love it?" Dom spoke into her back, face buried into her purple sweater. Allie fumbled with the web, the stupid thing evading her trembling fingers. It took her a while to get it in place, but Dominic was a concrete statue around her, not moving or asking her to hurry up. Eventually, he put her down, but his hands lingered on her waist, turning her skin into goosebumps.

"I..." She turned to face him slowly, his hands still on her middle. She rested her palms on his lower arms. "Because my mom had a unique tradition for Hallows Eve, and every year I prayed for my power to manifest so I could do it with her." Allie swallowed the rocks that threatened to close her throat. "She was also an elemental Witch, and she used the night's magic to balance out her power: if she had used too much during the year, she could charge herself. If she had extra, she would give some back." At Dom's confused look, Allie added, "It's like feeding the moon with your excess power. It's balance."

"Sounds like a great tradition," Dom whispered. "I'm sorry you didn't get to do it with your mom." Allie offered him a small smile, tightening her grip on his arms.

"I know she'll be there with me, but...I still don't want to do it alone." Her eyes lowered to Dom's tree tattoo, and she traced the thick, inky branches with her index finger. "This is a great tattoo," she muttered, bewitched by the colorless image that looked so good and told so much.

"I'll be there with you, if you want," Dom offered. His green eyes followed her greedy finger around his skin. "I've always felt like the trees here gave me the power to become a Mage. With my missions, I've traveled all around the world, yet my power is never fuller, stronger than it is here."

Allie smiled. "I'd love to share the Hallows Eve night tradition with you."

She would love nothing more than continuing her mom's tradition with Dom by her side. The Mage smiled softly and nodded his agreement.

§.

Dominic was on his way out of Mia's shop when he ran into Brandon. His sister wanted to hear all about the altercation rumored to have happened between him and Jared last weekend. The people of Sycamore Falls had a way with words, and the scene had been twisted horrifically into a bloody fistfight. Mia listened to the true story, including parts he'd learned from Allie about the scum of the earth, then proceeded to swear colorfully in her mother tongue for at least ten minutes. She threatened Jared's presence in her store, promising to sic the hungriest books on him if he ever had the audacity to show his face.

"Morning, Dom," Brandon said, his eyes roaming around the bookstore. Something had been going on between Brandon and Mia for a while, but it wasn't his business. It would become his business if Mia got hurt, but Brandon was his best friend and knew better than that.

"Did you save me some pumpkins for carving?" Dom asked.

"What? Are you running a fever again?" Brandon inquired, his interest switching from the shop to his friend. "You have never, *not once*, asked me to save you carving pumpkins. Ever. Do I need to remind you in how many years since we've known each other, you have *not* asked me to do that?"

Dom knew his friend was babbling some nonsense, but he heard nothing since Allie came out of the bakery across the street and meandered around the yard, sweeping the leaves and rearranging the spider web on the door for the thousandth time.

"Ah, that's why you want pumpkins now," Brandon mused. "You're smitten."

"You're ugly."

"Is this how you talk to your pumpkin provider?"

"Did you want me to say please?" Dom raised his eyebrows.

"Four okay?" Brandon took out a small notepad and a pencil.

"Six."

"You're really smitten, then."

"I really, really am," Dom admitted, his eyes still trailing Allie around the yard. She looked like she belonged there, surrounded by the fall colors that matched her hair. Next to his bakery. With him.

Brandon clapped him on the shoulder. "Really glad about all these reallys, Dom."

The day before the weekend was eerily quiet, and Allie spent her downtime in the bakery reading up on "Baking for Dummies." It was, of course, easier and much more enjoyable when Dom was teaching her in the kitchen, but Allie had slacked on enriching her knowledge on her own. She was flipping through "no-bake recipes" when Mia walked in, clad in a denim jacket with a thick scarf around her neck, brown leather boots, and jeans similar to Allie's.

"Come with me to Harper's coffee shop this weekend," Mia said, leaning over the counter and sticking her nose in Allie's book. "Her pumpkin spice latte special is finally for sale. Later than it was supposed to be," she muttered. "Besides. You've been here, what? Almost six weeks now?" Allie did the quick math and nodded, ignoring the pang of anxiety that came with the thought of her seven-week deadline. "And you've never been to Harp's."

Mia had a point, but Allie couldn't help but think about the reasons she kept more to herself during her time here. For one, she had been very busy with work. A huge part of her free time went to practicing, especially before she got her power under control. But if she were honest with herself, Allie hadn't frequented these places because she felt like it wasn't her place. Witches didn't join activities, or go to restaurants, or participate in society more than sourcing potions, doing Readings, or anything else their magic could contribute to someone's life. They were cunning creatures, and they lived socially only amongst themselves.

But Allie did not want to be like that.

"I'd love to," she told Mia. Her happy smile was worth however many sneers and scowls she'd get by going with her.

"Hey, Dom!" Mia shouted, angling her head to peer down the narrow hallway. Her brother stepped out of the kitchen, his black apron dusted with flour and speckled with dough, hands up like a surgeon's, covered with something gooey.

"What?" His question was less barked than usual, and Allie smiled at seeing him soften for Mia. Dominic blew a wild lock of deep brown hair out of his face. Once. Twice.

Allie chuckled. "Come here." As if under a spell, Dom leaned toward her, then checked himself, confusion filling his beautiful green eyes. Allie twirled his hair around her finger, which was entirely selfish and totally unnecessary, then placed the naughty strand behind his ear, combing it with her fingers to make sure it stayed put. "There."

Mia cleared her throat loudly, making them flinch and veer away from each other.

"We're going to Harp's this weekend. Come with us," Mia told more than asked her brother, pinning him with a daunting look.

"Brandon and I are going to the Sanders' this weekend."

"After you're back, then," she said with a dramatic eye roll.

"Fine." Dom turned back to the kitchen, though not before moving his eyes over Allie's face, down her neck, over her sweater, and back up.

"He's in a good mood," Mia noted. "Any ideas why?"

"None whatsoever," Allie lied, but she couldn't contain her smile, or the way her cheeks heated. "Let me tell you about this recipe."

Allie's attempt to draw Mia's attention to anything other than her brother failed spectacularly, and Mia dragged her out of the bakery, shouting to Dom that she was stealing Allie for a walk. A string of grumbles followed them out the door from the back of the shop.

They strolled down Maple Street to the huge park where the Harvest Festival would take place next week. It felt like yesterday Allie had followed Mia here to sign them up for the best booths. The weather had gotten colder and the days shorter, but Allie loved every minute of it. She was still in awe of the burnt orange landscape, the clean, crisp air, and the chilly mornings with her hot cups of coffee. Her favorite discovery was stepping on crunchy leaves, so she would sometimes walk funny to get the best ones.

"What's on your mind?" Mia asked her.

"I just love this place," Allie sighed. "Despite everyone counting the minutes until I leave."

"Pfft." Mia waved a hand. "Don't worry about that. People here hate outsiders, period. I know, I know. Your witchy roots don't help, but still." Her friend nudged her. "You could always stay longer, *amiga*."

Allie had a thousand arguments against that statement, all flocking to her mind at once. Yet none broke free because she still had a little time left here, and she did not want to waste any moment thinking about what waited for her after she left Sycamore Falls.

She smiled at Mia and changed the subject, and her friend did not bring it up again.

They checked the two booths for Mia's and Dom's shops, and the Archivist took note to bring extra shelves for the discounted books for the festival. Allie inspected the bakery booth, amazed by the space and the display case carved into it.

"It's turning out really well," Allie exclaimed. Two long rows of booths faced each other, and nestled between them were wooden tables and benches, a few chairs, and bins. Poles were being installed to accommodate the fairy lights. A myriad of hay bales were scattered around, surrounded by and piled with different kinds of pumpkins. It was still a work in progress, but Allie could see the magic that would come to life once everything was done. "What's going on there?" She pointed to the eastern side of the park, where a huge red and white striped vinyl canvas covered the ground.

"They're putting up a canopy to create a dance floor. There will be a band, and their instruments need to be covered in case of rain."

Allie thought about the last time she had been on the dance floor. With Dom. The flirtatious comments that transpired between them.

She only had two weeks left here, so she should be honest with him. Would it be the end of the world if Dom rejected her? Probably. But she would go back to Pearls Fields and forget about her embarrassment. With time.

The alternative, where he would *not* reject her, made all the hypothetical pain worth it, and her stomach filled with butterflies.

It was decided, then.

Allie would tell Dom how she felt when he returned from his trip with Brandon.

Chapter 29

THIS IS HIS LIFE

Dom and Allie worked quickly and quietly to prepare the pastries and bread before her boss left with Brandon. Allie didn't miss all the glances Dom stole at her through the silence, as she was doing some heavy glancing of her own. Dominic would be back later in the afternoon, so he decided to post a shorter schedule for Dom's Sweets today. Allie was happy to run the place until the lunch rush hour faded, then lock up and go on her daily walk through town.

Frustration bottled up inside her with every failed attempt at finding the place cursed by the Witch. Dominic had helped her conquer her fiery power, and now it was her turn to help him, but she felt useless. There must be something she was missing. Allie had resolved to roam the unexplored parts of the town until she found *something*. Anything.

"I'll be back soon," Dom said as he donned his jacket. Allie gathered the remaining pastry boxes and walked him outside to Brandon, who had been honking for the last five minutes. "What is wrong with you?"

Brandon, unsurprisingly, grinned as if this was the best day of his life.

"Just making sure you knew I was here."

"Everyone in the damn town knows you're here." The men exchanged a look that Allie couldn't translate, which ended with Brandon cackling and Dom muttering something to the gods.

"Drive safe," she said.

Brandon thanked her and got into the driver's seat, but Dom stood there, watching her for a long minute. He looked torn, like leaving was the last thing he wanted to do. He stood there, frozen, like the air was hard and compressed between them, and he wasn't sure if he should take another step.

Allie took that step for him. She grabbed the lapels of his leather jacket and smoothed them over, although there was no crease in sight.

"Don't forget to smile at the Sanders." Allie chuckled, raising her eyes to his. Dom had his hair loose, wild strands flowing on the chill breeze around his jaw. One corner of his mouth ticked up, almost imperceptibly, as if to show her this smile. "Something like that."

"Yeah?"

Allie nodded.

Dominic moved closer as if her nod meant more to him than just her approval of his crooked smile.

He grabbed the back of her neck and stared into her eyes. Allie read a silent question in the calm green and urged herself to sit still. Dom sighed, then leaned down and pressed a quick kiss on her forehead. His lips were soft and warm against her skin, his fingers squeezing her nape.

It was a silent promise, a wordless acceptance, a mute desire, yet all so loud and clear that Allie felt branded. If she looked into the mirror, she'd find a Dom mark in the middle of her forehead.

"I'll be back soon," he repeated, then jumped inside the car, leaving her wide-eyed and with her mouth open, quietly reaching for him.

❧

"Where's Dom?" Anna asked, as she always did, looking around the space for him. Allie had no doubt the woman had less of a sweet tooth and more of an interest in the man running the place, given the fact that she was here every day. Most times, her boss would only tip his chin at Anna, or give her a bitter "Hey." Not more or less bitter than any other greeting Dominic offered, to be fair, but Allie noticed how Anna deflated from his lack of attention. Her crush was evident, as were Dom's subtle replies hinting toward rejection.

"He's away today. What can I get for you?"

"I'll get the weekend special." This week was raspberry cheesecake cups. "Is there..." Anna cleared her throat. "Is there something going on between you two?"

She grimaced, like the question tasted bitter and made her sick. Allie scoffed and shook her head.

"I don't see how that's any of your business."

"Dom is my business!" she hissed. Allie had a strong feeling her boss might disagree.

"I doubt that," Allie mumbled to herself. She dropped the subject and silently handed Anna her order, who mercifully took it and left with a loud, frustrated groan. Allie waved her off, offering her a smile that was not reciprocated.

She'd done the same with all the customers today because she was excited for her plan to walk around town, and for Dom to get back. To her shock, her smiles weren't met with the usual sneers and distaste. No one smiled back at her, but most of the townsfolk kept their mouths in a straight, indifferent line.

Mrs. Chen came by at lunch and praised Ekko's form, the gleam of his purple scales, and the strength of his wings. She'd done that as if the dragon took care of himself all on his own, but

Allie enjoyed hearing this positive assessment. It was her confirmation that she was doing a good job caring for Ekko.

The creature was around her all day, sometimes perching on her shoulder, other times bringing Allie different items between his claws. Lately, every time Dom was away or Allie was on her own, there was nothing she could do or say to keep Ekko away. The baby dragon clung to her clothes and hair and puffed steam at her until she relented. Allie hadn't figured out if Ekko didn't like being alone, or if he didn't like *her* being alone.

The busy day passed by quickly, and Allie and her dragon went on their way with the sun still out. Allie followed the trail toward the farmlands today, a part of town she had only experienced from the car. She kept close to the river once it slithered out of the forest, its murmur a comforting noise in the quiet afternoon.

Ekko flew from tree to tree, happily creating swirls of steam among the red and yellow leaves. They stumbled upon a wild plum tree, and Allie sat at the base of its trunk, letting Ekko eat his fill, while she took a moment to think about Petra.

What clues am I missing, Mom?

Allie closed her eyes, memories of the two of them in the sycamore shade vividly coming to the front of her mind. She smiled at the fun coincidence of being in the town of the sycamores, missing her unique broom that her sisters had found distasteful.

Between the steady flow of the river and Ekko rustling the plum tree leaves, Allie heard a constant, long hissing sound. She strained her hearing to identify it, but it was as difficult as splitting a hair into three.

"Ekko," Allie called for her dragon, and he appeared immediately, chewing, his snout covered with plum juice. Allie wiped him with the back of her sleeve. "Can you fly over the trees in that direction? Is there something else other than the river?"

Ekko wasted no time and did as he was told, coming back with a loud flutter of chitters after a short moment. Allie followed him through a narrow path in the forest, unmarked and undisturbed, until that resonant ringing grew louder and deeper than the river, and...

Allie stood in front of a hidden waterfall. It flowed beautifully and untamed, foaming the water at its base, like a thick curtain protecting the rocks underneath.

Everything clicked into place at once.

Sycamore Falls.

Falls.

Waterfalls.

"Sycamore Falls is bordered by mountains covered in dense forests and hidden waterfalls." Brandon's words from the night he rescued her came to Allie's mind.

It was just like a conniving Witch to pick a place as much in your face as it was out of sight. Allie could swear that evil Witch thought, "This town *falls* because I want it to." She had no power to test her theory, but her gut instinct screamed that this was right. Maybe not this waterfall, but one of the hidden waterfalls in Sycamore Falls.

The wind picked up as Ekko led the way out of the forest and back to the main road, then plopped on Allie's shoulder and snuggled in her unruly hair. Dusk settled in, painting the forest pink and violet. Dom would be home soon, and Allie couldn't contain her excitement. She finally had a lead for him, a promising one, and—

A string of loud honks made Allie stop in her tracks as a red car pulled over, rolling the passenger's window down.

"Get in, get in, get in!" Mia screeched.

Allie nearly caught her fingers in the door while rushing into the car. She strapped her seat belt as Mia high-tailed it back onto the road, Ekko still clinging to her shoulder.

"What's wrong?"

"Brandon's farm is on fire."

"What?" Allie shouted. "Which part?"

"The part closest to his house," Mia answered robotically, driving like a maniac. "That place is his entire fucking life," she muttered.

"And he's out of town. Dom's with him, too."

"Shit. I forgot about Dom. I kind of hoped to find him at the farm, putting the fire out by the time everyone gets there." Mia's voice was low and lost in a way Allie hadn't heard before.

"Everyone?"

Mia took a sharp left, and a dark tower of smoke curling into the sky came into view.

Allie's heart raced as they drove the last length of road. As soon as the car stopped, Allie and Mia jumped out and ran to the herd of people gathered by the gates. The farmhands fought the wildfire with water hoses that were too small and too inefficient to put out the tall flames licking at the ground, the strong gusts of wind spreading them wide. Toward Brandon's green-roofed white house.

Everyone, every single one of the people there, crowded Mia.

"Where is your brother?"

"Where's Dominic?"

"We need Dom to be here!"

"Our strongest air Wizard, he can put it out!"

The utter shock and panic that registered on the townsfolk's faces when Mia told them Dom was away drilled a hole into Allie's heart. He was the hope everyone had been waiting for, a hope that suffocated in the heated wind.

"What about Tom and Andrew?" Mia demanded.

Yes. Tom and Andrew. Even if Dom wasn't here, there were two more air Wizards in Sycamore Falls. They had to be here. Had to be.

But Andrew was visiting his family three towns away, and no

one had gotten hold of Tom today. He was their last chance, everyone lamented, as they busied themselves with carrying buckets of water.

The fire department from Rocky Hills? On their way, but would they make it in time?

"Allie." Mia's voice trembled, her eyes glistening with terrified tears. "This is his life. Please."

"Wha—Me?" Allie's eyebrows rode her hairline, and she clutched her hands to her chest.

"No one in this town wields water or fire. Except you." Her friend kept her voice down, but the look in her hazel eyes was so, so loud. "I can't... I'm only an Archivist," she spat as if she hated the word with the intensity of the sun. Like she loathed herself.

And Allie knew that feeling well. Before she came to Sycamore Falls, before she found a way to her power, she had hated being a Witch. And before Dom and Mia, and Brandon, and Tina and Harper, no one had truly been there for her, not since her mom. Now she could be here for the people she cared about. The people she grew to love.

"Any water or fire wielders in Rocky Hills?" someone asked.

"No need," Allie heard herself say as she stepped out of the crowd. "Stay with Mia." She gave Ekko the most admonishing look she was capable of as Mia hugged the dragon to her chest. "If anything happens to me—"

"Wait. What are you doing?"

"Tell Dom it's the waterfalls," Allie said and broke into a jog.

"What is the Witch doing?"

"Where is she going?"

"Oh gods, is she an elemental Witch?"

Allie ran toward the fire, grabbing at thick strings of warm power from her heart.

"Is she crazy? She can wield from here!"

"Isn't she afraid?"

Terrified out of her mind.

She had stepped into a fire before, but that had been different. It had been *her* fire, and Dom had held her hand, looking at her like she was porcelain, and he'd never allow her to break. He had been her safety net, and now Allie was free-falling.

The sharp fear was not enough for her to back down. She was doing this for the town that had become her home, regardless of the mean faces around her. Allie was doing this for Brandon. For her friend.

Brandon had been the only one to help her that night, without a second thought. He'd convinced a skeptical Dom to let a homeless Witch into his house, into his life. Neither was here to defend what was dear to them, and Allie simply could not watch from the sidelines and do nothing. She had to try because...

Because she owed them everything.

The heat enveloped her with each step she took closer to the fire. Allie grasped at her magic, wrapping herself in what she hoped was some sort of protective shield. She bent the power to her will as Dom had taught her, praying she had learned enough to extinguish the monstrous fire. Allie took a gulp of air and stepped between the flames.

It's not burning me, it's not burning me, it's not burning me.

It was, surprisingly, not burning her.

The scorching heat clung to her limbs, yet was bearable enough for her to keep walking. As soon as she stood in the flames closest to Brandon's house, Allie readied her magic, wove it with the wildfire, and started to pull.

She pulled and pulled until the burning terror was far away enough from Brandon's house not to be considered an immediate danger.

Magic buzzed through her veins, heating her from the inside out. Allie managed to keep the flames away, but the strain on her power lit a fire inside her. With every pull, her breathing hitched, hot air scratching her throat and frying her lungs. But she couldn't give up now; she couldn't let the wind feed the flames.

Allie fell to her knees, gasping for air, not once stopping the pull of that magical thread.

"Roll the thread back."

Dom's words came to her like a caress as she did exactly what he'd taught her, stuffing the scalding fire inside her. She was an elemental Witch; she could take it. She had to. For Brandon. She had to. She...

Allie's eyelids became heavy, gluing together from the sticky sweat coating her skin. She coughed the burn from her lungs, panted for air through her open mouth. The flames laughed at her, dancing around carelessly with horrendous cracking sounds, grabbing at her with searing claws.

If this was the last thing she did, she had to do it well. Allie wanted to protect what was dear to her, and never before did she have enough power to do that.

Grasping at the last piece of thread, that ball of yarn sizzling hot, Allie thought about Dom. About his kind green eyes, his deliciously broody mood, his huge heart. She hoped with everything she was that he would find the magic rupture behind a waterfall. Mia would tell him.

Allie kept pulling.

Just a little more.

Just until she was sure the fire could be put out by other means.

Just...

WE'RE STRONGER TOGETHER

"How did we go there to deliver pastries and fresh produce and leave with two bags of food?" Brandon mused, casually propping his wrist on the steering wheel.

"Beats me," Dom muttered. "Drive faster."

"Relax, D. Allie's not going anywhere," his friend teased him.

Except she was. She was going back to Pearls Fields after Hallows Eve, and that was too damn soon. They didn't have enough time to learn what they could be. Dominic felt his heart shrink to the size of an almond.

"Just drive. In silence," he insisted to no avail. Brandon took jabs at his newly discovered soul, the fact that he was capable of feeling *something* with that "stone-cold heart," and how Allie was kinder, prettier, and just so much better than Dom's ex.

Like he didn't know.

But it didn't matter because Allie compared to no one. She was unique, and warm, and lit up his entire life.

"Can you just—"

"What the hell is that?" Brandon's voice rose, his brows furrowing. Dominic followed his look to the left, where dark smoke covered the clear sky they were leaving behind. "It's coming from... Is it..." His voice cracked.

"It's not. Drive faster," Dom ordered, this time for an entirely different reason.

It couldn't be Riverbend. It could not. Dom refused to entertain the idea even for a second. Riverbend was Brandon's home, and his home was safe. It had to be safe.

The deadly silence Dominic had wished for filled the car like a slick presence, licking at his face and arms. He contemplated throwing all his magic at the twirl of smoke, but he was too far away to have any impact. Better to preserve it. Just in case. Both men fidgeted incessantly as each minute brought them closer to Sycamore Falls.

To home.

To Allie.

The town was in an uproar as the car passed the "Welcome to Sycamore Falls" sign. Everyone waved at them frantically, recognizing Brandon's car, urging them to hurry, hurry, hurry. Dominic's heart thudded, his focus lasered in on his magic, grabbing and taking control of it, so he could unleash enough to take a fire of any size out.

"It's Riverbend," Brandon whispered, as the path wound down along the river. Dom wanted to contradict him, to tell him it was not Riverbend.

But it was.

Brandon's farm was on fire.

They jumped out of the car in front of the gates, since the driveway was flooded with people. The entire town was here, working on an inefficient way to bring water from the river in buckets, while the farmhands struggled with a garden hose.

A purple smudge of claws and wings attacked Dom, the chittering higher pitched and more intense than ever before.

"Where's Allie?" he barked at the dragon, advancing through

the crowd. Ekko flew chaotically, swiveling his head toward the fire.

No.

She was probably just somewhere in the mill of people.

"Dom!" His sister's voice. Mia came rushing, her hair a tangled mess, dark charcoal smudges on her face. "Dom..." she panted.

"Are you okay?" He grabbed her shoulders, steadying her. Mia nodded, breathing through her mouth.

"I tried to go after her, but it was too hot," she blurted.

"What?"

His sister pointed frantically to the monstrous flames. "Allie's in there. I think she's trying—"

"Watch Mia," he commanded a teary-eyed Brandon, positioning his sister to lean on his friend. Brandon snapped out of his shock and took hold of Mia, snaking his arms around her in a tight hug as she sobbed into his chest.

Dominic ran.

He dashed through the crowds with ease and speed facilitated by his magic wind. One thread of magic was woven close to him, a protection from the fire as well as a means for him to breathe clean air. He ran into the flames with no fear, no reserve, cursing the gods who dared put his future in danger.

Dom threw his magic at the wildfire, quenching the flames as he passed through them, leaving behind smoke and scorched grass.

"Allie!" he shouted, desperate to set his eyes on her. She was fine, surely, because no other outcome was acceptable to him. "Allie! Where are you?" His heart thrashed in his chest, one moment away from leaping out and looking for her on its own.

Dom ran like a possessed man, hitting the flames with sharp, harsh magic. They were keeping Allie from him, so they had to die. Swiftly.

Left. Right. He threw his arms out, quashing the simmering heat around him.

"Allie!"

"Dom?" A faint voice reached him from the edge of the flames closest to Brandon's house. Loud coughing and heaving sounds followed, but she was fine. Fine. Fine. She was fine.

Dominic was next to her in a heartbeat, pushing his magic to its limits to practically fly there.

"Allie." He kneeled and gathered her in his arms, instantly throwing his shield around her. The air met a fiery wall, a patched and wobbly shield of her own. Good girl. It had done the job to keep her skin from being burned, but her breathing was heavy. "It's okay. You're okay. Breathe, baby." Dom used magic to send clean air through her lungs. Allie coughed into him more, until the smoke left her body and her breaths evened into a normal, healthy rhythm.

Then she opened her big brown eyes and looked at him with a glimmer of something Dom recognized as if he was looking into the mirror. Relief.

"They were heading for the house, Dom. I couldn't do more. Couldn't pull more." She moved to rise to her feet, steadier now as she was breathing well, and Dom helped her because selfishly, he didn't want to let her go.

"You did more than enough," he assured her. It was true. Dom looked around, noticing the line of burnt grass too close to the house porch for comfort, but it hadn't reached it. Brandon's house was safe, and they all had Allie to thank for that.

Dominic had a personal vendetta against this fire now, and once he swept his eyes over Allie and made sure she wasn't hurt, that there was nothing else behind the dirty clothes, messy hair, and charcoal smudges, he brought hell to it.

Fitting, he thought, bringing hell to fire itself.

The flames died one by one, some faster than others, when Dom realized Allie kept working her magic as well.

"Allie—"

"Let me help. We're stronger together."

They were. The truth of that statement hit him in the chest like a boulder. He didn't argue, only because he was right there next to Allie, and wouldn't let anything happen to her. Would stop her if it got too much. She struggled but managed to put out a couple more flames with the little magic she had left.

Dom took her hand, her fingers clinging to his, and together, they stifled the burning red light.

Allie sat quietly, softly playing with one of Ekko's wings as he refused to leave her lap.

"You're going to be all right," Tom said, his eyes moving fearfully between her and Dominic. The Mage watched the pharmacist inspect her lungs and do another air cleaning—a better one than Dominic's, Tom promised, as he had vast experience with healing magic. Not that Dominic had done a poor job, gods forbid. The man stuttered and sweated as if he was on trial for his life.

Allie didn't blame him. The entire town had been on his case because he hadn't been here when they'd needed him. Apparently, Tom had decided today was a slow day and took the time to go gather some medicinal herbs from the fields outside of Rocky Hills. Allie witnessed the town's contempt quietly, not on the receiving end of it for once. Nothing was left unsaid, from, "Who goes gathering plants randomly in the middle of the day?" and "You should have put a sign in your freaking window," and "I really hope those plants are worth letting our town burn."

Tom attempted to defend himself once, but Mrs. Chen warned him not to have the audacity to speak and focus his efforts on making sure Allie was okay.

"Do your job and take care of Allie," she bellowed as if she'd been calling Allie by her name all this time. "She's the one who saved Brandon's home while you were dilly-dallying in the fields. And you." Then the elder lady turned to Brandon and Dom and tore into them for leaving together. They had the good sense to remain silent, although they could have argued that Brandon had no magic in the first place, and both of them visited the Sanders together frequently.

Allie was surrounded by so many people who, for the first time, were not scorning her. They were worried, and grateful, and didn't shy away from voicing these feelings. Someone brought her water, and someone else covered her with a blanket, rubbing her shoulders and hugging her sideways. She smiled and assured them she was fine, but in reality, Allie was overwhelmed.

She finally felt like she could become one of their own. Sure, one could argue the townsfolk accepted her only after she had saved them, but Allie wouldn't nitpick. Being part of a community had always been a privilege for a Witch like her, reason be damned.

"Thanks, Tom." She smiled at the blushing man and got up from the chair that had been brought to her at some point during all the ruckus. Ekko flew up and bumped his snout into the pharmacist's cheek, then hovered close to Allie.

Dom was in her face instantly, grabbing her forearms as if to steady her, the familiar glare overtaking his features. Searching her.

"I'm okay," Allie chuckled. She really was fine, exhausted if anything, but she was breathing without difficulty, and her skin was not burned. A win for the day. That, and also, keeping Brandon's house from catching on fire.

"Allie." Brandon came out of the crowd and shoved Dominic out of his way. He hugged her so tightly that her air supply was cut off, but Allie hugged him back. "I can't even begin to thank you," he blurted out as Dominic peeled him off her. Brandon scowled at his friend, who, not shockingly, scowled right back.

"You have nothing to thank me for," Allie said, squeezing his arm. "You're the one who saved me first, remember?"

"Let's go home." Dom pulled her to him and tipped his chin to his friend.

"Thank you, Allie," Brandon said again.

Dominic strolled through the crowd, oblivious to all the looks following them, especially the ones pinned on the arm he curled around her shoulder.

Mia drove them back to Dom's Sweets after she made sure Brandon didn't need her. Allie was curious about the story between them, since this was probably the first time they hadn't avoided each other.

"I'll see you tomorrow." Allie waved at her friend, who threw her a confused look. "You said something about a pumpkin spice latte?"

"Oh. Are you sure? We could go next week," Mia offered, worry lining her eyes.

"I promise I'm fine, Mia. Tomorrow. It's a date!" Allie turned and entered the bakery before Mia could argue, a broody Mage on her trail. Ekko had already flown to their room, and she expected to find him passed out on his belly.

Allie rubbed her shoulder mindlessly when a thought hit her with the intensity of a lightning bolt. She wheezed and whirled on her heels, panic wrapping around her like a curtain and dulling her senses.

"Oh gods." She was the one to grab Dom's arms this time, running crazy eyes over him in some sort of assessment of... Of what? It wasn't like she could check his magic reserves with a glance.

"What's wrong?" Dominic matched her panic in his cold, controlled manner.

"Are you okay?"

"What?"

"Oh gods," Allie repeated, still searching him for any signs of depletion. "You used so much power to put out the fire. Because I'm not strong enough." Her voice cracked, hot nails lodging inside her throat. "Please don't get sick again."

Dom's features smoothed into something beautiful, his emerald eyes crinkling at the corners.

"Allie." He said nothing and everything with her name, a scolding as well as a plea.

Dominic pulled her to his chest in a strong, warm hug. Her arms went around him reflexively as she rested her head on Dom's rock-hard chest.

"You're worried about *me*?" She nodded against the soft fabric of his sweater. Dom breathed into her hair, one hand firmly locked around her waist, the other rubbing circles on her back. The move was comforting and familiar, yet the last time he'd done this, Allie had been in pain and out of control. "I'm fine, Allie."

"Are you sure?" she whispered.

"Do you trust me?"

"Of course I do." Allie squeezed him harder to her, as if she could transpose the answer to his body. "Always have." Always will, she thought, but didn't find the courage to say it out loud. Always seemed like such a long time for someone who was bound to leave.

"Good." He sighed contentedly.

Allie melted into his arms, inhaling long breaths until she found that comforting cedarwood and leather scent under all the burnt smell. Exhaustion seeped into her body once she relaxed, and she took a moment to check on her magic.

That warmth behind her chest was gone, replaced by a cold and quiet feeling, just like the one she had before fully manifesting her power. Allie winced at this realization, but Dom's arms strengthened their hold around her.

"It will replenish," he assured her. "With time, and sleep, and food."

"Are you Reading me?" she asked with a hidden grin.

"Do you blame me?" His voice was raspy and accusatory in the kindest way. Allie shook her head.

Dominic took a step back, and Allie saw the reluctance in his eyes, as if this distance was hurting him. She, too, hated the cold air that swirled around her, missing his warmth immediately.

But his large hands cupped her cheeks, thumbs softly stroking under her eyes. Allie wondered if he could feel the skin heating up under his touch.

"Get some sleep. We're closed tomorrow."

He leaned forward and kissed her forehead, long and sweet, his body shuddering through an inhale. The spot under his lips burned in the most delightful way, the sensation spreading through her limbs and muscles like a shockwave.

Allie wished it had been her lips.

Chapter 31

LET ME

Dom didn't sleep a wink last night. He was moments from bursting with the restless energy coursing through his veins.

He should have kissed her. He wanted nothing more in his life than to taste her lips, feel her soften against him, make her body tremble under his touch.

He wanted her. All of her. Mind, body, and soul.

After climbing up and down the stairs countless times, convinced he must knock on her door and kiss her until she begged for air, then talking himself out of it, Dom spent the entire night in pure agony, as if someone was going to deny him his next breath.

Dawn arrived after what felt like a week of suffering, and Dominic jumped out of bed as if he'd been held prisoner. It was a miracle that his jaw was still intact, but it hurt while he brushed his teeth with more force than required.

He went about deep cleaning his apartment, an activity he hated with a passion, but which kept his hands occupied. His mind, on the other hand, was under the spell of the beautiful Witch, her gorgeous brown eyes, red mane of hair, and all the ways he could get tangled up in it.

When the purple light faded into a soft, stronger orange and the first rays of sun were out, Dominic moved on to another task that would keep him busy since the bakery was closed today. Some of the furniture needed repairing, he decided, and got to work on the wobbly drawers of his nightstands.

The morning was in full bloom when he heard the door open downstairs, followed by soft steps about the bakery and the sound of the coffee machine.

Dominic shoved the chair aside and got to fixing his perfectly fine desk, pounding unnecessary nails into it.

"Dom?" Allie's singsongy voice sent a thrill down his spine.

"Up here."

Footsteps filled the silence and matched his racing heart with each thud, and then... Then she stood there, smiling at him, bewitchingly beautiful and sexy.

"Morning. I made coffee," Allie said, hooking her thumb and pointing downstairs.

Dom dropped the hammer, slid out from under the desk, then slowly unfurled to his full height. Allie wore a soft white sweater paired with a short purple skirt and the long boots from the wedding. Her hair was loose and drowning her in the best way, draped around her shoulders and chest. The stone rings she rarely wore gleamed in the light on her slim fingers, and the crescent moon necklace was hidden under her clothes.

He never thought he would be jealous of the jewelry touching her skin.

"Dom?"

"Mmm?" He closed the distance between them.

"Coffee?" Allie breathed, weaker than before. Her lips parted, dark chocolate eyes fixed on him with an intensity that choked him.

"Let me."

"Wh—"

"Let me," he begged. "Kiss you."

Dominic would have given anything to steal that tiny gasp of air that left her lips. Then Allie placed her hands on his chest, lining her body with his.

"When have I not let you?"

Dominic was upon her before all her words were out. He crushed his mouth against hers, one hand cupping her cheek while the other snaked around her waist and pulled her into him. Allie's heart raced frantically, barely grasping the fact that she was kissing her boss. She gave herself to him, trusting Dom to lead her where they both wanted to go.

He parted her lips with ease, sliding his hot tongue into her mouth. Allie whimpered, and he squeezed her to him, deepening the kiss. She matched his desperate pace, feeding a need of her own. It was hot and hungry, and everything she never knew she needed.

Dom's hand trailed down to her neck, over her collarbone, and she was ready to rip the sweater open to feel his touch against her skin. Her arms hung around his shoulders, one hand fisting the loose locks at the base of his neck.

Dominic groaned.

He grabbed her ass and hoisted her up, her legs hooking around his hips. Dominic moved swiftly, as if she were featherlight, and set her on the desk. The shift put a small distance between them, and Allie whined, tugging him closer by his shirt. Dom chuckled against her lips, hands moving to her waist, down her legs, slowly pushing her skirt up.

"I've wanted to see this for so long," he panted, voice strained and raspy. Allie had no idea what he was talking about, but she was ready to show him anything. Everything.

His palm traveled up her thigh as if he had all the time in the world, revealing her tattoo. Dom turned questioning eyes to her, heavy with yearning.

"It goes around your thigh?" he asked, and Allie nodded. "What is it?"

"It's an olive branch," she forced the words through her winded breaths, "with...with small peonies."

Dom's fingers contoured it gently, revering the ink. He grinned, a charming, wicked thing, and lowered himself between her legs.

"Tell me about it," Dom ordered. But his mouth closed around the soft skin of her thigh as he trailed each leaf with his tongue. Allie gripped the edge of the desk so hard her palms hurt. She focused the last fragment of her mind that was not lost to pleasure on keeping her from screaming his name. "Tell me," Dom growled and bit her inner thigh, then sucked and licked the spot in consolation.

"Dom, p-please." Allie was a mess, completely at his mercy, and Dom... Dom was kissing around her thigh with the leisure of a man who had years to do only this. He wouldn't stop until she told him something, and Allie forced that intact piece of her brain that threatened to crumble to find an answer for him. "It's for peace," she managed. "So I always lead...with...p-peace."

He looked up at her through his lashes and smiled against her leg.

"Good girl." Dom stood up, hands roaming over the sides of her body and setting her on fire, until one settled under her skirt and the other on her face. His thumb pressed on her lower lip, craving green eyes drilling into her. "Where are the other ones?"

"Other..." She was drunk on him, feeling that last lucid piece giving in to the strong lust.

"Show me all your tattoos, Allie," he said, then lowered his head and kissed her.

Softly.

Once, twice.

Allie hated it. She wanted more, more, more.

"Under my sweater," she surrendered, then bit his lower lip. Provoked him. Dom made a deep, guttural sound in the back of his throat. He fisted her hair and opened her mouth, giving her what she wanted, twirling his tongue expertly around hers. Pressure built low in her abdomen, threatening to take her apart at the seams.

It was too much and not enough.

Dom let her breathe as he said, "Tell me you want this." She nodded fervently, as if her life depended on it. "Say it," he hissed.

Allie placed her hands on his jaw and drew back enough that her eyes could meet his. The thirsty, disheveled look he sported drove her insane.

"Dom." She placed a soft kiss on his lips, just like he had done to her. "I." Soft kiss. "Want." Kiss. "This." Kiss. "You."

"Fuck." He moaned into her mouth, impatient and hungry. Then he picked her up and walked them to his bedroom, not breaking away from her for a second.

Allie slammed the door closed with the heel of her tall boot.

It was late afternoon when they finally left the house, after Allie had argued multiple times that they'd be late meeting Mia. Dominic had growled in protest and kept her prisoner in his arms under the blanket until the last minute. He'd spent an obscene amount of time tracing her tattoos with his fingers and tongue. The lotus flower between her breasts was his favorite, he declared after taking hours to study every ink line. The one on her back received the same amount of attention, though: a full moon stamped in the center of her back with opposite moon phases up and down her spine.

The pleasure had been out of this world, and now that she'd experienced it, nothing else would ever come close to matching it. Dominic had smirked arrogantly at the image of her boneless and tangled up in his sheets.

Now they were walking hand in hand toward Harper's café, Dom's features schooled into that characteristic frown, Allie smiling uncontrollably, plastered to him. Everyone they passed by stopped to ask how Allie was feeling, and some played with Ekko for a bit, yet no one dared to acknowledge the closeness between her and Dom. She smiled and told the truth, that she was doing well and was happy to have been of help. Dom was back to his grunting and scowling self, and Allie felt privileged to be the only one who saw that sweet, wicked smile on his handsome face.

"You're la—Are you holding hands? Oh gods, it's finally happening!" Mia jumped up from the table by the window, nearly spilling her coffee, and threw her arms around their shoulders. "I knew it!" she muttered victoriously. "I'm so happy for you!"

"Thanks, Mia," Allie said. Dom grunted.

"Me too!" Harper attacked them just when they were untangling themselves. The cheerful blonde gave them a toothy smile before she started on their pumpkin spice latte order.

The three of them sat down, and before Mia showered them with a dozen questions about her and Dom that she was not ready to answer, Allie asked, "How's Brandon doing?" Dom winced, and a pang of guilt stabbed her heart, since she'd kept him from checking on his friend. Mia went deadly quiet, so Allie filled the silence with: "Why don't we get one of these fancy coffees to go and pay him a visit?"

Dominic turned to her with a stricken, surprised look. Allie smiled, and his features relaxed. He draped his arm across her chair and pulled it closer to him. A smirk bloomed on Mia's lips, silence forgotten.

"Tell me everything."

"How much do you want to know about your brother's personal affairs?" Dom provoked her.

Mia leaned across the table, interlacing her fingers, mischief shining in her eyes. "Everything." Allie laughed. "What's funny? For sure not my brother."

"You two. How easy it is for you to be around each other and tease each other. I haven't had someone like that since my mom." Allie's voice didn't wobble, and she was smiling, but Mia still threw her a soft look while Dom squeezed her shoulder.

"Now you have your pick," Harper said, approaching with a tray. "Me and Tina, Mia, Brandon, and Dom." She placed tall drinks topped with whipped cream on the table. The sweet smell filled the space, and Allie's mouth watered. Ekko had a similar reaction and stretched his snout to the glass.

"Ah-ah." Allie gently pushed him away, but her heart melted at the look in his eyes. "It's not good for you," she insisted, but the dragon's expression morphed into a dramatic pout. "Fine. Just a small taste." Ekko flew in happy circles around the table before sitting down in front of the glass. Allie swiped at the cream with her index finger and offered it to the longing creature.

"Gentle," Dom warned him. As if Ekko would ever hurt her. The baby dragon spat a cloud of steam in Dominic's direction in contempt, then—gently—licked the cream off Allie's finger. He chittered with happiness and settled on her lap.

Dom and Mia fell into conversation about the Harvest Festival preparations and booths, but Allie's mind wandered. She thought about Harper's words, how true they were. How fate had brought her to Sycamore Falls to meet all these amazing people who had started to feel like family.

The prospect of celebrating Hallows Eve here with them was

more exciting by the day. With the cool weather and the burnt colors, Allie felt like Hallows Eve was made for a town like this. She considered risking Lydia's wrath and delaying her return by one or two days to spend that night here, with the man next to her.

Mia pointed at the corner of her mouth after Allie slurped her sweet drink, still oblivious to their conversation.

"You have a little…"

Allie reached for a napkin, but Dom was quicker. His hand moved to her nape, setting dark green eyes on her lips as she turned to him.

"I got it." He leaned in and kissed her softly, once, then his tongue traced her mouth, sucking her lips between his teeth one by one, cleaning her up.

"You're right. It's better if I don't know too many details," Mia conceded. Allie laughed against Dom's mouth before he kissed her again and leaned back into his chair.

"Sorry," Allie mouthed the lie to her friend, who waved a hand and rolled her eyes.

"Allie, you told me to remember to tell Dom something right before you went into a living, raging fire like a crazy person. I obviously forgot, but—"

"Oh gods." Allie jumped up, a disoriented baby dragon soaring from her lap and spitting steam to defend them from unseen dangers. The discovery had completely slipped her mind, with the threat to Brandon's house and then… Well, then today. But this could be a real chance for them, and Allie didn't want to waste any more time. She grabbed Dom's hand and pulled him to his feet.

"What's wrong?" He went into full-scowl, offensive mode at the panicked and excited look in her eyes.

"Dom, it's the waterfalls."

Chapter 32

CAN YOU FEEL IT?

Allie dragged Dom out of the coffee shop, rushing in a flurry of coats and scarves, a confused baby dragon flying around them.

"Lead us to the waterfall!" Allie told Ekko, who took to the skies and led the way.

They ran to the end of Maple Street before Dominic stopped abruptly.

"Allie, wait." Dom tugged at her hand until she halted, loud, unladylike gasps coming from her mouth. Gods, she was out of shape. Dom smoothed the hair away from her face and placed his palms on her cheeks, forcing her to calm down, breathe, and get lost in his green eyes.

No.

Don't get lost, Allie. You have one job.

"Dom, let's—"

"I will follow you into the deepest, darkest forests, in this world and any other, but for the love of all gods, breathe, Allie. And tell me, why are we running like lunatics? I'm sure we can spare thirty seconds to exchange this information." His eyebrows rose playfully, and Allie couldn't resist laughing during the rare times he attempted a sarcastic comment. Dominic leaned down and kissed her, squeezing her cheeks so her lips smooshed together under his.

Allie inhaled loudly, making a show of proving to Dom she was *breathing*, as he had insisted.

"I think the magic is broken behind one of the hidden waterfalls." Dom furrowed his brows, and Allie took his hand and resumed walking instead of "running like a lunatic." She told him her theories as they followed the purple dot above into the thick forest.

"How far have you gone to search?" Dom muttered as they passed through the trees and bushes. He walked in front of her and kept any overgrown branches at bay until she ambled by them. The murmur of water grew with each step, and so did Allie's heartbeat. They kept quiet except for Dom's occasional sighs, which were loud enough for his sister to hear all the way across town.

"Should be around here," Allie mused. A moment later, Ekko flew down to them and pointed his snout ahead. Allie scratched him under the chin with her free hand. "Here we are."

They entered the secluded clearing where the waterfall tumbled down in a roar, peaceful and assailing at the same time.

"Have you already checked this place?" Allie figured she should have asked this before, especially when Dom looked at her with a very clear "You're only asking me this now?" expression.

He kneeled down and placed his palm on the ground, his focus visibly shifting from being her... Her what? He wasn't *hers*. Was he?

To a Mage. He was in his full Mage mode. Assessing.

"I haven't," Dom concluded.

Yes!

The chance that she might be right sent a fresh surge of excitement racing through her.

"All right."

Dom spread his palm wide and closed his eyes. That soft vibration buzzed through Allie, like a wave of feathers caressing her magic. The sensation disappeared abruptly, making her choke on air.

Allie waited for that familiar hum to rush through her again. And waited. And waited. Ekko had plopped on her shoulder a while ago. He kept nudging her jaw and looking pointedly at Dominic, who didn't move or speak. Dom kept still as a statue, down on one knee with his hand on the earth and his brows furrowed.

Allie placed her hand on Ekko's belly when she felt like he was going to jump up and fly to Dom. She shook her head silently, urging the baby dragon to stay put. The magic vibration she was waiting for didn't come anymore, and Allie found that she was rooted to the ground as much as Dominic was. They sat unmoving in a silence filled by the waterfall's whooshing, and occasionally by Ekko's soft chittering.

Sweat trickled down Dom's temples as his breathing became more labored. He ground his teeth and hissed through them until a deep groan escaped his throat.

Allie couldn't help him, but she moved to sit by his side. To be there when this was over and provide whatever comfort possible. She didn't know how long she sat there, cross-legged, fidgeting with the edges of her purple skirt. Ekko sat up straight in her lap, waiting, his eyes never leaving Dom. She scratched the scales on his tense back, but the creature refused to relax. Allie felt just like her dragon, but she trusted Dominic and his power with her life. He would be fine, but...

What if he got sick again?

The thought sent a row of unpleasant shivers down her spine. If that happened, she would be th—

A sharp zing ran through her, like an electric shockwave setting her nerves on fire, and Ekko jolted up like he'd been burned.

Allie raised on her knees and placed her hand on Dominic's back, caution be damned.

"Dom?"

He exhaled loudly and slumped to the ground, gasping for air. Allie inched closer to him and rubbed his back in slow circles, hoping he felt the same comfort Allie had when he did this for her. With her free hand, she swiped the wild locks away from his face. Then she spent a long moment smoothing that frown between his eyes with her finger until Dom's breathing balanced and he opened his eyes. He regarded her with something like awe, a shadow of a smile on his handsome, tired face.

"It's done. It was here, the rupture," he panted softly. "It's fixed. Can you feel it?"

Allie allowed herself a moment to study that feeling after she was satisfied with studying Dom enough to conclude he looked fine. Exhausted, but fine.

When that forceful zing snapped through her, Allie felt her magic hum, as if in response to this hidden power. It felt different than before, fuller and stronger and richer. As if she'd gained access to another source of magic than her own. This feeling of being whole was old and new, something she had before, but not quite. Something she had been wanting to obtain forever.

"I...I think I do?"

Dom chuckled.

"This is what whole magic feels like, Allie. Sycamore Falls was a place with disrupted magic. Until now."

"But I've been in places with whole magic before," Allie argued.

"Pearls Fields is old magic, which is different. Weaker." Dom pinned her with a look full of rage that wasn't targeted at her. He chose to ignore her time in Green Creek and added, "And your power was still buried under the seal. You've been here since your power manifested fully." Dom's eyes moved over her with curiosity.

"Oh." He was right. Sycamore Falls was the first place Allie had been in with full control of her power. Now that the magic was whole, Allie felt like... Like there was nothing she couldn't do. Like her magic was pure and powerful. Like she was exactly where she was supposed to be.

"I'm so lucky to be here with you now," Dom uttered, and Allie cocked her head. "You have the biggest, brightest smile on your face."

Allie felt the stretch in her cheeks, the warmth under her skin. Nothing compared to this feeling of wholeness. It was not something she could name or put into words, but it was everything she'd been looking for as a Witch. To feel whole. To feel like herself.

Allie cupped Dom's cheeks and kissed him. Slowly, unhurriedly, and for a long time, right there on the cold, leaf-covered ground.

❦

Dom felt dizzy and drained, seconds away from crumpling to the ground in a heap. But he held the hand of the most beautiful woman in the world as they strolled back to Maple Street, and that made the exhaustion hush. He prayed not to get sick again, only because he had other plans to keep Allie in his bedroom.

The town was alive with noisy celebration. Everyone was hugging and cheering, some were crying, others were laughing. Whether they had magic or not, Dom knew everyone had felt the moment he wove the magic back together. He'd felt it, too, like a shot of adrenaline that made him want to howl or wail, to make room in his soul for that fullness.

Ekko had not left his shoulder ever since he got to his feet, which he found strange because the creature preferred Allie to him any day. As much as Dom scowled at him, the baby dragon stayed put as if he'd grown roots inside Dominic's body.

"It's fixed! It's finally fixed!"

"After all this time..."

"Sycamore Falls is safe again!"

His fatigue made Dom feel more overwhelmed with everything going on around him. Their words drowned him in warm, comfortable water, but he longed for quiet air.

"Dominic! Allie!" All eyes turned to them like a choreographed move. "Where have you been?"

"Did you feel it?"

"There must have been a Mage in town. The Order didn't forget about us!"

Dom felt like his face was pressed between two hot rocks. His jaw clenched, and the muscles in his body locked, ready to be attacked. There were so many people, so many words, their lives pushing into his own, stealing his air. He shouldn't give them any reason to suspect him of fixing this. Dom's identity was his most prized secret, and only his family knew about it. His family, and...

"I wanted to show Dom this beautiful waterfall I found, just around—"

Allie spoke with unmatched enthusiasm about their romantic walk in nature, lying expertly and with ease about why they were there and how they'd found it. She held his hand and didn't flinch when Dom almost crushed it with his. He released his ironclad hold and rubbed his thumb on her skin in apology. Allie inched closer to him, grabbing his arm with her free hand and leaning her head on his shoulder as she navigated this social situation they found themselves in. The conversation moved from the utter miracle of the magical sycamores being restored to how they had become a couple.

The beautiful Witch held her own with not a word from him

and smiled, smiled, smiled, until she politely dragged him away and toward the bakery. Dom had no idea the pretense she'd come up with to get them to leave, but he was infinitely grateful to go home. With her.

He didn't remember how he ended up propped on one of the bar chairs in Allie's kitchen as she roamed between the stove and the fridge, cutting, mixing, tasting. The earthy and spicy flavor that filled his nostrils was the one to bring him back to reality.

"What are you doing?" he asked like an idiot. Allie must have told him what she was doing while he spaced out because of his depletion. But she gave him a bright smile that reached her caramel eyes, unbothered as she most likely repeated herself.

"I'm making lentil soup and beef stew. Just a little longer before they're ready." Her eyes fell to something in front of him. "More water?"

More?

"Please," he mumbled, then drained another glass in big gulps.

Ekko lay in the crook of his elbow, front claws gently holding on to his jacket. The dragon watched Allie move around the room, his beady eyes wide, and when his chitters turned loud and excited, Dom guessed he was getting something to eat, too.

"Here you go." Allie placed a bowl of pumpkin seeds, chia seeds, orange slices, and grapes in front of the salivating creature. Ekko feasted on his food with noisy, happy chewing.

Dom followed Allie with heavy-lidded eyes as she fidgeted around the kitchen in her short, swishing skirt and her bare feet. His heart raced with the memory of this morning that he wanted so badly to repeat. Maybe after a full night's sleep, though, if he was honest with himself.

"And now you, mister." Allie placed two bowls of lentil soup and two plates of beef stew with boiled potatoes and roasted tomatoes on the table. As if on cue, Dom's stomach growled, and Allie shoved some slices of bread toward him.

Dominic caught her wrist and grabbed her hand, playing with her long, delicate fingers. "Thank you, Allie."

"My pleasure. I love cooking."

"This too, but..." Dom cleared his throat and squeezed her hand. "Thank you for not giving up, for finding the waterfall. I never would have thought... I haven't been to the hidden waterfalls ever since I was six or seven years old. I made a rookie mistake searching all the obvious spots, and if it weren't for you, who knows how long it would've taken me to realize I was looking in all the wrong places?"

"You would have figured it out, I'm sure. And you made no mistakes when you gave all your effort to this endeavor, Dom." She squeezed his hand back. "Now, eat."

Dominic cleaned both plates in record time. The food was delicious and rich with flavors, and he knew he would be greedy and ask Allie to cook for him again. He blatantly ignored the thought of her leaving in a week and convinced his mind and heart that she would stay here with him for a long, long time.

Allie was setting down a steaming cup of tea on his nightstand when Dom exited the bathroom after a long, hot shower. His muscles were sore, his magic depleted, the source never so hollow as it was now. It would replenish with time and rest, but this had been by far one of the most tiresome weekends in his Mage life.

Allie's lips parted as her eyes traveled over his bare abdomen up his chest, over the dark tattoo on his arm.

"I..." She swallowed, her cheeks coloring the prettiest shade of pink. "Did you need anything else?" Allie asked his chest.

Dominic smirked.

"Come here."

She took slow steps toward him until Dom wrapped her in a tight hug. He inhaled her tangerine and vanilla scent and ran his hand through her long, red hair. Allie's arms went around his waist, the metal of her stone rings cold against his skin.

"Stay with me tonight." Allie looked up at him without breaking away from his embrace. Dom couldn't resist pressing a kiss on her forehead. One on her nose. As much as he wanted to kiss her more, always, everywhere, forever, his body felt heavy like lead, his mind foggy. "Please."

Allie nodded and kissed his chest. "All right."

That night, Allie fell asleep curled up to him under the blanket. In his bed, in his arms.

He was the luckiest man in the world.

Chapter 33

WITH HAZELNUT CREAM

Allie woke up caged by two heavy arms. She glimpsed the dark sycamore tattoo and wondered if being held down by one of its branches would feel the same. Yet nothing would ever feel as good as waking up in Dom's arms. Allie shifted under the covers, inching away from him, but Dom's ironclad hold activated, and the arms pulled her into a hot, naked chest. She inhaled greedily, again and again, stamping his scent into her mind and soul, so she could always remember it vividly. Remember him.

With each day, Allie's heart grew heavier at the idea of leaving Sycamore Falls. Mia had suggested she could stay longer, but Dom...hadn't. She didn't want to pressure him by asking because she was mostly convinced the Mage would allow her to stay longer. But Allie wanted Dom to *want* her to stay. And if she asked, and he said yes, would that be because she urged him, or because he wanted her here?

Allie hoped it would be the latter, and that was why she kept quiet about it.

The thought of going back to Pearls Fields, to old magic, to a house of sisters who barely tolerated her, and to that abominable, endless heat made her chest constrict. A twinge of sadness sneaked into her heart for her past self, for the Allie who had wanted that life because it was the only one she knew. She had spent years drilling into her brain that Witches didn't make their way into the world, didn't live outside a coven, unless they chose solitude.

And she didn't want to be alone.

Looking back, the coven's decision to send her away was the best thing that had happened to her. Allie had learned this new way of life, met all these wonderful people, and created a life of her own, one not dictated by her power—or lack thereof.

Giving it up was close to impossible, and she was in for a lifetime of heartbreak.

Dom squeezed her to his chest with a low purr that vibrated through her body.

"Good morning."

"Morning." Allie placed tiny kisses on Dom's chest as he rubbed her back.

Something shifted around her feet, and Allie looked down to see Ekko sprawled on his back, feet up, snoring between their legs. She laughed while Dom gave a hoarse chuckle.

This was the life she wanted. Waking up in Dom's arms, their cat-like dragon curled at their feet. A bakery to run—more like assist with, but a girl could dream. Friends to go out with for coffee and delicious food. Cold weather for Hallows Eve.

"How are you feeling?" she asked Dom, running her fingertips over his hip.

"Good." He inhaled loudly and moaned into her hair. "And I'm about to get so much better." Dominic rolled her over, pinning her body down with his and bringing mischief-filled green eyes to the center of her universe. She was addicted to his sexy, arrogant smirk, the way he kissed her and worshipped her body.

"Are you sure you're feeling well enough?" Allie asked, despite her instincts that screamed at her to shut up and take anything Dom gave her.

"Why don't I show you?"

Allie bit her lip and nodded before a purple smudge took flight from the bed and soared out the bedroom door.

§.

Maybe he was dead. And he must have done some good deeds, seeing as how he was living his happiest life. Or death?

Dominic couldn't remember when he'd ever been this happy before. He couldn't care less about the past anyway because his future was beautiful, and bright, and red-headed. He loved how easy it had been to convince Allie not to leave his bed. Short of asking her to move in with him officially, everything was as it was supposed to be.

They spent the first half of the week before Hallows Eve tangled up in sheets, running the bakery, cooking, talking about everything and nothing, *laughing*. Right. He was one of those men who laughed now. Because she was funny and witty, and interesting, and his.

Dominic planned to ask Allie to stay in Sycamore Falls during the Harvest Festival this weekend. Not longer. Forever.

If she had to go back to Pearls Fields to settle anything with the coven, he'd go with her. If she wanted him to. Regardless, Allie's place was in Sycamore Falls, with him, and not in some overly-hot place surrounded by wicked Witches who didn't care about her.

His blood pressure increased dramatically every time he remembered this. It hit him harder with every piece of Allie he got to know. From the moment she stood homeless at his doorstep, to her struggling with her fire, to the fucking seal—they'd shunned her when they should have helped her most, and Dominic would never forgive them. In fact, he'd love to go with Allie to Pearls Fields to become the first Mage who cursed a Witch.

"What did that dough do to you?" Allie wrapped her arms around his waist and looked at him over his arm.

He instantly relaxed and let that rage go. Well, not *go*, but he bottled it back up from where it had escaped. "Nothing. Sprinkle more flour over here, please."

Allie went around the table and did as instructed. "What else do we have on the schedule for today?"

Hearing her say "we" was the highlight of his day, every day.

"I have to make dulce de leche for Mia. She made it abundantly clear I haven't made her some in a while, and 'Do I even love her?'" he grumbled. "And I'll run a delivery in the afternoon to Mrs. Chen."

"Let me help with Mia's sweet treat," Allie offered. "I'd like to know how to make it for her, too."

Dom nodded once, his heart growing to the size of a carving pumpkin.

Dulce de leche was complicated in its simplicity. Allie needed to observe Dom at least three times more before she gave it a try herself. But this was Mia's favorite, so the effort was worth it.

Allie was cleaning the table by the window when the doorbell rang.

"Welcome—oh."

Jared freaking Finn stood by the door and stared at her. She hadn't seen him since the day he was all too friendly with her manipulative ex. He looked as uncomfortable as she felt, and Allie Read him instantly. She'd take no chances around a man like him. His aura was conflicted, feeling like he wanted to repent, but at the same time like it was the last thing he wanted to do.

His eyes moved awkwardly around the shop, where the other patrons enjoying their pastries had gone quiet. Jared walked up to the counter, and Allie followed him, rolling her eyes so hard they almost made a popping sound.

"What can I get you?"

"Just a coffee, please. To go." Allie turned her back on him, reaching for a to-go cup even before he'd mentioned it. Jared cleared his throat. Twice. "I came to apologize."

Allie heard him loud and clear, but unfortunately for him, he spoke over the buzzing sound of the coffee machine. She suppressed a smile before turning to face him.

"I'm sorry, what was that?"

Jared's face grew red, and Allie thought that at any moment, smoke would be coming out of his ears.

"I'm sorry!" he shouted. "I had no idea Sam put a—" Allie's eyes turned to saucers, but thankfully, the moron stopped talking. No one in Sycamore Falls knew about the seal except Dom and Mia, and she wanted to keep it that way. Jared cleared his throat again. "I didn't know."

Allie nodded and handed him the cup of coffee.

"Thanks." What else could she say? Allie hadn't thought about Jared all this time, and she wasn't going to start now. "Have a good day."

"So...we're good?" He placed the money on the counter and raised his stupid eyebrows.

"We're...nothing. But I appreciate the apology."

Allie left for the kitchen to do exactly nothing but wait until the unwelcome guest left. She stared at the oven timer, which had twenty-two minutes left, until she heard the doorbell ring in the bakery.

She was not one to hold a grudge, having always considered them a waste of energy on people who did not deserve the effort. However, she did not want to look at his face anymore, and that was a perfectly valid excuse for hiding in the kitchen.

"Allie?" Her favorite voice boomed from the narrow hallway

before Dom's body filled the doorframe. He wore his unfriendly glare, and his hands fisted at his sides as he scanned her from head to toes. "You okay?" She nodded honestly. Besides the scare she took from Jared almost announcing the seal to the entire town, nothing about him fazed her. "I really need to put up one of those signs," Dom muttered.

"What sign?"

"Never mind."

"Let's go over the Harvest Festival preparations," Allie suggested instead, putting her arm around Dom's waist and cuddling to his chest. "I have some ideas."

The crease between his eyebrows shifted into intrigue.

"Baking ideas?"

Allie smiled widely and nodded, then said the thing she knew might give her a glimpse of Dom's smile.

"With hazelnut cream."

She was right.

"Tell me all about it," Dom said, charming Allie by giving her his full, undivided attention.

He listened patiently to everything she said, not frowning once, to his credit. Allie suggested adding caramel chocolate cookies for quick bites, choux filled with hazelnut cream for obvious reasons, and lemon cream pie, as everything else was sweet, and she wanted to offer something a bit sour, too.

"I'm impressed," Dom said, placing his hands on her hips and pulling her to him. "Everything sounds great, Allie. But you know you just gave us more work, right?"

"I know." Allie hugged him, resting her head over his heart. "I can do all of it." She made an empty promise, knowing that one, Dom wouldn't let her, and two, she was not ready to take all of this upon herself. But she could help with more than half of the baking tasks, and that flooded her heart with a soft, warm joy.

Despite knowing those things too, Dom said, "I know you can," then kissed her on the top of her head.

The doorbell rang with more force than usual, breaking their blissful moment.

"D, you in here?" Allie recognized Brandon's voice with a hint of urgency in it.

Dom sighed loudly.

"I'll be right back. Will you take care of those?" He tilted his chin toward the oven where the cupcakes' timer was about to go off.

"Of course. I'm a pro now," Allie said with no small amount of pride.

"Dominic!" They both startled at Brandon using Dom's full name and exchanged a worried look.

"I'm coming!" Dom barked loud enough for the entire town to hear.

Something was definitely wrong.

Chapter 34

THEN COME BACK TO ME

"What's stuck up your a—"

"Is Allie back there?" Brandon blurted out, wearing a preoccupied and grim expression instead of his usual grin. Dom's spine stiffened as he picked up a vibe he did not like, but he nodded. "Can you make sure she stays there?"

"What's going on? And why are you whispering?"

"Just answer my question," Brandon hissed. Then he leaned over the counter and grabbed Dom's arm, dragging him out to the floor.

"She's frosting cupcakes for the next twenty minutes."

Brandon stopped abruptly a few steps before the door. Dom knocked into him, his annoyance and heart rate increasing exponentially.

"Can you make that thirty?"

"What the fuck is going on?"

Brandon opened his mouth to speak, then sighed in defeat. He pushed Dom to the door, where he saw—

Four Witches stood on the sidewalk, red hair mingling with the auburn fall landscape around them.

"I found them roaming around Harp's. They were looking for Allie, and someone told them she's working here."

"Fuck." He'd find out who that someone was and give them a piece of his mind.

"What do you want to do?"

Dominic considered. The Witches were here for one of two reasons: one, they came to tell Allie not to bother coming back. The thought made his skin crawl, even if the outcome worked in his favor. The other option was that they were here to check on her power and take her back with them. He had procrastinated asking Allie to stay in Sycamore Falls in hopes of asking during the festival, which might come and bite him in the ass. Regardless of his efforts, it was ultimately Allie's choice. And as much as he wanted to run these Witches out of town, to not let them an inch closer to the woman he had fallen in love with... Allie could hold her own with her coven.

"I'll go get Allie," Dom snarled against all his instincts. The words stung his throat as if he'd swallowed a hive.

"Are you unwell? What if they're here to get her back to Pearls Fields? How can you let her get away?" His friend punched him in the chest.

"I'm not letting her do anything, Brandon. It's her choice." And it would hurt like hell if her choice was not him. Yet it was still hers to make.

"You're finally happy—"

"Allie!" Dominic shouted, her name wringing a sweet pain inside his chest.

"Dom..." He avoided Brandon's look, which, by the tone in his voice, was full of pity. Instead, he focused on the Witches, standing casually on *his* sidewalk, staring at the trees in *his* town, threatening to get *his* girl.

"What's up?" Allie came out in a mild jog, wiping sticky hands on her apron. Her bun was messy, untamed strands running wild around her face. Dominic's hand itched to tug the hair safely behind her ears, but he knew that if he touched her, he would never let her go.

His jaw clenched hard, teeth grinding together as he spat, "There's someone here to see you." Then he jerked his head toward the window and watched her mouth open, eyes growing wide.

He couldn't bear not knowing what was going on in her head, in her heart. The stakes were too high for him to just...wait. Yes, it was her choice, and yes, he respected it. But he couldn't possibly stand there without a fucking clue about his future.

So Dom Read her.

His magic was not back to its fullest yet after fixing the magic on the sycamores, but it was enough to get an idea of her feelings. Genuine surprise washed over him, mixed with curiosity, and... Was that fear?

Was Allie afraid of these Witches? Had they ever done anything to her? Dominic felt his body heating, breathing faster as rage took command of his own feelings.

Allie had nothing to be afraid of as long as he was by her side. As long as he was alive, nothing and no one would get past him.

"I'll be right back," Allie said and reached for the doorknob.

Dom acted without thinking. He grabbed her by the wrist in a swift movement, bringing startled brown eyes to his. The rage was not targeted at her, so he inhaled for a long moment, dulling it, softening his features so she wouldn't, gods forbid, be scared *of him*. He gathered the courage needed to make this demand, to ask her to change the course of her life. For him.

It would only take one word. Or four.

"Stay."

Allie froze. Not because of Dominic's sudden touch. Not because his green, icy glare drilled into her like a sharp blade. But because she could see behind it, could feel that iciness melt the longer he held her hand.

"What do you mean?" she whispered.

"Stay here. With me." His voice was loud and clear, not even remotely wobbly. The grip around her wrist tightened, and he pulled her to him, laying her hand over his heart, the frantic beats tickling her palm.

"I have to check what they want," Allie tested him. She selfishly wanted to make sure Dom was asking her to stay here, in Sycamore Falls, not here, in the bakery. That he wanted her in his life.

He nodded once, brows furrowing deeper, creasing his handsome face.

"Go. Then come back to me." The plea in his voice grabbed her heart with an invisible hand and squeezed it until Allie found it difficult to breathe.

Except nothing about this was difficult. Not at all. It was the easiest decision she had ever made. She rose on her tiptoes and placed a quick kiss on his jaw.

"I'll be right back."

The sigh that followed her outside the bakery felt like a gust of wind caressing the back of her neck. Yet Allie held back her smile, knowing what she would face. *Who* she would face.

"Lydia!" At the sound of her voice, the four Witches turned to face her. The Magistra was accompanied by Freya, who looked sick to her stomach, and Marla and Aurora, the elder Witches who openly disliked Allie. It was an interesting choice for a party, but Lydia didn't do anything without a reason.

"Alecsandra." Lydia twirled the ends of her red ponytail between her fingers as she looked Allie over like she was a prize calf.

"Such an...interesting choice." Allie crossed her arms over her chest, raising an eyebrow. "Sycamore Falls. New magic? I thought you didn't like being around it." Allie felt as though a blunt arrow punctured her throat.

"What?"

"You thought I didn't know about your life in Green Creek? How you ran away from it?" Lydia scoffed. "It is my responsibility to know everything there is to know about a Witch who joins my coven."

Allie straightened her spine, willing some of that initial confidence into her voice. She would not let them intimidate her.

"And you took me in knowing that."

"I don't care whose bed you warmed before coming to the manor, Alecsandra. I only care about your power. An elemental Witch is a great addition to the coven."

"Is that supposed to be a compliment?"

"It depends. Were you the one who almost set the town on fire?" Her burgundy-painted mouth twisted into a challenging grin.

"Are you high on potion steam?"

Before Lydia turned her sour grimace into words, Freya spoke.

"It's why we're here. To...to check on you, make sure you're fine." She rushed the words, yet Allie didn't miss the lies. Lydia threw her a menacing look that shut the Witch up. Freya was kind but spineless, and even if there was some truth behind her words, it was only she who was interested in Allie's well-being.

The others... They genuinely came to check if her power was so out of control that she was the reason Brandon's farm caught fire. They came to laugh in her face, to prove to her they had been right to kick her out.

Allie heard the doorbell ring but resisted the urge to turn around. She felt a warm, comforting presence at her back and imagined Dom standing by the door, arms crossed, glaring at the Witches in front of her. A smile slipped onto her lips.

"What are you simpering about?" Lydia barked. "Did you, or did you not, start that fire?"

"She didn't, you bitch." Allie looked to her right and saw Mia crossing the street. She was next to her in a few strides, grabbing Allie into a side hug.

"What did you just call me?" Lydia's face was fully red by now, a prominent vein pulsing along her temple.

"Witch," Mia said innocently. "Not only did Allie *not* start the fire, she was the one who put it out." Allie held in a laugh at Mia's exaggerated pride.

"You're joking." The Magistra's enraged expression morphed into a stupefied one. She studied Allie as if it was the first time she had laid eyes on her. "You can control your power?"

"Show them," Mia hissed.

Allie did not want to make a spectacle of herself in Sycamore Falls. Yet now that everyone knew she was an elemental Witch with power over fire, and they had finally welcomed her, maybe she could show off. Just a little bit.

Allie focused on the warmth in her chest, grabbing the magic in a strong grip and weaving it into a thread around her and Mia. Her friend didn't even flinch when a string of fire surrounded them both like a bow.

Lydia's eyes grew impossibly wide, and Allie pulled her magic back with an easy thought.

"Don't be so surprised, Lydia. I just needed a little help." Allie leaned into Mia's embrace, and her friend hugged her tighter.

"Hmm. Well." Lydia smoothed the skirt of her dark blue dress. "I suppose you can come back to the manor now." She found something interesting on which to fixate on the ground, while the other three Witches stared at Allie with their mouths open. Freya's eyes held a spark of joy, but her mom's sisters simply looked stunned.

"If only any of you had bothered enough," Allie went on her own tangent. "All you did was come up with excuses. Why should I go back with you now?"

"Because it is your place. You're still a Silverbark as long as I have your broom," Lydia said with bristling pride.

"My place," Allie said, doing her best to replicate one of Dom's glares, "is not with you." As if summoned, the Mage came to her other side, placing a hand on her hip. Brandon shuffled next to Mia, arms crossed. Warmth filled her chest, different than the magic one that hummed steadily in her heart. This one was sparkly and wild and so, so beautiful.

Allie was surrounded by her friends. Her family. In fact, she should thank Lydia for kicking her out. It was the reason she had walked into her fate and ended up in Sycamore Falls. Petra had always warned her not to live a lonely life, but she had never urged her to live in a coven. Allie knew she would be infinitely happier here, for as long as she stayed in Sycamore Falls.

And even if life happened and she left, Allie had gained the confidence that she would be all right. She did not have to settle for a life in a sweltering town, surrounded by people who didn't care for her, just out of fear of being alone.

"Thanks for stopping by. I'll come pick up my broom soon."

"What—"

"Get the fuck out of my town," Dominic growled. "While I'm asking nicely."

The wind picked up around the four Witches while Allie and her friends stood shielded, facing them. Lydia watched them with horror through wild strands of red hair, moving her eyes between Dominic and Allie, and had the good sense to shut her mouth. She muttered something that might have been a curse, turned on her heels, and walked away, the other Witches trailing behind her.

"Does this mean you're staying?" Mia asked and clapped her hands. Allie turned to look at Dominic, at the man who had done so much for her, who had helped her gain the confidence she exuded today. He stood there frozen, emerald green eyes burning into hers.

Allie decided to end his suffering.

"I'm staying."

Chapter 35

FOR BEING YOU

"I hate it already," Dom muttered from behind the wheel. He and Allie were driving to Pearls Fields, two days after the Silverbarks had come to Sycamore Falls. Allie wanted to pick up her broom and tie any loose ends with them, and Dominic... Dominic wanted whatever she wanted. He wanted her.

"It's not that bad," Allie tried to convince him. She almost did, as she was playing with the hair at the base of his neck, distracting him from the road. But the heat grew with every mile south, and he truly, honestly hated it.

"I'm sweating so much that I'll lose weight."

"Did you just try to make a joke?" Allie laughed. He did try, more and more often, just to hear the crystalline sound of her laughter. "Don't worry, Dom. I'll stuff you with pastries. And hazelnut cream." He couldn't resist glancing at her and caught the shimmer of mischief in her big brown eyes. Gods, he was gone for her.

"I'll hold you to that," Dom promised.

They drove for another thirty minutes before reaching Pearls Fields. The town was charming in its old magic way, yet Dom could never survive in this abominable heat.

"This it?" He parked the car on the curb of a dirt road leading up to a manor. Allie nodded, climbing out of her seat.

Dominic circled around the car and took her hand, but only after he had wiped his sweaty palm on his jeans. They walked along the path through the river birches and magnolia trees, but Dom's eyes were on Allie. He wanted to make sure she did not have any regrets, that she did not long for this place. Dominic understood if she did, but he wanted to be there for Allie if any of these feelings surfaced.

Allie's face remained unsmiling but carefree. When she caught him staring at her, Allie wrinkled up her nose and stuck her tongue out at him. Dom shook his head.

He had nothing to worry about.

As they approached the manor, a Witch came out through the heavy wooden door and stood outside the entrance.

"Freya," Allie said.

"Hey, Allie." She looked from her to Dominic, but his scowling made her eyes jump back to Allie instantly. "Let me go get your broom," she said and went back inside.

"This is anticlimactic," Dom mumbled. Allie chuckled.

"Did you expect another stand-off? Wasn't the one two days ago enough?" He shrugged. It hadn't been enough for him because he didn't get to turn any of those sneering Witches into raisins.

The Witch came back and handed Allie her broom, who took it with new light in her eyes.

"For whatever it's worth..." the Witch started, but stopped abruptly when Allie's eyes moved from the broom back up to her. She offered Freya a tight-lipped smile, and the Witch snuck back inside without another word.

Dominic waited, thinking Allie might want to take a moment to say goodbye to this place. To look it over. But her brown eyes were plastered to her broom as she turned around and walked away from the Silverbarks' manor. Forever, if he had any say in it.

"Is this sycamore wood?" Dom asked after he took a moment to look at Allie's dear possession.

Allie grinned and nodded.

"My mom's broom was also sycamore. I guess Lydia damned tradition when it came to keeping such a powerful Witch in the coven. I wonder..." Allie held the broom at arm's length, regarding it with love in her eyes. "Maybe Mom made it for me as a clue. That I don't need a silverbark broom because I wasn't meant to be a Silverbark?" She scoffed and shook her head. "It's silly."

"It's not." Dom stopped by the car's door and turned to face her. "Sycamores suit you so much better, Allie."

She beamed at him, and Dominic stared at her beautiful face, framed by those untamed red curls. He leaned down and pressed a kiss on her lips, fighting the urge to linger there forever. Dom drew back and put effort into what he hoped was a charming smirk.

"Let's go home."

Allie was slipping the stone rings on her fingers when she heard a knock on the door.

"Come in!"

Dominic entered, his cedarwood and leather smell filling the studio room. His chestnut hair was up in a messy bun that she would love to untangle, almost as much as she would like to unbutton his dark blue shirt. He swept his green eyes over her tall boots and short purple skirt, which he had called "his favorite clothing item" Allie owned.

"Did you plan on us staying in?" he said, closing the distance between them in two long strides. His hands went to her hips as Allie clasped her fingers behind his neck.

"We have a booth to run." Her argument was weakened by

Dom's touch, his minty cologne, the smoldering look in his eyes, the way his hands tightened around her hips.

Allie shook herself and stepped away from the bewitching man, knowing they would be late opening their festival booth if she spent another second in his arms. His frustrated growl followed her around the space as Allie grabbed her jacket and her dragon and went out into the hallway.

They walked along Maple Street, Ekko flying between them until Dom shooed him away, complaining he wanted to look at his beautiful girlfriend and not at Ekko's chubby ass. The dragon enveloped the Mage in a thick puff of steam, then sat on Allie's shoulder...next to Dom. She laughed heartily. Their constant bickering was rapidly becoming one of the highlights of her daily life.

Her daily life, which was now full of joy, and laughter, and love. Of family, and friends, and Dom. Allie thanked whatever gods were listening for this fortune, and for all the pain and struggles of her past. If it weren't for them, she would not be here now.

The park was busy with vendors opening up their booths, attendees from Sycamore Falls and the neighboring towns milling about, children and pets running around hiding behind the hay bales, and the band setting up their instruments under the red and white striped canopy. Even with the heavy dusk settling over the dark auburn landscape, the place was coming alive, lit by fairy lights hanging between the poles and the booths.

A line of customers had already formed in front of Dom's Sweets' booth when they arrived. The two of them made quick work of opening, with occasional help from Ekko. Everything had been set up that morning, so they started serving customers just a few minutes later.

Allie loved the full circle moment of smiling at her customers with her entire heart throughout the Harvest Festival. During her first days in Sycamore Falls, she'd forced out polite smiles to counter all the sneers... Now everybody was smiling back, complimenting their sweets and pastries, asking Allie about Ekko. The townsfolk had become her neighbors, and some of them, her friends.

"Your cookies and choux are the stars of the show," Dom told her when the crowd died down. "We're almost out."

Allie felt like she could burst with happiness. She wore a smile so wide her cheeks hurt, hardly keeping the urge to squeal and dance and clap under control.

After the next few customers left, they were out of everything.

Her Mage boss was content and decided to close the booth so they could enjoy the night's festivities. They stopped by Mia's booth, and she waved from behind a group of kids who were listening intently to one of the books reading itself. Allie waved back and blew a kiss to her friend, who moved to catch it midair and smack it on her face. Ekko flew to Mia, quickly becoming an equally interesting attraction for the kids.

Music notes sounded on the night's breeze, and Allie craftily changed the course of their walk toward the festival's dance floor. Dom was caught up in his story about the time he and Brandon had messed around with the electric installations for the festival and short-circuited all the lights, leaving everyone in the dark.

"What gave you that idea?" Allie laughed.

"We were convinced we could make it brighter." He shrugged and gave her a boyish grin, one she was seeing more and more often.

Dominic halted by the edge of the dance floor and said, "Sneaky."

"Who? Me?"

"If you want to coax me into stepping on the dance floor, there is something else we must do first." Allie threw him a puzzled look. "You have a Hallows Eve tradition to uphold."

"I can multitask," she countered.

Dom looked at her with confusion.

"Don't you need to be...under the moonlight, or something?" He scratched the back of his head, muttering something about needing to learn more about Witches.

How much deeper could she fall in love with this man?

Allie dragged Dominic onto the dance floor and wrapped her arms around his neck.

"I will teach you everything there is to know about a Witch," Allie said as they swayed to the slow music. "As long as you keep teaching me to bake."

Dom's chuckle rumbled in his chest and vibrated through Allie's body.

"Deal."

"Look, over there! She's right there!" Small voices made everyone turn their heads to the group of kids that had finished the book reading and were now bordering the dance floor. They elbowed each other and waved to Allie, who waved back with no little amount of surprise and confusion.

"The fire Witch of Sycamore Falls!" one of them yelled.

Allie liked the sound of that.

She and Dom laughed and resumed their slow dancing. The fairy lights played around his handsome face, illuminating the beginning of an encouraging smile.

"Are you ready?" he asked, and Allie nodded.

She leaned her head over his chest, listening to his steady heartbeat. She centered herself and leaned into her magic, steadily grasping at the threads of her power. The fire was there, burning peacefully, beckoning her to bend it to her will. Allie held on to it while she reached for the moon, to that warm, pure light that always made her feel whole.

It buzzed and poured with renewed strength, that veil that thinned tonight letting it flow without restriction into Allie's heart. She felt its presence prickling her skin, balancing the magic she had and the magic she used.

But Allie had barely used any magic since she had manifested, so she flooded the moon with her power, strengthening and enriching its pure magic.

Allie knew her mom was with her, watching over her, and this first time carrying on the Wells' Hallows Eve tradition.

Mom? I have found my place.

"All good?" Dom asked, worry fizzling into his heart. Allie had been silent and barely moving for the last two songs, and there was only so much multitasking a man could witness without interfering.

"Perfect." Allie straightened, and he immediately missed her warmth against his chest, even if she was still in his arms. But she directed that blinding smile at him, and the warmth he had missed filled him on the inside. She was so fucking beautiful, and perfect, and his.

How did I get so lucky? Does she know how I feel?

Dominic had always believed that actions speak louder than words, yet he found that this time, with Allie, he wanted to tell her. Tell her what was in his heart, as best as he could, and in probably very few words.

"Allie." Dom cleared his throat. "I'm not a man of many words."

"Understatement of the century." He pinched her, and Allie shrieked, inching closer to him. "Please, continue, Mr. Ranford."

Dom rolled his eyes but focused on getting out the words he desperately wanted her to hear.

"I am..." She looked at him from beneath thick eyelashes, root-colored eyes warm and kind, freckled cheeks stained red by the chill, lips stretched into a wide smile. Dominic was holding his future in his arms, and he would never let her go. "I am so madly in love with you."

Allie's mouth parted for a second, then morphed back into a huge, gorgeous smile.

"I am in love with you, too, Dom."

He leaned down and kissed her. Slowly, like they had all the time in the world. Because they did. Allie kissed him back, and when she wanted to come up for air, he let her. For a second.

Then he kissed her again. On her forehead. Her cheeks. Her nose.

"What's this for?" She chuckled.

"For being you. For giving me your heart, and...for accepting mine."

Epilogue

THAT'S MY LINE

"Stop squirming," Allie scolded her husband. "You know you are not going to fall."

Dominic gripped the broom so tightly with both hands that the wood could've snapped. His body trembled, and he couldn't find his balance, even though they had been doing this together for the past year.

"I am not s-squirming," he hissed, leaning back and forth on the broom.

Allie didn't like to ride straddling her broom, so she and Dom sat on the wood next to each other as if they were sitting on a bench. Her magic enveloped them and the flying broom, and Allie knew with the certainty of her next breath that they would never, ever fall.

"The car is a perfectly fine means of transportation," the Mage snapped when he managed to keep his balance for a few seconds at once. "I don't get why you insist we travel through the skies when we have all this vast land at our disposal."

Allie laughed. It was always like this, but she would never give up on flying, and as with everything else she loved in this life, she wanted to share it with her husband. As much as he was against it.

They had been married for two months and spent the last two weeks traveling. Dom took Allie to his favorite beach, favorite rivers, favorite diners, favorite everything. As a Mage, he'd seen so much of this world, and Allie was the tiniest bit jealous, yet immensely happy he was sharing everything with her.

Before the wedding, Allie and Dominic had finished renovating and rebranding the bakery. The room she used to live in was now open to the floor of the bakery to allow more tables inside for customers, and a tiny part of it was used for extra storage room.

Now they were traveling back to Sycamore Falls, Ekko flying in circles around them and leaving trails of steam behind, showing off how easy it was for him to fly. Dom grabbed for the dragon once, trying to keep him in place, but lost his balance and immediately cursed at the creature.

There was only one way Allie could make him feel better.

She leaned closer to her husband and kissed him on the cheek. Once. Twice. Then, as he slowly turned his head toward her, Allie kissed him on the lips, hard and loud, smearing her pink lipstick all over his mouth.

"I would never let anything happen to you," she said sweetly. Dom scowled.

"That's my line."

Nothing was only his anymore, and Dominic didn't miss that one bit. No lines, no space, no room. Everything he had, everything he was, he shared with his beautiful wife, and he wouldn't have it any other way.

When he came up with the idea to rebrand the bakery to include Allie in the business one way or another, she had cried and laughed for an hour straight, asking him over and over if he was sure about that.

Dominic had been so sure that he got down on one knee and proposed to her, making her continue to laugh and cry for another hour. Allie had yelled her answer, a sharp and resounding "yes" that vibrated in his heart, filling it with the purest love.

They renamed Dom's Sweets to Ekko's Treats and made the dragon their ever-proud mascot. Customers clamored to spend time with the creature, and Ekko basked in all the love and attention.

Dominic had been away for a couple of missions, during which time Allie had run the bakery all on her own. There was little left for her to learn, even if she argued that she needed a couple more years to practice. Dom always said, "You don't. Trust me."

And she did.

Allie trusted him with everything in their life. Every time he was away from home, every time she was scared of trying something new. Just every time.

When his lovely Witch wife gave him her heart, Dominic started a life-long mission that would end on his last breath: cherishing and protecting it.

And this was on repeat in his mind while they descended from the flight of hell down to Sycamore Falls, the recently-painted purple roof of the bakery coming into view.

As soon as he set his feet on the ground, Dom muttered thanks to the gods that they made it in one piece. He also trusted Allie with his life, and deep, deep down—really deep, buried under all his organs—he knew nothing bad would happen when he was flying with her. But there was a severe disconnect between this knowledge and the facts, one that grew with each foot of distance they put between them and the earth.

Dominic eyed the wicked broom and would have set it on fire, had it not been so dear to his wife.

"See?" Allie smirked, as she always did. She threw her arms

around his neck and kissed him, her red, wild curls tickling his cheeks. "Nothing to worry about."

"Never, as long as we're together."

THE END

Acknowledgments

"Sweets and Sycamores" is the lovely book that you have read today because of all the amazing people who have supported me during this journey, and I am beyond grateful to each and every one of them.

Monica, I cannot tell you how happy I am that producing and promoting this book was not a "one woman show" anymore. You are a wonderful PA and cheerleader, and I couldn't have done even half of the cool things we did for "Sweets and Sycamores" without you. Thank you for always being there for me, for brainstorming with me, and for keeping me on schedule.

Allie, you have been more than just an editor to me. You have been a partner in making this book shine and polishing my words without changing my voice. I am so thankful that you took the time to teach me while making all these improvements, and for squeezing me into your busy schedule.

Alina, I am filled with happiness and gratitude that we have met. More than an amazing illustrator, I have found a friend in you. You have brought my story to life in a way I could have never expressed in words. I cannot wait for our next collaboration!

Ramona, thank you for helping me iron out the tiniest details in this book and making it better. You are a great proofreader, and I am excited for us to work together again!

To all the artists I have commissioned multiple times and who will likely never be rid of me: Mori, Paula, Snoozie, Yeollie—thank you for bringing my characters to life.

To my Street Team, thank you for taking the time to show all the love to "Sweets and Sycamores." It was so fun to go through our weekly challenges together, and I am very grateful for all your support.

A special shout out to my beta readers: Vroni, Mica, and Petunia—I am so grateful for the love and care you showed me and my book while helping me make it better.

To my readers, thank you for loving my stories. You are the ones who keep me going, who nudge me to find inspiration even in the hardest moments.

Last, but not least, I would like to thank my family for their unwavering support. To my wonderful parents, who have always been my biggest supporters, thank you so much for all your encouragement and love. And to my husband, my rock, my everything—thank you for constant patience and love, and for always pushing me to be the best version of myself.

About the Author

Arianne Nicks is a writer who weaves romance and magic within her stories, in a mix of cliffhangers and comfort reads. She is a coffee-fueled self-published author whose debut is a paranormal romance trilogy, the Soul Erosion series, completed in 2024. Her newest release, Sweets and Sycamores, a cozy witchy slow burn romance, is a fall-themed book published in September 2025. Originally from Romania, Ari now lives in the US with her husband and their house plants. She loves to exercise so she can keep eating, and your chocolate is never safe with her.